Dear Ma[...]
Thank yo[u]
for buying a copy [—]
much appreciated. Hope you
enjoy it (no refunds!) Love
Ca[...]x

Gingerbread Children

Carol Carman

Gingerbread Children

First published in 2018 by McCaw Press

© Copyright Carol Carman 2018.
Carol Carman has asserted her right to be identified as the author of this work in accordance with the Copyright, Designs and Patents Act 1988.

All illustrations by Lisa-Marie Damant
© Lisa-Marie Damant 2018
Lisa-Marie Damant has asserted her right to be identified as the illustrator of this work in accordance with the Copyright, Designs and Patents Act 1988.

Cover design by Martin Carman.

All rights reserved. No part of this publication may be reproduced, distributed, stored in a retrieval system or transmitted in any form or by any means, including photocopying, recording, or other electronic or mechanical methods, without the prior written permission of the copyright holders.

ISBN: 978-1-9998523-0-6

Printed and bound in Great Britain by
Impressions Print and Label, Cambs PE28 3EE

McCaw Press

mccawmedia.co.uk

For Martin

without whom this book would not have been written

and for Terry Pratchett

without whom this book would not have been written

What was coming was only a matter of time.

For Dominica,
waiting and watching,
it would be the most important time…

…for Imelda,
summoning her failing strength to perform one last duty,
it was the time of her life…

…for Helena,
staring at the words she already knew by heart,
surely this time was her time…

…for the magic,
burning green in an otherwise black, black ledger,
it was time for a change…

~•~

NOTES ON

The Origins of
The University of Nature

No-one knows when The University of Nature first appeared. Nobody's that old.

Some say it evolved gradually, being built upon the ruins of a long-abandoned temple dedicated to Artifax, god of trowel and brush, which itself incorporated the findings of an archaeological dig on the site of an ancient castle, constructed to reinforce old fortifications on top of a prehistoric burial barrow where the original inhabitants of the town of Maund were laid to their not-quite-eternal rest.

Some say it's as ancient as time itself, the result of a massive collision of all the molecules in the universe which then started bonding, forming what's technically known as 'stuff'; people call this the Big Prang Theory, and it's usually propounded at closing time in The Lamb and Werewolf when the brains of the young men of Maund are swimming in an ocean of Carson's Gutwrencher.

Some say it's so old they're surprised it hasn't fallen to bits by now.

However, the some who say these things have never actually been inside it, otherwise they might hold different views.

Everybody calls it 'The Union', primarily because people can't resist shortening perfectly good names, and a name such as 'The Union' speaks of solidity, strength, power and durability, whilst 'The University of Nature' whispers of botany, aromatherapy and meditation.

Neither name says a dicky bird about witchcraft.

Presided over by the Matriarch, The Union is the biggest thing in Maund, and big things need careful handling just as much as small things. Especially when they're full of magic.

~✦~

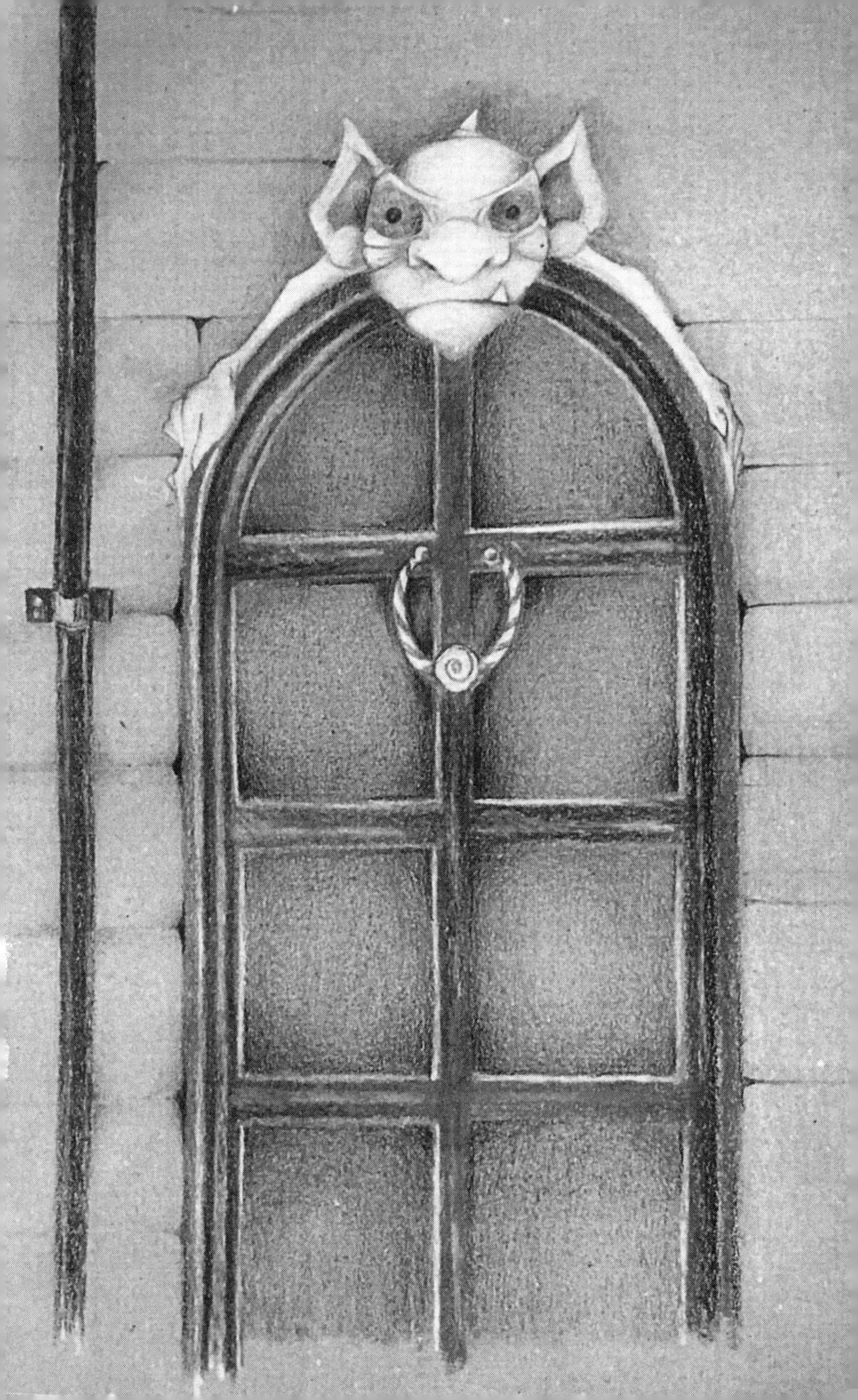

The annals of The Union show that in the time of Matriarch Imelda McGinty, there was not much of that time left. Measurements had been taken, wood was being sawn, silks cut and cold meats ordered. There was little left to do but wait for the silence.

As was her duty, Vice-Matriarch Dominica Tort sat by the large, oak-framed bed and waited; as was her love, she held the hand of the elderly Matriarch. The air and each passing moment seemed as heavy as the black and maroon tapestries which draped and swagged around the ancient four-poster. The rhythmical rising and falling of the matching blanket and the accompanying creak of bedsprings were the only indications of life left in the dying woman. The solitary candle burned low, its flame giving little true light, but merely hinting at animation where there was none.

Dominica looked round the room, as she had done many times over the past fortnight. Everything was exactly in its place, as if the dust had already begun to settle on the ledgers of Imelda's life. The mirror had begun to cloud over, and the cut-glass trinket bowls and tray on the dressing table no longer caught the candlelight. The broomstick lay in its cradle attached to the footboard, the conical hat was locked away in its case and the black cat with the white eye-patch sat on the mattress, the model of ancient felinity, staring, staring, as still as stone.

Death inevitably meant change, which usually entailed chaos; for the moment, though, all was calm. As far as Dominica and Imelda were concerned, if time had not actually stopped, it was certainly having a long hot soak before deciding what to do next.

There was a faint click and the door inched silently open, just far enough for a serving-girl to enter. She carried a silver tray bearing a silver tea set, a china cup and saucer, two gingerbread men on a china plate, a starched napkin and a new candle in a silver candlestick. Her long skirt shushed the carpet as she set the tray on a small bedside table and lit the new candle from the old one. Turning to go, she looked towards Dominica and whispered, 'Ma'am?'

Dominica shook her head. 'No. Thank you, Truda.'

'Ma'am.'

Truda bobbed, picked up the old candle and headed for the door. The curtain of darkness parted in front of her and soon filled the space she vacated with every step.

She had almost reached the door when it swung open to greet her, smacking her on the arm as the Bursar strode into the room. Hearing a thud, the Bursar moved the door and revealed Truda, anchored to the spot by a large silver candlestick on her left foot. The Bursar stared at Truda, who could not respond in likewise fashion, because not only is it not done for servants to return the gaze of witches – or bray the Bursar with the nearest thing to hand, although many people wanted to – but her eyes were squeezed shut in pain.

The Bursar hated to see people lounging about.

'What are you doing there? Have you no work to do?'

'Mm,' Truda piped, without moving a muscle. Years of domestic training had taught her to maintain her composure at all times, even if it meant she gritted her teeth so hard she had toothache for three days afterwards. Wordlessly she picked up the candlestick and limped out of the room, valiantly ignoring the flames licking at her hemline. As she gently closed the door, the slight breeze wafted the smoke from her uniform back into the room, and for a few moments the aroma of burning serge drifted like incense.

Dominica looked at the cat. Although it had never taken its gaze off the Matriarch nor altered its position by a whisker, all its fur stood on end, giving the impression it had grown two inches all round and become a porcupine. She felt some sympathy. She knew what was coming.

The Bursar gripped the footboard, sending shudders through arthritic carpentry joints. She stared at the Matriarch but spoke to Dominica.

'Has she said it, Minnie? Has she? Has she said it yet?'

From outside the room there was a scream, a sloshing of water and a hiss of steam.

'Do not call me Minnie,' said the Vice-Matriarch flatly. 'My name is Dominica. Or you can call me Vice-Matriarch.'

The Bursar tutted. 'Yes, yes, whatever you say, Minnie. Anyway, has she said it yet?'

For seven years Dominica had asked the Bursar to stop calling her Minnie; to hear it again engendered murderous thoughts in her heart and she bared her teeth momentarily. However, she realised where her duty lay, and with a heavy heart she realised it didn't lie in taking the Bursar out into Concentric Yard and giving her a good slapping. But one day.

She turned to face the Bursar.

'I take it you are referring to the Deposition of Succession. No, Helena,' she said, injecting as much venom as she could into the Bursar's name, 'the Matriarch has not said it yet. Not all of it.'

'Well how far has she got?'

'So far her words have been, "I pass to you the power to appoint as my successor". That is all.'

'But she was up to there five days ago! She must have said something since then!'

'Do you doubt my word, Helena?'

'No... no... of course not... it's just...'

'Until the Deposition is completed, nothing is certain. I would be failing in my duty to even think otherwise. And up until now, the Matriarch's words have been, "I pass to you the power to appoint as my successor".'

Imelda stirred and mumbled; Dominica bent close to her. The Bursar heaved herself over the footboard onto the bed, dislodging the broomstick from its cradle and cannoning into the cat, which shot under the bed, resurfaced near Dominica and leapt onto the pillow at the side of Imelda's head. The bedframe, unaccustomed to the extra weight of the well-upholstered Bursar, began to creak ominously.

'Did she say it? Did she?'

'Shh! If you want to hear who the Matriarch nominates I suggest—'

Dominica's suggestion was cut off as she felt the Matriarch squeeze her hand. She leant closer, and was swiftly followed by the Bursar. The Matriarch whispered a three-syllable word which sent the Bursar bouncing and leaping from the bed. This unexpected activity strained desiccated timbers and cracked ancient dovetail joints.

The Bursar's joy was unencumbered by decorum.

'Yippee! It's me! It's me! I'm the new Matriarch!'

Dominica closed her eyes, listening intently to Imelda.

The Bursar made her right hand into a fist and jerked it towards her shoulder in a traditional victory salutes.

'Yes! Good old Imelda! You heard her – "Helena," she said. Oh, yes! Got a certain ring to it, eh? Matriarch Helena Jacket. Oh, yes, very nice.'

Dominica held a hand up.

'You are not there yet, Helena. The Matriarch still lives.'

This insignificant detail didn't worry the Bursar, who was dancing on the spot and mentally assembling the new Senior Council she'd bring in after her inauguration. Dominica's face did not figure in it.

'What? Oh, yes, of course. Well, can't hang about here all day. Things to do, plans to make, gowns to order.'

The Bursar jigged her way towards the door. Unfortunately enjoyment does not give off light, so she didn't know about the broomstick until she caught her foot in it and went face down onto the carpet. The resultant vibrations travelled across the floorboards and into the bedframe, setting up muted but deadly resonances along the uprights. The Bursar struggled to her feet, stomped to the door and wrenched it open.

'And let's have some proper light in here!' she commanded, smacking the wall. The thick window curtains flew open, sending dust motes tumbling in the sunrays.

'That's better!' she snapped, then she skipped out of the room and slammed the door.

Dominica had to let go of the Matriarch's hand as the reverberations from the slam hastened the demise of the dovetails and the four-poster collapsed. The breeze from the falling drapes and poles snuffed out the candle flame as surely as the weight of them snuffed out the life of Matriarch Imelda McGinty.

When the dust had settled, Dominica stood for a moment.

'Oh, dear,' she said. 'Oh dear, oh dear, oh dear.'

Turning to go, she noticed small movements under the pile of tapestry and oak. She delved into the heap, pulled out the cat, set him down on the floor and watched him as he walked round unsteadily.

'At least you seem unhurt, Bertie.'

The cat stretched his legs out, arched and flexed his spine and turned his head from side to side.

'No thanks to that bloody woman,' he said. 'How do you put up with her?'

Dominica shrugged her shoulders. 'I treat her as a life

lesson. If I get through a day without actually walloping her, I consider myself a better person.'

Bertie paced up and down. 'What's wrong with her? Doesn't she understand about— about death? My mistress is in her last agony and all the Bursar can think about… If she'd been through this as many times as I have… it never gets any easier. Never.' Tears came to his eyes, so he sat down, wiped them away and started to wash his face. 'At least… my mistress is in no pain now.'

'No,' said Dominica quietly, fighting back tears herself.

Bertie hooked his foreclaws into the carpet and stretched out again, opened his mouth wide, then shook his head and returned to the sitting position. 'Time for the blessing?'

Dominica nodded. She knelt on the carpet, cupped the cat's jaw lightly in her hand and looked steadily into his eyes.

'Spirit of the Western One, I give you your freedom. May you wander without hindrance, and always carry your home with you. Be true to yourself and fair to others, and walk the world in peace.'

He closed his eyes very slowly, and breathed deeply. Dominica kissed him lightly on the head. He opened his eyes again and gazed into hers.

She stood up. 'So what will you do now?'

'Well,' he sighed, 'I'll have to wait until the new Matriarch's inaugurated and see if her familiar needs any help, but after that… who knows? At some point, of course, I'll have to go back and wait for another body and another mistress… start another adventure. Until then, I don't know what I'll do.' He walked towards her, rubbed against her leg and looked up at her hopefully. 'You're not in the market for a spare familiar, are you?'

She smiled sadly. 'I'd love to… but what would Spirit of the Wind say? He gets a bit touchy about that sort of thing.'

Bertie sat down. 'Oh, Dennis, yeah. A good old boy, but he doesn't like anybody on his turf. Shame, that.'

Dominica smiled.

The cat shook himself briskly, took a deep breath, lifted his head and closed his eyes. 'All right. I'm ready.'

Dominica clasped her hands. 'Spirit of the Western One, I ask you this: will you stay within the confines of The Union until such time as the ceremonies be complete?'

'I will.'

'And do you do this of your own free will?'

'I do. Of free will, of honour, and' – he opened his eyes and tapped straight into Dominica's already full heart – 'of love for she that loved me.'

A lump came to Dominica's throat. 'Thank you, Bertie.'

She turned and walked towards the door.

Bertie spoke again.

'If you need me at all, let me know. I'd do anything for you, you know that.'

'I know.' Tears welled in her eyes again. 'I, erm, I have to lock the room. Do you want to stay with her, or…?'

'I can't… I'm too…'

He sighed, turned towards Imelda's bed and bowed.

'Goodbye, Mistress,' he whispered, then he ran out of the door before his sobs could stop him.

Dominica quietly left the room, locked the door and

sealed it with a barrier spell to prevent any intrusion.

Another chapter in the history of The Union had reached its conclusion. All she had to do now was tread firmly in tradition's footprints and close up the circle of long-established ritual demanded by such events.

The Bursar danced round her room, fists in the air, utter joy on her face and a song in her heart.

'Matriarch Helena Jacket, Matriarch Helena Jacket, na na naa naa, na na naa naa.'

She sashayed over to her wardrobe and pulled the doors wide open. From a box on the wardrobe floor she took an old envelope, which had been opened so many times the flap had long since fallen off and been lost. She kissed the envelope and clasped it to her heart with both hands.

'Not long now, Daddy. Not long now.'

Dominica entered her own study. Over the years, this room had absorbed so much of her personality, her attitudes, her tastes and her moods; now it returned some to her, as if sensing her need for reassurance. The familiar scent of her own life drove out the smell of death from her nostrils, and she was as comforted as if she had been wrapped in the arms of her mother. Leaning back on the door, her face crumpling, she slid to the floor where she wept over things past, things to come, and the loss of a valued mentor and dear friend.

When she had exhausted her tears, she lay on her bed and whilst she slept, the breeze through the partly open window brought scents of orange blossom, lemon grass, lavender and thyme from the garden to colour her dreams and soothe her aching body and soul.

It also blew in a bundle of ginger feline fur, a marmalade cat of the three-fruit variety. One of his ears was bent, and there were thin patches on his coat indicating the sites of old wounds. His rough, battered appearance often lulled new cats on the block into thinking he was a pushover; however, a short temper kept him fighting fit and there was many an alley cat now stalking with a limp after provoking him. A scar ran across his head from above one eye to behind the other ear, making his fur grow awkwardly, giving him a quiff to go with his attitude.

Spirit of the Wind padded gently across the desk by the window and dropped expertly to the floor. A silent walk and an agile leap onto the bed and he was beside Dominica. He put his face close to her body. His nose twitched at the smell of death on her clothes and salt water on her handkerchief. His eyes narrowed at the aroma on her leg, his quickening heart beat cold blood when he smelt her hands, and every hair on his body stood on end as he put his nose to her lips.

Horrified, shaking his head but unable to take his eyes off her, he backed away. Disbelief numbing sensation, he felt no pain as he lost his footing and thudded onto the floor.

~ ⋅ ~
NOTES ON

Systers and Familiars

'When a Novice shall graduate from The University and be welcomed as a Syster in Full Membership of the Systerhood of The Black Cauldron, she shall inform The Familiar Office (hereinafter known as the F.O.) whereupon she shall be entered into The Register of Systers without Familiars. At that Time shall she state whether she has Need or No Need of a Familiar, this being a Spiritual Essence housed, for the Purposes of Convenience, within the Body of a Cat.

If No Need has been stated, the Name of the Syster shall remain in The Register of Systers without Familiars until such Time as Need is stated.

If Need has been stated, then within a Period of fourteen Days the Syster shall be issued with a Familiar in the Body of a Cat. If, after a Period of fourteen Days, she shall not have been issued with a Familiar in the Body of a Cat, she shall contact the F.O. whereupon she shall be issued with a Familiar in a temporary Body to be determined by the F.O.

Once a Syster shall have been issued with a Familiar, there shall be a Period of Grace of fourteen Days during which Time, shall either find Fault with the other, they shall together return to the F.O. to state their Grievances and apply for Re-issue. A Maximum of three Applications for Re-Issue shall be permitted per Syster and per Familiar.

Should no Fault be found by either Party during the Period of Grace, then at the End of the Period of Grace there shall be a formal Bargain struck between the Syster and the Familiar, and The Ceremony of Matching shall be performed according to the Rules laid down in The Book of Ceremonies Volume III: The Ceremony of Matching.'

The Book of Procedures Volume III:
The Procedure of Graduation

Whether or not a witch has a familiar depends upon her future employment. Familiars are mandatory for witches who graduate from The Union and take their place in the wider world, because everybody needs someone to talk to when they start a new job. Familiars are also mandatory for all Union teaching staff and members of the Senior Council, the reasoning being that people in positions of authority should always have someone keeping an eye on what they're doing.

All other witches make do without a familiar, unless there's a very, very good reason. There's a lot of planting, tending and harvesting within the confines of The Union and witches are generally green-fingered from successful horticulture, not from plunging their hands through premium-grade topsoil into something unexpectedly paste-like and possibly toxic.

Animals housing familiars are the envy of other animals outside the walls of The Union. No Union animal ever goes hungry or has to raid bins for its survival, and any ailment, illness or injury is treated by someone who knows what they're doing and has access to potions money can't buy.

They can talk, so any complaining and demanding is a lot easier because people can understand what they're saying, and they can drink alcohol in quantities way beyond what would normally be considered poisonous, although they are not immune from the headache that follows.

And if they're really lucky animals, the familiars may bring with them extra powers such as invisibility, shapeshifting or supernatural strength.

Witches and familiars bond for life, and once that bond has been struck, the animal housing the familiar no longer ages; their clock is paused so that they can live for at least as long as the bond between the familiar and the witch exists. The bond can only be broken by two things: death or proven misfaith.

If the bond is broken by the death of the witch, the familiar is given a period of freedom, both in recognition of their service and to allow them to grieve. Once freed, familiars have a maximum of six years and six days in which to do as they please; after that time they are recalled to be available for re-issue. They can, of course, hand themselves back into the Familiar Office at any time, but Senior Council familiars are bound by courtesy to stay on to offer to help their successors settle into the job.

If the bond is broken by the death of the animal – and

accidents do happen – the familiar will make its home in the nearest available living thing until it can get back to the Familiar Office for formal re-issue in another body. This is why the Familiar Office usually has one or two surprised-looking pot plants on the window-sill.

If the bond is broken by proven Misfaith on either side, all parties must go back to the Familiar Office for a rigorous inquest and probable repercussions.

~∗~

When sleep had done all it could for her, Dominica rose and went over to her desk. The marmalade cat was sitting on the window-sill, staring out through the glass. He did not move his gaze.

'It's over, then,' he said.

Dominica sighed. 'Yes, it's over.'

Although this was the response Spirit of the Wind had been half-expecting, he was still fully shocked to hear it. His claws protruded from beneath his fur.

'Just like that?'

'Everything happens "just like that". A thing is either something, or it's something else.'

'And this is the start of something else?'

'I'm afraid so, Dennis,' she said softly, reaching out to him but he moved his head away, avoiding her touch. She withdrew her hand and tidied the papers on her desk.

He observed her for a few moments before speaking.

'I must say you're taking the end of this long partnership remarkably calmly.'

'All things must end, however painful it is when they do.'

She started to look through the desk drawers. 'And it's not as if it was unexpected.'

Dennis's jaw dropped as he gasped. Not unexpected? Well, he hadn't seen it coming, that's for sure. All he knew was that one day his mistress tells him she's going to tend to a sick friend, and then he finds her sprawled on her bed, covered in the scent of another familiar. Not unexpected? A bolt from the blue, more like.

Dominica was still rooting through the drawers. 'And I have to remain calm. There are things to be done and I'm the person to do them. I am the Vice-Matriarch, after all.'

'And I'm just a cat,' said Dennis, bitterly.

Dominica closed the drawers and straightened up.

'Dennis, what is the—'

The window-sill was empty. There were several fresh, deep scratches in the woodwork.

'And now, girls, as ever, we need a little practice to consolidate the theories. I will give each of you a piece of vegetation, and I want you write about whatever I give you in the most original terms you can think of.'

The Tutor of Creative Chronicling moved through the class, placing before her disbelieving students a variety of produce. From her wicker basket she brought potatoes, carrots, yellow waxpods, purple globe artichokes, sticks of giant red celery, silverskins, peppercorns, coriander leaves, nutmegs and garlic bulbs.

'Remember what we talked about. Use all your senses to describe these things, to draw out their hidden stories, to say what their impact is on you. I don't mind what you write – poems, prose, monologues, plays – but no recipes, please.'

On the desk in front of an Assistant Graduation Administrator called Naiba who'd fancied having a go at chronicling, the Tutor placed a dried root. Naiba thought it looked just like a small, deformed, boneless chicken wing recently unearthed after being buried in sand for five hundred years. She also wondered whether she shouldn't have joined the pottery class instead.

Truda limped in to Dominica's study wearing a natty little above-the-ankle singed skirt with matching damp patches. She bobbed as best she could, even though Dominica did not look up from her work.

'You rang, ma'am?'

'Ah, Truda. I want you to—'

Dominica broke off as she caught sight of Truda the trooper, carrying on regardless, despite a possibly broken foot and a definitely charred uniform.

'Truda, go to sick bay and see Matron about your foot.'

'Foot, ma'am?'

'Foot, Truda. The thing on the end of your leg that's throbbing with pain after the application of a candlestick.'

'Oh, that, ma'am. That'll be right. 'S only bruised.'

'It'll still need to get better, so run along – I mean go – to sick bay and Matron will sort you out.'

'Right y'are, ma'am. Will that be all?'

'No. When your foot's better, go get a new uniform.'

'Beggin' your pardon ma'am, but Bursar says uniforms

has to last ten year.'

'Did she?'

'Summat to do with…' – Truda screwed her face up in concentration – '…fiscal strictures and austerity measures in the current economic climate, I think. Summat like that, anyway, ma'am. Though what the weather's got to do with it, I've no idea.'

'When did you last have a new uniform, Truda?'

'Seven year last Walpurgis Night, ma'am, so this one's another seven year to do.'

Synapses twanged in Dominica's brain.

'Seven years? Really? Why?'

'Two year ago Bursar told me I had to wait another five year afore I could have a new uniform, ma'am, and she said that's how I could tell how long it'd be afore I got another. I'd had it five, and I had to wait five. So now I've had it seven, I reckon I got to wait seven.'

Dominica caved in under the burden of the logic.

'Well, let's save you the wait, shall we? See Matron, then take this note to the dressmaker in Caxton's Passage and ask her to make you a new uniform.'

'But—'

'Now don't you worry, Truda, Bursar will pay for it. And send one of your sisters to me, please. I need some help.'

Truda opened her mouth to protest her fitness, but Dominica overrode her.

'That'll be all, Truda. Go see Matron. And don't—'

Too late.

'—curtsey.'

Truda stopped in mid-bob, standing on her one good leg, giving a passable imitation of a black flamingo with cramp. She thought for a moment, then turned on the spot and hobbled towards the door.

'How old are you, Truda?' asked Dominica, immediately wishing she hadn't as Truda again pirouetted like a clumsy ice-skater.

'Don't know, ma'am. Older'n seven, I reckon.'

Dominica didn't have the heart to fight.

'Yes, I suppose you must be. Off you go.'

Showing remarkable strength in one ankle, Truda turned again and left the room. Dominica liked Truda. A devoted hard-worker, an extraordinary intuition as to when people needed tea, a heart of gold – and unfortunately a brain made of the same mineral.

~•~
NOTES ON
Bargain-Tokens

'During the Ceremony of Matching, the Bargain-Tokens shall be exchanged:

A Lock of Hair shall be cut from the Head of the Syster and set in a silver Clasp; this shall be given unto the Familiar as a Token of the Bargain struck between Syster and Familiar.

In likewise Manner, a Lock of Fur shall be cut from the Body of the Familiar and set in a silver Clasp; this shall be given unto the Syster as a Token of the Bargain struck between Familiar and Syster.

These shall Syster and Familiar keep until they be separated by proven Misfaith or Death.

After the Exchange of the Bargain-Tokens:

The Name of the Syster shall be struck from the Register of Systers without Familiars and immediately entered into the Register of Systers with Familiars.

In likewise Manner, the Name of the Familiar shall be struck from the Register of Familiars without Systers and immediately entered into the Register of Familiars with Systers.'

The Book of Ceremonies Volume III:
The Ceremony of Matching

The bargain-token is the symbol of the life-long bond between witch and familiar. It is one of the few truly personal things a witch ever owns, and she accords it great respect, keeping it either on a silver chain around her neck, sewn into her hat, or locked away in a silver casket along with her Insignia of Systerhood.

What the animals do with them is anybody's guess.

~•~

Dominica lifted the brass candlesticks. Nothing under there. She opened the glass doors on her bookcase, ducking, out of habit, as Playtown's *Theory of Poltergeist Activity* threw itself across the room. She ran her hand behind each row of books – nothing. She scrabbled amongst the boots and shoes at the bottom of her wardrobe, but to no avail. She contemplated the filing cabinet. Would it be under C for 'cupboard', S for 'safekeeping' or I for 'important'? Only one way to find out.

She trawled the cabinet from A for 'all the things I'll file later' to Z for 'the spare folder at the back of the drawer because people don't have things to file beginning with Z'. A fruitless search. Only one place left. And if it wasn't there, she'd have to resort to magic, which she didn't want to do, because not only was it a bit of a sledgehammer to crack a nut, but it would be extremely embarrassing to be the highest authority in The Union at the moment and to have lost the key to the stationery cupboard.

She sat on the edge of the bed, upended the rigid conical hatbox, held it between her knees and unscrewed the lid, lifting it away to put it on the bed. A faint smell of roses greeted her and for a moment she remembered her days as a student in the arts and crafts department, making the rose-tissue which now filled the inside of her hat. Carefree days, choosing the roses for colour and scent, selecting only the best petals; but that was before she had climbed the managerial tree to the – for now – topmost branch. She removed the rose-tissue, carefully laid it on the bed and gingerly ran her fingers around the inside of the hat, feeling at the pockets which lined it, until it was too narrow to allow further probing.

Nothing there. Damn! Dominica brought her fist down on the rim of the hatbox. From way down at the point, there came the chink of metal. She shook the box. Chink, chink. Pulse racing, she spread her arm over the rim to keep her hat in place and flipped the box upright. Out dropped a copper keyring holding one bronze, one silver and one golden key; she snatched them up, kissed them and put them in her pocket.

But something else had fallen out as well: a lock of ginger fur in a silver clasp. Dennis's bargain-token. A bell rang in the back of her mind but for what, she was not sure. Her previous euphoria evaporated, leaving her distinctly uneasy. She brushed the fur against her cheek. What was he up to? And where was he up to it? And why now?

There was a knock on the door.

'Come in,' she called, her look turning from expectation to puzzlement as the serving-girl entered.

'Truda?'

The serving-girl bobbed.

'Beggin' your pardon, mum, it's Bebe. Truda's sister. We do look very much alike. You want some help, mum?'

She put the bargain-token back inside the hat, replaced the handmade rose-tissue and screwed the bottom back on the hatbox.

'Come on, Bebe, we're going to the Library.'

In her room, Naiba examined the dried root. Knobbly and gnarled, the places where it might have divided into branches were merely stunted limbs. Overall it had the bleached appearance of driftwood marooned by a high tide many generations ago, but Naiba looked closely and saw purply mud browns tinged with grey, fading to beige and rich cream.

Where the outer covering remained, it was crinkled and wrinkled like shrivelled skin, but where it had worn off, the surface was smooth and felt powdery, although no dust came off onto her fingers. There were striations and fine ridges twisting this way and that, signposting the direction in which the fibres had grown. Naiba was reminded of an old blackboard, pitted with wear and finely dusted with chalk.

She prodded it. Hard and unyielding, it broke unexpectedly when she tried to bend it. Fine particles swirled and melted into the air, and fibres jutted from the cream-coloured centres of the ragged edges of the break. Feeling suddenly flushed, she put the pieces back down onto her desk and studied them for some minutes, pushing them around with a pencil. A soft seductive aroma suffused the air, and her nose kept sending messages to her brain along the lines of 'Get me closer; I must have more of this.'

Unable to resist any longer, she picked up a piece and rolled it around in her fingers, its rough surface providing a good grip despite its small size. She held it to her ear and heard her fingers rasping over it; she brought it to her nose and inhaled its spicy aroma, warm and prickly like thick tweed. Her fingers closed around the root, her eyes glazed over, and she began to write:

THERE WAS A CLEARING IN THE WOODS, a perfect round clearing. In the centre of the perfect round clearing was a well, a perfect round well, complete with a wooden roller to haul up the bucket hanging deep inside. The young witch stopped on the edge of the clearing, rested her handcart up against a tree, clambered over all her worldly possessions, stretched up and began to climb. On a branch overlooking the clearing, she scanned the area, noting the position of the sun, the proximity of the mountains and in which direction the wind blew the rain clouds. She smelt the air, the forest breezes bringing her razor-edged pine, warm oak, brittle birch and pungent ginkgo; artemisia and mock orange jostled with juniper, eucalyptus, sweet apple and almond.

She rested her head on the tree trunk and let the sounds fill her ears: the tapping of death-watch beetle and the rasping of grasshoppers; the caressing shush of leaves and the impatient snap of twigs; the brrr of ruffled feathers and the soft swish of flight. Underlying everything was the distant rumble of grinding stones, and from directly beneath her came the yawn of a cat as a patch of tortoiseshell fur stretched and snuggled down again on the tarpaulin covering the handcart. She smiled, climbed down and put her mouth close to the cat's ear.

'Wakey wakey, Axy, we're here.'

He kept his eyes closed and muttered, 'Go away.'

She laughed, scooped him up, kissed the top of his head and threw him into the air. Reflexes outran any considered reaction, and he flexed and twisted before landing lightly.

'Aw, that's a rotten trick!' he protested. 'I was asleep!'

'You're awake now.'

She dug her heel into the ground several times before bending down to examine the disturbed earth. It crumbled easily in her fingers, but was not so dusty that the mischievous breeze would take it away. She stood up and brushed the remaining soil from her hands.

'Excellent!' she said, and in measured paces she strode across from the southern edge of the clearing to the well.

Axy leapt on the well-wall and walked a circuit of it, tail high in the air.

'There's not much here.'

'You're very picky for someone who's been living rough on a handcart for a month,' the young witch replied, measuring from the well to the easternmost point of the clearing. She picked a large leaf from an overhanging branch, folded it into a dart and threw it, watching as it glided smoothly across the clearing and nosedived down the well without touching the walls.

'Bullseye!' said the cat. 'But it'll have to be a big pub if the dartboard's this far away from the oche.'

She placed another leaf on the ground with the stalk

towards the well and started to walk around the perimeter of the clearing.

'We're not having a pub.'

Axy walked on the wall, keeping pace with his mistress.

'What are we having then?'

'A home.'

He sat down. 'Here? Not only in the middle of nowhere but very handy for the back of beyond? What do we do for entertainment? Who am I going to talk to?'

The witch stopped by her leaf marker and smiled at him, her hands on her hips. 'We'll just have to make our own entertainment, like every generation before us has.' She walked towards him. 'And as for your social life – well, you'll soon find some little friends.'

'Oh, great. "Little friends",' he sneered. 'I need friends of all sizes.'

The wooden roller creaked in protest as she cranked the handle of the well, reeling in a tattered and fraying rope until it hauled up a slimy, dribbling, rust-banded bucket, holding stinking water which was dark green, almost black, with brown noodles of weeds swaying superciliously from side to side under the surface.

'Fancy a taste?' she grinned.

He screwed his nose up.

'Not likely. But good wine is a good familiar creature comfort...' he said hopefully.

'Well, we don't have any wine yet, so let's see what we can do with this.' She let the bucket fall back into the water, and from a pocket in her dress she pulled out a small leather pouch secured by a brass ring.

Axy padded over to investigate, trying to get his nose into the pouch. 'What have you got there?'

She whipped it away out of reach.

'Naught for nosies. Out of the way.'

She elbowed him gently and he slunk off to the opposite side of the well and peered down it.

From the pouch she picked a small, white lozenge, dropped it into the well and stood back. Almost immediately a dense, muddy cloud shot out of the well, followed by coughing, spluttering, a thud and a call of 'Aw, thanks a bundle!'

'I told you to get out of the way,' the witch laughed, as the cloud dispersed and Axy staggered from behind the well. She cranked the handle again, this time reeling in a strong, tightly braided rope which held a brand new wooden bucket full of clear, sparkling, liquid crystal water. She scooped some up in her hand and tasted it; sweet and ice-cold, it giggled in her mouth. She swallowed.

'Perfect!'

She bobbed down to Axy, who licked her palm.

'I suppose this means we're staying,' he said.

'Of course we're staying. This is our home. Now come and help me get this lot unpacked – we've a lot to do...

When Naiba awoke, she had writer's cramp and lines down her face where sheets of manuscript had been her pillow. She did not feel rested.

NOTES ON

The Architecture of The Union

The Main Tower of The Union can be seen from miles around, dominating the landscape like a giant black witch's hat. In Maund, hardly anybody actually looks at it, mainly because it's always been there so everybody's seen it and it's so tall that trying to see the top makes you fall over.

The only breaks in the exterior surface of the Main Tower are the windows, which are a variety of round, crescent and star shapes. The masonry between the window frames is home to thousands of small black amphibians called heliolamina whose purpose in life is to absorb sunlight then plunge into pools of water to cool off, the heated water then being siphoned off for use throughout The Union buildings.

Completely encircling the base of the Main Tower, much like the brim on a witch's hat, is a covered walkway. Its slate roof is bordered by guttering, thus affording shelter not only from the rain but also from any wayward experiments daft or desperate enough to make a sudden exit through one of the windows.

At the apex of the Main Tower is The Point, where the sloping circular construction can accommodate no more bricks and the resultant gap is covered by a crystal cone, which tapers from a few inches at its base to a single micron in width at the tip. However, it is impossible to see The Point from ground level, chiefly because the Main Tower is so high its upper reaches are constantly above several layers of cloud. From a distance it looks like an upturned cast iron icing bag punching through cotton wool doughnuts.

Inside the crystal cone of The Point is a spherical air bubble, in perfect imitation of the spherical glass Globe Hall which is the main assembly area and auditorium that fills the base of the Main Tower and resembles nothing so much as an enormous hollowed-out crystal ball in which someone has had the good sense to lay a flat wooden floor.

Looking up through the glass roof of the Globe Hall there is a startling symmetry and concentricity to the interior of the Main Tower, which houses rings of classrooms and dormitories like a child's 'stack the rings inside the cone' toy. Each ring of rooms is fronted by a galleried landing, the doors and banisters as regular as the pictures on a zoetrope. Light bounces merrily from polished marblewood doors and handrails which are supported and complemented by wrought iron handles, hinges and spindles. Each successive landing echoes the one before, and they seem to frame The Point as celestial rings frame a far-distant planet, eloquently demonstrating happens when you lock an architect in a room with nothing for company but a barrel of turnip burgundy and a spiral-drawing machine.

The designs of the Main Tower were re-used, greatly scaled down, when The Union's new Library was built, and all the plans are still held on file in case an enterprising student develops a hitherto unknown branch of magic which needs its own premises, or a Matriarch wants an extension.

The circular architecture of The Union reflects the cyclic

rhythms of Mother Nature, and circular construction ensures concentration of magic, which is why the perimeter wall of The Union is circular. The area within the wall is known as Concentric Yard and it encloses most things necessary for life and studies to continue, including not only the Main Tower and the Library, but the Magic Pool, Brew Shed, Art House, Herb Wheel, crop circle, vegetable rotatory, orchard, frog pond, apiaries and countless other things which have been built, planted, installed or modified as necessary. Or unnecessary but aesthetically pleasing.

However, for the sake of safety The Union Flying School is located just outside the perimeter wall with an invisible rebound barrier in place to stop any trainee broomstick pilots losing control over Concentric Yard and baling out into the Magic Pool. It's not that they wouldn't survive the fall; it's the fact that they might drop in the pool as a trainee witch but what they'd come out as would be another matter, possibly one which would keep scholars guessing for years.

~•~

Dominica and Bebe crossed the floor of the Globe Hall. In a few weeks' time, Dominica thought, there'll be another portrait up on the wall. Another link in the chain. It'll show that Imelda was another pair of capable hands through which The Union had safely passed. Another steady, measured study of calm Matriarchal efficiency. It won't show her doing sleight-of-hand tricks for kiddies, or thumping the table at a Senior Council meeting, or topping up Matron's elderflower spritzer with something stronger at the Walpurgis Night revels. It won't show the jewel that was Imelda; it'll only show the box the jewel came in. And after a few years, the box will be the only thing most people will recall, for those who have seen the jewel will be few, and the many will not believe that such a box could hold such a jewel.

Stepping out into the garden, where life carried on as normal principally because it hadn't been told not to, Dominica suddenly became aware that she was the temporary link in the chain. In her hands lay the threads of the past, and only she could ensure they carried on into the future; she had to be the bridge between history and possibility, and with Mother Nature's help she would not fail.

She filled her lungs, glad to be freed from the four walls, in a place where she could stretch her body and let the sunshine feed her soul, a place where Mother Nature was all around her. As she stooped to smell a rose, there was a thrash of leaves and a flash of ginger; she didn't see which way it went, but it did remind her that Bebe was at her side and courtesy demanded conversation.

'Bebe's an unusual name, isn't it?' she commented as they walked to the Library.

'Oh, it's not me real name, mum, it's only me nickname. Me real name's Buda.'

'Buda?'

'Dad says he called me that 'cos he knew I were goin' to be a pest, but he lives in a world of his own, mum.'

'Buda and Truda. Are you twins?'

'Lords, no, mum. Truda's the eldest, then there's me, Duda, Fuda, Guda, Juda, Luda and Muda.'

Dominica opened her mouth to speak, but her brain got

there first and closed her mouth again. It then sent the unused words down her nose, where they came out sounding like a sigh. She tried again, using different words.

'Why are you all called something ending in "uda"?'

'Well, our Mam has trouble with her letters, mum, and after Truda she wanted summat a bit simpler, so she knocked the first two letters down to one and then it were easy for her just to change one letter, rather than change 'em all.'

'Why isn't there a Cuda?' Dominica asked, somehow knowing there'd be a good reason she'd never think of.

'Dad says if you called somebody Cuda, people'd always say you Cuda chosen a better name. But like I say he lives in a world of his own, mum.'

'Quite. But doesn't it get confusing, all of you having names that sound similar?'

'No, mum, 'cos we've all got nicknames 'cept Truda. I'm Bebe, and there's Deedee, Effie, Gigi, Jay, Ellie, and Emmie.'

'Oh. Gigi is quite an exotic name, isn't it?'

'Dunno, mum. We call her Gigi 'cos she looks like an 'orse.'

~•~
NOTES ON
The Library

Many generations ago the Library was within the Main Tower itself but increased numbers of both students and books forced the construction of a separate building, not just as a matter of storage but one of sorcerial necessity.

More students meant more magic of a practical nature; more books meant more magic of a theoretical nature. Unfortunately, wayward experiments and excess practical magic from the Upper Levels which couldn't get out of the windows tended to plummet down the centre of the Main Tower, heading straight for the Library Area. A shimmering thaumaturgical shield across the inside of the Main Tower ensured they were caught and burnt up before they could do any serious damage, but it took such a battering it had to be renewed every year.

With the serendipitous timekeeping witches are renowned for, the Library was built not a day too soon. Twenty-four hours before the topping-out ceremony, the shield was overdue for renewal and an intense but misjudged incantation punched a hole through it. As the words were falling towards the roof of the Globe Hall, someone opened a door into the Library and the resultant draught sucked the words in. The aura of the Library changed the words from air to liquid, which a quick-thinking Library assistant caught in her tea mug. Holding it at arms' length, she dashed outside and poured it over the Orbital Rockery which has had a damp patch ever since, even in a drought. Apparently her tea never tasted the same afterwards, either.

Once the books had been removed to the new Library, the shield was retired and a complicated series of drains, gutters, ducts and channels was installed in the Main Tower to drain the excess magic and collect it in the Magic Pool, making it the only pool in the world to grow talking bulrushes. Unfortunately, possessing the power of speech is not the same as being able to comprehensibly communicate well-reasoned argument, hence the expression that people are often said to be 'talking bul'.

The Library, the Main Tower and the Magic Pool are the three points on an equilateral triangle inside the perimeter wall of The Union. Each of the triangle's sides is bisected by a golden flashrod; the point where the flashrods meet marks the exact centre of The Union. The main purpose of the flashrods is to stop cross-pollination of magic from the Library, the Main Tower and the Magic Pool; magic leaking from any of these points will be earthed by the flashrods.

However, on hot summer nights when the elderflower spritzers have been flowing, witches may be asked to walk a straight line along a flashrod to prove they're fit to spell.

The Library used to be cool, dark and quiet. If you nodded off in the Library, the chances were you'd never be able to tell whether you'd woken up; it was an excellent place to go if you wanted to get some practice in for eternity.

Then Libby Waveshaft became Librarian. Libby's field was Light Engineering, and once she entered that field, everybody else might as well have picked up their picnic baskets and headed for the coast. She walked into the Library one day, blew away some dust from the counter top, and saw polished glasswood. Where there was polished glasswood, there was reflection, where there was reflection, there was light, and where there was light, Libby could engineer.

Which she did, brilliantly. As an architectural echo of the Main Tower, the Library has a Point at the top where the bricks are too big to fit and a tapering crystal cone tops off the building. By installing strategically placed mirrors and prisms, and keeping the whole place highly polished, Libby was able to reflect and refract the light from the Point around the whole Library. Pools of light collected in previously gloomy corners, and refracted light found its way along the floors between bookshelves where once the dust had lain undisturbed for months, sometimes years on end.

Libby based her lighting system on one of the basic tenets of The Union's teaching, the 'pea principle': any solution to a problem or any work to be done must be practical, economic and appropriate. So, as you walk along between the gleaming bookcases, a vertical shaft of light shines from the top of the bookcase to the floor and keeps pace with you, allowing enough light to see what's on the shelves at the point where you stand, but not enough light to disturb the other books in the vicinity.

Glancing across the Library will show the various disciplines illuminated by colour: in the Nature section the light is lush and verdant; in Sciences there's a cool blue glow; Politics and Economics have a faint yellow haze; History and

Biographical Studies a lilac softness. Everywhere you look you can see something, but if you're not looking the light isn't there. Libby's light only goes where it's needed, and if it's not needed it goes for a lie down somewhere to conserve its energy. Consequently, the books enjoy the cool darkness they've come to expect, the users of the Library have the appropriate lighting for their task, the light only has to do a fraction of the work it used to and successful applicants for the cleaning jobs in the Library undergo several months of intense duster training and must pass a stringent practical polishing exam.

~•~

Dominica and Bebe approached the counter. A column of light illuminated Libby, making it seem that she had just stepped out of the shadows. Her crystal pendant earrings flashed and shone in the column of light, breaking it up and casting a hazy corona round her head; her long, parchment-coloured gown was covered in writing. She looked like an angel someone had been using as a notepad.

'What's the gown all about, Libby?' asked Dominica.

'Dopple's Theory on the Duplication of Entities,' Libby replied. 'Rather smart, don't you think?'

'Very nice. Give us a twirl.'

'No point. The back's exactly the same as the front.'

Libby laughed, and several pinpricks of light danced around the Library and slowly faded. 'Right then,' she said. 'What can I get you?'

'I need these books.' Dominica handed Libby a list. 'Bebe, would you wait over there until the Librarian has got all the books together and then carry them to my study, please? I'll be back later.'

'Yes, mum.' Bebe bobbed, then went to sit and wait.

Dominica turned to Libby again.

'I also need access to Legal, if that's alright.'

'Certainly, Vice-Matriarch.'

The Legal Chamber was at the far end of the Library – something not possible with any other round building. Dominica swept past Home and Social Studies, where an orange warmth briefly flickered into life then faded as she passed. The red glow from the Romantic Fiction section beckoned to her and she veered down a pink passageway. Hardly anybody came this way any more, and then it was usually on their way somewhere else. The light seemed surprised to see someone. It shimmered all the way from coral to vermilion, and made Dominica feel queasy.

At the end of the passageway was a door, and as the scarlet glow faded behind her she could just make out the nameplate. Not that she needed to read it – she already knew what it said: *Legal Chamber: Unauthorised Access Prohibited.* A previous Matriarch, the security-conscious Edgarina Vacuum, had put the nameplate on the door when she had been head of the Legal Department, overlooking the fact that only Senior Council members had keys to the Legal Chamber. In point of fact, only the Librarian and Senior Council members *knew* about the Legal Chamber, and even then only during their term of office. Once they left the Senior Council, all their knowledge of the Legal Chamber vanished. A sign prohibiting unauthorised access was as useful as a notice whose sole function in life was to advise people, 'Do not throw stones at this notice.'

Dominica took the copper keyring from her pocket. Using the bronze key, she unlocked the door, stepped inside and closed the door behind her, listening to the tumblers in the lock falling back into place by themselves as she took a moment to adjust to the dimness of the room. The light was grey, soulless, dull and flat; it was the sort of light which was rarely invited to parties and only then it was because they were family affairs and everybody had to be invited, so it would sit at a table away from the music with half a shandy droning on in a nasal whine about the beneficial aspects of Hawthorne's *Laws of Administration*.

The room was lined from floor to ceiling with shelving stockpiled with pads of pre-printed forms, most of which were to do with some aspect of security. One shelf did contain useful items, such as blank Graduation Insignias and pointy hat order pads, but the rest was all that remained of Edgarina Vacuum's Fabulous Bastion of Impregnability – unloved, unwanted and unused.

The grey light reluctantly illuminated a painting of Edgarina, hanging half-way up the wall opposite the door through which Dominica had entered. However, Edgarina had been keen to the point of paranoia on preserving the secrets of The Union, and the painting showed an empty chair in front of a bookcase in which were lined up volumes whose titles had been carefully obscured. Dominica touched the bottom of the frame and the painting silently swung to one side on carefully concealed hinges. Behind the portrait was a recess in the wall containing protective goggles, protective gloves and a lead safe. A sign on the front of the safe said UNAUTHORISED ACCESS STRICTLY PROHIBITED. Dominica donned the goggles and gloves before carefully inserting the silver key into the lock on the safe. The sign on the safe changed.

ACCESS FOR MEMBERS OF THE SENIOR COUNCIL ONLY.

She turned the key once.

ARE YOU AUTHORISED FOR THIS ACCESS?

Twice.

CAN YOU PROVE YOU THAT THE KEY YOU ARE USING IS YOUR OWN?

Thrice.

ACCESS IS RECORDED IN CASE OF DISPUTE. DO YOU WISH TO PROCEED?

Fource.

IF YOU'RE NOT ALLOWED TO DO THIS, YOU'RE GOING TO BE IN BIG TROUBLE. DON'T SAY I DIDN'T WARN YOU.

As Dominica turned the silver key for the fifth time, there was a whisper as well-oiled mechanisms slid into place.

ON YOUR OWN HEAD BE IT.

Dominica opened the safe.

The Tutor of Creative Chronicling looked up from the manuscript.

'You've certainly made an interesting start.'

'Thank you,' said Naiba.

'You've included quite a bit of detail in this first section. Did you research it? Readers look for veracity of detail. Paint a broad picture and the reader will accept whatever you tell them; describe something to the *n*th degree and they will seize upon any inconsistency. Is it possible all these trees and shrubs will grow in the same place at the same time? I'm ashamed to say botany's not my—'

'*Do not concern yourself with trivia; this is my world, not yours.*'

The Tutor and Naiba looked at each other as if neither of them knew where the voice had come from. Naiba remembered forming some words in her head, but she was sure they weren't the ones which came out of her mouth.

The Tutor cleared her throat.

'Er… quite. Ahem. Are you all right?'

'Fine. I'm fine thank you.' Naiba could hear the relief in her own voice at hearing her own voice.

'Oh, good, good,' said the Tutor, mentally filing the incident away; at a later date it could be expanded, enriched, cut and polished ready for publication. 'What did I give you to write about?'

'A piece of dried ginger root.'

'It doesn't seem to figure very prominently.'

'I know, but that seems to be its story.'

'Not its entire story, surely? I feel that this is only the scene setting, the curtain-up, as it were, of the—'

'*I know,*' said the voice. '*It's not finished yet.*'

Dominica left the Library with what looked like a very expensive shoe box under her arm. With every step, she felt the box becoming increasingly obvious, as if it knew that what it contained was of vital importance, otherwise it wouldn't be out here in the sunshine. Also, she had the distinct impression that what was in the box was impatient to be out and about, doing what it was meant to do. She quickened her pace in order to reach the Main Tower before the box persuaded her to open it.

A pair of green-gold eyes with black almond vertical pupils watched her path.

Once back in the relative cool and shade of the Main Tower, the box settled down and Dominica relaxed a little. As she reached the door of her study she was just about to heave a sigh of relief when she heard a noise. She put the box to her ear and listened carefully, but the noise seemed to be coming in via the other ear, which meant it was coming from within her room. She opened the door.

'Dennis, is that you?'

'No, mum, it's me,' answered a pile of books supported by a pair of arms with interlocked fingers. It tried to curtsey, but instability soon put a stop to that.

Dominica swept past it into the room.

'Oh, Bebe, do put those on the desk,' she said, bending down to put the box under her bed – the coolest, darkest place in the room. 'Your arms must ache.'

Bebe wandered to where the desk might have been, but wasn't; Dominica straightened up just in time. She took hold of Bebe's shoulders and steered her from behind.

'There you are – right by the desk. You can put the books down now.'

'Can't, mum. Me fingers is locked. Can't get 'em apart.'

Dominica removed the books one at a time, gradually uncovering a red face. As Bebe's arms emptied, the desk filled. When there were no more books, Dominica attempted to prise open Bebe's fingers, but the knuckles had locked and Bebe was condemned to stand like a choirgirl about to attempt an aria.

'Oh, I'm so sorry. I didn't know it'd do this to you.'

'Nowt that cold water won't fix, mum, don't you fret.'

'Then go and get it fixed it right away,' said Dominica, suddenly thirsty at the mention of cold water.

'It'll be right, mum. It's always happenin'. Me fingers lock up like it's goin' out of fashion.' Bebe moved towards the door. 'It's why I can't play the piano – that and the fact we haven't got one.' She opened the door with both hands and bobbed. 'I'll send some tea up, mum.'

'Thank you Be— how did you know?'

'Family trait, mum.' She closed the door.

Dominica sat at her desk and looked out of the window. He was out there somewhere, she was sure, but he was keeping a very low profile.

She sorted through the books on her desk. Mrs Egg's *Festive Fare* – that could wait, so it went on the floor, as did Askey's *Bee-keeping* and Rayalan's *Voice Projection Made Easy*. Her immediate need was for *The Book of Procedures Volumes X and XI*; unfortunately, *Volume X* was not there.

Dominica checked through the books on the floor again and then through the books in front of her. She leant over the desk and checked the floor at that side, swiftly followed by a search to the left and right.

'Lost something?' said a voice from the window-sill.

'And where have you been?' asked Dominica. She looked up. 'Oh, sorry, Bertie. I thought you were Dennis.'

'Alas, no. I just thought I'd get a bit of fresh air but this window happened to be open…'

Dominica started to write a note.

'If you really want some fresh air, I don't suppose you'd do me a huge favour?'

'Anything.'

'Take this note to Libby and wait for her reply. Please.'

'Your wish is my command.'

'You're a familiar, not a genie.' She rolled up the note and put it into Bertie's mouth. 'Thanks.'

'Mo probms,' he replied and leapt off the window-sill into the garden just as there was a knock on the door.

'Come in!' called Dominica.

The door opened and a serving-girl carrying a tea-tray backed into the room.

''Scuse me, miss – Bebe sent me,' she said, turning round. 'She's still got her hands in iced water.'

Dominica smiled. 'You must be Gigi.'

'That's right, miss,' said Gigi. 'How did you know?'

'Oh, just a lucky guess.'

Spirit of the Wind paced backwards and forwards under the Ancient Apple Tree, choking back tears. How could she? After all their years together? They'd had their ups and downs – everybody did – but they'd always been there for each other. More than once he'd limped home after a fight and she'd patched him up, dressing his wounds and chiding him gently for being hot-tempered. Many an evening he'd sat on her knee, sharing the firelight, perfectly content as she smoothed his fur with her soft, caressing hands, talking about the day's events… and now it all seemed a lifetime away.

All right, so he wasn't as handsome as some of the other cats he could mention – and one he couldn't – but she wasn't the sort who worried about looks. She wouldn't be swayed by smooth fur and an unscarred body and perfect ears. She looked past the packaging to the familiar inside.

So why did he hurt so much?

Part of him still couldn't believe it. Not Dominica. Not her. But yet a faint smell still lingered in his nose…

No. It must be some new magic they're trying out. Or… or maybe because she'd been sitting with the Matriarch for so long. You're bound to pick up different smells when you're in someone else's room for so long waiting for them to d—
…waiting for it to be over. Bound to.

Over. Waiting for it to be over. She said it was over. Maybe that's what she meant. Not him and her; the Matriarch. Yes, that must be it! The Matriarch's time was over, and it was time for something else! She wasn't leaving him! Oh, fool. And to think he'd nearly— well, never mind. He just hoped he hadn't said anything to upset her, that's all. Time to get back in there and act as if nothing had happened. Least said, and all that.

He sat down and washed his face. Best to look well-groomed, especially if there's apologising to be done, which was a possibility. Right then. All clean; best foot forward.

Here we go, round the Ancient Apple Tree and…

He looked up to Dominica's window, which was still partly open. He froze in his tracks. Standing on the window-sill was Bertie.

'Hewwo,' said Bertie to Dominica, bending to put his head under the bottom of the window. In his mouth was a rolled-up piece of paper. 'I've bwought you Wibby's wepwy.'

Dominica took the paper. 'Oh, you angel, Bertie.'

'Anything else I can do?'

Dominica's brow furrowed slightly as she read the note.

'No… no thank… er… you didn't see Dennis on your way round, did you? He was acting strangely earlier on and I haven't seen him for hours.'

'How can you tell when he's acting strangely? He's probably having a f— oof!' There was a flash of gold in the sunlight. Bertie's head hit the woodwork with a thud and he disappeared from the window-sill.

One eye-witness said she thought a first-former's fireball had escaped when the blur of orange streaked past her and up the wall, knocking something from the window-sill. It was only when both things had fallen to the ground that she saw both things were cats.

When Bertie hit the earth, a couple of things troubled him. Firstly, why he'd been dragged off the window-sill, and secondly, deciding which hurt more – his head or his stomach, where Dennis's paw had winded him. He didn't have long to ponder.

Dennis stood over him, snarling. 'That's it. I've had

enough. It's time we settled this.'

'Settled what?'

'You've got some bloody nerve, I'll give you that.'

'What? What's happened?'

'Nothing yet. But I'm going to give you the biggest hiding of your miserable life.'

'Now, now, Dennis, let's not be too hasty about this. You don't want to do something you'll regret.'

'No. What I do want to do is push your teeth so far down your throat you'll have to sit down to eat your dinner!'

Bertie liked his teeth where they were, so he made a dash for it across the garden. Dennis streaked after him and, being fitter, soon caught up with him. A carefully stuck-out paw sent Bertie sprawling across the grass. As Dennis loomed over him again, Bertie knew he was beaten, but he was damned if he knew why.

'Dennis, Dennis— before you go rearranging my features don't you think I deserve to know what I've done?'

'You deserve a bloody good hiding!'

'What have I done?!'

'What have you done?' Dennis prodded Bertie, who started back-pedalling. 'What were you doing on my window-sill, eh?' Prod. 'What were you doing in her room, eh?' Prod. 'Why are you trying to take over my' – prod – 'mistress' – prod – 'eh?' – prod.

Bertie pushed Dennis's paw aside. 'I'm not trying to t—'

'I smelled you. I smelled you on her! You've started moving in, haven't you? You scumbag!'

'I haven't! I swear!'

'Don't give me any of that. You lie like a bloody tab rug!'

'I'm not lying! Ask her!'

'I don't have to. She told me. I smelled your filthy scent all over her and I asked her if it was over and she said yes. And all for you, you bastard!'

Dennis lunged at Bertie, who had nowhere to run. For the next couple of minutes the air was full of the primeval sound of teeth clashing, claws skittering on stone, flesh tearing and bone thumping, a body in pain and a soul in torment.

Heads popped up from behind rockeries, under bushes, over the tops of walls and below the water line in the pond. Those who dared moved closer to the action. A fight always draws a crowd; a good fight attracts specialists.

'Tonight's dinner says the ginger feller'll win,' said Spirit of the Ocean.

Spirit of the Twin snorted. 'Don't waste your breath. I wouldn't bet on Bertie – and I'm his brother.'

'Aren't you going to help him?'

'Against Dennis? If I look that stupid, it's time I got a new body.'

As the writhing combatants started to rip up a flower bed, the crowd parted. The two cats found themselves facing one another in mid-air, each held by the scruff of the neck in a grip of iron. Bertie managed to find a voice.

'You must've been the last one left when she came in!'

'Why you—'

'You're so stupid! You don't deserve her!'

'Well, you're not having her!' Blind rage made Dennis lunge at Bertie. His claws scored flesh. He didn't care any more. He'd take whatever punishment came his way now. What he couldn't take was the sight of blood pinpricking in parallel lines along Dominica's face. His eyes opened wide in horror, then his body went limp as he fainted.

Naiba opened her copy of *Scribe That Chronicle! Your Tale From Start To Finish*, the first words of which were 'Anybody can scribe a chronicle'. Encouragement and dismissal in equal measure. If any old fool could do it then she was as well-qualified as the next witch; but what was the point in trying to be a scribe if any old fool could do it? Mother Nature, if she spent that long pondering about every statement in *Scribe That Chronicle!* she'd never scribe anything herself. She decided to skim through the rest of it. One paragraph caught her skimming eye:

'Unfortunately, the Muse is a fickle creature; when she is with you, the words will cascade from you in an unstoppable torrent; when she leaves you, it can feel as if your meagre oasis has dried up. Therefore, when the Muse is upon you, take full advantage.'

Something whispered to Naiba that full advantages were the best sort and should be grabbed with both hands. The rest of the introduction went unskimmed as the story tumbled onto the page:

THEY WALKED OVER TO THE HANDCART. The cat tugged at the tarpaulin strings on one side of the cart while the young witch untied the other side. The tarpaulin made a skidding noise as she dragged it away to reveal a large black stove and a substantial candywood chest.

From under the base of the handcart the witch pulled a length of wood as long and as wide as the cart itself. Securing one end of it to the tailgate of the cart, she let the other end rest on the floor. She climbed onto the cart, braced herself against the backboard, planted her feet on the side of the stove and pushed. The tiny castors under the stove began to turn and it rumbled slowly towards the tailgate, where it waited for a few seconds as if considering its course before rolling down the slope and careering off across the clearing, raising clouds of dust.

'Watch out for the well!' shouted Axy.

'Circle!' called the witch. The stove swung violently and circled the well. The witch observed three revolutions before shouting, 'Stop!' The stove obeyed the command, and settled forever in its place, facing her, in the area designated the kitchen.

'Axy, go and stand by the stove and face me, please.'

The cat did as he was bidden.

'And now walk towards me.'

'If you wanted me over there, what did you send me over here for?'

'Just do it.'

He had walked about twice his own body length when she stopped him.

'Sit down there.'

The witch bent down to the candywood chest on the handcart.

'Right,' she said to its lock. 'Over to Axy, then circle the well and come to rest opposite the stove where Axy's sitting.'

Again she braced herself on the backboard.

'Hey! You're not using me for target practice,' said Axy, getting up.

'Sit down!' she yelled.

He sat, but covered his eyes with his paws.

She pushed the chest off the handcart. It sped towards the cat, and just when any spectator would have thought that nine lives were down to eight the chest veered, circled, and came to a halt opposite the stove and a whisker away from the end of Axy's nose. The witch leapt down from the cart.

'Excellent! You can look now.'

In taking his paws from his eyes, Axy moved his head a little too far and banged his nose on the candywood chest.

'Typical,' he said, rubbing his nose. He could have sworn the lock on the chest was smiling.

From the chest, the witch took a bowl, a spoon, a bag of white powder, a small bottle of dark liquid and a funnel which tapered down to an extremely fine point. She shook some of the white powder into the bowl, splashed cold well-water onto it and started to stir, lifting the spoon every so often to check the stiffness and adding more water as necessary. When she was satisfied with the consistency of the mixture, she added three drops of the dark liquid from the small bottle, and they appeared like bloodspots on the surface of the white paste. As she stirred them in, swirls of colour overran the white and eventually the mixture was brilliant carmine red throughout.

She scooped some of the mixture into the funnel, holding

her finger over the point so that none escaped. When the funnel was full she held it over the track left by those wheels of the chest which had been closest to the trees, and let the mixture flow out. She followed the track all the way round the circle back to the chest again, filling up the channel with the red mixture.

'What are you doing?' asked Axy, watching her repeat the process on the track left by those wheels of the stove nearest the well.

'I'm putting down the building lines.'

'Building lines?'

'When I start building, I'll follow these lines when I lay the bricks. But for now, they're just marking out the plot.'

Soon there were two vibrant red rings marked on the perfect round clearing...

Take full advantage of the Muse, *Scribe That Chronicle!* said. It didn't say that the Muse herself is no shrinking violet when it comes to seizing an opportunity.

'It's coming along very quickly, isn't it?' said the Tutor of Creative Chronicling.

'It appears to be,' replied Naiba.

'You're building the characters nicely, and it's obvious there's a strong relationship between the witch and the cat.'

'Thank you.'

'I notice your main character doesn't have a name.'

'*I know her name,*' said a familiar unfamiliar voice, as a helpless look crossed Naiba's face.

As a cold dread clutched her heart and a hot flush suffused her body, the Tutor suddenly felt she knew what it was like to be a baked alaska, and realised she needed to make a note of it when Naiba had gone. She took off her horn-rims and started to polish them furiously on a handful of her gown especially gathered up for the occasion.

'Do you— ahem!' She clutched at her voice with both hands to bring it back down a couple of octaves and made every effort not to look Naiba in the eye. 'Ahem. Do you think, er... ha!... do you think you ought to continue this – this work? I feel you may be... er... overdoing it.'

'Not overdoing it. Just telling it like it was.'

The Tutor was in danger of polishing her glasses into oblivion.

'Well, I... er... ha! – I still think you should um...' – she held her glasses up to the light to see how well she was polishing, but seeing as she didn't have her glasses on, she couldn't tell, so she breathed heavily on them – '...should go and see Matron. Ha! Yes, that's it. Go and see Matron.' The polishing continued apace.

'Oh, all right then – if you think it'll help.'

The Tutor of Creative Chronicling juddered and whimpered as there was a loud crack of horn-rim.

NOTES ON
Matron

Matron's attitude to illness was simple. As a trainee witch, you were supposed to be learning to be able to treat yourself. If you suffered from something more advanced in the curriculum, Matron would treat it. If it was visible, she'd treat it with ointment, bandages and compresses; if it wasn't visible, she'd assume it was all in the mind and as such, the mind could treat itself.

But as some people took more convincing of this than others, she kept a standard range of pills which students with non-specific ailments could work through. This started with yellow pills, which were just slightly too large to swallow comfortably and were mildly distasteful, and increased in size and revulsion through green, brown, blue and pink until you got to black. Black pills had to be sliced up to be swallowed and were so awful that only a complete breakdown of smell and taste buds allowed you to open the bag to look at them, and even then your eyes still watered. Black pills came with a complimentary bowl of curried horse manure to take the taste away.

Consequently, very few students were ever ill enough to get past the blues, and witches who graduated under Matron's regime never had a day's illness in their lives until they dropped dead.

Dennis started to come round as Dominica approached the sick bay. However, pain, heartbreak and fear of Matron meant he closed his eyes again and silently beseeched Mother Nature to keep him out of there.

Keeping a tight hold on Dennis, Dominica put Bertie down on the floor and knocked on the door.

'Just a minute!' called a voice from inside.

Dennis pretended he was dead.

The door opened and Matron ushered out a witch carrying a rolled-up manuscript, a paper bag and a sickly look.

'Two yellows three times a day,' Matron advised, 'and if it hasn't cleared up in a week, come back and we'll try something worse. Dominica! Come in! Oh, look at your face. What happened? Let me see to it for you.'

'No, thank you, Matron. I'll do that myself. I want you to have a look at one of these. There's been a bit of a scrap.'

'Oh, look at him, poor chap. Been in the wars, hasn't he? Come on – let Matron look at you.'

What was left of Dennis's heart sank as Matron's minty breath warmed his face. Mother Nature, let me die…

'Don't worry,' said Dominica, 'I'll sort this one out.' She shook him roughly. 'Any wars *he* gets in are usually of his own making. Can you look at Spirit of the Western One? I fear he's been' – she lifted Dennis until his ears were close to her mouth – '*the innocent victim of a vicious attack.*'

Dennis's eyes started to bulge behind their closed lids, but the wrath of his mistress was a small price to pay for not seeing Matron.

'In you go, Spirit,' Dominica said to Bertie.

He limped into the sick bay.

'I'll take care of him, don't you worry,' Matron reassured her, closing the door.

Dominica took Dennis in both arms and looked down at him.

'Right, you,' she said, as a single drop of blood fell from her jaw and stained the fur on his belly. It stung him worse than any injury he'd ever received.

Back in her study, Naiba glanced inside the paper bag which Matron had given her. Beautiful, glossy, custard orbs like little balls of sunshine. She put the bag on the desk next to the gnarled and wrinkled root, and the warm, spicy, slightly prickly smell of the ginger wafted towards her. She poured herself a glass of water and reached into the bag for one of the pills. As she drew it out, the malodour of sulphur shot straight up her nose, slapped her taste buds about and then raced off to give her stomach a good kicking.

Nausea is a powerful prompter of action. She dropped the pill back in the bag and scrunched up the top. Deciding that the potential cure was worse than the alleged ailment, she threw the pills in a drawer and slammed it shut.

Dominica sat on the edge of her bed. Dennis lay across her knees, feigning as near death as he could possibly manage. She opened up her medical kit beside her.

'Come on – let's hear it,' she said. Dennis kept silent. 'I know you're not dead or unconscious, so let's hear it.'

He remained motionless, hoping that if he could just hold on a few moments longer, Mother Nature might have pity on him and call him home. Dominica poked him in the belly, causing him to bend and flex.

'Unless your vocal cords have been severely damaged, I suggest you start talking, Dennis.'

'I'm sorry,' the tiniest of voices said.

She started to clean him up and dress his wounds.

'Did you say something?'

'I'm sorry. I'm sorry I'm sorry I'm sorry I'm sorry I'm sorry. You have no idea how sorry I am. I wouldn't have hurt you for the world. I didn't mean to, truly—'

'It was an accident.'

'Of course it was! I was angry... mad... so I behaved... madly.'

'And you're sorry.'

'Deeply.'

She pulled a bandage almost to the point of ripping.

'And can you give me one reason why I shouldn't take your sorry little carcass back outside and kick it all the way round Concentric Yard until my foot hurts?'

'Because it couldn't hurt me more than I'm hurting now.'

'Because I have learned to control my temper, unlike some I could mention.' With more force than was strictly necessary, she rubbed the spot where her blood had stained his body. It did not come out. 'What's got into you, Dennis? You've been in some scraps before, but never like this.'

'I've never had to fight for you before.'

She seemed not to hear this as she groaned when she

parted the fur on his flank to reveal gravel embedded in his flesh.

'I've never see you so – so vicious.' She gently eased the gravel out of his skin. He did not protest. 'So reckless.' She massaged soothing balm into his body. He made no sound. 'So – so like you didn't care whether you lived or died.'

She became aware that where his head lay on her thigh was damp. His eyes were closed. She lifted his head.

Tears streamed down his face.

'I don't care,' he said.

'What?' she snapped.

Dennis shook. 'I don't care.'

She sat him upright. 'Look at me, Dennis.'

He did not open his eyes. 'Please put me on the floor.'

'Look at me!'

'I can't. Now please – please – put me on the floor.'

She was surprised by his calm. She stared at the wet face, the closed eyelids, the battered body. She shook her head and gently set him on the floor. She watched as he lowered his head and limped to his bed in the corner, where he sat for a minute, sobbing.

Dominica sighed, a mixture of sorrow, anger and bewilderment. She thought for a minute, trying to find some logical explanation for today. Perhaps the Matriarch's death was subliminally affecting everything. Perhaps Dennis had been crossed in love. Perhaps it was, after all, just one of those days when the best thing to do is sit in the corner drinking elderflower spritzers until you can't focus.

She dampened some cotton wool and cleaned up the

dried blood from her cheek. As with most scratches, they looked worse than they actually were. That it had been an accident, she was sure; that he was sorry was more than evident. But what had caused it?

She felt something tap at her foot. Looking down, she saw Dennis take a couple of steps backwards and then sit down. He still did not look at her. On the carpet between the two of them lay a lock of hair in a silver clasp.

'What's this?' she asked.

'It's the most precious thing I have to give you.'

She counted to ten, then sat on the floor next to him.

'And why do you give it to me?'

Dennis didn't understand. Isn't this what you were supposed to do when it was over?

'I have nothing else,' he said.

'*"These shall Syster and Familiar keep until they be separated by proven Misfaith or Death."* Isn't that the rule?'

'Yes…'

Dominica was past caring. If Dennis wanted to drag this thing out, drag it out she would. 'Is one of us dead, then?'

Dennis's brow furrowed even further. 'No…'

'Then what have you done that qualifies as misfaith?'

This was more than feline flesh and blood could stand. Dennis's body may have been ravaged, but his temper was as quick as ever. His eyelids flipped open.

'Me? It's not me who's been consorting with another. It's not me who's broken our bond.'

'Are you telling me that I have?'

Dennis gasped. How could she be so cruel when he was

so vulnerable? Did she want it spelling out for her?

'I smelled him on you, for Mother Nature's sake!'

'Who? Smelled who? When?'

'When you came back from the Matriarch! You were asleep, and I came over to say hello, and all I could smell on you was him! Spirit of the Western One! All over you. On your leg. On your hand. On your – on your lips.'

'Oh, so that's it...'

'And I asked you if it was over and you said yes. So I've brought you your bargain-token back so you can go and give it to him and I'll just crawl away in a corner and die somewhere while the two of you live happily ever after!'

Dominica caught hold of his head with one hand and brought him close to her face. She was breathing hard; her grip was so tight he thought she would crush him. Her eyes glittered with a fire that he had never seen before and frankly never wanted to see again, but he could not look away as she snarled at him.

'How... how *dare* you talk to me in this way! I thought we understood each other, Spirit of the Wind, but now... you accuse me of misfaith? You smelled him on me because I gave him his freedom. I gave him his freedom because his mistress – *my friend* – had just died. That's what was over. Her life. The long wait. Their life-bond was broken by death. *We* bonded for life, don't forget it, *life* – spirit to spirit and soul to soul – and death is the only thing that will separate us. And if you doubt me, remember these scratches and that bloodspot. And if you ever, ever, say or do anything like this again, then we will be separated sooner rather than later, for I will kill you myself.'

Dennis had never been so terrified. He looked past the flames into her soul, and saw his paw-print.

Naiba told herself it was curiosity about the remainder of the story and a brave pioneering spirit to push back the frontiers of chronicling which made her carry on writing. And the Muse was upon her, wasn't it?

AXY WAS IN THE MIDDLE OF ONE OF THOSE DECISIONS which catch the dreamer unawares at the cusp of waking and sleeping. Am I dreaming, or can I smell shortbread? Or am I having one of those dreams where I know I'm awake, because in my dream I've just woken up? He opened one eye, and the truth laughed at him. This must be real life, he thought; under normal circumstances I wouldn't dream of sleeping under tarpaulin, however cleverly arranged over a handcart.

He twisted and fidgeted, rubbing his back on the floor of the cart to get the circulation going again. He stretched his forepaws out to the side, and his ears flattened at the scraping noise his claws made as they came into contact with metal. He investigated further and found one of the many cheap tin trays which his mistress had gathered during her baking training. Axy had the paw to execute any mischief, and what he really enjoyed when things were slow was to play, skilfully and with a loud noise. He tapped on the flat-bottomed tray with his claw, and smiled.

At the end of the slope down which his mistress had

rolled the stove and the chest, two large branches supported the tarpaulin, which formed a large flap. He padded down the slope to the flap and pushed it gently. It wasn't fastened. As quietly as he could, he manoeuvred the tray to the top of the slope and sat on it. He curled his tail onto the tray, hooked his foreclaws over the tin rim and took a full breath.

'Cast off forr'rd!' he shouted in a whisper. 'Cast off at the back end!'

As he told himself he was 'Casting off, Captain!' he pushed with his back foot and started sliding down the slope. Accelerating rather more rapidly than intended, he only just had time to assume a more streamlined shape as he burst through the tarpaulin flap. The corner of the tarpaulin ran along his back, leaving a parting down which the wind whistled as he shot off across the clearing, dust clouds billowing. He leaned forward.

'Meeeeowwwwww!'

He laughed as the sound streaked out behind him. He was still laughing as he hit the small stone which sent the tin tray clattering, wheeling across the clearing and into the trees. Axy bowled over and over in the dust, straight into a pile of shortbread which came raining down on him like a ton of what they were.

'Hey, mind my bricks!' shouted his mistress from the edge of the clearing.

Axy fought his way up through the pile of sugar-coated shortbread and shook himself. Slipping and staggering down the unsteady surface, he came to rest near a coil of caramel rope.

'What's this?' he called.

'Haven't you ever seen a toffee cable before?'

'Only in Dr Poonser's Dictionary.'

He noticed a mountain of broken biscuit gravel nearby. It was too tempting; he leapt and sloughed his way to the top.

'I'm the cat of the castle!' he sang.

'Get down, you dirty rascal!' came the reply.

Round an overhanging tree branch, the witch was tying off one end of a caramel rope cradle in which her cauldron was suspended. Inside the cauldron she had fitted two offset paddles, and the cauldron was at an angle so that she could throw things into it.

'Come here a minute,' she said. 'I've got a job for you.'

Axy lifted his back paws in the air, hooked his front paws round them and slid down the mountain on his back, deftly putting his paws down in the right order when he reached the ground. He padded over to her, the heat from the working stove stinging his eyes when he passed. He looked up at the cauldron.

'What are you doing?'

'You'll see,' grinned the witch. 'Hop on.'

What he hopped on to was a thick black liquorice conveyor belt running over rollers of seaside rock. As long and wide as a tall person's bed, the conveyor was supported by a candywood frame which stopped the liquorice dragging on the ground. When Axy hopped on it, the liquorice moved over the rock rollers; he lost his footing and fell on his back with his legs in the air. The conveyor carried him along and dumped him off the end.

'Oh, I like that!' he giggled.

'Good, isn't it? See if you can walk on it.'

Never one to resist a challenge that looked like fun, he had another go and this time kept his footing when he landed on the conveyor. As he padded along, the liquorice again moved over the rock rollers and although he was walking quite briskly, he was getting nowhere fast.

'Brilliant!' he shouted, trying out a variety of side-steps, dance routines and backwards walking.

'Thought you'd like it,' his mistress laughed. 'Now mind your head.'

He rode to the back of the conveyor to get a better view and narrowly missed cracking his head on the cauldron as the witch adjusted its rope cradle and lowered it slowly until it was in contact with the liquorice. Once the cauldron touched the black strip, there was a gentle rumbling as it rotated within its cradle, powered by the liquorice drive belt.

'Keep going,' said the witch.

Axy walked, and the cauldron turned. The faster he walked, the faster the cauldron turned.

'Now what?' he called.

She lifted him off the liquorice.

'Now we have some tea, then I'll mix up some lemon and lime mortar to hold all these bricks together, and you start your new exercise regime…

The end of the Matriarch was the start of well-regulated procedures, which was why Dominica was knocking on the door of a certain study.

'Come in!' sang a voice obviously having a better day than she was. She opened the door.

The Bursar was standing in front of a full-length mirror, arms outstretched and draped in thick velvet. Her long straight hair glistened as she posed right and left, and its rich autumnal colours contrasted vividly with the aquamarine of the velvet. From the back, she looked like a sunset over the sea. 'What do you think, Minnie?'

Dominica was willing to let this one go on the grounds that she didn't want to spend any more time with the Bursar than she had to. 'Very nice. Is it for something special?'

'It's going to be my Inauguration gown,' said the Bursar, adding condescendingly, 'surely you can see that, Minnie.'

Dominica needed no further provocation but as she strode into the room, from in front of the Bursar emerged the smallest, most wizened, round-shouldered woman in Maund. Round the woman's neck was a tape measure and on her wrist was a pin cushion. She reached up to measure the Bursar's outstretched arms, wheezing as she went.

'That'll be all, Mrs Placket,' said Dominica. Mrs Placket duly folded up again, still wheezing like a battered self-operating concertina.

The Bursar waved imperiously. 'Hang on, Minnie, this won't take a moment.'

Mrs Placket started to unfold…

'That will be all, Mrs Placket, and you will have no memory of this.'

…then thought better of it. Picking up her basket with one hand and deftly flicking through her appointments book with the other, she shook her head and left silently.

'Now really, Minnie,' said the Bursar, turning to face Dominica, who was rather more angry and certainly closer than the Bursar had realised. The Bursar started to back away but was hampered by the velvet draped around her. As she divested herself of the cloth, she lost her balance and grabbed at a bedpost for support. Unfortunately, the Bursar was not the sylph-like creature she had once been, and as her chubby fingers closed round the newel it broke off, causing her to fall on the bed.

'Ow! What the—?'

The Bursar fished around under herself for the cause of her discomfort. She pulled out something which was the colour of thunder at midnight, and along its spine the gold letters glistened: *The Book of Procedures Volume X.* The Bursar looked startled and tried to stuff the book back.

Dominica's foot anchored the Bursar's skirts to the bedframe. She bent over the supine figure, and spoke through gritted teeth.

'My name is Dominica. And if you don't give me that book, yours will be forever forgotten.'

~•~
NOTES ON

Transition
(Procedures following the Death of the Matriarch)

'All this shall be done under the Direction of the Vice-Matriarch:

1. There shall be official Certification of the Death of the Matriarch, according to the Rules laid down in The Book of Procedures Volume XI: The Procedure of Certification. Upon such Certification, the Matriarch shall be known as the Matriarch Morte.

2. There shall be a General Assembly of The University, at which there shall be made the Announcement of the Death of the Matriarch Morte.

3. There shall be a formal Visit to the Apiaries, at which there shall be made the Announcement of the Death of the Matriarch Morte.

4. There shall be a Period of Mourning of not less than one Week, during which Time the following Events shall happen:

> 4a. There shall be a Meeting of the Senior Council, at which the Last Will and Returning Wishes of the Matriarch Morte shall be read, and the Pronouncement of the Name of the

Matriarch Designate shall be made.

4b. The Matriarch Designate shall be summoned. Should the Matriarch Designate:

- have pre-deceased the Matriarch Morte, or
- prove to be a Character of Myth, or
- fail to take up Office within thirty Days of summoning

then there shall be held an Election according to the Rules laid down in The Book of Procedures Volume XIV: The Procedure of Election.

5. There shall be a General Assembly of The University, at which there shall be made the Pronouncement of the Name of the Matriarch Designate.

6. There shall be a formal Visit to the Apiaries, at which there shall be made the Pronouncement of the Name of the Matriarch Designate.

7. There shall be held a Funeral Ceremony for the Matriarch Morte according to her wishes.

8. There shall be held an Inauguration of the Matriarch Designate according to the Rules laid down in The Book of Procedures Volume VIII: The Procedure of Inauguration.

9. There shall be held a Returning Ceremony for the Matriarch Morte according to the Rules laid down in The Book of

Ceremonies Volume XX: the Ceremony of Returning, taking into Account the Wishes described in the Last Will and Returning Wishes of the Matriarch Morte (Funds sufficing).·

> *The Book of Procedures Volume X:*
> *The Procedure of Transition*

The Procedure of Transition is now in its third edition, in which the rule about electing a Matriarch first makes an appearance. This is because Matriarch Joselina Spigot was so batty that she named her late brother-in-law as her successor, thus precipitating the Great Scrap (two spells, two submissions or complete destruction of the Known Universe to decide the contest).

The Great Scrap produced several interesting results: one golden flashrod was so bent out of shape by wayward spells during the contest that it had to be taken into the local forge to be straightened out; an overflow sump had to be built for the Magic Pool to drain into because it was in danger of flooding from all the thaumaturgical fallout; a new variety of geranium sprang up which is much the same as the other members of the geranium family except it brings itself in for the winter; a path through the gardens was created after a magical flame ran round trying to put itself out. It proved impossible to grow anything on the scorch marks, so the bare earth was lined with wooden slats to form a path. This is the answer to the often-asked question as to why Zig-Zag Walk doesn't start anywhere useful and ends abruptly at a flashrod.

The Winner of the Great Scrap was Meg Straweaver, a

Marshlander who became known as The Ironic Matriarch. Years earlier she had been asked whether she thought a Marshlander would ever be Matriarch, and she replied, 'Not in my lifetime, I don't think.' By the time her reign was over, many people wished she'd stuck to that principle.

One of Meg's first acts was to civilise the mechanism for determining the new Matriarch, and to that end she carried through the legislation which introduced elections into The Union and which became Rule 4b in *The Procedure of Transition*. And a good thing she did, too, for after a few years the pressure proved too much and she descended into madness, speaking of herself in the plural and naming as her successor a fictional character who was brought up by apes.

The election to find her successor was the first one to be held under Rule 4b.

~•~

On the way back to her study, Dominica encountered Gigi, who was mopping the corridor.

'Ah, Gigi. I want you to go and find the Head of Faculties and ask her to come to my room immediately.'

'Yes, miss. You want me to go immediately, or you want Faculties to come immediately, miss?'

'Both, Gigi, both.'

'Very good, miss.'

Gigi leant her mop up against the wall, bobbed, and set off on her appointed task.

Once she was safely out of sight, Dominica picked up the mop, whispered to it and set it down again. The mop started to clean the corridor by itself.

'Now don't forget to stop when she comes back,' said Dominica. After a few steps further down the corridor she remembered something, and spoke to the mop again. 'And for Mother Nature's sake, don't upset the mice – especially the large black one with the big ears and the high-pitched voice.'

One of the problems about having the Muse upon you is how to get it off again.

The writing continued, unabated.

IT WAS BECOMING LESS OF A CLEARING and more of a builder's yard. Neatly piled around the building lines were shortbread bricks, liquorice gutters and downpipes, glazed pastry doors and crystal toffee windows in rock frames. Brandy snap chimneys stood to attention next to grissini roof trusses, swiss rolls of insulation and egg-varnished crispbread slates. The witch was happy in her work and Axy had more than enough to exercise him…

Oblivious of his physical pain and freed from his mental one, Dennis was asleep in his basket, dreaming those dreams which seem perfectly rational while you're in them, but just you try explaining them afterwards without sounding like a megalomaniac or a complete lunatic.

He was leading his victorious troops through the town in a massive parade. The streets were thronged with people, cheering and clapping, celebrating the return of their heroes. Artemisia leaves were strewn across their path and flower petals rained down on them from their adoring public. Dennis led the way into the town square which was bedecked by gaily coloured bunting and flags, and the smell of frying sausages invaded his nostrils. He was about to go over to the hot-dog stall when the mayor called him back and led him into a banqueting hall. Although the room was laid out with tables set for hundreds of people, Dennis was the only guest.

As he sat down, the mayor clapped his hands and a procession of waiters entered carrying large salvers with domed silver covers. He inspected the contents of each platter as it was brought before him. He waved away cod, whitebait, trout, and salmon; he dismissed chicken, duck, quail and pheasant. He rejected a salver of cheeses and eggs, and the selection of beef, lamb, pork and venison did not tempt his jaded palate. The final platter was laid before him, and the waiter removed the domed cover. Walking round on the silver salver, hands and feet manacled and dragging chains along, was Dominica. Dennis looked up at the waiter.

It was Bertie, who started to smile, then grin, then laugh, until all Dennis could see was a gaping mouth and teeth, and all he could hear was Bertie's laughter filling the room. He screamed and lunged at Bertie, knocking the silver dome from his hand and sending it clattering across the room.

There was a resounding crash from the corridor outside Dominica's study. Dennis twitched in his sleep, then rolled over and started happier dreams.

Dominica opened the door. The Head of Faculties was sprawled across the corridor, and the mop was frantically trying to soak up spilled water, a task not helped by the fact it kept wringing itself out over the upturned bucket, so all it was doing was giving the water a change of scenery.

'Sorry about the noise, Dominica,' she said, kneeling up and righting the bucket, which greatly relieved the mop. 'Didn't see the bucket. Shouldn't take too long to clean up.' She took a piece of chalk from her pocket and started to write on the floor. 'If the bucket held a gallon of water, and let's call the absorbency of the mop a and each mopping and wringing time t, it should be done in 1 gal / a x t.'

'Which is not very long at all,' said Dominica, looking down with affection at her oldest friend and helping her up, after which she had to look up with affection at her, because Marianna Land – mathematician and Head of Faculties – was the tallest member of the Senior Council. As a student, she'd swept the board at most of the track events on sports days. Some people said her innate numerical abilities meant that throughout a race she was constantly able to balance distance, speed, track circumference, angle of curve, wind resistance and height and weight of other runners, thus giving her a distinct advantage over her opponents. Other people said she won through sheer length of leg.

'You've got parallel lines on your face,' she said. 'What happened?'

'Let's call it the result of friendly fur on a Union peacekeeping mission.'

'Enough said. So, what's the problem? How can I help?'

'It's Imelda. She's gone.'

'Oh, Dominica, I am sorry. Is that why the Bursar's

walking about with a smile like a semicircle?'

Dominica frowned. 'Decorum and Helena would appear to be mutually exclusive.'

Marianna nodded. 'No respect for anything, that woman; just shoves numbers about from one column to another, adding and subtracting 'em with no admiration for their power and no sense of wonder at all. Treats numbers like people most of the time. Worse in fact.'

She straightened her gown indignantly, causing clouds of dust to rise up and fall onto the clean floor. She had a natural affinity for chalk; the pockets of her gown were stuffed with odds and ends of chalk in all colours, even down to those little triangular pieces which have to be held with the very tips of the fingers and there's always a danger you'll scrape your fingernails on the blackboard and set everybody's teeth on edge. Consequently, she was always surrounded by a faint aura of rainbow dust, but she could explain complicated mathematical theory at the drop of a hat, especially if there was a handy wall or floor nearby.

The mop glared at the settling dust and slapped round Marianna's feet. Dominica took her friend by the elbow and led her away from the irritated cleaner.

'Will you help me do the Official Certification of Death?' she whispered.

'Certainly, but don't you need somebody a bit more qualified? Someone medical, perhaps? Matron?'

'No, I need someone with a pocket mirror. And you know what Matron's like. She'd probably take one look at her and say, "Take two black pills and come and back in a week" and we'd all be in limbo from here to Graduation.'

'True. Sorry – don't know why I suggested her. Put it down to brain fade. Been experimenting with magnets and think my brainwaves are a fraction out of sync at the moment. Be all right dealing with death. I've kicked the bucket myself today, haven't I?'

The Tutor of Creative Chronicling didn't want to reach the end of the manuscript, because then she'd have to say something. So, she read with one half of her brain whilst the other half searched her mental card index for something non-committal. Eventually the inevitable happened, and the words ran out. She handed the papers back to Naiba.

'Did you go and see Matron?' she asked.

'Oh, yes. She gave me some yellow pills.'

'Have they done the trick?'

Just the smell of them had done the trick.

'Oh, yes,' said Naiba. 'I feel a lot better now.'

'Good, good.' The Tutor relaxed. 'I think what you've written here is very well-described and you certainly have a vivid imagination.'

'*It's not imagination, it's fact,*' said a familiar unfamiliar voice.

The Tutor hurried a blank-faced Naiba towards the door. 'Well, must press on, you know, postcards to sort, sawdust to plait. Come back and see me when you've got less time.'

Naiba found herself outside the door of the Tutor's study, without really knowing how she'd left the room.

~✦~

NOTES ON

Certifying the Death of the Matriarch

These Tasks shall be done under the Direction of the Vice-Matriarch; a Member of the Senior Council shall perform these Tasks and at least one other Member of the Senior Council shall bear Witness to these Tasks.

1. A Looking-Glass shall be held unto the Lips of the Deceased, and be held there for a Minute; if there be no Clouding of the Looking-Glass, this shall be one of the Primary Signs of Death.

2. The Pulse shall be felt for at the Neck, Wrist and Ankle of the Deceased; if there be no Pulse detected, this shall be one of the Primary Signs of Death.

3. A Member of the Senior Council shall place her Hand upon the Chest of the Deceased and leave it there for a Minute; if there be no Rising and Falling of the Chest, this shall be one of the Primary Signs of Death.

4. A Feather shall be placed upon the Lips of the Deceased, and be left there for a Minute; if the Deceased blow not the Feather away, this shall be one of the Primary Signs of Death.

5. The Feather shall be applied to the Inside of the Elbows, the Palms of the Hands, the Soles of the Feet and the Environs of

the Nose of the Deceased; if there be no Reaction from the Deceased, this shall be one of the Primary Signs of Death.

6. When all the Primary Signs of Death detailed above have been given by the Deceased, a Member of the Senior Council shall say these Words to the Deceased: "The Wizards are at the Gate, demanding Entry."

If the Deceased replies not: "Tell the Wizards to bugger off!", this shall be the final Sign of Death, and the Deceased shall be known as the Matriarch Morte.'

> *The Book of Procedures Volume XI:*
> *The Procedure of Certification*

~•~

Marianna looked surprised when she saw the wreck of the Matriarch's bed.

'Have they started to clear the room already?'

Dominica started to pull at the tapestries.

'No, she's still under this lot.'

When the four-poster had collapsed, the top frame had dropped onto the base, trapping Imelda inside like a withered rose in a flower-press, then the posts had fallen across the top frame.

'A sudden death, was it?' Marianna asked as they lifted one of the posts and laid it on the floor.

'Not until Helena arrived.'

There was a sharp intake of breath and Marianna's eyes widened at the prospect of a scandal. 'Murder?'

'Not unless we put it down to death by exuberance.'

'Meaning?'

'Well, she – oh, it doesn't matter. But it wasn't actually murder.' Dominica caught a glimpse of Marianna's face: relief thinly tinted by disappointment. 'Don't worry, I'll give you the whole story when all this is finished – and by that time I'll probably need somebody to talk to – but I've got to get this done first.'

'I'm here for you on both counts.'

Dominica patted Marianna's arm. 'Thanks, Marianna. You're a good friend.'

They moved the other posts but the top frame proved too heavy for them to lift off and the thick fabric stretched across it prevented them getting to Imelda.

'Hang on,' said Marianna. 'I have an idea.' She took out a tape measure and carefully measured the width of the bedframe and the length of the poles. She rolled back a rug, knelt on the floor and started to chalk geometric shapes accompanied by complicated mathematical formulae. After about five minutes, she sat back on her haunches.

'I reckon if we build an A-frame out of the bedposts then throw a rope over the top of it and tie one end of the rope to that end of the top frame, we should be able to tilt it up on this end, thus freeing up the bed. Simple, really,' she said. 'What do you think?'

There was no reply. She looked up to see Dominica straddled across the top frame, cutting the last piece of material from the frame with a penknife.

'Or we could just cut the material off, I suppose,' said

Marianna, as Dominica clicked the penknife closed.

On the bed there was a mass of blankets, covers and tapestry under which, somewhere, were the last, mortal, slight remains of Imelda McGinty. They peeled back layer after layer of fabric. It was like trying to find the meat in a cheap puff pastry pie.

Eventually they were down to the sheets and then to Imelda herself, who appreciated not one little bit all the effort they had gone to. 'So,' sighed Dominica. 'What's first?'

Marianna stood at the foot of the bed, balancing *The Book of Procedures Volume XI* in one hand and fishing in her gown with the other.

'The Mirror Test,' she said, handing over a small pocket mirror covered in chalk-dust.

Dominica cleaned the glass on a handkerchief.

'Libby'd have your guts for garters if she saw this.'

'You don't have to tell me – if I want anything from the Library I have to send one of the domestics.'

'What?'

Marianna looked slightly shame-faced.

'Banned. Too dusty. I give to dust, that is, a little guilt.'

'And the rest of the guilt?'

'An ill-favoured thing, but mine own.'

'Y'know, you could've done Classics instead of Maths.'

Dominica held the mirror to the Matriarch's lips, and waited. She knew what the result would be, but she wasn't going to risk the future of The Union on a technicality. She handed the mirror back.

'There is no Clouding of the Looking-Glass.'

'I witness,' said Marianna. 'Next, Feeling for the Pulse.'

Dominica felt the Matriarch's neck. She knew Imelda was dead, but she was unprepared for the shock that the cold of the body sent through her fingertips. You never realise how warm people are until you touch someone whose warmth is just a memory.

She felt the Matriarch's wrist. It was strange to think the mechanisms to make the hand work were still in there, and it was only the power that was missing.

She felt the Matriarch's ankle. It was the first time she'd seen it – pale and bloodless; usually Imelda's feet had been encased in stout black boots which the sun did not penetrate.

'There is no Pulse detected.'

'I witness,' said Marianna. 'Next, the chesh tesh – chest tesh – test chesh – oh, dammit – the Test for the Rising and Falling of the Chest.'

Dominica put her hand on the Matriarch's chest. Her hand felt incredibly, conspicuously heavy and she couldn't make it feel comfortable before the minute was up.

'There is no Rising and Falling of the Chest.'

'I witness. Time for the first Feather Test.'

'Ah,' said Dominica. 'The feather.' She picked a pillow from the wreckage of the bed, held it against her body and smoothed it with her hand. She flipped it over and did the same again, then laid the pillow over one arm and eased out a small feather from the ticking. 'Here we are.'

'Lips first,' advised Marianna.

Dominica bent toward the Matriarch's face, then looked back at Marianna and grimaced. 'Bit of a problem.'

'Oh?'

'Her mouth's open and my feather's not big enough to cover both lips.'

'Ah. Can't you close her mouth?'

'Not really,' Dominica winced. 'That's manual intervention, isn't it? I think it contravenes the small print.'

'Hmm. And, come to think of it, negates the whole point of the exercise.'

'What about if we just did one lip?'

'Well, logic says if she hasn't got enough wind to blow it off one lip she certainly hasn't got enough to blow it off two, so it's either do one lip or go out and find a swan.'

Dominica balanced the feather on the Matriarch's bottom lip then moved away as slowly as she could. For the longest minute of their lives, Dominica and Marianna watched the feather, breathing out of the side of their mouths lest their breath be taken as a sign of life in the Matriarch.

'The Matriarch did blow not the Feather away,' said Dominica.

'I witness. Second feather test.'

Dominica dutifully applied the feather to the Inside of the Elbows, the Palms of the Hands, the Soles of the Feet and the Environs of the Nose of the Deceased.

'There is no Reaction.'

'I witness. And I, Marianna Land, witness and declare that all the Primary Signs of Death have been given by the Deceased.' She handed *The Book of Procedures Volume XI* to Dominica. 'Your turn.'

Dominica faced the Matriarch. 'Imelda McGinty, the

Wizards are at the Gate, demanding Entry.'

For all that Imelda knew, or cared, or could do anything about, the wizards could have been doing a conga through her bedroom and eating the world's largest knickerbocker glory out of her upturned hat.

Dominica looked at Marianna. 'Has the Matriarch replied, "Tell the Wizards to bugger off!"?'

'I witness that the Matriarch has replied not.'

'Then also witness that this be the final Sign of Death, and that Matriarch Imelda McGinty shall now be known as the Matriarch Morte.'

Marianna bowed her head. 'I witness.'

As the Assembly Bell struck its first sonorous note, the Vice-Matriarch and the Head of Faculties stood alone on the central dais of the Globe Hall. At the second stroke, all animal movement in Concentric Yard was stilled as families of fur, feather and scale turned towards the Main Tower. In the classrooms, pens and pencils were laid down as lessons ceased, and in the kitchens the bubbling of liquids and the hissing of steam was silenced. Dennis was roused from his slumbers; he sat up in his bed and faced the door of Dominica's study. The Library darkened as students streamed out of its doors and across the gardens. Throughout The Union, lowered voices murmured variations on 'I bet I know what this is about' as women and girls gravitated towards the Globe Hall until at the ninth stroke, the Hall and the landings encircling the inside of the Main Tower were crammed with females of all shapes and sizes.

There were gardeners, who came still with the secateurs and trowels in their hands. There were physical scientists in white overalls and protective goggles, and domestic scientists with floury hands and fruit-stained aprons. There were herbalists carrying mortars and pestles, and builders carrying hawks and handsaws. All the staff, students and domestics answered the call of the bell.

All except one.

Because even as the Assembly Bell struck its first sonorous note, Naiba was already completely oblivious to it.

IN DUE COURSE, as people always say when the timespan is unknown or too tedious to detail, the shortbread bricks were laid, the grissini roof trusses placed and the crispbread slates overlapped. Sugar-glass gargoyles with gobstopper eyes headed liquorice gutters and downpipes which directed rainwater into a series of nougat water-butts. The kitchen was completed, and the two handcart-dwellers moved into a very desirable, if basic, one-roomed residence. It was comfortable and warm, mainly because the oven was in constant use churning out replacement stock.

Once he'd provided the motor power for enough mortar to cement the kitchen together, Axy was as fit as he ever wanted to be and the novelty value had worn off considerably. So one day, when the witch was pebbledashing the exterior walls with hundreds and thousands, he took a jaunt into the forest. His keen senses soon led him to a place where a rabbit was lapping at the edge of a golden pool.

If Axy had had a middle name, it would have been

Stealth, and consequently the rabbit had no hint that Axy was there at all until he saw a feline head next to his own reflected on the surface of the pool. The rabbit flinched.

'Gmph!' he spluttered, golden bubbles filling his nostrils.

'Hello,' said Axy. 'What's this?'

The rabbit quivered. 'It's a g-glucose p-pool.'

'What's it for?'

'To g-give us e-energy. To ou-outr-run the d-dogs.'

'Why are you t-talking like th-that? L-local d-dialect?'

'I'm n-nervous.'

'Of me? Why?'

The rabbit nodded, but never took his eyes off Axy. 'You might be wor-working for the d-dogs.'

Axy stood on his hind legs. 'I'll have you know I'm one of the highest orders of felines and I work for nobody. Get it? Nobody!'

The rabbit quaked under his shadow.

Axy softened and dropped down again. 'I'm sorry. Tell me about the dogs.'

'They ch-chase us.'

'What for?'

'Sport.'

'Oh, so they chase you 'til half-time then you chase them, is that it?'

'Ahaha,' sputtered the rabbit, to the sound of one paw clapping over his mouth.

'That's not it, is it?'

Still holding his mouth, the rabbit shook his head.

'They chase you all the time, don't they?'

Nod.

Axy sat down and stared into the glucose pool.

The rabbit, sensing this cat to be more friend than foe, sat beside him and returned to lapping the sparkling golden liquid. But he kept one eye on Axy all the same.

Axy stared for so long the rabbit thought he'd fallen asleep with his eyes open. Suddenly, Axy breathed in sharply.

'Got it! Come on. I'll take you to meet my mistress. Not that I work for her, you understand.'

'H-how do I know you're n-not taking me for the p-pot?'

'We're vegetarians with a very sweet tooth. Besides, I could've attacked you at any time, but—'

He broke off as his ears pricked up. He'd heard, far in the distance, the snapping of a twig under the weight of a large pad foot, and the slop-slop slobbering of hanging jowls. His nose twitched. Dog breath. Heading this way.

'Come on. Better get going.'

They left the glucose pool and walked back to the clearing. Axy kept one ear pricked up all the time; he knew the dog was gaining on them, but he didn't want to panic the rabbit. Not when he'd only just thought of the plan. He summoned up all his nonchalance.

'I hope you don't mind me commenting, but you don't smell like any rabbit I've ever smelt before.'

'Oh, no. That's p-perfume. We c-cover ourselves in it to throw the dogs off our s-scent.'

'Does it work?'

'N-no. They just f-follow this smell instead…

The fact that the Assembly Bell struck for the tenth time made no difference to Naiba, but the hubbub in the Main Tower fell silent. Windows had been opened in the glass dome of the Globe Hall, and as the sound of Dominica's words filled the building, only her closest friends could hear the waver in her voice.

'Sisters all. It is with great sadness that I have to tell you that this day, the Head of Faculties and myself have had cause to certify the death of our beloved friend, sister and Matriarch, Imelda McGinty.'

The silence of the crowd remained unbroken, but there was much nodding of heads and heavying of hearts.

'We shall miss her greatly for her love, friendship, advice and teaching. May she rest in peace.'

The assembly took their cue.

'And be renewed in Mother Nature.'

'This moment,' Dominica continued, 'marks the start of a Period of Mourning, at the end of which the funeral of the Matriarch Morte will be held. Tomorrow afternoon, the first steps will be taken towards securing the Matriarch Designate. Once the Matriarch Designate is in agreement, there will be another Assembly at which there will be happier news. Until such time, please continue your business as before, and remember the Matriarch Morte in your thoughts and prayers. Mother Nature be with us all.'

'And with our spirit.'

The low murmuring began again as the throng dispersed in as disciplined and orderly fashion as they had gathered. In Concentric Yard, the animals turned from the Main Tower, and went about their daily lives a little less strenuously. Dennis snuggled down in his bed again, and sought the sleep which would heal his body and give his over-active imagination free reign with no adverse consequences.

'Shall I go with you?' Marianna asked when she and Dominica stood alone in the Globe Hall.

Dominica seemed smaller, as if the weight of the day had physically ground her down. She rested her hand on her friend's arm.

'Oh, Marianna, I would be so grateful.'

In contrast, there was positive lightness of step as one member of The Union tripped back to her room to continue practising gravitas and stateswomanship. Oooh, only a few days to go, Daddy, thought the Bursar. Then we'll see some changes round here.

THE WITCH'S EYES STARTED TO WATER and she opened a window. 'Axy,' she called over her shoulder, 'what on earth have you been eating? And why have you brought it in here? Get it back outside, now.'

'It's not me!' he protested.

She turned to locate the source of the smell.

'Then what in the name of— oh, hello! Who's this? See, Axy – I said you'd find a little friend, didn't I?'

Axy was indignant. 'He's not a little friend, he's—'

'Ed-Edgar, m-mistress. P-pleased to m-meet you.'

'—nervous,' explained Axy.

She smiled and shook his paw.

'Edgar. I'm very pleased to meet you too.'

The warmest, most comfortable feeling he'd ever had in his life soaked up his arm and drenched his whole body; he would be her slave for life.

'And there's no need to be nervous here,' she said.

He was beaming. 'Oh, I'm not in the least bit nervous now, mistress, thank you very much indeed.'

She bobbed down, still holding his paw.

'Edgar,' she whispered, 'do you mind if I just… turn it down a bit?'

He gazed into her eyes and shook his head slowly.

She ran her hand down his back, removed most of the perfume from his fur and threw the smell outside as a green cloud. She smiled. 'That's better.'

Edgar almost collapsed from happiness. She'd held his paw, smiled at him, called him by name and run her hand down his back. Surely life couldn't get any better than this.

Axy chuckled, then reassumed command of The Plan.

'Come on, Edgar, we're going to play Rabbit's Revenge.' Edgar didn't move. 'Edgar? Edgar!' Axy grabbed the besotted rabbit's paw and dragged him outside to the end of the liquorice conveyor.

'What's this?' asked Edgar.

'You'll see,' said Axy, squinting and measuring. He led Edgar away from the end of the belt. 'You sit right… there.' On the last syllable he plonked Edgar on the ground. 'Now, how can I get hold of some of that perfume?'

Edgar giggled. 'Easy.'

For a split second, Axy realised he could be on very

dangerous ground so he was greatly relieved when Edgar simply ran his paws through his own fur and held them up.

'That do you?' asked Edgar.

'Great!' said Axy. He ran over to the witch, whispered to her and seconds later was standing in front of Edgar holding a lace handkerchief. 'Here. Wipe your paws on this.'

Edgar did so, but it was with great reluctance he handed the handkerchief back again.

'Sit there and watch,' instructed Axy. 'Don't move from that spot, and don't be afraid of anything you see.'

Edgar giggled again. Axy ran off through the trees, carrying the lace handkerchief. Finding a favourable breeze, he wafted it into the air and shouted, 'Here, liddle doggy-dog-dog! Come and see what nice Uncle Axy's got for you… come on, dere's a good dog.'

As he heard the slop-slop slobbering growing louder, he ran back to the clearing, gave Edgar the handkerchief and was leaning against a tree nonchalantly cleaning his claws when the large dog ambled along. It looked like it was made of well-worn tan suede; there wasn't a sharp corner on it and its guileless features made it Mother Nature's gift to cartoonists. The sort of dog whose school reports consistently said 'Good-natured but none too bright'.

'Hi there,' said Axy.

'Well, howdy,' said the dog. 'Ain't seen you round these here parts afore.'

Axy gritted his teeth and wondered whether to say 'Shucks, no, we done come in off the last stage and this looked like a mighty fine place to stop' but he had his pride.

'No, we're new in the woods and I was just wondering what people did for fun around here.'

'Gee,' said the dog, 'there's a whole heapa things—'

'What are you doing?'

'Me? Ah'm a-chasin' rabbits.'

'What fur? I mean, what for?'

'Ain't fur nuthin'. Just is, an' that's the truth, mister.'

Axy walked towards the dog.

'Chasing poor liddle bunny wabbits around? That's not the game of the professional, is it? That's for namby-pamby nerdy dogs who sit in their kennels all day, playing imaginary fetch. Dogs who don't know the meaning of the word thrill. Where's the challenge in that?'

'Challenge, mister? I ain't sure what—'

'Challenge, son.' If he'd been tall enough, Axy would have put an arm round the dog's shoulders. 'You look like a dog who knows a thing or two about real hunting…'

The floppy tan suede stiffened.

'…a tough individual with the grim determination to succeed…'

The lolloping head was held high.

'…a true hunter with the skill to take on the trickiest opponents and beat them at their own game…'

The friendly round eyes narrowed.

'…and I know where there's a rabbit nobody has been able to catch. He's the undisputed king of the wood, and' – Axy gritted his teeth again – 'gittin' mighty uppity with it. He needs cuttin' down to size an' lickin' into shape. It needs a real special kinda dog to do it.'

The slobbering jaws were pulled back as the dog growled. 'Lemmeaddim!'

'Are you dog enough for it?'

'Yes, sir! Ah'm ready for it!'

'Prepared to face any obstacle, overcome any hurdle to catch that uncatchable rabbit?'

'Yes, sir! Hell, fire and seven kindsa tarnation, sir!'

'Attaboy! Come on then, let's go get him.'

The witch was giving the kitchen door a second coat of salt glaze when a variety of noises assailed her ears. The bass line was provided by the rumbling cauldron being rotated at high speed. The dog's paws landing on the liquorice strip provided a regular backbeat, with an interesting asthmatic counterpoint from the dog's heavy breathing. Piercing through all this was the soprano giggling, which came from Axy and Edgar. They rolled about at the end of the conveyor helpless with laughter, occasionally holding their bellies, pointing at the dog and wiping their eyes. The more they laughed, the faster the dog ran, the faster the cauldron whirled and the more they laughed. Eventually, to save their aching sides, Axy had to drag the dog from the conveyor belt and send him home with a commiserative 'Better luck next time, son'.

'Ya mean Ah c'n come back tomorrer and try agin?'

'Sure thing, son, but it'll cost you. What'll it cost you? It'll cost you... a bag of flour. Bring a bag of flour, son, and you can have another go.'

And thus was born Mr Axy's Canine Gymnasium. Dogs were soon queuing up to have a go at its star attraction,

Gingerbread Children

Edgar the Uncatchable Rabbit, who took to leaping about at the end of the conveyor in a variety of costumes. Some days he was Edgarro, Rabbit in Black, a masked avenger; at other times he was Quick Furpin, the highwayrabbit; sometimes, complete with cutlass and gold earring, he was the dashing pirate Furbanks Junia.

Axy ensured that exclusivity generated attraction. Not everybody could get in; admission depended on what the witch was baking. When the cauldron was used to capacity, usually for bread dough, or when speed was the priority, as when making candy floss to be used as quilt filling, the large dogs had their turn on the liquorice strip. When swirling together mixtures for marble cake, gently folding flour into a sponge or meringues into a soufflé, the smaller dogs were allowed to pad along the drive belt.

Axy soon realised that a single running track was not enough to satisfy his growing list of customers. Commercial acumen being the mother of unnecessary invention, he devised other ways for the dogs to get their exercise. When the bread dough had risen and wanted knocking back and kneading, it was wrapped in the tarpaulin and used as a bouncy mattress for dogs to jump up and down on. A variety of bags were hung from the trees; their contents, ranging from biscuits to royal icing, were punched into the required size of gravel or hardcore. Whenever the witch wanted some new paving slabs, pastry was flattened by being passed through the equivalent of a large mangle, powered by dogs birling the top roller like lumberjacks. If the oven fire needed boosting, small dogs would be admitted to use the bellows chest expander. Axy designed specialist weight-lifting equipment: for the highly-strung weak dogs, the dumb-bell was a cheese straw with a meringue ring weight at each end; at the opposite end of the scale, it was a large stick of rock with several fruit cakes slotted on.

Because the dogs came in all shapes and sizes, so did the admission fee. Anything the witch could use in her baking was acceptable, and soon her store cupboard was regularly restocked with baskets of eggs, cones of sugar, hessian bags of flour, tubs of lard and pails of milk. In return, she maintained and repaired the equipment in the gymnasium.

The dogs were healthy, the woodland rabbits lived in peace, Axy had something to occupy his time and the witch was never short of ingredients or mixing power. Over time, surrounding the perfect round well in the perfect round clearing, a perfect round house took shape, and the last thing to be added was a sign in the shape of a black cauldron which swung from a tree branch, and a nameplate which read *Doughnut Cottage*.

The witch settled down to her life as the nearby village's wise woman, healer, and object of curiosity and fear.

And so it continued until…

'Until?' said an eager yet apprehensive Tutor of Creative Chronicling. 'Until what?'

'*Until the next time*,' said a familiar unfamiliar voice.

A small figure in a black and yellow stripy jumper dashed across Concentric Yard to the edge of the Herb Wheel and burst through the door of the Hive of Activity, the shed which served as her workshop. She whimpered as she assessed what she had to move; so much to do, so little time. Nekta Bonnet, expert apiarist – the Archivist – was going to be as busy as a bee with a deadline.

Humming tunelessly, she cleared a table at the back of the hut. Trays holding tubs of experimental honey in a startling variety of colours and consistencies were shifted onto a shelf; lolly sticks polished with a new range of coloured beeswax gleamed briefly before being gathered up and put into a drawer; trifling dishes of flavoured royal jelly were set aside in a cupboard. When the table was cleared, she propped it up against the back wall and set about moving the cases of tightly sealed jars that had been under it. Evicting whole families of spiders and woodlice which scurried off for safer habitation, she re-stacked the cases behind her, blocking off her access to the door. As she moved the last case, the glint of a brass escutcheon indicated a keyhole in a floorboard.

The Archivist delved into her pocket and pulled out a large brass key. Turning it in the lock released two floorboards that folded back to reveal a cubby-hole the length of a broomstick, from which she lifted a long thin bundle wrapped in black cloth secured at each end by a brass spring-clip. She leant the bundle up against the cases of jars and climbed over them; once on the other side, she reached up to a peg on the back of the door and took down a wide-brimmed hat with what looked like a giant bedroll on the top, fastened by a bow. She donned the hat, tugged at the bow and almost immediately disappeared under a cone of very fine mesh net which stretched from the top of the hat to the floor. She patted the mesh inside to find the sleeves, put her arms through and picked up the long thin bundle. Gently prising open the spring-clips, she unwrapped a stout black rod with a brass finial at each end. She was just in time to step outside to greet two callers.

'Good afternoon, Archivist,' said Dominica.

'Good afternoon, Vice-Matriarch,' the Archivist replied, slightly out of breath. She tipped her head towards Marianna. 'Faculties.'

Marianna tipped back. 'Archivist.'

'How do they seem today?' asked Dominica.

'Unsettled. Your visit will settle them.'

'Will we need, er…?' asked Marianna, indicating the Archivist's outfit. If Marianna could have seen the Archivist's face, she would have seen the scorn with which the Archivist treated such a question.

'Course not. They won't hurt you.'

'Then why…?'

'Ceremonial – you know I like to do things the Apian Way. My babies wouldn't hurt anybody. Unless I say so.'

Marianna wished she was back inside the Main Tower, solving some problem or other. Dealing with numbers was a lot easier than dealing with things which had a mind of their own – or a mind of someone else's for that matter.

'You'll be needing this though.' The Archivist handed the rod to Dominica. 'I'll wait here for you.'

The Head of Faculties was not encouraged by this.

There was a hum in the air, a hum at a frequency which had one foot in comfort and one foot in 'get me out of here'. Dominica and Marianna stood on a round patch of grass in the centre of the Herb Wheel; between Dominica's feet was a small, circular brass plate. She glanced at Marianna, then at the black rod. 'Oh, well. Here goes.'

Marianna swallowed hard.

Dominica held the rod vertically and with it knocked three times on the brass plate. The hum stopped, leaving behind a silence that startled.

From each of the nine hives encircling the patch of grass came a single Sentry Bee which hovered just outside the entrance to its hive. They buzzed in unison.

'Who knockzz for the Beezz?'

Dominica gripped the summoning rod.

'The Keeper of the Bees.'

'Whozze Beezz?'

'The Queens' Bees.'

'And who comezz azz the Keeper of the Beezz?'

'Vice-Matriarch Dominica Tort.'

'And what doezz the Keeper of the Beezz dezzire?'

'I desire to speak with your pages.'

The nine bees went back into their hives. There was a series of short sharp buzzes, barely perceptible, after which another nine bees emerged. Marianna assumed they were different bees; short of asking to see identification, there was no way to tell.

'We are the Page Beezz.'

Of course, they could have been lying.

'I come to bring you sad news,' said Dominica.

'What zzad newzz do you bring?'

'The news I bring is of the Death of the Matriarch.'

'Zzad newzz indeed. What do you azzk of uzz?'

'I ask you to tell your Queens and your families.'

'Zzo be it.'

The bees returned to their hives. After a while, there came the collective sigh of hundreds of thousands of souls, and the nine Page Bees emerged again.

'Our Queenzz and our familiezz thank you for your courtezzy and zzend their condolenzzes.'

Dominica took from her pocket a bundle of small black strips of material, hand-hemmed into perfect rectangles. She held these up one at a time, and each bee took one and draped it on the top of its hive. When all nine hives had been so draped, the bees reassembled in front of Dominica.

'Live in peazze, Keeper of the Beezz.'

'Live in peace, bees.'

The bees re-entered their hives. Marianna sighed with relief. As she and Dominica walked away towards the Archivist's hut, the hum of the hives returned.

The Archivist was waiting for them, as she had promised.

'Are they told?'

Dominica lifted the rod to hand it back. 'They are told.'

The Archivist caught the other end of the rod and pulled it towards her. 'Thank you, Vice-Matriarch.'

Dominica held on.

The Archivist tried again with a little more force.

'Vice-Matriarch, I'll take the summoning rod.'

There was no reply.

Marianna took hold of the rod. 'Dominica, let go. The Archivist needs her rod back. Dominica. Dominica!'

Dominica's knuckles were turning white and her nails were beginning to dig into the palm of her hand as she gripped the rod.

'Oh-oh,' said Marianna.

The Archivist looked on in amazement as Marianna prised open Dominica's fingers, then caught her as she collapsed. Despite being encased in very fine mesh net the Archivist ran for help, dropping the summoning rod as she did so. Marianna laid the unconscious Vice-Matriarch on the ground, lifted Dominica's feet and rested them against her own body.

'Dominica... come on, Dominica... can you hear me? Say something.' She patted Dominica's legs. 'Come on, talk to me. Vice-Matriarch? Dominica?'

There was no response.

'Come on... say something, even if it's only "shut up".'

Nothing.

The ground started to thump as heavy footfalls signalled the arrival of the Archivist and four very similar serving-girls, one carrying a blanket. The girls laid Dominica on the blanket, picked up its corners and carried her to her room.

'Knew we should have used nets,' muttered Marianna, loping alongside them, unaware that the distant hum of the hives had suddenly stopped.

The Archivist picked up the summoning rod.

'It's all right, my babies,' she called. 'She didn't mean it.

She's worried, is all. Calm yourselves.'

There was a second more of silence, and then the steady drone of the hives at work once more filled the Herb Wheel, but not before there had been a collective 'Hmph!'.

Naiba paced up and down her study. She had rolled the manuscript along its length, making a tube; it popped as she patted the end and it swished as she slid it back and forth through her curled hand. She pushed out her bottom lip as she concentrated, absent-mindedly bouncing the manuscript on the walls, the fireplace, the chair back and the window as she walked. When she tapped it against her chin, she caught a familiar, warm, prickly smell. Back at her desk, she held the manuscript tube to her eye; screwing her face up, she looked down the grey cylinder and in the perfect round circle at the end of it she could see the ginger root.

'I need some fresh air,' she said, tossing the manuscript carelessly onto her desk, knocking the ginger root onto the floor. She automatically bent down and picked it up.

The fresh air waited ages for her but she didn't turn up so it breezed off to be of service to others.

AND SO IT CONTINUED UNTIL the witch decided to experiment with some new recipes. She wanted to try unusual combinations of tastes, and needed a more informed opinion about food than Axy's, which was usually a short burp followed by a long snore.

During her travels she had noticed that people would put stalls by the roadside, inviting the passing public to part with a few hard-earned coppers for tomato plants, vegetables, small posies, large bouquets, grow-your-owns, pick-your-owns, pretend-they're-your-owns, take-'em-home-plant-'em-and-watch-'em-dies, large cats, small dogs, unwanted furniture and even stable manure (as if anyone would want to buy unstable manure).

Pulling out her best Stylten East Slopes Hard-Roasted table, she set up a stall at the side of a path through the woods. She arranged salt and sweet biscuits, fruit flapjacks, exotic frangipanis, coloured meringues, iced buns and plain fancies on the table, and against a table leg propped a slate, on which was chalked 'Try me!' in a meticulous hand.

She muttered a few well-aged words and passed her hands over the table. When she'd trained in confectionery, one of the first things she learnt to make was an invisible food net, and insects which previously had been merrily zipping in eccentric squares over the site now found themselves taking an unscheduled detour as they came up against the exclusion zone covering the delicacies. Several flies zig-zagging their way home arrived at their own door complaining of a severe headache and no excuse for it, having run into a very thick wall of absolutely nothing.

Each day she would lay out the stall, then hide in the bushes and watch as people passed by. Some ignored the stall completely; others glanced round furtively, snatched something and then ran away; some would stop and take their time, sampling this and that. She watched their faces and made note of their comments. She saw what was popular, soon cleared from the table; she saw what was left and had to be taken back in at the end of the day.

One day, two figures approached the table. Their clothes were no more than rags covering frames so thin they might snap in the breeze. They reached out with dirty hands and snatched two buns each, then ran and hid behind a bush opposite the stall. All the witch could see were the tops of two auburn heads bobbing up and down as they wolfed the food. At first she thought they were woodland sprites, but when they returned to the table less than a minute later, she could see that under the grime and grubbiness they were children. They each stuffed another cake whole into their mouths, and the smaller one held out her ragged grey pinafore to form a makeshift sack. The larger one then swept his dirty arm across the table, gathering all the cakes into the pinafore. Before the witch could stop them, they had melted back into the woodland as swiftly as they had come.

The following day the children returned, bringing with them a sack into which they threw all the cakes, clearing the table before running away.

On the third day she put out small flagons of honey beer alongside the baking; after the children's visit, there were no more cakes and ale.

On the fourth day, the boy seemed to be in even more of a hurry. He tugged at the sack, making the girl overbalance. Putting out a hand to steady herself she scraped the side of her palm on the table edge; on instinct she put her hand to her mouth to take the sting out of the graze.

Her eyes widened. 'Cor!'

The boy was busy sack-filling. 'What's the matter?'

'I can taste... what is it?' She licked her hand.

'Stop messing about. Get a move on!'

She rubbed her finger hard on the table. The surface powdered and stuck to her finger. She tasted it. 'Try it.'

He did as she had done, then grabbed a corner of the table and pressed on it until it broke off. He snapped the broken corner in two and handed half to the girl. They nibbled the pieces.

'Blimey!' said the boy. 'It's a coffee table!'

The witch emerged from behind a bush. 'Yes,' she said. 'Do you like it?'

The two children stared at her.

'Oh, it's all right,' she smiled. 'I can make another one.'

The boy tried to pick up the sack and make a run for it, but found it a lot heavier than he was expecting.

'Don't go,' said the witch. 'I'd like to talk to you...'

The serving-girls put Dominica on her bed and covered her with the blanket. 'Will that be all, miss?' one of them asked.

Marianna looked at her and felt a sudden impulse to start calculating racing odds.

'Tea. Bring us some tea, please.'

'On the boil already, miss.'

The girls bobbed and left the room, closing the door quietly.

Marianna studied her sleeping friend, whose pale skin was blemished only by three long ruby scratches on her cheek.

'Worn out, aren't you?' she said softly. 'No lavender needed for your pillow.'

She walked to the slightly open window and stared across the gardens, so familiar, yet ever-changing. A smell of baking wafted across from the kitchens. The evening sun was casting golden hues and long shadows, painting a picture of a day much happier and more contented than reality could have proven. It suggested warmth and comfort, which brought its own penalty. Marianna suddenly felt tired, as though someone had whispered that now was the time to let go; it was the instantaneous drain of energy which tells you you don't know how tense you've been.

She looked towards the Herb Wheel. 'Sorry, bees.'

There was a small movement beside her as Gigi set down the tea-tray, complete with two gingerbread men.

'Will that be all, miss?'

'Yes, that'll be all.'

Gigi withdrew as silently as she had appeared.

Marianna felt uneasy about the gingerbread men. Probably something to do with the eyes, she thought, remembering the two golden rules of food: never eat anything bigger than your head, and never eat anything that's looking at you, especially if it's trying to hypnotise you. She quickly turned them over and snapped them. An unexpected sensation of relief flooded her and she couldn't help feeling she'd had a lucky escape.

The snap of the biscuits had another effect; it echoed through the ears of Dennis who, despite sleeping through the kerfuffle of four serving-girls putting his mistress to bed, was always awake to the prospect of food. He rolled over, stretched, winced and shook himself, after which he winced again. Opening his eyes, he looked under the bed and saw a pair of boots at the other side, so he got up and walked towards them, carefully avoiding the box residing in the cool shade under the bed. Lifting his head past the edge of the bedframe he was surprised to be staring straight up the nose of the Head of Faculties.

'What's happened?' he said. 'Where is she?'

Marianna's tongue was busy probing in her teeth for impacted gingerbread, so she glanced sideways at the dormant figure under the blanket. Faster than anyone would have thought capable, Dennis was up on the bed, staring wide-eyed at his mistress.

A fathomless drowning sleep consumed Dominica. It swallowed her tiredness, her mind and her soul, plunging the waking world into oblivion. So far was she in another realm that any disturbance might have seen her lost forever, her mind struggling to return before her body was active. Not only did her slumber knit up the ravelled sleeve of care, it made a new collar and cuffs and sewed on the missing buttons. Not so much a sleep, more a short course in death.

'You do that?' Marianna asked, pointing to Dominica's face. Dennis blinked back tears and nodded. Marianna sniffed disapprovingly. 'Ought to be ashamed of yourself.'

Dennis's lip curled momentarily. That's right, he thought. Throw a drowning cat a glass of water. Damned woman. Couldn't she see how ashamed he was? How he would've given one of his lives not to have done it?

'Well, whatever it was about,' said Marianna, 'she needs

your help now. She needs your strength.'

'What happened?' asked Dennis.

Marianna tried to imagine what he was feeling.

'She's worn out. Needs rest.'

'Will she be all right?'

'Should think so.'

'How can you tell? She's so... not there.'

'If she'd been in mortal danger, you'd have been awake in an instant. Wouldn't have spent so long snoozing.'

Dennis swallowed hard, put his paw on Dominica's body and looked at Marianna. 'Will you stay with her tonight?'

'Of course. But will you, Spirit?'

'Always.' He snuggled down at Dominica's side and prayed to Mother Nature to give her strength.

Outside, under the window, a black cat with a white eye-patch paced backwards and forwards, and did the same.

And so it was for most of the night.

Dominica's only dream found her in the Senior Council Chamber, about to read out the Last Will and Returning Wishes of the Matriarch Morte. She held the document open before her, cleared her throat and faced the Senior Council. In front of each Senior Council member hovered a bee, and all were waiting for the news from the will. As Dominica opened her mouth to speak, one Senior Council member closed a hand round a bee, and very slowly crushed it. Dominica stared at the member; a pair of golden eyes with black almond pupils glittered back.

GINGERBREAD CHILDREN

THE WITCH HEFTED THE SACK ONTO THE TABLE. The boy helped her to carry them both back to the cottage; the girl followed on behind. Axy saw this procession enter the clearing but was too busy with his thriving fitness empire to stroll over and enquire further.

The witch made the children wash their hands and faces in fresh well-water, and once they were less grubby she could see a strong family resemblance. 'Brother and sister?'

They nodded.

She gave them glasses of sparkling, laughing lemonade and large slices of apple pie with cheese; they ate and drank as if tomorrow it would be banned.

'Why do you steal all my cakes?' she asked.

'We can't pay,' said the boy, between mouthfuls.

'I didn't ask you to. I simply asked why you did it.'

'Because we're poor and hungry,' the girl piped up, 'and part of the downtrodden masses of underclass which society prefers to forget.'

The boy put down his lemonade glass. 'That's what Father says, anyway. I know we're poor and I know I'm hungry, but I don't know about the rest.'

'Father says that's just the sort of blinkered helpless attitude which the ruling classes depend on to keep us all in subjugation.'

'How old are you?' asked the witch.

'Eleven. He's thirteen, but only because he's two years older than me. Father says that in terms of political astuteness I'm streets ahead.'

The witch thought Father had a lot to say for himself. She

sliced up more apple pie and cheese.

'And what does Mother say?'

The boy's cheeks bulged out as he ate. 'She's dead.'

'Oh, I'm sorry to hear that.'

'She was a martyr to the cause,' said the girl, emptying the lemonade jug. 'She died for her beliefs.'

'Oh?'

The girl waved the jug at the witch. 'She believed she should go without so her children may have a better chance when the oppressed masses rise and seize control.' Her mouth was so busy eating and talking she must have been breathing through her ears. 'So in order to secure a glorious future for us she went without.'

'Without food,' said the boy, with a large slice of pie in one hand but no hint of irony anywhere.

The witch put down a refilled jug and a plate piled high with confectionery of all shapes, sizes, colours and tastes.

'And I take it food is still in short supply?'

The boy closed bony fingers round a bakewell tart.

'All the time.'

'At the moment,' stressed the girl, topping up her glass. 'Father says that come the revolution, there will be more than enough to go round everybody fairly. From each according to his ability, to each according to his needs.'

'What does your father do?'

The girl reached out for a rice cake. 'Do? He doesn't do anything. He is. He's an equalist.'

'An equalist?'

'He wasn't always,' said the boy, pouring more lemonade

and handing the empty jug to the witch once more. 'Used be a leatherworker. Used to make decorative leatherwork for the big shops in town. Got a big order one day from one of the shops and went out celebrating. Come back drunk and knocked a red-hot branding iron onto a pile of straw in the workshop. Didn't notice until the place was burning down around his ears. Lost everything. Workshop, our house, even the tools he used for working the leather.'

'Oh, how terrible,' said the witch.

'And then,' chirped the girl, 'thing got worse when the corporate conspiracy started.'

'Conspiracy?'

The girl nodded. 'Because he didn't have a house, he couldn't get a loan to buy tools. Because he'd no tools, he couldn't work. Because he couldn't work, he couldn't earn. Because he couldn't earn, he couldn't buy a house, so he couldn't get the loan for the tools, and so on. And because he never delivered the big order, the shops blacklisted him anyway.'

'Didn't he have any savings?'

The girl cut a slice of orange meringue pie. 'He had some money in the bank, but not for very long.'

The witch put down the re-refilled jug. 'I don't suppose it would last long with a growing family to feed.'

'Oh, it wasn't that,' said the boy. 'The fire spread from our house to the bank and burned that down as well.'

'Ah…'

'Only thing he had left was his wedding ring, so he pawned it and put the money on a horse at twenty to one.'

'Don't tell me – it came in at half-past three,' said the witch.

The girl seemed bemused. 'No, it won, but he was a victim of the escalating violence symptomatic of the growing schism between those who create wealth and those who dispose of it.'

'Got mugged on the way home from the bookie's,' the boy explained, helping himself to a rock cake.

'Which just goes to prove that a society engaged solely in the pursuit of wealth will eventually collapse under the weight of its own avarice.'

'Well, I don't know about that, but I do know he didn't have the money when he got home.' The boy licked his finger and mopped up the crumbs from the plates.

The witch could scarcely believe two such skinny frames could pack away so much food and drink, but the evidence was there in front of her on the table. Or rather it wasn't.

'It sounds like your father's just had a run of bad luck.'

The girl snorted. 'Father doesn't believe in bad luck. I told you, he's an equalist.'

'An equalist?'

'He says the whole world has to balance. For everything that happens somewhere, the opposite must happen somewhere else.'

'I don't quite…'

'Look.' In one word, the girl's voice betrayed her irritation. This woman was a grown-up, right? Why couldn't she understand? 'Some people are happy, some are sad. Some babies are born, some people die. It all balances, see?'

'So why doesn't he believe in...'

'For him to be having such bad luck, someone somewhere must be having a really good time.'

'Oh.'

'And Father says there just isn't that much good luck in the whole world.' She drained her glass and put it back down on the table.

The witch picked up the glass. 'Would you like to take some food back for your father? I could...'

The boy burped and pointed at the sack. 'Think we've already got some.'

The girl got to her feet. 'Come on, we'd better be going. You know what he's like if we're late back.'

'Mmm.' The boy picked up the sack and turned to go.

Before the girl stepped outside she said to the witch, 'You're just the sort of helper we're looking for in the struggle for freedom from oppression and tyranny.'

'Am I? Really?'

'Oh yes. You'd be a valuable asset to the cause...

In the morning, the Head of Faculties and Spirit of the Wind sat at the table playing cards. Marianna fanned her hand of cards with ease, spacing them with precision. At her elbow were a large number of broken matchsticks, grouped in tens. Dennis's cards were laid face down, jutting over the edge of the table, next to four pieces of matchstick. He put his head under the edge of the cards and looked up to read them.

'Trumps is the roundy black ones, right?'

'Roundy black ones it is,' said Marianna, laying down the

two of pointy red ones.

'I thought you'd have that,' said Dennis. 'Second right.'

Marianna took the second right from Dennis's paw of cards and turned it over. The seven of pointy red ones.

'Ha-ha,' said Dennis. 'I won one!'

'Could be the start of your lucky streak,' Marianna said without quite believing it.

This was where Dennis's game went to pot. He was all right as long as he was reacting to someone else's lead, but when it was his turn to lay the first card, he never knew what to do for the best. 'Middle one.'

Marianna took the card. The five of squirly blue ones. She swept it away with the four of roundy black ones. 'Sorry, no squirly blue ones.'

Someone's lip curled slightly.

Marianna laid the eight of pointy red ones.

Dennis's head went under the table then came out again.

'Left.'

Marianna picked up the card: the one of roundy black ones. 'Bit of a Pyrrhic victory there, Dennis,' she said, laying the cards by the four matchstalks.

He smiled as only a cat can. 'A victory all the same.'

He was still smiling as Marianna turned over his final card – the Jill of roundy red ones. Get out of that.

He couldn't believe his eyes as she did get out of it, taking the trick and the game with the minus two of roundy black ones.

'And that looks like Goodwood to me,' she grinned, scooping up the last of Dennis's matchstalks.

Dennis pawed at the cards and screwed his nose up.

'I reckon you're playing with a bent deck.'

'Now, now,' said Marianna with the supercilious magnanimity of the victor, 'don't get personal, little kitty.'

'She's a mathematician and a witch. She doesn't need a bent deck,' said a voice from the bed.

Dennis streaked across the table over to where Dominica lay. It could have been entirely coincidental that as he did so, he put his back foot into the pile of matchstalks which were Marianna's winnings, spraying them across the room.

'You're awake!' he cried.

Dominica's eyes remained closed and her breathing remained deep and even. Dennis started to knead the blankets on her thigh with his forepaws.

'Come on, you're awake. I heard you. Say something.' There was no reaction. He pressed harder. 'Come on, wake up!' He looked at Marianna. The kneading became more agitated. 'I heard her. I did. I heard her!'

Marianna was picking up matchstalks. 'You sure?'

Dennis's voice rose half an octave.

'Am I sure? What do you think these things on my head are for? Keep my hat on?'

'You don't wear a hat.'

'I know I don't wear a—' Dennis buried his face in his paws. 'Look, didn't you hear her say something?'

'Don't think I heard anything.'

'You must have!'

'Gustave? Who's Gustave?'

'Aaagh!' he said, slumping onto Dominica's leg. The

reverberations made the bed shudder. And shudder. And shudder. Dennis lifted his head, then walked up Dominica's body until he was peering into her face which was trying to keep itself under control. He licked the end of her nose. She burst out laughing, put her arms round him and kissed him.

'Oh, you're hopeless. You flare at the least provocation. You should have been called Spirit of the Trouser Bottom.' She smiled at her friend. 'Thanks, Marianna.'

'What are friends for?'

'Mother Nature, I was tired. I didn't realise.'

Marianna peered at her. 'Are you going to be all right? You've been far away for a long time.'

'I'm back now. I'll be fine. Thanks for staying.' Dominica secretly prodded Dennis.

'Ow! What? Oh, er, yes, thanks for staying with us.'

Marianna gave him a look which said, 'I know you wouldn't normally say that, no matter how grateful you are.'

The returned look said, 'I know, but I am.'

Marianna yawned. 'I'll send up some breakfast for the pair of you, then I'll refill my own rest reservoirs. You know where I am if you need me.'

'Before you go…' said Dominica. She whispered in Dennis's ear and he dropped onto the floor. There was the sound of cat straining against wood, and slowly from under the bed there emerged what looked like a very expensive shoe box pushed by two marmalade paws.

Marianna raised a hand. 'Oh, don't worry about it now.'

Dennis sat down and glared at her.

She glared back.

'Just push it under the door when you're ready,' she said. 'What time will it be?'

'Three o'clock this afternoon,' said Dominica.

'I'll be there.'

Outside, under the window, a black cat with a white eye-patch walked off, lay down in the morning sun under the Ancient Apple Tree and fell fast asleep.

The Tutor of Creative Chronicling was on her way to the Library when she passed the slightly open door. Curiosity quite naturally pushed politeness out of the way and she glanced inside. Naiba was sitting at the desk, writing.

THE FOLLOWING DAY THERE WAS A KNOCK ON THE DOOR of Doughnut Cottage. When the witch opened the door, she saw the girl carrying the sack and the boy holding the crescent shape of half a door-knocker. The witch glanced at the other half still hanging on her front door. 'Never mind,' she said. 'I'll make another one. You might as well finish it.'

The boy looked blank. 'Finish it?'

'Yes. Eat it. It's sweet rock.'

He broke the crescent in two and gave half to his sister. They crunched on it.

'Is everything in this place edible?' asked the girl.

'More or less,' said the witch. 'Although I shouldn't try taking a bite out of the stove. Or the cat.'

The boy smiled; the girl carried on crunching even as she kicked his ankle. He flinched.

'Ow! What? Oh, yes,' he said. 'Father says we must thank

you for the generous gifts you've provided.'

The girl kicked his ankle again.

'What?' he moaned.

She said nothing, but glared at him and gave a sharp nod with her head.

He sighed. 'All right.' He smiled at the witch again. 'Father says we must thank you for the generous gifts you've provided to deliver us from starvation and further the cause of the poor and downtrodden.'

'It was only a few buns,' said the witch.

Having finished eating, the girl pushed her way into the kitchen.

'Father would have come himself,' she said, 'but he is sharing the bounty with others and is, at this moment, distributing your food to those less fortunate than himself.'

'He's using what I gave you in order to help others?'

The boy ambled into the kitchen. 'You could say that.'

'Father says this will make their miserable lives more bearable,' said the girl, 'and possibly give them the strength to survive one more day.'

'Are things really so bad?'

'Father says any help at all is more than welcome. The greater the contribution, the greater the good he can do. The need is massive but the resources are tiny.'

'How old did you say you were?'

'I'm still eleven.'

'Then help you shall have, my dear. You must call on me twice a week and I will give you food for your father to distribute to the poor and needy. How does that sound?'

The children smiled broadly at each other and looked back at the witch.

'Father's joy will be unconfined,' said the girl. She held out the sack. 'Shall we start today?'

'Of course, child. It's funny – I don't even know your names.'

'I'm Hansi,' said the boy, 'she's Greta.'

'And my name is Auregia…

After breakfast, Dominica put the box on her desk and contemplated it for a long time. The reddish wood was dramatically marked in shades of auburn, mustard, beige, purple and blue; it was as if someone had varnished a box on fire, trapping the flames under the clear, smooth surface, and there they blazed for evermore. The rounded corners and seamless construction were an object lesson in the carpenter's arts, and tiny gold filigree escutcheons embellished the four locks at the centre point of each side. In style it was simple, elegant and understated, and as such it commanded immediate and total attention. It sat on the desk much as a queen might sit on a throne – sure of its own position in the world and confident in its purpose. This box knew its time had come.

Dominica took the copper keyring from her pocket, carefully removed the golden key, put it in the first lock and turned it clockwise. There was the snap of metal jaws abruptly closing, and a small clunk as a piece of metal dropped inside the box. Dominica withdrew the key and examined it. The end had been sheared off, and the circular shaft had been flattened at the sheared end, leaving it looking like the world's most elegant and expensive sardine tin key.

In the second lock, she turned the key anticlockwise. There were rapid mechanical movements within the box and the key was spat out through Dominica's fingers and onto the floor. She picked it up; the shaft was circular again, but had been concertinaed up to half its original length. She inserted it into the third lock, and turned it clockwise again. There were more mechanical movements and Dominica was left holding the bow of the key between her forefinger and thumb. She pushed the remains of the key into the fourth lock until she heard it clunk.

'Open sesame,' she whispered, taking hold of the lid and pulling gently. Her fingers slipped off the box. She gripped more tightly and tried again. Her fingers slipped off again, and she broke her thumbnail. 'Blast!' she said, sucking her thumb and biting off the jagged nail edge.

She opened a desk drawer and took out a large flat circle of ridged rubber with which she gripped the lid of the box. She gritted her teeth as her fingers strained. 'Open sesame!'

No use. She stood up, held the box tight against her body and tugged at the lid. She ran her fingers round it, trying to insert one of her remaining fingernails into the gap where the lid met the base, to see if she could prise the two apart. She couldn't even find the gap.

'Come on, open up, damn you,' she growled as she banged the box up and down on the desk, but still the lid would not budge. She placed the box on its side and waggled the end of a paper-knife in the first lock; when that failed, she held the knife in the lock with one hand and with the other took off her shoe and brought the heel crashing down onto the knife's blunt end. Her ears rang with the resultant 'twoing!' as the metal reinforced heel made contact with the metal handle of the paper-knife, and the rough patterned sole rasped the skin on her fingers as the shoe bounced out of her hand and shot off across the room, denting the plasterwork as it hit the wall. She dropped the box and knife onto the desk, pressed her sore fingers close to her body with her other arm and limped off to retrieve her shoe. She ran her unrasped fingers over the wall's new dimple: not too bad, considering the speed at which the shoe had been travelling.

She donned the shoe and stomped back to the desk. Leaning on her fists, she narrowed her eyes and flared her nostrils as she looked the box straight in the lock.

'For the last time, will you please open up!'

There was the softest of clicks and then that embarrassing noise which happens when a tight-fitting lid is parted from its box. The lid rose and hovered above the base. Sometimes all you need to do is say the magic word.

'Oh, har har har. Thank you so very bloody much,' snapped Dominica, snatching the lid and laying it on the desk. In the box lay several sealed envelopes and a perfectly re-formed golden key.

From the doorway, the Tutor of Creative Chronicling watched her pupil write. Naiba's action was fluid and continuous, determined yet seemingly requiring very little effort. As the Tutor went to tiptoe away, her shifting bodyweight made the floorboards creak and she knew she had to come clean. She turned back.

'Sorry. Didn't mean to disturb you. I was just passing…'

There was no reaction from Naiba.

'…and I thought I'd dance a jig in my underwear,' said the Tutor slowly, as she steadily moved across the room and inched into Naiba's sightline.

The writing continued, unperturbed.

THE CHILDREN'S SACK WAS NOT BIG ENOUGH to take all the cakes Auregia made, so they started to bring an old sack-barrow, its peeling paintwork a testament to its age. Auregia made two candywood crates which, when filled with her baking, could be stacked on the sack-barrow for ease of transportation. The twice-weekly run continued for some months, until one day Auregia made the mistake of asking the girl how her father was.

'Father thanks you greatly for your contribution, and says he could not hope to continue his good work without you. He is at present struggling with the problem of dividing the confectionery between the poor and oppressed, and the local orphanage. Unfortunately, the volume of your production no longer covers adequately both needs, but no doubt Father will find the best solution.'

'He's taking care of the orphans as well?' said Auregia.

'The winter is a great collector for the Grim Reaper, and the orphanage has many new occupants.'

'Well, I'm sure I can stretch to a few more buns.'

Twice-weekly grew to thrice-weekly.

Outside in the gym, Axy noticed that the equipment had started to sag a little. The parallel bars, in particular, would soon have to be renamed…

Dominica rang the bell on her desk. The letters in the box had written and addressed themselves at the Matriarch's behest; all she had to do was ensure they were delivered.

She set aside the internals first: invitations to the Extraordinary Meeting of the Senior Council in the afternoon. Then she separated the external post: letters destined for people who no longer resided within the confines of The Union, but who were still to be formally notified of the Matriarch's death.

Two envelopes were left: the large, black-bordered one holding the Matriarch Morte's Last Will and Returning Wishes, and the small blue one holding what Dominica considered the linguistic equivalent of gas – the one that would make the balloon go up. She locked these in a drawer, looking up as the door opened.

'Ah, Bebe. Fingers fixed?'

'Oh aye, mum,' replied Bebe, lifting her hands and performing the kind of exercise normally reserved for concert pianists. 'Nowt that cold water and willpower won't sort out. Our Mam says that'd cure a lot of the world's problems – cold water and willpower.'

Rounding off a dazzling display of digital dexterity, she interlocked her fingers and lifted her hands high above her head with a flourish and a dramatic crack of knuckles.

'Excellent,' said Dominica. 'Glad there's no harm done.'

Bebe grimaced. 'There wasn't — not until I did that. And me elbows is locked as well.'

Dominica crossed the room and held the door open.

'Go get yourself some more cold water.'

'I'll send one of me sisters up, mum.'

Bebe bobbed, partly out of custom and partly to enable her to get out of the room more easily.

'Please. And be careful how you go down the stairs.'

Returning to her desk she saw, out of the window, that The Union was alive with normality. The joint venture that is education was in full swing: teachers trying to impart wisdom along with fact; students inclined not to learn from someone else's mistakes. Animals and plants were living mostly in harmony, too wise to question the natural order of things. All around, Mother Nature was regenerating, nurturing, providing, pollinating and reclaiming, cleansing the earth of detritus in preparation for the next generation. Born, flourish, die. We all ride the same life-cycle, thought Dominica. The only difference is the speed.

A knock at the door interrupted her reverie. She turned away from the window and so she did not see a marmalade cat pad across the gardens towards the orchard. 'Come in.'

Gigi entered. 'Miss?'

Before Dominica strode out to hand-deliver the relevant invitations, she first passed the post to Gigi.

'Please can you make sure these letters go with the courier today?'

'Yes, miss. You want me to make sure today or you want 'em to go with the courier today?'

'Both, Gigi, both.'

'Very good, miss.' Gigi bobbed and left; left Dominica wondering whether she needed lessons in plain speaking.

It was nearly lunchtime when Spirit of the Western One awoke to the smell of something very familiar close by.

All his fur stood on end.

He opened one eye very slowly and saw a cat sitting beside him, looking up into the Ancient Apple Tree. Feigning oblivion, he rolled over and was about to nonchalantly saunter off when a marmalade paw rested on his shoulder.

'What's your hurry, Bertie?' said Dennis.

Bertie rolled back. 'Oh, you know. Walks to take, muscles to stretch, breakfasts to eat.'

'Breakfast? At this time? You're a late sleeper.'

Bertie's nervous laughter didn't fool anyone in the immediate vicinity. 'Oh, well, I... er... I had a late night last night. You know, doing... er... tomcat-type things.'

'Is that so?'

'Oh, yes. Tomcatting. All night. Very tiring, tomcatting.' He swallowed hard. 'Now, if you'll excuse me, I'll just go get my breakfast.'

He tried to slip out from under the paw, but Dennis was a professional when it came to pinning someone to the ground.

Dennis laughed. 'I was right. You do lie like a tab rug. And a bad 'un at that.'

'Oh, Dennis, let me go. Please. I haven't done anything.'

'Oh yes you have. And you're going to get what's coming to you.'

Bertie moaned and laughed at the same time. 'Oh, no, not again. You're bigger than me, you're faster than me and you're harder than me. What more do you want?'

'I want you to come with me.'

Bertie sagged. 'If I must.'

It was pointless trying to run, anyway. He was still tender from yesterday's mauling.

'I know what you were doing all night,' said Dennis. 'I saw you. And I've just got two words to say to you.' He led Bertie towards a pile of small fish behind the Ancient Apple Tree. 'Thank you.'

'But—'

'I know you were worried, and I know you were praying. And I just want to say thanks.'

Bertie was taken aback.

'Er... you're welcome,' he said, at a loss for something more appropriate.

'And I want to say sorry for yesterday. But I'm warning you – I'd do the same thing again.'

Bertie looked Dennis straight in the eye. 'So would I.'

'I know.'

There was a moment of silence as each understood.

Dennis waved a paw dismissively as he turned to go.

'Anyway,' he said. 'Bon appetit. See you.'

Bertie smiled. 'So long. And thanks for all the fish.'

The Bursar knew what it was as soon as it came under the door. She picked up the envelope and waved it towards an elegant creamy-blue cat posing on the window-sill.

'Oh, look at this, Claude,' she gleefully teased. 'What have we here? An invitation, perchance?'

'Almost certainly, mistress,' he said languidly.

The Bursar put the envelope to her nose and inhaled, her face one of pure rapture. She opened the envelope and squealed with delight. 'Why yes! An invitation to an Extraordinary Senior Council Meeting. What fun!'

She put the invitation in the box at the bottom of her wardrobe, next to an old envelope with a missing flap.

'And so it begins,' she whispered, patting the envelope. 'Not long now, Daddy. Not long now.'

The Tutor looked into Naiba's eyes. The lights were blazing all right but there was nobody home.

The writing continued, incessant.

ONE DAY AUREGIA WAS BUSY loading yet more baking into candywood crates. Who was it for now? Did that really matter as long as it went to a good cause? The thoughts didn't stay long in her head because they were driven out by the sound of arguing from outside her front door.

'Don't blame me – I'm not even a man yet!'

'Well, when you do finally grow up, remember what you've seen and modify your brutish behaviour accordingly.'

'I'm not brutish! I've never been brutish! I don't even hit you and you're my sister!'

'I'm just saying it's in the nature of man to prove his strength over the physically weaker species of this earth and that frequently includes women.'

'Bet it won't include you.'

Auregia wrenched open the door. 'What's all this noise?'

Greta sighed in irritation. 'I am trying to ensure that when my brother grows up, he is not the cause of misery to his wife and family.'

'Why should I be?' moaned Hansi.

'I don't expect you to be, having seen at first hand the damage that can be done by strength without mercy.'

'Greta, what are you talking about?' asked Auregia.

'A group of severely beaten women came to us last night, seeking sanctuary from their violent husbands.'

'Why did they come to you?'

'They had heard of Father's charity work, and came to him because they had no other refuge.'

'But—'

'Father took them in for the night. He's trying to find somewhere for them to live safely so they can support each other in times of distress.'

Another day, another good cause. Outside, the parallel bars sagged a little more, and a broken dumb-bell went unmended…

'What are you doing?' asked Dennis, very close.

Dominica's supine meditation came to an end.

'Getting ready for the Senior Council meeting.'

'With those things on your face?'

'Yes.'

'What are they for?'

'To soothe tired eyes. Although right now, I wish I'd got

one on each ear.'

'Why, have you got tired ears as well?'

She breathed in, then changed her mind about what she was going to say.

'No, Dennis.' She took from her eyes the small linen sachets stuffed with cold tea-leaves. If only it were so simple to get rid of the bags from *under* my eyes, she thought.

'Can I try them?'

'No.'

'Why not?'

Dominica sat up. 'Because your head's the wrong shape. You wouldn't be able to balance them.' She put the tea-bags on a saucer on the bedside table and walked over to the wash-stand. 'Anyway, you don't like tea.'

Whilst she was washing her face, Dennis retrieved one of the tea-bags, lay down on the bed and slapped the tea-bag over his eye. 'Ta-da!'

'Very clever,' said Dominica. 'Now try both eyes at once. And do it on the floor, not on my bedspread.'

She unlocked her desk and took out the large, black-bordered envelope and the small blue one. From the bottom drawer she took a small wooden gavel which had obviously seen better days and plenty of them.

As Dennis writhed on the floor with two tea-bags, Dominica tried to think of anything else she might need, but as she didn't possess any armour, she decided to go with what she'd got.

'Right. I'm off.'

'Wait!' called Dennis. 'I've done it!'

She looked down. He was flat on his back, all four legs in the air like an upturned table. His tail twitched as he tried to keep his balance, and over his eyes were the two tea-bags.

'Congratulations,' she said.

'How long do I stay like this?'

Dominica sucked in her breath in the manner of a builder over-estimating. 'Oooh, I'd say about… an hour.'

'An hour?!'

The tea-bags fell from his eyes and he toppled over onto one side.

Dominica laughed. 'I said you wouldn't be able to do it.'

'Haven't you got a meeting to go to?'

'On my way.' She picked up her things from the desk. 'Will, Name, gavel, specteswalwatch.'

'What?'

'What what?'

'What was that last thing you said? Spectes something or other.'

'Specteswalwatch? It's an old Universal chant to make sure I've got everything. Now I must go. Duty calls.'

Duty did indeed call, but standing behind it was expectation, which said, 'Take one cat; take one bowl of pigeons; mix vigorously.'

OUR CHARITIES ARE SO BENEFICIAL TO THE COMMUNITY,' said Greta, 'that Father wishes to help more and more of those in need, and to that end he's started a shelter for the homeless…

Around the large polished walnut table in the Senior Council Chamber, most of the members of the Senior Council of The University of Nature were waiting with a decent level of curiosity and excitement. The Bursar, however, was full to the brim with self-generated entitlement and was busy drawing what looked like a very short, very wide garden rake on her notepad.

Dominica banged the wooden gavel once on a battered oak block in front of her.

'I call this gathering to order and by the power vested in me as Vice-Matriarch of The University of Nature, I declare this Extraordinary Meeting of the Senior Council open. I now ask you to state your name and the capacity in which you attend this meeting. Stephanie, you start.'

'Stephanie Forgeson, Head of Personnel.'

Stephanie wore an immaculately pressed uniform given extra definition by shoulder pads big enough for an eagle to perch on. Her combined diary, address book, notebook and 'To Do' list lay open on the table like a portable office; a thick and weighty tome bound in black leather, it doubled up as a weapon whenever anybody suggested to her that humans were just 'resources'.

Under one of the tines on the rake, the Bursar wrote *Human Resources.* Stephanie twitched slightly.

'Josephine Codling, Head Girl.'

Tall, thin, angular and eminently sensible, Josephine was a future Matriarch in the making. If she'd been born a boy, the wizards of Maund would have been a much better organised bunch.

Another time, another place: *Senior Student Representative.*

'Marianna Land, Head of Faculties.' Tall, thin, angular, and just the sort of person the Head Girl could become if only she had some fun.

Strategic Departmental Lectureship Co-ordinator.

Matron was there in body if not in mind.

'Matron, Head of Health and Safety.'

Nobody could quite fathom why Matron never used her proper name any more. Opinion was divided between the camp which said she'd been Matron for so long she'd forgotten her own name, and the not-so-camp which said it was because she was left alone with powerful medicines.

Occupational Well-being and Hazardous Incident Management.

'J. W. Arcrite, Head of ADAM.'

'Full title, full title,' the Bursar tutted impatiently, scribbling again in her notebook.

JW narrowed her eyes. What she wouldn't give to have a piece of four by two in her hands right now.

'J. W. Arcrite, Head of Administration, Domestics And Maintenance for The University of Nature, which takes in a damned sight more than' – she tapped on the Bursar's notepad – 'bloody *Facilities Management.*'

The Bursar slapped at JW's hand, turned the page in her notebook, and put down her pencil on top of the clean page. She looked around as though nothing had happened.

Everybody waited. Eventually Dominica said, 'Bursar?'

'What? Oh. My turn. Helena Jacket, present Bursar of The

University of Nature.'

Eyebrows were raised at the word 'present'.

'Not *Financial Services Manager* then?' asked JW.

The Bursar's mouth remained closed, but her nostrils flared and her body language said, 'Twenty minutes from now you're going to be out of a job, mate.'

Dominica banging the wooden gavel on the desk cut off any further discussion.

'Sisters, I thank you for your attendance and your attention.'

The Bursar picked up her pencil and doodled. She was a natural artist, and it wasn't long before the shape of a gavel appeared on her notepad.

'There are two items on the agenda for this meeting,' Dominica announced. 'These are The Reading of the Will of the Matriarch Morte, and The Pronouncement of the Name of the Matriarch Designate. We shall deal with the items in that order, if there are no objections.'

The Bursar opened her mouth.

Dominica inhaled noisily. 'Bursar? Any objection?'

'Well,' said the Bursar, but the combined weight of six stares changed her mind. 'Of course not. Carry on, Minnie.'

'Full title, full title,' mimicked JW, resulting in several smirks and a flare on the Bursar's nostrils which suggested that in twenty minutes' time not only would everybody be out of a job but she would personally make sure they never cast spells in this town again.

'No objections, Vice-Matriarch,' she said through gritted teeth, and returned to her drawing.

'Are we disturbing you at all, Bursar?' asked Dominica.

The Bursar didn't even look up. 'Nope.'

'Are you sure?'

'Yep.'

She added to her drawing a circular platinum disc that the gavel would be used upon. No battered oak block for her.

'So you don't mind if we carry on?'

One of the Bursar's hands was still fully occupied sketching, so she waved the other one dismissively.

'Fill your boots.'

Dominica clenched her fists. She'd have loved to have filled the Bursar's boots, preferably with someone else's feet. Failing that, some concrete and a nearby lake should do it.

'Don't worry, Bursar,' she said. 'Boots will be filled.'

The Bursar kept drawing.

'So,' Dominica continued, 'as I see that I now have what's left of your attention, I shall read the Last Will and Returning Wishes of Imelda McGinty, Matriarch Morte of The University of Nature.'

**The Last Will and Returning Wishes of
Imelda McGinty,
Member of the Systerhood of the Black Cauldron,
Matriarch of The University of Nature
(hereinafter known as The Union)**

I, Imelda McGinty, being of sound mind (relevant certificates attached) do hereby give & bequeath my possessions in the following manner:

Part One

My Bracelet of Life do I return to the Thaumetallurgy Department for recycling; all my books do I bequeath to the Library; all my topclothes & bedclothes do I return to the stores to be re-used; my cut-glass decanter & six cordial glasses do I bequeath to the Matriarch Designate; my silver pinkie-ring & hoop earrings do I bequeath to Dominica Tort in remembrance of our friendship.

*

'Practical as ever. Always keen on recycling,' said JW.

'The Matriarch's books will enhance our knowledge,' said the Head Girl.

'They're nice glasses,' said Matron.

On the back of the platinum disc in the Bursar's drawing was her family crest; on the front – the side that would take the hammering – was the Main Tower of The Union.

Part Two

The following items are to be shown to various dealers to ascertain their fiscal worth with a view to their sale: my bookcases, writing desk, chest of drawers, dressing table, wardrobe, bed, silver-backed hairbrush & hand mirror, silver teapot, milk jug & sugar basin, china tea-service.

Incognito enquiries are to be made of other dealers as to the cost of procuring such items; then do I wish for the dealers to pay a fair & honest price for the said items.

*

'That'll be worth a bit – it was already antique furniture when she bought it and she had a good eye,' said Marianna.

'I could do with a new writing desk myself,' said the Head of Personnel.

'There may be a precedent for such a purchase,' said the Head Girl.

Set into the milling around the edge of the platinum disc were tiny gemstones spelling out the Bursar's family motto: *Family Money.*

Part Three

The proceeds from the sale of the said items shall be augmented with any monies I leave behind (details of which I leave in a sealed envelope for the attention of Marianna Land) & used for the financing of my Returning Wishes, which shall be carried out under the direction of Marianna Land. Any monies left over after the completion of my Returning Wishes shall go into the general fund for the upkeep of The Union. Should there be not enough money to complete my Returning Wishes, then it is my will & command that I be returned to Mother Nature at the point where the money runs out.

*

'Like I said – practical as ever,' said JW.

'Marianna, do you accept this task?' said Dominica.

'Without question.'

Dominica passed her a long cream envelope.

Platinum platework covered the business ends of the gavel in the Bursar's drawing and the rest of the gavel head was encrusted with precious stones.

Part Four

Any items deemed to have been borrowed by me shall be returned to their rightful owners if such can be proven, with my gratitude for the loan of such items & apology for delay in returning them.

*

'I offer my assistance to the Vice-Matriarch in tracing any rightful owners,' said the Head Girl.

'As do we all,' said JW.

'Mother Nature,' said Matron. 'You mean I'll get my silver syringe back?'

Adorning the handle of the gavel was gold filigree work culminating in a golden eyelet.

Part Five

All such other items as may be deemed to have belonged to me shall be disposed of at the will of the Vice-Matriarch.

*

'I accept this task without question,' said Dominica.

Looping through the golden eyelet, a silken thread coiled seductively.

The Returning Wishes of Imelda McGinty.

It is my will & desire that my mortal remains be taken from The Union unto the area known as the Styltens, specifically to Colmlet Tarn, & from the highest point closest to Colmlet Tarn shall my mortal remains be cast into the waters to be reunited with Mother Nature.

*

'Colmlet, Colmlet... Why do I know that name?' asked Marianna.

'The Matriarch returns to her birthplace,' said the Head of Personnel.

'Colmlet is a place of immense geological significance,' the Head Girl began, only to find herself not as a soloist, but merely one of a chorus round the table who intoned, 'where Mother Nature, through prehistoric fluvial deposits, has bequeathed to us a unique variety of fossilised remains as signposts to the very start of life itself.'

'Remember now?' said JW. 'Geography field trips?'

Marianna smiled. 'Oh yes. I hated every minute of them.'

The Bursar had entitled her drawing *Plans for the Ceremonial Gavel of Matriarch Helena Jacket.* The drawing itself was a work of art worthy of any gallery; the gavel produced from it would be something very rare indeed.

Dominica folded the papers, put them on the table and picked up the blue envelope.

'I now declare that the Last Will and Returning Wishes of Matriarch Imelda McGinty have been read, and it falls to me to make the Pronouncement of the Name of the Matriarch Designate.'

The Bursar put down her pencil and sat upright.

Waving a hand in front of Naiba's face produced no reaction; gently calling her name achieved nothing. Physicians were of the opinion that rudely awakening a sleepwalker was dangerous; presumably the same was true of sleepwriters. The Tutor of Creative Chronicling decided that doctor knows best, and pried no further other than to glance at the manuscript being produced.

The writing continued, relentless.

AS IT DID EVERY DAY, the slight breeze brought the smell of baking across from Doughnut Cottage to Axy's nostrils. He sauntered over and went into the kitchen where Auregia was rolling out wafer-thin pastry.

'Mistress, any chance of having a new punchbag, please? The old one's lost most of its stuffing and Big Lenny's just put his fist through it.'

She didn't stop rolling out.

'Sorry, Axy, not today. I've got to finish these pastries for the orphanage.'

'When then?'

'Maybe tomorrow.'

'Tomorrow you'll be making stuff for the old people's home all day.'

'The day after, then.'

'That's the women's centre day.'

Her voice started to rise. 'Well the day after that!'

'The homeless shelter.'

The rolling pin thumped and swished on the pastry.

'Axy, just go away and stop bothering me for a while. I'll make you a punchbag when I get time.'

'Oh, don't bother. I'll patch it up myself and refill it with leaves or something.' He walked towards the door.

Auregia slammed the rolling pin on the counter.

'Look, I've said I'll make you a punchbag, all right? But just now I've got to finish these so Hansi and Greta can collect them.'

'Oh, Hansi and Greta,' Axy sneered. 'That's all I hear these days, Hansi and Greta. I'm sick of Hansi and Greta. I wish I'd never clapped eyes on 'em!'

'Axy!'

'Well, it's true. They're—' He stopped short.

'They're what?'

'Oh, forget it.'

'No, no, say what you were going to say.'

'They're taking advantage of your good nature.'

'How?'

'Look at you. You're working every hour Mother Nature sends and it's all for Hansi and Greta.'

'It's for the poor, the hungry, the oppressed.'

'Oh, yeah, that lot.'

'What do you mean "that lot"?'

'It's always "the poor, the hungry, the oppressed". What about me and Edgar?'

'A-ha!' Auregia said, pointing at him. 'You're jealous.'

'Oh, face it! They've got you for a mug and you can't even see it!'

'That's it – you're jealous!'

Axy thought that if the judge had already decided on the verdict, the defendant might as well leave the courtroom. He sighed.

'Yeah, yeah, whatever you say. If you say I'm jealous, I'm jealous. Now excuse me, I've got a punchbag to stuff.'

He turned abruptly and marched away. The slight breeze sided with Axy and slammed the door after him.

Auregia stared at the door for several seconds, tapping her fingers on her lips as she always did when she was puzzled. When she smelt the flour, dry and dusty on her fingers, she remembered that she must get this finished before Hansi and Greta arrived. She'd talk to Axy later. When she had time…

As Dominica opened the blue envelope, the Bursar smiled benevolently at everyone round the table, her eyes sparkling and meaningful. In the Bursar's dictionary, benevolence was defined as 'if you want me to be nice to you, it's going to cost you – big time'.

Dominica took out a sheet of paper from the envelope.

'To ensure the safe continuation of The University of Nature, I hereby nominate as my successor—'

The Bursar's notebook spontaneously burst into flames.

Matron gallantly prevented the fire turning into a conflagration by smothering the flames with her bare hands.

'Health and Safety, you know. Health and Safety,' she said, nonchalantly dusting the ashes from her unscathed palms. There was unspoken consensus around the table: firstly, how alert Matron had been and how quick to respond; secondly, how stupid Matron had been to respond in such a manner; thirdly, how amazing that Matron was unhurt; and fourthly, Dominica, isn't it time Matron had a holiday?

'Oh, that was childish,' said the Bursar.

Dominica raised one eyebrow. 'I'm sorry?'

'Burning my book – childish. Very unlike you, Minnie.'

'*I* didn't burn your book.'

'You must have done!'

'Why?'

'Because I'm the next Matriarch and you're not!'

As soon as the metaphorical horse was galloping towards the next county, the Bursar shut her stable door by clapping a hand over her mouth. She stared wide-eyed around the table to see if anyone had noticed what she'd said, because the echo of her words in her own ears had drowned out the collective sharp intake of breath which was enough to bow the walls of the Senior Council Chamber.

The room temperature dropped noticeably as Dominica slammed her gavel down into the remains of the Bursar's notebook and rounded on her, eyes blazing.

'Do you not think, *Bursar*, that I've got better things to spend my magic on than you, *Bursar*?'

The force invested in the last word shocked everybody.

Marianna provided an escape valve.

'Perhaps a break might be in order here,' she said gently but firmly.

The Head of Personnel knew a bandwagon when she saw one, and she leapt straight on it. 'Excellent suggestion. A comfort break. I'll organise some tea and biscuits. A relaxed atmosphere is always... er... we're about to face a historic moment... er... I'll organise the tea.'

'Fair enough. Back here in fifteen minutes then,' said JW.

When most of the others, Bursar included, had left the room, Dominica brushed ashes from the head of her gavel.

'I didn't burn her notebook, Marianna.'

'It wasn't any of us in the room. Well, nobody we could see, anyway.'

Dominica's face clouded. 'You don't think it was...'

'Imelda? Possibly. Not been returned yet, so her spirit's still very strong.'

'And she did have a wicked sense of humour.'

'Wicked enough to make the Bursar wait as long as possible?'

The Tutor of Creative Chronicling lifted Naiba's free hand, which was tightly clasped. There was no response. She tried to prise open the fingers, but they remained determinedly curled, as if clinging to life itself. She took further manuscript pages from the desk, and gently placed Naiba's hand back down.

The writing continued, remorseless.

AUREGIA LAY ON HER BED watching her bedside candle fluttering. She had a headache, her hands were chapped, she was exhausted and to cap it all she couldn't get to sleep. Even the lavender oil wasn't working. And she had to be up early in the morning to bake for the nursing home.

Her bedroom door opened slightly and a small voice whispered, 'Mistress? Are you asleep?'

'No, Axy, I'm not asleep. Come on in.'

'Can I come too?' said a smaller voice.

Auregia smiled. She always smiled at Edgar. He was that sort of rabbit. 'Yes, Edgar, you too.'

Axy and Edgar hopped up onto the bed and sat facing her. She looked so pale in the flickering candlelight that Axy almost lost heart and abandoned his mission.

'Now, what can I do for you two?' she said quietly.

Axy swallowed hard.

'Well, we just want to tell you what we've heard, and what we're going to do about it.'

'You don't need to do anything to start with,' said Edgar. 'Me and Axy'll do it, and if we're wrong it won't matter, will it? You won't need to do anything at all, will you?'

'Apparently not. Have I missed something here? What have you heard?'

Axy took a deep breath.

'We've heard,' he started, 'that a couple of years ago a man called Grandel started selling cakes and pastries from a handcart in town…'

Edgar didn't want to be left out. 'And he only used to appear a couple of days a week…'

'But his cakes were so delicious he used to sell out very quickly…'

'Even though his cakes were more expensive than anybody else's…'

'And he made enough money to buy a shop…'

'And he now opens up five days a week…'

'And rich people queue up outside the shop, waiting for it to open…'

'Even though he charges a fortune for the stuff…'

'It all tastes so good they can't get enough of it…'

'And the poor people can't afford it…'

'And now he lives in a big house…'

'With servants and stuff…'

Auregia held up a hand. 'Hold on a minute. Are you telling me I should open up a shop because you want to live in a big house with servants?'

Axy was shocked. 'No! Just listen, will you?'

Taken aback his vehemence, Auregia listened.

'And now he lives in a big house…' Axy repeated.

'With servants and stuff…'

'Just him and his children.'

Auregia smiled.

'Axy, there's no law against a man making an honest profit.'

'But what about a dishonest one?' asked Edgar.

'Dishonest?'

'It's Hansi and Greta's father.'

'Oh, is it now?' said Auregia in a tone of voice which suggested that this could end in a shouting match, a visit to the local constabulary, or murder. Possibly all three.

'Don't say it like that,' said Axy. 'We're only telling you what we've heard.'

'And where have you heard this? Big Lenny, I suppose?'

Edgar sprang to Axy's defence.

'N-not just Big Lenny. Q-quite a few of the t-town dogs have s-said something.'

'And we just put two and two together,' said Axy.

'And came up with six hundred and forty-seven, as usual, no doubt,' scowled Auregia.

Axy bit back his planned reply and said, 'All right, it's only hearsay, but tomorrow me and Edgar are going looking for evidence.'

'Such as?'

'We're going to follow them when they come to collect the baking. See if they say anything or do anything that might prove them guilty.'

'Or innocent,' Auregia stressed.

'Or innocent,' echoed Axy. 'That's why we want you to come with us.'

'What? Spy on my friends? Are you mad?'

Axy looked at Edgar.

'I told you she wouldn't. Come on, let's go.'

Edgar put a restraining paw on Axy's shoulder and looked at Auregia.

'P-please, mistress. We all used to be so happy together, and this thing is driving a wedge between you and Axy. Please. The only way to fix it is if we all see the evidence together.'

'Or not,' said Auregia firmly.

'Or not,' agreed Edgar...

'Tea, mums?' said a voice belonging to a body whose bottom was easing open the door to the Senior Council Chamber.

Dominica turned to open the door properly.

'Yes, thank you, Gigi.'

The owner of the bottom bobbed slightly, causing a chink of crockery and revealing someone else following her. When she stood up again and faced forward, she exactly fitted the outline of the girl behind her. They were like two slices of the same person.

'Beggin' your pardon, mum, it's Ellie and Emmie.' The girls marched into the room and each laid a large silver tray on a side table. 'Gigi's at the gate, awaitin' on the courier.'

'Oh, yes, of course. Sorry, Ellie.'

'Emmie, mum,' bobbed the girl.

'Emmie – sorry – thank you – both of you.'

The girls left.

Dominica nudged Marianna. 'Can you tell them apart?'

Marianna shook her head. 'Only Gigi.'

They walked over to the refreshments. One of the trays held the cups, saucers, teapot, milk jug, sugar bowl and teaspoons; the other was covered in an intricately embroidered and beautifully laundered cloth, on which was a pile of plates alongside a selection of biscuits. Gingerbread biscuits. Gingerbread men with fudge hats, currant eyes, icing waistcoats, chocolate trousers and liquorice boots, but for all that, underneath they were still gingerbread men.

'I'll pass on the biscuits,' said Marianna, tapping her chest and hinting at indigestion.

JW breezed in. 'Thought I could smell tea so I've brought my own mug. You can't get a decent drink out of them little 'uns. Well, I can't, anyway.' She put down a mushroom-coloured mug on which, in brown lettering, was: *Old witches never die, they simply leave the broom.* 'Oh, gingerbread men. Haven't had a gingerbread man for years.'

'That's not what it says in the Craft Room toilets,' sniped the Bursar, coming through the doorway.

'Oh, good, you've finally learnt to read,' JW retorted.

'Now, now, children,' said Dominica, pouring the tea.

Marianna stepped into the breach. 'How have you managed to escape the gingerbread glut then, JW? What's your secret?'

'No secret. Rather than keep traipsing up to my room with a tray every five minutes, the kitchen gave me what innkeepers call "my own tea-making facilities". So, I don't get the biscuits but I do have an endless supply of the witches' brew.'

Dominica chuckled. 'I don't know why you don't have it piped intravenously.'

'Hey – I would if I could, but I can't so I don't.'

The Bursar opened her mouth to speak, and was naturally taken aback when she found it full of gingerbread man's boots, courtesy of Marianna.

'Oh, good shot,' said Matron, gliding past and picking up a cup of tea.

She was followed by The Head of Personnel and the

Head Girl, earnestly discussing potential new ways of student development.

Dominica caught JW's arm. 'Any chance you could issue the non-teaching staff with name badges?'

'If you like... why?'

'Well, I'm ashamed to say that since Truda hurt her foot I can't tell who's who.'

'Ah, you mean the sixteen sisters.'

Dominica laughed. 'There's not sixteen!'

'Well, no, not actually. To my knowledge there's...' JW pulled a face as she mentally counted, '...seven. No— tell a lie, eight. It just seems like there's sixteen of 'em. Or two of 'em running round very, very quickly.'

'Name badges, I think.'

'Fair enough. Mind you, Gigi's always easy to tell from the rest – there's not many people round here suit a sheepskin noseband.' She grinned, bit the head off a gingerbread man and moved to sit down.

When all were settled again, Dominica banged the gavel on the battered oak block. The Bursar's face suggested that this was a personal insult.

'Before we start again,' said Dominica, 'I'd like all those present in this room, *seen and unseen*, to ask Mother Nature for the grace to conduct ourselves properly through this meeting, and the maturity and patience to accept the Matriarch Morte's decision on her choice of successor. Do we do this with a sincere heart?'

A faint smell of burning paper wafted around the room.

'We do,' the Senior Council said.

Dominica picked up the nomination letter again.

'Very well. I shall continue.'

The Bursar paid full attention and smiled broadly.

AUREGIA PILED CONFECTIONERY INTO CRATES and stacked them outside the cottage door. 'Won't they get suspicious if I'm not here? I'm always here when they come so if I'm—'

'It'll be all right,' said Axy. 'Just leave them a note saying you've been called away.'

'Where to?'

'Does it matter?'

'Well…'

'Look, if it makes you any happier, say you've been called to help one of your sister witches and you don't know when you'll be back.'

'But that's lying,' said Auregia.

'Then just say you've been called away.'

'But I haven't.'

Axy rolled his eyes. 'Yes you have. I've called you away.'

'I suppose that's technically true.'

'Then write them a technical note!'

'Axy…'

'Sorry.'

Auregia scribbled a note on a sheet of baking parchment and left it on the topmost crate of confectionery, then she and Axy walked past the gymnasium to where Edgar was dabbing at a broken shortcrust door leant against a tree. His paw was bright red, as was a pool of liquid by his side.

'Edgar, are you all right?' she said.

He looked up. 'Taking care of the customers.'

Auregia and Axy looked at the door. The red-pawed message read: *Closed today, open tomoro*. Auregia took hold of Edgar's wrist and looked at his paw.

'Cochineal,' he grinned.

'Who's a clever bunny?' Auregia teased.

Edgar blushed, but not enough to disguise his paw.

The three of them set off through the trees, and after a while reached the rough road which snaked past the wood on its way to the village.

'What now?' asked Auregia.

'Now we hide and wait,' said Axy.

The witch muttered to herself, circling her hands over the three of them.

'What are you doing, mistress?' said a bemused Edgar.

'Just putting us inside a cloak of inaudivisibility. We can see and hear everybody else, but they can't see or hear us. It's a lot easier than hiding behind trees and whispering.'

'Ooh, I've never been part of a magic spell before. I always thought it involved top hats and stuff.'

'There's somebody coming,' whispered Axy. 'Shush!'

Auregia tutted. 'Sometimes I think you don't listen to a word I say.'

The Somebody Coming proved to be a local farmer on a horse, slowly plodding along the road. The farmer was swigging ale from a stone flagon and singing *I'll Give You A Seed From A Stalk Straight And True*.

'How on earth does he find his way home when he's as drunk as that?' said Edgar.

'He doesn't need to,' replied Axy. 'The horse knows where they live.'

'But isn't it dangerous, drinking and riding?'

'No, why? The horse isn't drunk, is he?'

Edgar giggled, and when nothing else happened the three of them sat on a nearby tree-stump and waited.

Axy stretched his back legs out in front of him and banged his paws together. 'Should have brought a picnic.'

Auregia poked him in the ribs. 'You've only been away from the house five minutes.'

'Which means it's nearly time for afternoon tea.'

'Which you could have been having if we weren't out here spying on my friends. How long are we going to wait?'

'Until they get here...

'To ensure the safe continuation of The University of Nature, I hereby nominate as my successor Eleanor Lynin.'

The Bursar was still smiling broadly, but only because her face hadn't caught up with the news that her ears had heard. However, her hands were faster than her face and she snatched the paper from Dominica. By the time her eyes scanned the shaking note, the rest of her face was keeping pace and going scarlet, like a tomato ripening at high speed.

'What? What? No! It can't be! You can't do this to me! I was there! She said me! I heard her! Give me that envelope!'

She leapt to her feet, grabbed the blue envelope and turned it inside out. Finding it empty, she shredded it into tiny pieces which fluttered like blue feathers during a pillow fight. She slapped the palms of her hands on the table and gave everyone a stare which could have burnt the paint off a pine wardrobe at twenty paces.

'It's a conspiracy. You've never liked me, any of you. You all know it should be me. Especially you, Minnie. You were there. You heard her say it was me. You got her to change her mind.'

'Helena—' Dominica began, but a Bursar in full spate brooked no argument.

'That's it! Enough's enough. I'm off. I've had it up to here with this place and its petty jealousies.' She swept towards the door. 'You're getting a new Matriarch, so you can find yourselves a new Bursar!'

She slammed the door so hard that the teacups on the desk rattled and one gingerbread man's leg broke. After a few moments The Head of Personnel said, 'Do you think I should go after her?'

Dominica shook her head.

'No, leave her. She'll only be polishing her Miss Sunny Disposition award.'

'As gracious in defeat as she would be magnanimous in victory,' said Marianna.

'If her nose was much further out of joint it'd be round the back of her head,' said JW.

From somewhere high above and far out of the reach of ordinary mortals came the sound of supernatural sniggering.

Dear Marianna,

I know your loyalty to The Union will have prompted you to accept without question the task I've given you. You never have been able to resist a challenge & so I know you'd have accepted any problem set you regardless & worked it out later.

Details of my finances are attached. I chose you because you can calculate exactly how my investments have grown, without having to bring the figures back to The Union & pore over them for six weeks with a team of assistants like some people I could mention.

Furthermore, you're the only one I trust to carry out my Returning Wishes to the letter regarding 'where the money runs out'. <u>Absolutely no Union funds</u> are to be expended on my Return to Mother Nature & you'll have to work out how to finance it solely from my investments.

I know you hated my field trips & I know you don't feel particularly at ease with the unrestrained side of Mother Nature – indeed I've heard you on many occasion say that you 'don't do Nature well'.

However, we must confront our fears or forever live in their shadow. You're a dear & valued friend, Marianna, & you will be tested, but I wouldn't have chosen you if I thought you'd fail.

Besides, you're the only person in The Union who can correctly calculate the trajectory & velocity required to return me to Mother Nature from the edge of the Tarn.

I commend myself to your safekeeping until Mother Nature reclaims me.

Your friend, servant & Syster in The Union,
Imelda.

'When do you want me to start Imelda's returning journey?' asked Marianna when she and Dominica were the only ones left in the Senior Council Chamber. 'Straight away?'

Dominica gathered her papers and the remains of the blue envelope.

'You can't. The Matriarch Morte can't leave The Union until the new Matriarch's been inaugurated and has given the farewell address. We've got to have what you might call a continuous presence of Matriarch, otherwise... well, it's a bit like those pharmacies you go to where they can't sell you certain potions unless the pharmacist is actually there to take responsibility. If we don't have a live Matriarch in office or a deceased Matriarch on the premises, we can't cast any spells.'

'What? None at all?'

Dominica shook her head. 'Not a one. Imagine: the entire thaumaturgic power of The Union suddenly rendered useless. Orthographic Incapacity – that's what the ancients called it.'

Marianna's brow wrinkled. 'But orthographic means spelling using letters, not spelling using magic.'

Dominica sniffed. 'I know. It seems the ancients had orthographic incapacity themselves – they obviously couldn't spell "thaumaturgic".'

IN ALL DRAMAS THERE COMES THAT MOMENT: the hero is just about to give up and admit defeat when the thing he's been waiting for happens, validating whatever extreme action he's been advocating. Axy's moment arrived amid much jangling of horse brasses and creaking of springs when a coach and four hurtled round the corner and halted.

Two flunkeys jumped down from the driving board; one unfastened a travelling case from a large flat platform at the back of the coach whilst the other opened the coach door. On the back of the door was a full-length mirror, reflected in which Auregia could see an intricate cream lace dress, dripping with crystals and pearls, sitting on a deep-buttoned leather bench. The dress started to move, made its way down the coach steps and soon sunlight was playing around the copper-flashed ginger hair of its wearer.

'Blimey!' said Axy, luckily still masked by the cloak of inaudivisibility.

The girl was followed from the coach by an older boy wearing white silk stockings, blue satin breeches, turquoise silk shirt and a waistcoat woven with silver and gold thread. He bore a striking resemblance to the girl, including the same copper-flashed ginger hair.

'Blimey O'Reilly!' said Axy.

'Come on, come on, we haven't got all day,' the girl snapped. 'Open the canopy.'

From under the coach the servants pulled two carved wooden poles with spiked ends which they dug into the ground five paces away. They then unfurled a large canvas awning from a roller on the roof of the coach; half-way along they hooked it onto the poles to form a rudimentary roof, letting the rest of the canvas drop to the floor to form a flap. From the front and back of the coach they unfurled two more large canvases which also hooked onto the poles. In under two minutes the side of the coach had been made into a tent, with the boy and girl inside it.

One of the flunkeys lifted the side awning and passed the travelling case under it, then helped his fellow flunkey unfasten a battered sack-barrow with peeling paintwork from the platform at the back of the coach.

After a while, two grubby, unkempt urchins dressed in rags came out from under the awning and set off into the woods, pulling the sack-barrow behind them.

Axy and Edgar looked up at their mistress with love and pain in their eyes and their hearts. She gathered them up into her arms, buried her face in their fur and wept silent tears of bitterness and betrayal.

After a while she straightened up. 'Come on. Let's see what we've been working for.'

The proud, powerful horses shied nervously as an invisible hand stroked their gleaming coats. Auregia examined the coach, noting no self-reflection in the highly polished paintwork. Gold leaf had been used to impress rather than highlight, especially in the painting of the capital 'G' which covered most of the bottom panel of each door. This motif was on the door handles, wheel hubs, screw heads and anywhere else it was possible to paint or engrave.

The flunkeys assumed it was the forest winds which lifted the canvas awning and gently swayed the coach.

On the ground under the awning was the travelling case. In the lid, a well-used hairbrush had been thrown; in the body of the case was an assortment of ragged clothes. Clean, pressed, fresh, ragged clothes. From the unhemmed edge of one of the garments she pulled a long thread, and from the hairbrush she pulled a single golden hair.

'What's that, mistress?' asked Edgar.

'Let's just call it a hair of the dogs that bit me.'

On the coach steps a smaller box held coloured powders and crayons, mainly in drab greys, browns and greens. Auregia picked up a crayon and smeared it on her hand.

She sighed. 'Even the dirt is dishonest.'

'Mistress?' said Axy.

'They are painted children of dirt that stink and sting…

The Tutor of Creative Chronicling had just finished reading when a small movement disturbed her. She watched in silence as the autoscribe opened a hand, let fall a piece of dried ginger, rose from the desk and collapsed on the bed. The sightless eyes closed.

The Tutor lifted Naiba's feet onto the bed, put a pillow under her head and covered her with a blanket. She tiptoed towards the door, then looked back and said, 'Mother Nature send you some rest.'

'*I shall not rest until my story is told,*' said a familiar unfamiliar voice.

The Tutor shut the door quickly and ran all the way back to her own study.

Dominica hesitated outside the door of the Bursar's room. Through the marblewood panels she could hear a regular dull thud, each sound accompanied by a scream of 'Me!'. Discounting the theory that the Bursar had started giving singing lessons, Dominica knocked on the door.

Neither the thudding nor the screaming stopped.

She knocked louder. 'Helena?'

No reply, and no cessation of noise. Fearing for the Bursar's safety, Dominica opened the door and rushed in.

By the side of the Bursar's bed lay the head of her broomstick. The shaft of the broomstick was in the Bursar's clasped hands, being slammed down repeatedly onto the bed. Generations of concussed mattress mites dropped under the bed in heaps too small for the eye to see.

The Bursar's body bowed with each whack of wood on mattress. Her scarlet face was wet and her eyes tight shut as she bared her teeth for each scream. All-consuming rage made her oblivious to Dominica, who stared at her.

An elegant creamy-blue cat oozed into the room.

'Good afternoon, dear lady,' he said, sitting down next to Dominica's feet. He polished his claws on his fur and raised one eyebrow in disdain. 'In days gone by, I was a Matriarch's familiar, you know.' He sniffed. 'Now look what I have to put up with.' He held one paw out in front of him and examined his gleaming claws. 'Temper tantrums are so unbecoming, don't you think?'

Dominica tore her gaze from the Bursar and looked down at him. 'Is she always like this, Claude?'

'Let's just say,' he said drily, 'that it must have been *exceedingly* bad news.' He sauntered over to the Bursar and stood by her side. 'Mistress, we have a visitor.' His voice was quiet, authoritative and completely ineffectual. The Bursar was still beating like some toy whose motto is 'Perpetual motion is for wimps'.

Dominica heard a refined, resigned, feline sigh. Claude

braced himself, bit on the hem of the Bursar's gown and tugged. His head jerked back and he almost somersaulted as the fabric was yanked from his mouth by the Bursar's arm movement. Determinedly, he again approached the Bursar and started to climb her gown. Once he had all four claws securely hooked into the fabric, he dug his two front paws firmly into the Bursar's thigh.

The Bursar came to a sudden stop, with her hands still tightly grasping the shaft of the broomstick above her head. Breathing hard, jaw thrust out and lips pulled back, she glowered at Dominica. There was rage in her heart, a dangerous glitter in her eyes and a cat swinging on her gown.

'Give me one good reason why I shouldn't strike you down where you stand,' she snarled.

'Because I am unarmed.'

'Not good enough. Try again.'

'Because you can't use a witch's broomstick to harm another witch.'

'Not a broomstick any more. No broom. Just a stick. Last chance.'

'Because it's not me you're angry with.'

The silence was broken only by the Bursar's rhythmical hard breathing, which became more and more ragged as she gave up the unequal struggle to hold back tears. She dropped the stick and fell backwards onto the bed, wailing. Claude, still attached to her gown, looked round at Dominica with panic in his eyes; she stepped forward and gently released him from his cotton prison.

He massaged his paws on the floor.

'Thank you, dear lady. Now please excuse me; I am expected at The Club.' He left the room as quickly as dignity would allow.

'Should've been me... my job...' sobbed the Bursar. 'I've got to get it sorted...'

Dominica lifted the Bursar's feet onto the bed.

'Helena, what are you talking about? Get what sorted?'

The Bursar thumped the pillows as she made herself comfortable. 'How could Imelda do this to me? How could you do it? You could've told me. Why didn't you tell me? Why did you let me make a fool of myself?'

Dominica pulled a tapestry blanket over the Bursar.

'You know full well the Vice-Matriarch can't divulge the identity of the Matriarch Designate until the meeting of the Senior Council. It's the rules.'

The Bursar blew her nose. 'So you put rules above friendship?'

'Now wait a minute. Even you'd admit that you and I get along because we have to, not out of choice. That's not what I'd call friendship.'

'So, if we're not friends, why are you here?'

Dominica sat down on the bed and mentally worked her way through each option. Should she say what she came to say and leave the Bursar feeling victorious, thereby boosting the Bursar's self-esteem and giving her something to take her mind off her disappointment? Or should she say nothing, thereby giving the Bursar even more to worry about by potentially giving her less to worry about? No contest.

'Well... I'm here to—'

'Gloat over my misfortune?'

Dominica stamped her foot.

'Mother Almighty, Helena! This is why we don't get on. I come here to ask for your help and all you can do is—'

'Help? The Vice-Matriarch wants my help? I must tell all my friends.'

'Go ahead. I can wait thirty seconds.'

The Bursar picked imaginary fluff off the blanket in stony silence.

The end of Dominica's tether was rapidly coming into sharp focus. She rubbed her face with her hands.

'Helena, I know you're upset about Eleanor—'

The Bursar snorted.

'—but I'll make no bones about it: I want you to stay on.'

'What?'

'I'd like you to stay on as Bursar because I can't do everything myself. We've got the Inauguration Ceremony and Graduation Day practically on top of each other and I don't want to have to worry about budgets as well.'

'Can't Faculties help you? She usually does.'

'Right now I need everybody's help, and Marianna's going to be busy organising Imelda's Returning Journey. And anyway' – Dominica crossed her fingers behind her back and bit her lip – 'she doesn't have your flair for money matters. She's a teacher, not a doer.'

The Bursar seemed mollified. 'That's true.'

'Look. Help me now, and when the new Matriarch's in office you can resign away to your heart's content and I'll back you to the hilt. Please?'

The Bursar picked at the blanket again for a few moments. Suddenly, her expression changed very slightly, as if a new thought had rushed into her brain yelling, 'Yes! Yes! Say yes!' and she said begrudgingly, 'Oh, all right then. But it's only temporary, mind.'

'Of course. Thanks, Helena. I knew I could rely on you. Now you must be tired – I'll let you sleep.' She stood up.

The Bursar snuggled down under the blanket. 'Good idea. Shut the door on your way out, Minnie.'

'Of course…' Dominica replied sweetly, '…'elena.'

THE FOLLOWING DAY, AXY AND EDGAR appeared to be play-fighting, but in reality they were watching as Hansi and Greta trundled away another sack-barrow full of baking. When the children were safely out of sight, Axy padded through the house to Auregia's bedroom door and knocked.

'It's all right, they've gone!' he called.

The bedroom door opened.

Axy tilted his head to better look at the woman who stood there; she was the most wizened, bent-over old crone ever to lean on a knobbly stick.

'Good day, young Axy,' said a voice worn out from at least a hundred years of giving advice.

'Mistress?'

Auregia's normal voice returned as she straightened up.

'Pretty effective, eh?'

'Not half. I'm very impressed. But what's it for?'

'I'm going into town.'

'Oh.' He followed her into the kitchen, where she opened

a cupboard and took out a wicker basket and two clean tea-towels. Putting the basket on the table, she laid a tea-towel in the bottom of it and then put in a layer of bakewell tarts from a cooling rack by the window. Axy leapt onto the table and stuck his head in the basket.

Auregia pushed him gently.

'What have I told you about jumping on the table?'

He ignored this, being too interested in and slightly unnerved by the contents of the basket.

'What are *they*?'

'You've seen iced bakewells before.'

'Not like them, I haven't.'

Each round bakewell had a basic coating of icing; some were chocolate, some caramel, some pale pink. Each one had two white chocolate drops with liquorice centres as eyes, a round mulberry icing mouth and dark chocolate icing curls. Each one was encircled by a blood red pleated paper case. It looked like the decapitation of a boys' choir.

Axy shuddered. 'What are you going to do with them?'

She covered them up with the other clean tea-towel.

'I'll tell you when I get back…

In Dominica's study, Dennis had challenged Marianna to a game of shove ha'penny. He was way out in front, only needing to get one more coin in a bed to have wiped the floor with her. Trouble was, it was her go and she seemed to be taking an interminably long time about it, measuring this and calculating that.

Dennis strolled alongside the slate, impatient for victory.

'Oh, come on. Just push the damned thing!'

'Now, now, you're not going to rush me and make me spoil my game. That's cheating.' She held her coin up to the light and examined it.

Dennis bridled. 'It's not cheating – it's tactics. Psyching your opponent out – that's what they call it.'

Marianna breathed hard on her coin.

'Is it really?' she said, rubbing the coin on her gown. 'Clever little kitty, aren't you?'

His eyes narrowed. 'Are you going to play that thing or put it in your coin collection?'

'Don't know yet.' She placed the coin carefully on the slate, bent down and squinted along the table. 'Haven't quite decided.'

'Aagh! Get a move on before money goes out of fashion!'

'Tut, tut. Temper, temper.'

Marianna stood up, cracked her knuckles and brought her hand back. Just as she was about to strike the coin, the door opened; she whirled round to see who it was and her sleeve swept all the coins from the slate. She grinned at Dennis. 'Oh, dear. Game null and void, I believe.'

'Oh, what?!' protested Dennis. He slumped down and put his head on the slate. 'You are such a cheat!'

'You're a fine one to talk,' said Dominica, coming into the room. 'You're the one who stops the coins by flicking his tail when he thinks no one's looking.'

'Ohhh,' he groaned. 'It's a conspiracy.'

'Ahh, never mind, little kitty,' said Marianna cheerfully, tickling him behind the ears.

He stuck his tongue out at her. She stuck hers out at him.

Dominica flopped into a chair. 'Well, I've managed to persuade Helena to stay on until after Graduation.'

'Oh, well done,' said Marianna.

'It wasn't easy. I had to make some pretty disparaging remarks about you.'

'I could've done that,' said a voice from the slate.

Marianna laughed. 'She bought the whole story, then?'

Dominica looked uneasy. 'I think so, but to tell the truth, I'm not quite sure who I'm dealing with any more.'

'Oh?'

'When I went into her room, she was beating seven bells out of her bed with her broom handle. She was raging.'

'We all have our ways of handling disappointment,' said Marianna, glancing at Dennis, whose head still graced the shove-ha'penny board.

'Hmm. But there's more to it than just disappointment – there's something else, something almost… fundamental. And I need to find out what it is before the other two wheels come off her trolley. Dennis, do me a favour, please?'

'As long as mathematicians aren't involved, gladly.'

'No,' Dominica laughed, 'no mathematicians. I want you to talk to the Bursar's familiar.'

'What, Toffee-Nosed Claude?' said Dennis, getting up.

'Haven't you got a good word to say about anybody?'

'Not usually, no. What do you want to know?'

'Find out how the Bursar's been since Imelda took ill. See if her behaviour's changed. If she's said anything unusual. Anything peculiar.'

'Such as?'

'I don't know. Anything.'

'Well, thanks for being so specific. Anyway, I don't think Toffee-Nosed Claude'll talk to me.'

Dominica raised her eyebrows. 'Whyever not?'

'Let's just say we don't move in the same social circles. Don't forget…' – Dennis mimicked Toffee-Nosed Claude's refined accent and smooth saunter – '…"in days gone by I was a Matriarch's familiar, you know".'

Dominica chuckled. 'So I understand.'

'Don't worry, I know somebody he'll talk to.'

AUREGIA THE OLD CRONE hobbled about amongst the townsfolk. Mother Nature, it was busy! How did people live like this? Cramped, pushing, shoving, side-stepping, always moving but never seeming to get anywhere.

She put her hand out and it landed on the arm of a young woman, laden down with a sack of old vegetables. Three young children tagged along behind.

'I'm sorry, my dear,' Auregia croaked, 'but could you tell me – is there such a thing as a women's refuge in this town, where an old woman might rest her weary bones awhile, free from the constant grind of life?'

The young woman sighed. 'No, old mother, there's no such place. If there were, I would go there myself.'

'Thank you, my dear. May Mother Nature bless you.'

Inside the sack the vegetables took on a new lease of life, and by the time the young woman came to use them, they were as fresh and tasty as a first crop.

Auregia walked on for a few minutes and when she next put her hand out, she stopped a merchant carrying two money-bags. His dark attire was lightened only by two red sashes running from his waist, over his shoulders to his waist again, holding his lower garments in place. He tried to brush her hand from his sleeve but the crone had a surprisingly tight grip.

'Excuse me, sir,' she whispered. 'Is there a place in this town where a lonely, sick old woman might stay and rest her weary bones awhile, free from the constant grind of life?'

'Unhand me, hag!' he snapped. 'An old folks' home? For you to idle away your time at the expense of others? Indeed, no. Earn your keep, crone – the rest of us do.'

'Thank you, sir,' she said, letting go of his arm. He had gone but a few steps from her when his twin red sashes broke, leaving the bottom half of his body naked to the jeers and catcalls of the passers-by. As he gathered up his garments, he dropped his money-bags; the contents spilt out and were promptly seized upon and spirited away into the crowd. Auregia laughed and started coughing to cover it.

A young man carrying a sheaf of papers came up to her.

'Are y'all right, missus?'

'Why, bless you, son, I would be if I had anywhere to live. Is there a shelter for the homeless in this town, where an old woman might rest her weary bones awhile, free from the constant grind of life?'

'Not yet. Come and sit down here for a bit.'

He guided her to a low wall in front of an inn.

Auregia lowered herself gently as if the wall were the

finest seat in the county and she had the oldest bones.

'Not yet, you say?'

'No. We're trying to raise funds for such a shelter by selling this.' He held up his sheaf of papers. Across the top of each page were the words *The Large Topic*.

She peered at the papers. 'What is it?'

'It's an information paper telling people what's happening and what it's like to be homeless and how they can help and stuff like that. People buy it, and the money goes towards building a shelter for the homeless.'

'Sold many copies today?'

His face fell. 'Well, none actually. But it's early days yet, missus, don't you fret yourself.'

'Then let me be the first to buy one.' She groaned and leaned heavily on her stick as she stood up to hand him a coin. 'Here, is that enough?' she asked, knowing it wasn't.

He glanced at the coin. 'Yes, that's grand, missus. Here you go.' He folded up a copy and put it in her basket.

'I think it needs a change of name, son,' said Auregia. 'Something with a bit more oomph. Help me up here.'

He held her hand as she climbed onto the wall. As he'd never played housey-housey with his granny and her friends, he was startled that one little old lady could produce so much noise.

'*The Burning Question*! Get your copy of *The Burning Question*! If you don't know what *The Burning Question* is, you don't know anything. Not available in any shops! Get *The Burning Question* now!'

As the young man was engulfed in people clamouring for

his paper, he noticed that the title on all the sheets had changed to *The Burning Question*. He didn't have time to notice the old woman get down from the wall and melt away into the crowd.

Auregia hobbled on through the streets, following her instincts until she was on the end of a long line of well-dressed townsfolk. She rested her hand on the large, jittery, well-upholstered arm of the man in front of her.

'What are you queueing for, my dear?' she croaked.

'Oh, it's so exciting!' the stout man quivered. 'Grandel's got some new confections in today and everybody wants them. I hope I'm not too late, being this far back in the queue. Oh, I do hope there'll be one left for me.'

'I'm sure there will be, my dear,' Auregia said, before hobbling alongside the queue. Silk, cashmere and brocade were much in evidence, as were babbling voices and the jingling of money-bags. When she reached the point where the queue blocked the doorway, she stopped and looked in the shop window. Rows of bakewell choirboys looked back. She tapped her cane on the ground.

'I must have some of those for my grandchildren,' she warbled, and made her way into the shop by adept use of her elbows coupled with a blatant disregard for other people's toes. Those who objected soon experienced the pain of an old lady leaning very heavily on a cane on their instep.

'Yes, Madam?' said the large, round man behind the counter, a man she could only assume was Grandel, bearing in mind the ginger hair and strong family resemblance.

'I'll take six of those face things.'

'Our Angel Heads are very expensive, you know,' said Grandel patronisingly.

'It's all right. I have money here somewhere.'

She lifted the top tea-towel from her basket. A gasp went round the shop as the other customers saw what was in there.

'Grandel! She's stolen some of your cakes!' claimed one.

'Look! There in the basket!' said another.

Grandel reached over the counter and snatched the basket. Something dropped from it and was picked up by one of the wealthy clientele who held it between a gloved thumb and forefinger and waved it in the air. His face contorted in disgust. 'Oh, look – it's that subversive paper that boy sells! She must be – ugh! – homeless!'

Silk, cashmere and brocade flattened itself against the wall and started edging out of the door in an effort to get as far away from the old woman as possible.

She surveyed her new-found space.

'I've stolen nothing,' she cackled, mainly for effect but also to cover her laughter.

'I saw her do it on the way in,' called someone further down the queue.

'And she's got my wallet,' shouted another hopeful.

Grandel wasn't going to let a little thing like a homeless old woman ruin his profits. As he walked from behind the counter he raised his hand to calm the situation and his voice was velvet reassurance wrapped around steel.

'Now, now, ladies and gents, no need to be alarmed. We'll soon sort this out.' He grabbed Auregia by the arm and manhandled her into an empty storeroom at the back of the shop, pushing her so hard she fell over. He threw her basket in after her, scattering bakewell choirboys along the floor. 'I'll deal with you later,' he snarled and locked the door, brandishing the key to the applause of his customers.

Auregia sat up and looked round the storeroom. Light fizzled in through a four-pane frosted-glass window. She laughed as she picked up her basket.

Grandel never had leftovers to store, so he had only paid rudimentary attention to security. The storeroom window had a catch on it, of course. But it was to stop people getting in, not getting out...

Naiba knocked on the study door. There was no reply. She knocked again.

'Tutor?'

Silence flooded back at her. She tried the door. It was locked. On the other side of it the Tutor of Creative Chronicling held her breath, and was prepared to do so, if necessary, for ever.

NOTES ON
The Brew Shed

The Brew Shed is where overabundant fruit, vegetables and flowers are transformed into a dazzling variety of beers, wines, spirits, liqueurs and cordials. During the day it's off-limits to all except the brewers and distillers and their trainees; after all, if staff and students can't get through the day without resorting to alcohol, then the curriculum needs a very serious looking-at.

In the evening it's open to all, even the first-formers; by demystifying alcohol, the students learn about its effects rather than being attracted by its allure as a forbidden pleasure. And the Brewmistress makes sure that until they've demonstrated a certain level of responsibility, no student is served anything stronger than a homeopathic solution. On the other hand, the staff are deemed capable of making their own decisions – which most of them are – and therefore can drink whatever lurid combination of colours, flavours and viscosities takes their fancy as long as they can get up for work the next day. This is *how* students learn about the effects of alcohol rather than being attracted by its allure as a forbidden pleasure.

Magic won't work in The Brew Shed; any witch who even attempts to utter a spell will find herself spouting the first verse of *My Broomstick Has Flown Off Without Me*. For witches, it's the equivalent of leaving your weapons outside:

everybody can relax, knowing that no matter how raucous the party or how bad the argument, everybody's going to leave the Brew Shed the same species as they went in. It's one of the basic precepts of The Union that those who hold the power will do no harm — unless there are exceptional circumstances coupled with far-beyond-extreme provocation and there'd better be solid proof of that at the subsequent enquiry — but nobody's taking any chances when there's alcohol involved.

Above the Brew Shed are meeting rooms; being magic-free, they're the perfect location for disciplinaries, performance appraisals, discussions about the finer points of thaumaturgical lore, or any other occasion where people of differing views want to put their point across without fear of personal physical rearrangement.

Under the Brew Shed is Cookie's, the hottest spot for the coolest cats around, because whatever is fermenting, stewing, brewing or settling, one barrel of each is always left for the familiars.

By the front door a notice at ankle height warns *No familiar may consume alcohol before six p.m. unless for medicinal purposes, and then only for an exceptional reason accompanied by a note from Matron.* And if anybody tries to sneak a snifter before six, they'll find themselves on the wrong end of a bouncing from the Brewmistress's familiar, The Spirit of Antiquity, the cat himself — Cookie, who stands no nonsense and takes no prisoners.

The barrels of refreshment are arranged to accommodate the very different types of clientele frequenting Cookie's.

Gingerbread Children

One end of the hostelry is known as The Club, where the wines, liqueurs, cordials and highly-combustible-with-fruit-and-paper-umbrellas are sipped and familiars can drink until they think they're hilarious and then fall over and start hiccupping, farting and giggling in a high-pitched nasal whine.

At the opposite end is The Pub, where the ales, bitters, stouts, ciders and lagers are guzzled and familiars can drink until they think they're hilarious and then fall over and start burping, farting and giggling in a bronchial wheeze.

In the middle is The Bar, where the spirits are knocked back and familiars who are miserable can sit, bore the fur off anybody passing and drink until they can't find their ears with both paws. Then they fall over and start snoring, only to wake up the next morning with their bottom jaw in a pool of something that might once have been the Brewmistress's peapod vodka, a hangover the size of the Globe Hall and Cookie standing over them with a mop. And, in most cases, they wake up no closer to remedying the cause of their misery.

~•~

It was happy hour in The Club; the crowd in The Pub considered themselves too intelligent to have their moods dictated to them.

An elegant creamy-blue cat sat alone, sipping beetroot liqueur on the rocks and keeping an eye on the door, searching out the company that misery loves so much. A black cat with a white eye-patch had hardly got through the door before a refined feline voice addressed him.

'Bertrand! Do came and join me.'

Bertie strolled over to him. 'Evening, Claude. You're in early tonight.'

'Oh, my dear, the day I've had. It shouldn't happen to a *dog*. In days gone by I was a Matriarch's familiar, you know.'

'So was I, Claude, so was I.'

'What? Oh, yes, yes. Terribly sorry. Bad business.'

There was one of those silences which are much, much deeper than they are long. Then, just as Toffee-Nosed Claude thought he'd picked a wrong 'un, Bertie said, 'So tell me about your day, Claude.'

Claude leapt on this as if it were the last chocolate in the box and his granny was walking up the path.

'Well, my dear, my life is in ruins. Absolute tatters.'

'How come?'

'I've been *so* badly let down. You wouldn't believe it. You simply would *not* believe it.'

'Not another of your dead certs turning out cert dead?'

'Oh, no, dear boy. Much worse. Much worse. It's *her*.'

'Your mistress?'

One of Claude's paws tapped rapidly on the floor.

'Promised me *everything*, that woman. Said I'd be a Matriarch's familiar again. Said it was *her* job.' He looked around to see if anyone was within earshot and then whispered harshly, 'Well that's all gone to a ball of chalk, hasn't it?'

'So it would seem.'

'Not to her.'

'Really?'

'Keeps saying there must be some mistake. Insists it was her *destiny*, if you please, to be Matriarch. Says she *will* be Matriarch. Barking.'

'Dog impressions?'

'Mad, dear boy, mad. Lost the plot entirely. *Such* a disappointment. And such an *embarrassment.*'

'Oh, dear. Another beetroot, Claude?'

'Don't mind if I do, Bertrand; I don't mind if I do.'

From The Pub end of Cookie's, a three-fruit marmalade cat watched and waited.

THE TREACLE FORMED A LARGE TEARDROP on the edge of the spoon then fell lazily into the pan, starting an elegant flow from silver spoon to blackened pan. As the golden strand slimmed to a trickle it cast dignity aside and hurried into the pan, melting into itself to form a shimmering pool, regaining its composure before flowing over the butter and sugar like lava from a volcano.

Satisfied there was enough, Auregia propped the spoon across the treacle jar to drain then gently heated the pan, stirring the ingredients with a wooden spoon until they gradually resolved into a smooth, sweet, buttery syrup which she then set aside. In a bowl, she prepared air-lightened flour, soda and spices, and when the syrup had cooled sufficiently she poured it into the bowl and combined the ingredients into a dough, repeatedly pressing and kneading it – the technique born of long years' practice, the force born of recent misery.

She rolled the dough flat, and taking her sharpest knife

swiftly cut out two person-shaped figures and lifted them onto a lined baking tray. Into the dough at the head end of each figure she pressed two currants and a semicircular slice of cherry, then she slid the tray into the oven and went into the utility room, whence came slopping and slapping sounds.

After about ten minutes she returned to the oven, withdrew the baking tray and slipped the baked figures off the tray onto a cooling rack. A quick glance at them might have suggested the figures were of equal size; a closer look would have revealed that one was slightly larger than the other, but only by about two years. She left them to cool, and resumed her work in the utility room.

Axy heard a crash.

'Mistress? Are you all right?' he called, racing round the outside of the house. He was stopped in his tracks by the sight of the utility room window, cracked and broken on the ground outside the cottage. In the wall, there was a square hole through which Auregia poked her head and smiled broadly at him.

'I'm fine, thanks, Axy.'

'What are you doing?'

'Improving the utility room. Nothing to worry about.'

'Are you sure?'

'Yes, yes, off you go. It won't take long.'

Axy decided an improvement to the utility room was far more attention-worthy than a gym which practically ran itself, so he sat down and watched as Auregia placed five evenly spaced sticks of rock upright in the window hole and cemented them in with chocolate concrete, the dessert which has bent far more spoons than celebrated mystics ever could. After a while, when it seemed there was nothing more to be seen – and hadn't he got better things to do than watch concrete set? – he was about to pad back to the gym when he heard the swish of an emulsion brush glazing the wall, and the sweetest, most inviting smell tickled his nostrils and made fun of his taste buds.

'Yummy,' he said.

She looked out from between the sticks of rock. 'Nice?'

He inhaled as much aroma as he could, and a banquet of flavours assailed his senses. 'Mm. What is it?'

'That, my dear Axy, is the sweet smell of a dish best served cold.'

'Ice cream?'

She laughed. 'No, not ice cream. What are you doing watching me, anyway? Haven't you got a gym to run?'

Axy strolled off, trying to be miffed, but the delicious aromas kept lifting his spirits.

Repainting finished, Auregia went back to the kitchen where the baked figures had were ready to be decorated. She tipped icing sugar into a basin, mixed it with warm water until it was smooth, then dropped in two stigma of safflower. Yellows and reds suffused the icing, and she mixed again until the glossy flowing paste was a uniform orange colour. Over the top of the basin she held the single strand of ginger hair from Greta's hairbrush, and with silver scissors snipped the hair into minuscule pieces, peppering the surface of the icing. She stirred the mixture again and when it was ready, she lifted a teaspoonful of the icing and slowly drizzled it around the edges of the gingerbread heads.

Next she crushed a blackberry between her fingers until its dark juice dripped into the bowl of icing, turning the orange a muddy brown. Lifting the thread taken from the children's ragged clothes, she snipped it into tiny fibres and added them to the smooth paste which she then spread, in the shape of a ragged shirt, over each gingerbread figure.

Then she washed up, and waited…

It was late at night when a drunken Dennis banged his head on Dominica's window because he'd misjudged the opening. His back leg slipped off the window-sill and he had to reach inside and hook his claws in the curtains to stop himself falling off entirely. As he slid himself sideways under the window, the curtain-rings clacked with each movement he made and, fearing they would wake his mistress, he shushed them loudly.

He dropped onto a chair with a heavy thump which caused him to burp and wince, and the springs in the chair seat creaked in protest as he shifted his weight and prepared to jump down onto the floor. Looking down from the chair seat, Dennis suddenly felt sick and straightened up again, breathing in deeply. This sudden influx of fresh air only made him feel more drunk; overbalancing, he clasped at the chair arm with his two front legs, a gesture born more of hope than expectation. He missed the chair arm but caught the upright supporting the arm, and slowly slid down it until his head was on the corner of the seat.

Having his apex lower than his base made him feel sick

again, so the best thing for it was to slide his back end off the seat, dropping it lightly onto the floor. This gentle movement took on an alarming turn of speed as weight overcame intention and soon Dennis was swinging from the arm support like a furry pendulum and two of the chair legs started to lift off the floor. At this point he gave up the unequal struggle with gravity and let go. He hit the floor with a dull thud as the chair legs did the same with a considerable bang.

'Ssshhh!' he hissed, holding the chair down to prevent further noise. When he was satisfied the chair could be silent, he gingerly let go and started to pad slowly across the room past the end of Dominica's bed. He'd gone halfway when his claw caught in the fringes of a rug, which started to roll up behind him; stopping to untangle his foot, Dennis sat down harder than he had intended, thereby prompting hiccups. As he freed his foot, the rug slapped back down onto the wooden floorboards. He smoothed the rug and patted it down with his paw, then jerkily hiccuped his way to his basket. The wicker creaked as he climbed in, but he was sure it was only loud because he was so near it; she wouldn't be able to hear it at all.

As he closed his eyes and hicsighed, congratulating himself on being so stealthy, Dominica said, 'And where have you been?'

'Oh,' said Dennis, 'I thought you'd be hicsleep by now.'

'That's not answering my question. Where've you been until this time?'

'On a find-facting mission. Like you hicsaid.'

'And did you find any facts?'

'Not me. Bertie.'

'What did Bertie find?'

'Dunno. Still in The hicClub with Toffee-Clawed Nose. Left 'em to it.'

'Goodnight, Dennis.'

Hic. 'Night, Mstrss.'

The Tutor of Creative Chronicling spent a restless night, waking frequently, unable to push Naiba's story completely from her mind. She felt ashamed for running away but, if honest, also scared in case she heard the familiar unfamiliar voice again. However, she was the Tutor and technically Naiba was under her care, so she really should see how she was getting on. And it was a good story; it'd be a shame not to find out how it ended. And who ended it.

HELLO, MY DEARS,' AUREGIA SAID BRIGHTLY as the children trundled the sack-barrow towards her to pick up the day's baking. 'I've got everything ready for you.'

Greta smiled. 'Father sends his most grateful thanks to you, and marvels at your skill.' She motioned to Hansi to load up the sack-barrow. 'Your baking delights the people so much they are impatient for it, and Father was almost robbed yesterday as he went about his good works.'

'Really? Oh, dear. I don't like the sound of that. We can't risk your father's safety for the sake of a few buns. Perhaps I oughtn't to bake any more.'

Hansi almost dropped a crate. 'No!' he said with a hint of

panic. 'I mean... no, he wouldn't want that.'

'No? You're willing to put your father in danger?'

'What my brother means,' said Greta, in the placating tones Auregia had heard quite recently somewhere else, 'is that Father has no special regard for his own safety in this matter. It is reward enough to him to distribute your wares, and he is more than willing to face the associated dangers. It was an isolated incident and he expects no further trouble.'

Auregia looked concerned. 'Well... if you're sure that he'll be all right...'

'Perfectly,' Greta reassured her. 'Father is well able to can take care of himself.'

Auregia smiled. 'I'm sure he is. Want some lemonade before you go?'

The children pushed into the kitchen but the lemonade was forgotten as delicious aromas wafted towards them. Hansi saw visions of an almond-wafer shell overflowing with vanilla ice cream, topped with fresh wild strawberries drizzled with mint toffee; Greta was seized with a longing for mandarin segments and whipped cream, encased in a ball of coffee and orange gateau, rolled in crushed walnuts and dusted with icing sugar and sliver curls of dark, dark chocolate.

'What is that smell?' she asked, mouth already awash with expectation and probably something far nastier.

'Oh, it's just something I'm trying out,' Auregia said innocently. 'Do you want to some? It's in the utility room.'

They needed no other encouragement. Their noses led quickening feet to the source of the delight; they rushed into the utility room but it was empty apart from themselves, and so it remained after Auregia locked the door.

'There's nothing here!' said Hansi.

'What are you doing?' called Greta. 'Why have you locked the door? Father will worry if we don't return.'

'Surely he'll understand if I wish my friends to stay a little longer,' said Auregia from the other side of the door.

Greta tried reasoning. 'Of course, we'd love to stay, but we must take the confections to Father so he can distribute them to the less fortunate.'

'Oh, yes, the less fortunate,' said Auregia. 'Do you know, I must have no sense of direction: I went into town yesterday and I couldn't find the shelter for the homeless, nor the old folks' home, nor the women's refuge… and I couldn't even find the orphanage. And you'd have thought I'd have been able to find a building as big as that, considering how many children there are in it and how hungry they all are.'

'Which town did you go to?' asked Hansi.

'I went to the town where the rich people queue outside a cake shop to pay vast sums of money for no doubt exceedingly good cakes. A cake shop where I was accused of stealing. A place run by a man named Grandel. Do you know of it, by any chance?'

'All right, all right, you've made your point. Let us out, we'll call it quits and we'll not bother you again. What do you say?'

'I say no.'

'It'll be the worse for you, when Father finds out,' screamed Greta, banging on the door.

'I suspect Father's joy will not be unconfined,' said Auregia as she walked away…

The third day of the Period of Mourning was, for Dominica, much less eventful than the first two. She had absolutely no reason to deal with the Bursar, so her stress levels plummeted and she could concentrate on the Matriarch Morte's funeral service. Imelda left no specific instructions for her send-off; just as she would have no Union funds expended for her Returning Journey, she would have none expended on her funeral above and beyond a standard service. This saved everybody a lot of work, because there were no complicated scenarios involving a release of doves or troupe of acrobats. The only real worry was who would read what and who would sit where.

Dominica and JW discussed the logistical aspects of holding a Funeral, an Inauguration, a Graduation and – unlikely but possible – an Election, all within the space of a month. In her usual pragmatic fashion, JW had the answer.

'Leave all the chairs out just change the bunting.'

The Bursar went about her business as normal, but it was generally agreed that when bumped into, she displayed a surprising and unnerving level of cheerfulness.

~✦~
NOTES ON
Parturicia

Should a witch need to, she has the power to summon Parturicia – Earth Mother, the Bringer of Life, she who provides the spark to ignite new being. However, she and her work are invisible to the general population, who solely see the end result: a red-faced, howling miracle.

Only appearing in her full form when actively summoned she is instantly recognisable, being modelled on the best architectural constructions: solidly built and beautifully proportioned. She wears flat, black, comfortable shoes, and black stockings cover stout but shapely legs; her full-hipped body is encased in a starched, royal blue uniform with a thin white line piped around the short sleeves and the collar, where a circular metal badge adorns each lapel; a black elasticated belt encircles her waist, fastening with three silver buttons; on her generous bosom a small watch hangs upside down on a strap, underneath a name badge bearing the words *Natural Health Service* and *Parturicia*.

Her stiff black leather holdall contains bags of Time which she will provide on request for certain spells. If she gives out more than four hours' worth of Time, she will provide a Timekeeper – a flame-shaped black crystal – to go with it. Once the Time is activated, the Timekeeper will glow white for an instant before fading to green; as the Time is spent, the green will turn to a coppery amber, then red, eventually returning the crystal to black when the Time is at an end.

Whilst the Time is working, Parturicia or the witch who has asked for it can have a vision of where the Time is being used, simply by holding the Timekeeper. This is extremely useful when you've brought an inanimate object to life and sent it out to do a job; it's also very handy if you lose Time, as you'll be able to find out where the Time has gone.

Parturicia's work as the Bringer of Life is non-stop, because some women put themselves through prolonged excruciating agony more than once in order to have someone else to worry about for the rest of their lives, whilst some men casually impart their certain knowledge-from-no-experience that childbirth is a pain quickly forgotten. Many people think that were Parturicia to start visiting the male population, the birth-rate would drop dramatically and she'd be left with hardly anything to do.

But until biology takes a violent swerve away from the norm, Parturicia is kept very busy indeed; busier than Death currently as birth rates exceed death rates, but it only takes a moment's lack of vigilance over hygiene, common sense or government to reverse that situation.

Death comes to us all, childbirth does not. However, in bestowing life Parturicia often pays return visits to a mother; for someone to have more than one visit from Death in a lifetime could be construed as extremely unlucky, even if deserved.

~✦~

GINGERBREAD CHILDREN

BACK IN THE KITCHEN AUREGIA COULD STILL HEAR the children demanding to be set free so she closed all the doors, made a pot of tea, and on the kitchen table set out a tea tray with two cups and a plate of cakes.

Reaching down into the bottom of the candywood chest, she pulled out a small, battered pine box which filled her hand. Its top and sides were scuffed, ingrained with the dust and grease of too many years, despite the fact that all its owners treated it with the greatest of care and kept it in the darkest of corners, only bringing it out when absolutely necessary. The longer you looked at it, the tattier it became. A robber would not think twice about it in the search for gain; it conveyed its own worthlessness very successfully.

Auregia opened it and took out a white silk pouch. From this, she withdrew a finely engraved silver bangle which she slipped onto her left wrist. Clasping the bangle and her wrist with her right hand, she held her arms above her head.

'I call on the Power of the Bracelet of Life:
A favour I need, in the quest to do good.
Please give me some Time, to a task undertake
In order a man can live life as he should.'

She removed the bangle and replaced it in the silk pouch within the pine box and buried it back at the bottom of the candywood trunk. She had just closed the trunk lid when there was a knock on the door, which opened and a cheery voice lilted, 'Hello-o, anybody ho-ome…

The Tutor of Creative Chronicling balanced a tray of food with one hand as she knocked on Naiba's door with the other. There was no reply, in which case there was no option: she had to go in. She pushed open the door, and was not surprised to see Naiba at her desk, writing, as she must have been for some considerable time judging by the manuscript sheets piling up on the floor.

'Please come in, most bounteous Earth Mother,' Auregia said as she bowed, 'and take a seat. Tea's ready.' Every Union-trained witch knew that Parturicia didn't ask for much but she did like a cup of tea, and it was only common courtesy after a summoning.

Parturicia plonked her bag on the table and sat down with a small gasp.

'Oh, that's better – I'm glad to take the weight off for a few minutes. Please, call me Pat. I can't stop long; a woman's work is never done, and all that. What is that infernal noise?'

'Two children.'

'Not yours, though, are they?'

Auregia sat down. 'Indeed not.'

'No, I didn't think we'd met before. Ooh, coconut tarts, lovely.' As Auregia poured the tea, Parturicia bit into a tart and her face creased in delight. 'Ooh, these are gorgeous,' she said through a mouthful of crumbs. 'They'd go down a storm at christenings. You'd make a fortune selling these.'

'Yes,' said Auregia wearily, 'I know.'

Parturicia finished her tart.

'Mmmm, lovely. Now, what can I do for you? Time, wasn't it?'

'Life Time, if I may, Earth Mother.'

'What's it for?'

'To rescue some of your progeny from the evil path of greed and exploitation.'

Parturicia gulped her tea. 'A worthy cause. I hate it when a baby turns out bad; I always feel slightly responsible. Isn't that ridiculous? I mean, it's not my fault – I only make 'em, I don't bring 'em up – but it still makes me sad. How much do you want?'

'A single hour is all I ask.'

'And what will you do with the Life Time I give you?'

'Give it to others to try to bring a man to his senses.'

Parturicia laughed. 'You'll need more than an hour!'

'Still, an hour is all I ask.'

'Then you shall have it.' She unclasped the top of her holdall, delved inside and pulled out a small brown paper pouch, gathered up and tied at the top with a noose of string, the long end of which had then been wrapped around the fastening. She handed it to Auregia. 'Use it wisely, my dear, for Time is precious.'

'I will, Earth Mother, and great are my thanks.'

'Well, I'd best be off. Now, you don't need a Timekeeper do you, because it's only for an hour, so... I think we're done. Do you mind if I...' she said, indicating the cakes.

'No, please, help yourself.'

'Thanks ever so.' Parturicia tipped the remaining cakes into her black bag and snapped it shut. 'They'll keep me going for a while. And thanks for the tea. Bye-eee.'

She dashed out of the kitchen and was gone...

With one hand, Naiba ate and drank mechanically, oblivious of who had brought the food and drink, and equally oblivious of its temperature and taste. It was simply fuel, consumed to keep the other hand writing.

AUREGIA PUT THE TWO GINGERBREAD FIGURES on the floor and unwound the string from the brown paper pouch until only the noose was left keeping it fastened. Holding the long end of the string she let the pouch hang by her side until it skimmed the floor; she brought the pouch back to her hand and upended it.

She stared at it, weighing her next move very carefully, then took a deep breath, pierced the bottom of the pouch with a silver pin and let the pouch hang by her side again.

Sands of Time trickled out onto the floor, forming a large golden, silver, black-flecked circle as she walked round the gingerbread figures.

'This Circle of Life I give to you now:
Once outside this Circle, an hour is yours
To do as you're bidden in any way how.
I ask for your help in pursuit of my cause.'

Once all the Time had run out, Auregia crumpled up the paper pouch and placed it in the circle with the gingerbread figures. She lit the long end of the string and watched tiny starbursts pop as brilliant white flame ate its way along the string and consumed the paper pouch, lighting up the kitchen in an orgy of colour. When the lights faded, the gingerbread figures started to move and grow.

When Axy put his head round the door to see what was

happening, Hansi and Greta stood in a circle of sand. Well, he thought it was them, anyway…

The Tutor of Creative Chronicling left word with the kitchen staff that they were to send regular meals to Naiba's room and clear the empties, but on no account were they to try to wake her or tidy the paper constantly falling from her desk.

Bertie spent much of the day sleeping; it just seemed so much easier than opening his eyes. Whenever he woke he summoned the courage to lift his head and have a good drink of water, then he slumped back to sleep. However, by late afternoon he'd drunk as much water as he could stomach and, hoping it would stand him in good stead, he forced down a meal and dragged himself back to Cookie's for a second evening with Claude.

Meanwhile, Marianna busied herself making plans for Imelda's Returning Journey, sending Gigi over to the Library to ask Libby for atlases and gazetteers so she could determine the route and the stopover points, and calculate distance, time to be taken and potential costs. Costs! There was still the sale to organise! Maybe after the funeral she'd get JW involved in that – she'd know which dealers to go to.

And once she'd got Imelda to Colmlet Tarn… What then? What had her letter said? '*…you're the only person in The Union who can correctly calculate the trajectory & velocity required to return me to Mother Nature from the edge of the Tarn.*'

Trajectory and velocity, no problem; method of delivery was something else. It might involve the Engineering Department, and possibly a big rubber band.

THE LIVERIED FLUNKEYS CAME RUNNING OVER as they always did when the children returned with a fully laden sack-barrow. While the flunkeys secured it onto the back of the coach, the children ducked under the canvas awning into the dressing room, emerging shortly afterwards; the boy carried breeches and shirt, and the girl carried a cream lace dress. They sat down on the same tree-stump previously occupied by Auregia, Axy and Edgar.

'Take down the dressing room,' said the girl in a voice which the flunkeys had learned to obey. 'We won't need it any more.'

The flunkeys did as they were bidden, re-rolling the canvas and putting the carved poles back on the coach.

'Tell Father we'll return within two hours.'

The children sat on the tree-stump and waited until the coach was well out of sight. Then they walked into the wood, and halfway to Doughnut Cottage they lay down on their rich clothes and went to sleep.

That night, for the only time in their lives, a vixen and her growing family feasted on two small iced gingerbread figures she had found in the wood...

Dominica had just finished lunch in her study and was about to start final checks on the Matriarch's funeral arrangements when the door opened and Dennis and Bertie strolled in.

'Oh, hello,' she said. 'What news, weary travellers?'

Dennis snorted. 'Weary drinkers, you mean.'

'Sorry we're late,' said Bertie. 'I've only just got up.'

'Snoozing till gone one o'clock? Not like you, Bertie. Now Dennis, I could understand.'

Dennis stuck his tongue out at her then leapt onto her lap. She rubbed his head and kissed him; Bertie looked wistful. She winked and grinned at Bertie; Dennis frowned. Dominica laughed.

'Oh, mistress,' Bertie sighed, 'did you know the severity of the task you set?'

'Sitting in The Club chatting? Hardly severe. Although I do know someone here who came back the worse for wear.'

'And that was only after one night,' Dennis groaned. 'Poor old Bertie's had two full evenings of Toffee-Nosed Claude's whingeing and whining.'

'Oh, dear, was it as bad as that?'

Bertie looked up from under the remains of a thick head.

'The words "self-indulgent ramblings" come to mind. And boy, can that cat drink.'

'Well, you didn't have to,' Dominica, not unreasonably, pointed out.

'I had to burn the taper of conviviality at one end in case he suspected my ulterior motive.'

'Claude burns it at both ends and in the middle once he starts,' Dennis added. 'Mind you, he's so self-absorbed I'm not sure he'd notice an ulterior motive if it bit him.'

'Hence the late arrival,' said Bertie. 'It's a good job we're on long evenings or I wouldn't see daylight at all. Ooh…'

His neck ached from looking up at Dominica, so he leapt onto her desk for more comfort, forgetting the brain-bouncing that would result from doing it.

'Ow! Ah. Not sure I should have done that.'

'Your self-sacrifice in the face of tremendous hardship is commendable,' said Dominica. 'So what can you tell me?'

'Well, the long and the short of it is,' said Dennis, 'the Bursar has got it into her head that she will be Matriarch.'

'I meant what can you tell me that I don't already know. Besides, the Bursar knows our next Matriarch will be Eleanor,' said Dominica, adding hastily, 'which is top secret at the moment so don't go blabbing about it.'

Bertie waved a paw. 'Don't worry. All the Senior Council's familiars are bound by a code of silence.'

'I wish Claude was bound and gagged,' said Dennis.

Dominica's face clouded. 'Why, what's he said?'

'Oh, it's not what he says, but how bloody long he can string it out.'

'But—' Dominica started.

'It's fine,' said Bertie. 'Claude knows what he can say and who he can say it to. After all, in days gone by…'

'…I was a Matriarch's familiar, you know,' the three of them said.

'Quite,' said Bertie. 'Anyway, the thing is, when my mistress took ill, the Bursar started making plans to step into her shoes. Thought this was her big moment.'

'And when it wasn't,' added Dennis, 'she spat the dummy out and climbed out of her pram.'

Dominica was momentarily surprised at the mental

picture this conjured up. 'And when she climbed out of her pram – as you so eloquently put it – did she toddle straight into a sweet shop? Because that's how she's behaving.'

'Ah, well, this is down to you, I'm afraid.'

'Me? What did I do?'

Bertie chuckled. 'When you went to see her, you said something about when the new Matriarch's inaugurated, you'd back the Bursar if she wanted to resign.'

'Ye-e-es…'

'So,' said Dennis with a hint of glee, 'she realised the show's not over until the soprano's deafened the back row, so to speak.'

Realisation dawned on Dominica. 'O-o-o-h.'

'Until the new Matriarch's inaugurated, the Bursar's still in with a chance.'

'And,' said Bertie, 'Toffee-Nosed Claude says she's convinced it's only a matter of time before she's centre stage, drowning out the orchestra.'

IN THE CELL, HANSI AND GRETA HAD REALISED that shouting wasn't going to get them anywhere – certainly not out of there. Greta paced round the cell, pulled at the window bars and rattled the door handle.

'Give me your shoe,' she said.

'What for?' asked Hansi.

'I'm going to see if we can knock our way out of here.'

'Have you seen the thickness of these walls?'

'They're only cake and biscuit, stupid.'

'Can't you use one of your shoes?'

'Do you know how much these shoes cost me?'

Hansi looked at her shoes, which were out of shape, dirty, scuffed and fraying. Her toes poked through the uppers and the heels were worn down. 'Not much by the look of them.'

'Listen, mate, these are not just any old tat, these are very expensive designer tat. Now give me your shoe!'

He took off his shoe and handed it over. Greta knocked it hard on the wall. Holding it in both hands, she thwacked it against the window bars. She hammered on the door with it. All it did was echo round the cell and make her arms ache so she threw it back at her brother.

Hansi sat on the floor conserving his energy whilst all this was going on, and watched impassively as she stood on the window-sill and tried to squeeze herself through the bars; two years ago she might have been able to do it, but now she was built for fraud, not burglary, and her corpulent frame would fit no further than her shoulders.

Abandoning a window escape, she examined the door. She could find no hinges to unscrew and close inspection of the door handle revealed nothing at all.

Still Hansi made no move. 'In a bit of a pickle, aren't we?' he said. 'Although I suppose it's more of a jam, really.'

'What are you talking about?'

'We're stuck inside *Doughnut* Cottage so we must be... in a... jam...'

His voice trailed off as his sister's gaze bored through him. Suddenly, her face brightened.

'Brilliant!' she said. 'We'll eat our way out!'

'What? Even you can't eat a whole room.'

'Not all of it, just a hole big enough to crawl out of.'

'Good idea!' exclaimed Hansi, getting to his feet and walking over to the door.

'Not in the door, stupid – round the window!'

They tried to take a bite out of the window corners. As the saliva hit the fanlight and their taste buds sucked the flavours from the wall, they recoiled in nausea at a combination of salt, lemon sting, hot pepper, mustard, vinegar and sour milk. All the sugars in nature would not sweeten this little room…

Naiba gasped, sucking in breath as if someone had uncorked her lungs. An empty dinner tray was on one side of her desk, a greatly increased sheaf of manuscript paper was on the other and a surprised Tutor of Creative Chronicling sat opposite her.

'Wow!' said the Tutor. 'You're awake! Welcome back.'

'Where have I been?'

'Geographically, here. Literarily, I'm not exactly sure. How are you feeling?'

'Honestly?'

'Give me your best description.'

'Groggy – you know, when you can't wake up properly. Hung over but not sick. Like I need a really, really long walk in some fresh air.' She stretched her back. 'Ow! Stiff. Confused. What are you doing here? Is this my tray? I don't remember ordering a meal. What's all this?' She pointed to the pile of paper. 'Where's this come from?'

'*From me*,' said the familiar unfamiliar voice.

The Tutor clenched every muscle she possessed from the neck down.

'Ahhh... right...' she said, before swallowing hard. 'And why... why have you woken her? Why have you stopped writing now?'

'*I'm waiting.*'

'For what?'

'*Something to happen. Then the end can begin.*'

'What something?' cried Naiba. 'What will happen?'

But the voice was silent.

Four days passed.

The letter had been burning a hole in Dominica's pocket since it arrived that morning and the time had come to put the fire out. She stood outside the Bursar's room and raised her hand to knock but before she could, the door opened and the Bursar cannoned into her.

'Get out of my— oh, Minnie, didn't see you there.'

'Obviously.'

'So what can I do for you?'

'Can I come in?'

'Well, I am rather busy.'

'It's about the Matriarch Designate.'

'What about her?'

'Can I come in? I'm not discussing this in the corridor.'

The Bursar tutted. 'Oh, if you insist.'

As Dominica went into the room, it struck her that this was much more like the Bursar of old.

'Now, I know you were upset about Eleanor being nominated—'

'Well, I'm over that now.'

'—and I didn't know whether you were harbouring any hopes that you might get your chance in an Election, if Eleanor proved to be unavailable.'

'I might have been,' the Bursar sniffed.

The words 'Toffee-Nosed' rose in Dominica's mind.

'Then I'm sorry, Helena, but she is available, and she'll be arriving in time for Imelda's funeral.'

'Oh well, there you go, never mind, that's life,' said the Bursar brightly, opening the door and ushering Dominica out. 'Now if you don't mind, Minnie, I have things to do, places to go, people to see.'

Dominica listened at the closed door for a while to see if there was any thumping and screaming, but her fears were unfounded. However, she did think she heard chuckling.

Naiba's life had gone from one of suspension to one of suspense. She didn't know where or when the Muse would be upon her again, but she did know that this return to almost normality was only temporary and sooner or later the story would continue. She took to carrying a sheaf of paper around with her so that if the Muse did come back, she wouldn't have to scrawl on her own arms and legs. She kept the ginger about her, for safekeeping; it was in her pocket when the ten strokes of the Assembly Bell called everyone to attention.

As before, the Globe Hall and the galleried landings of

the Main Tower were packed; this time, ripples of excitement ran through the crowd.

Dominica was on the dais.

'Sisters all,' she began. 'This morning came confirmation that the person named as the Matriarch Designate has accepted the honour of becoming our next Matriarch. It is therefore my pleasant duty to read to you this letter.'

Dear sisters,

It is with the greatest of sadness that I learn of the death of my old friend and mentor, Matriarch McGinty, whose influence, knowledge and warmth will be greatly missed by those who knew her, and whose principles will be an example for all those yet to come.

I am greatly honoured by the Matriarch's legacy to me and be assured that I will use her firm foundation to build upon and strengthen The Union.

I shall be at The Union for the funeral, but of course shall not take up office until the Inauguration. Until such time, may I prevail upon the Vice-Matriarch to hold The Union steady in her capable hands.

Mother Nature bless us all.

'And the letter is signed by Eleanor Lynin.'

It was as though the entire building took a step backwards, pulled in its chin, furrowed its brow and said 'What?' in a puzzled voice.

Dominica continued. 'I can only echo the sentiments expressed by Matriarch Designate Lynin in her letter; may

Mother Nature be with us all at this time.'

'And with our spirit,' came the chorus.

As Dominica left the Globe Hall, the building echoed to the ripping-up of more betting slips and the sound of mathematicians calculating payouts for the winners, of whom, it must be said, there were very few.

'Did you try writing your own ending?' said the Tutor of Creative Chronicling.

'Yes,' said Naiba gloomily, 'but it didn't work. Somehow I don't think they all lived happily ever after.'

The Tutor shook her head. 'No, me neither. The thing about this particular writer's block is that it's not actually your block, is it? It's not you who's writing this story.'

'No.'

'So, the only advice I can offer you is make sure you're fed and watered and fit for when it starts up again. Get a good night's sleep, and I'll pop round tomorrow lunchtime with some different writing exercises. Let's see if they help.'

At the edge of the Herb Wheel, the Archivist had already retrieved the summoning rod.

'How do they seem today?' asked Dominica.

'Unsettled. Your visit will settle them.'

'Are they always unsettled?'

'No, only when they know there's news coming. No Faculties today?'

'I decided to come on my own this time.'

The Archivist raised one eyebrow.

'I'll be all right,' said Dominica. 'I'm well-rested.'

The Archivist handed the rod to Dominica, who walked away and was soon in the middle of the constant hum of bee-life, a hum which stopped when she held the rod vertically and knocked three times on the brass summoning-plate.

The nine Sentry Bees emerged.

'Who knockzz for the Beezz?'

'The Keeper of the Bees.'

'Whozze Beezz?'

'The Queens' Bees.'

'And who comezz azz the Keeper of the Beezz?'

'Vice-Matriarch Dominica Tort.'

'And what doezz the Keeper of the Beezz dezzire?'

'I desire to speak with your pages.'

The Sentry Bees flew back and sent out the Page Bees.

'We are the Page Beezz.'

'I come to bring you joyous news.'

'What joyouzz newzz do you bring?'

'The news I bring is of the Matriarch Designate.'

'Joyouzz newzz indeed. What do you azzk of uzz?'

'I ask you to tell your Queens and your families.'

'Zzo be it. Who izz the Matriarch Dezzignate?'

'It is Eleanor Lynin, Graduate of The Union and Sister Outwith The Walls.'

The Page Bees returned to the hives, and soon came a sound which Dominica would have sworn was hundreds of thousands of bees saying 'Really?'.

The Page Bees emerged again.

'Our Queenzz and our familiezz thank you for your

courtezzy, and would azzk one quezztion.'

'A question? What else can I tell you?'

The bees looked around briefly to check no-one else was listening, then hovered in a huddle in front of Dominica and whispered, 'Doezz the Burzzar know?'

Dominica put one hand on her hip and tried to look nine bees straight in the eye. 'Yes, the Bursar knows. Why do you ask, bees?'

The bees became the picture of collective innocence. They shrugged and laughed falsely. 'Oh, no reazzon. No reazzon at all.' They coughed. 'Live in peazze, Keeper of the Beezz.'

They shot back into their hives.

Dominica felt like a hostess whose guests had just read about her court appearance for poisoning.

'Well, live in peace, bees,' she said shortly. As she walked away, the hum of the hives was that of gossips gathered on a thousand honeycomb street corners.

The Archivist was waiting at the hut. 'Are they told?'

'Yes, they are told,' said Dominica, handing back the summoning rod. 'Has the Bursar been round here lately?'

'Don't think so. Not seen her myself. Why?'

'Oh, no reason,' said Dominica. 'No reason at all.'

Naiba got a good night's sleep and ate a hearty breakfast full of protein, fruit, fibre, vitamins, minerals and anything else it was necessary and possible to cram into one meal for one person. Which was just as well, because come lunchtime, she was already filling page after page, unaware of her own actions; unaware of the Tutor of Creative Chronicling sitting opposite, nervously bouncing one knee, spirits wavering between excitement and terror.

EVENING WAS PAINTING THE SKY with inky emulsion as Grandel kicked open Auregia's kitchen door and strode in, carrying in his large, fleshy hands blue satin breeches, a turquoise shirt and a cream lace dress, all covered in muddy foxpaw prints.

'I've come for the children.'

'I'm sorry?' said Auregia, drying her hands.

'My son and daughter. Little Hansi and Greta. The only joy of a poor father's life.'

She hung the towel up to dry. 'Why would they be here?'

'I found these on the way to this place.'

He threw the clothes at her; she made no move to catch them and they fell to the floor.

'Those clothes are far too rich ever to enter this house. I would remember clothes like those.' Despite the heat from the stove, the atmosphere would have suited polar bears.

'I know they're here. You've made your point, so hand them over.'

Auregia gave Grandel such a look that a patch of giant hogweed half a mile behind him withered and died for no apparent reason, leaving a family of insects very suddenly bewildered and homeless.

'I tell you, the children whose clothes those are cannot be here. My only guests are two poor waifs and strays who are filthy, ragged and constantly hungry. And their father could not afford such finery as that.'

'Cut the crap. Let me explain. I'm a very busy man with many powerful friends. You don't want to upset me and my friends, because you don't want any trouble, do you?'

As an explanation, his words left a lot to be desired but they did sound as if they'd been used before to some effect.

'No, but I do want an apology and some reparation.'

'What?'

'Repayment of that which you have stolen.'

'Stolen? You gave it away of your own free will.'

'You duped me – a fact of which I am not proud – but worse, you did it on the backs of others much less fortunate than yourself.'

Grandel took a fat wallet from deep in his heavy cloak.

'All right, how much do you want?'

'I want nothing for myself except the apology. But I do want you to do all those things you said you were doing.'

'Like what?'

'The orphanage, the old people's home, the women's centre, the homeless shelter.'

'Hah! Are you mad? I can't afford that!'

'I thought you were a man of considerable means and powerful friends?'

Grandel put his wallet back in his cloak.

'And I intend to stay that way.'

'So you refuse to do this?'

'You're damned right I do. I'm not running a charity, you know.'

'Not yet.'

'Not ever.'

'Then your children shall remain here.'

'Safe and sound and out of harm's way.'

Auregia was surprised at this.

'Do you not fear my hold on your children?'

'A powerful man like me – fear you? A white witch who can't resist doing good but can't bear to do evil? Fear you? Fear your mumbo-jumbo and sleight-of-hand tricks?'

To have the secrets of Mother Nature and the tradition of the ancients dismissed so lightly was almost more than she could stand, but years of training kept her temper in check and Grandel was unaware of any change in her voice.

'Do you come to my house and show me no respect?'

'What respect do you deserve for kidnapping?'

'And what would respect be worth from a man who uses charity as a cover for greed and exploitation, and seems to care nothing for his children?'

A patronising smile spread across his vast face. 'Not strictly true.'

'Although with children like yours, I can understand.'

The smile vanished far quicker than it had spread.

'Careful, hag, you go too far.'

'I've come this far without success; why should I not venture further?'

'Don't push me. I warn you – I'm a very powerful man.'

'Who constantly needs to reassure himself of the fact.'

Grandel purpled. 'Lady, do you know who you're dealing with?'

'I fear you've been watching too many second-rate barbarian morality plays.'

His eyes narrowed; one started to twitch uncontrollably.

'Don't push me. Not if you know what's good for you.'

'I appear to have found out what's bad for me.'

He grabbed her wrist and squeezed it hard. 'Not by a long chalk, witch. Hand over the children before this gets nasty.'

'Is this your idea of a pleasant evening?'

'Your flippancy does you no credit.'

'Nor your posturing you.'

'Posturing? Posturing? I'll show you who's posturing. If you won't give the children back, I'll take them back.'

'It is not within your power.'

'No? We'll see about power.'

'Father!' screamed Greta, and her voice poured straight into Grandel's already overflowing barrel of anger.

'Let me see them! If you've harmed one hair…'

'But I couldn't, could I? I'm a white witch, am I not?'

She picked his hand from her wrist, lit a candle and handed it to him. 'Outside. Turn right and keep walking. They're in the utility room.'

'Utility room? What's that?'

'Utility. From "utilise", meaning "to use". I keep things in there which can be of use…

The funeral service for Matriarch Morte Imelda McGinty took place on a suitably unusually damp and cold morning. JW had ensured that all the necessary logistical operations had been carried out: chairs had been set out; flowers had been chosen, cut, trimmed and arranged; aromatic oil burners had been replenished and lit.

From The Point, light filtered down onto the dais and softened the silver handles and screw-heads on the simple oak coffin which stood on a silk-draped bier. Eight tall, thick, cream wax candles burned reverently in large, floor-standing silver candlestands around the coffin: one at the head, two at the shoulders, two at the hands, two at the feet and one for the soulspace – that square yard which the body occupies on earth in order to hold the soul.

Bertie sat silently at the head of the bier, staring unseeing at the grain of the oak, trying to believe it wasn't happening, that it wasn't his mistress, that really he was sleeping under a tree and this was all just a terrible, terrible dream.

The Globe Hall and the Main Tower landings were, of course, full of grieving students and staff who were all aware of the rhythm of life and the necessity of being reborn in Mother Nature, but nonetheless sad that you had to die in order to do it.

Dominica led the Senior Council and the whole of The Union in the funeral rites: thanks were given for the Matriarch Morte's life; there were eulogies and anecdotes from those who wished to be heard; there were silent thoughts from all. Finally, there were prayers beseeching Mother Nature to grant success to the Returning Journey and, when the time came, to take back to her bosom her faithful daughter Imelda McGinty.

After the prayers, Dominica stood at the head of the bier and swallowed back tears. It was nearly over.

'I now ask Spirit of the Western One to take our sister to the Chapel of Rest, where her body will lie in state, her spirit watching over us, awaiting her return to Mother Nature.'

Bertie led the funeral procession, Imelda's bargain-token on a silver chain round his neck glistening with his tears. Six Senior Council members each picked up a candlestand and accompanied the bier and coffin which glided silently out of the Globe Hall, across to the gardens to the Chapel of Rest, where Dennis stood, as still as the stones of the chapel itself, head bowed, waiting to pay his respects.

Once the procession was out of the Hall, Dominica addressed the gathering again.

'Sisters all. Today there was an empty chair in the midst of the Senior Council, the chair of Matriarch Designate Lynin, who sadly has been delayed. However, we know she was with us in spirit. Therefore until she arrives, we shall keep a candle burning to symbolise her presence. May she be with us soon.'

She picked up one of the two remaining candlestands and placed it in the centre of the Globe Hall's circular dais.

'Our lives are the poorer for the loss of our sister, but they are lives still, and must go on. As is customary, today is declared a Union holiday. The Valediction Breakfast will take place in the refectory; all are welcome, and none compelled. This Period of Mourning is officially at an end, sisters all. Mourning has broken.'

MAY I ASK A FAVOUR, WISE WOMAN? *I have a fine steeplechaser who caught his fetlock on a fence at last week's Cerloyne Stakes. The wound festers and nothing eases it – my darling limps worse every day and I fear for his life. Please come and look at him. Many people have told me that I should seek* *your counsel and I believe you are the only one who can help. Thank you. Lady Arabella Clematis.'*

Auregia looked at the stable-boy. 'Tell her ladyship I shall prepare some ointments and be there this afternoon…

When the symbolic presence of the Matriarch had used up four candles, Dominica was reluctantly forced to take an unprecedented decision.

'Cancel the Inauguration?' said JW.

'I've no choice,' said Dominica. 'Unless she turns up in the next twenty minutes, there won't be time to go through all the formalities and preparations. We'll reschedule it when she gets here.'

'When's that going to be?'

'I've written to her again asking her, but I'm not prepared to keep the entire Union on standby just in case she turns up. We've only got four days before Graduation.'

'She must know how important that is.'

'That's what I can't understand. Eleanor's a stickler for this sort of thing. She sets great store by the rules and procedures. She wouldn't miss it if she could help it.'

'But if she's not here…'

'I know – I'll have to do it. I'm already doing the graduates' leaving interviews. I can't see there's any time for an Inauguration.'

JW sniffed. 'I'll change the bunting then.'

That night, in Naiba's room, the candle flame flickered and drowned in its own wax. Moths stumbled about in the unexpected dark, shivering at the drop in temperature. Silver moonlight streamed in, searched round the desk, and rested on the twisted and gnarled root which lay upon a pile of manuscript. The light cast deepening shadows from the ridges of the outer skin, shadows which threatened to absorb and engulf the light itself; the root seemed to grow stronger, feeding off the light and growing ever hungrier. The moonlight, sensing the inadvisability of such an association, tore itself away and moved on to light up the corners of other, safer rooms in The Union.

All these things went unregarded by the figure at the desk, whose handwriting covered reams of paper but whose open eyes were as sightless as those of the moths.

AXY SENSED THE FOOTSTEPS long before he could properly hear them. He looked wildly around the cottage garden. Lavender? Mint? Coriander? Basil? Chameleon plant, that'll do. Grabbing Edgar by the paw, Axy dragged him across the garden and pushed him into the mass of leaves.

'Stay here. They won't smell you above this lot.'

'But—'

'Just stay. And keep your head down!'

If Axy said stay, Edgar would stay.

Axy climbed a tree, flattening himself along the length of a branch, and watched as Grandel and three Huge And Heavies strode into the garden, each carrying a sledgehammer. Grandel also carried a thick leather strap, at the end of which was a slavering, growling, foul-breathed, seek-and-retrieve hellhound.

'Witch! Are you here? Or do you tend Lady Arabella's fine steeplechaser with the festering fetlock?'

As Grandel's amusement boomed round the wood, all birdsong and insectsound stopped.

'Father!' yelled the children.

At Grandel's signal, one of the men started to smash the liquorice strip and rock rollers of Axy's running track. Another man was set to work on destroying the front of Doughnut Cottage. Axy flattened his ears, trying to blot out the noise of crumbling brickwork and falling struts. Grandel and the third man walked round to where the children were waving their arms through the bars of their prison.

'Hurry!' snapped Greta. 'Before the bitch comes back.'

'Soon have you out of there my dears,' said Grandel. 'Stand back.'

The arms retreated as the henchman swung his sledgehammer against the wall of the children's cell. The hammer bounced off and made no mark. The Huge And Heavy tried again. Not a scratch.

Grandel tutted. 'Come on! Put your back into it!'

The henchman put his back, heart, soul and every fibre of his being into it, but raised not so much as a sprinkling of icing sugar.

Grandel tied the hound to a nearby tree and swung his own sledgehammer. It embedded itself in the wall. Grandel tugged; the sledgehammer ignored him. He put one foot on the wall of the cottage and pulled with both hands on the shaft of the sledgehammer, straining until the veins stood out on his neck; the sledgehammer was resolute. Nothing would persuade it to come out again, not even the brute force and ignorance being so eloquently displayed.

'What's happening, Father? Knock this wall down this instant!' demanded Greta. Grandel had a mental picture of his daughter standing in one corner of the cell with her arms folded, stamping her little foot.

'I will do, darling.' He turned to the henchman. 'Roof.'

The henchman used the window-sill and the handle of the embedded sledgehammer to hoist himself up on to the roof. Straddling the apex, he swung his own hammer again. It bounced out of his hands and clattered down the crispbread slates, plunging to the ground and almost parting the hair down the back of Grandel's head on the way.

'Why is it taking so long?' shouted Hansi.

'It'll be all right – it's just a little local difficulty. Nothing to worry about.' The henchman came down, retrieved his sledgehammer, climbed back on the roof and tried again.

'Father?' said Greta, coming to the barred window just in time to see the sledgehammer whizz past.

'Darling, just amuse yourself for five minutes while I sort this out.'

'You know how you always said I could have a rabbit?'

Grandel sighed. 'Yes, darling.'

A pudgy arm came through the bars.

'Can I have that one in that patch of green and red stuff over there?'

'Yes dear, in a minute.'

'Now!'

'If it'll keep you happy, darling.'

He set off towards the chameleon plant.

'Edgar!' Axy screamed at the top of his voice. 'Run! Run for your life! Go!'

There was a flash of white tail as Edgar shot out and raced into the woods. Grandel untied the hellhound, exhorting, 'After him, boy! Fetch the rabbit! Fetch!...

The day before Graduation, Dominica sat cross-legged on the floor in her study. Her eyes were closed, her fingertips lightly pressed together and the only sound to be heard was her slow, regular, breathing. She was the picture of serenity.

On her desk stood small bottles of essential oils, the only clues to show she'd pulled out all the stops to achieve this profoundly calm meditative state. The air was heady with sandalwood, camomile, petitgrain and sweet fennel; drifting through were hints of ylang ylang, cedarwood, marjoram and palmarosa. Not to be left out, lavender wafted from her pulse points. The words 'danger', 'toxic' and 'give me a mask' might have been used by an outsider, but Dominica was going to be calm if it killed her.

She had just wound down to the point where she could reasonably be described as 'only fraught' when there was a knock on the door. Gigi entered and almost immediately started coughing. She left the room, closed the door and knocked again.

Dominica inhaled slowly and deeply. A lesser body would have had an immediate severe migraine followed by a fortnight's sleep; Dominica simply opened her eyes, stood up, stretched and opened the door. Gigi ducked to one side as the aromas were given their freedom and wafted off down the corridor, calming everybody and everything in their path.

'You can come in now, Gigi, they've gone.'

Dominica walked over to the window and threw it wide open. Fresh air peeked in, thought, 'Oooh, this is a nice place to be' and promptly flooded every corner. Dominica started to put the small bottles of oil away.

Gigi held out an envelope. 'Sorry to disturb you, miss, but I reckoned I ought to bring this straight away. It's just arrived. With Cedric.'

'Cedric?'

Gigi blushed along the whole length of her face, which took a while. 'The courier, miss.'

Dominica took the envelope, slit the end open and drew out a single-page letter. As she read it, her face went from serene acceptance of her lot in life, through disbelief, veered towards despair and then rampaged in the direction of fully wound-up apoplexy, all in the space of three seconds.

'Oh… Shapeshifting Shirley! Bugger bugger bugger bugger bugger! Gigi, get me all the members of the Senior Council in here as quick as you can. I don't care what they're doing or who they're doing it with just get 'em all in here NOW!'

Gigi didn't even stop to bob.

THE PARLOUR HAD BEEN DEMOLISHED, the bedroom was a heap of rubble, the dining room was dust and the henchmen were about to start work on the wash-house when one heard Axy scream. He reached up and picked him off the branch, holding him by the scruff of the neck. Axy twisted and contorted but couldn't swing round far enough to take a bite. The henchman laughed as he walked past what was left of the cottage and dangled Axy in front of Grandel.

'Look what I got, boss.'

Grandel smiled. 'Well, well, well. It's a liddle puddy tat.'

Axy lunged, but Grandel backed out of the way.

'A lively little one, aren't you? Bet you like playing games, don't you? Well I don't, so tell me where the key is.'

'Key? What key?' said Axy.

'Don't mess me about, cat. I want my children out of that cell. Where's the key?'

'There isn't one.'

'A cell with no key? Hard to believe. Like a punch with no pain.'

His fist smashed into Axy's stomach. Axy doubled up; waves of hurt washed over him as the henchman grabbed his back legs and straightened him out again.

'Right,' said Grandel. 'Let's look for that key, shall we, puddy tat?' They moved to what had been the front of Doughnut Cottage. 'Is it in the parlour?'

Grandel looked around, clapped a fat hand over Axy's head, holding his jaws closed.

'No, not in the parlour.'

He pulled out one of Axy's whiskers.

'Is it in the dining-room? No, not in the dining-room.'

Pull.

'Is it in the bedroom? No, not in the bedroom.'

Pull.

'Is it in the wash-house? Let's see.'

Two henchmen soon reduced the wash-house to a pile of crumbs.

'Can't find a key in here, boss,' one shouted.

'Not in the wash-house.'

Pull.

'Where can it be?'

An increasing swish of ferns heralded the arrival of the hellhound, who held a shaking Edgar in his great jaws. Blood ran down Edgar's fur from a puncture wound made by a vicious fang. Grandel let go of Axy's head and took the terrified rabbit from the dog, which immediately started jumping up to attack Axy, but the henchman held him out of the way and laughed.

Grandel shook Edgar by the neck in front of the bars on the utility room window. 'Darling – I got you that rabbit.'

A pair of pudgy arms came through the bars.

'She's got the key with her!' screamed Axy through his pain. 'She carries it everywhere!'

Grandel turned his head, Edgar still swinging wide-eyed and panting at the end of his outstretched arm.

'I thought you said there wasn't a key.'

Axy breathed heavily. 'She has the key. Please leave us alone. I'll— I'll talk to her.'

Pudgy hands tugged at Edgar's back legs. Grandel kept hold of Edgar's neck.

'No! Please! Let me talk to her!' Axy begged.

'You're damned right you'll talk to her.' Grandel let go, and the pudgy hands snatched Edgar into the cell. Grandel walked towards Axy. 'Tell her I want those children and I'll be back tomorrow.' He took hold of Axy's back legs and smiled. 'Now you won't forget, will you, liddle puddy tat?'

Revolted by the hot, rancid fumes Grandel breathed over him, Axy lunged and his claws ripped through the waxy flesh of Grandel's cheek. For a moment there was silence in the woods as the cat and the man glowered at each other; a silence shattered by the snap of the bones in Axy's back legs and a scream that chilled the sap in the trees.

The henchman laughed, curled Axy into a ball and threw him onto the broken bricks and struts of the parlour.

'Tomorrow? Get us out now!' Hansi called.

Grandel walked back to the cell. Hansi's knuckles were white where he gripped the bars. Grandel touched his hand. 'Tomorrow. These walls are much stronger than the others – we can't get through them. When she sees the rest of the house, she'll come round to our way of thinking.'

Greta came to the window. 'Tomorrow?'

'Yes, darling. You play with your new friend and Daddy will be back tomorrow to get you out of here.'

Greta passed Edgar back through the bars to her father.

'He's no fun any more.'

On his way out of the clearing with his henchmen, Grandel towered over Axy. 'Don't forget.'

He dropped Edgar across Axy's broken body before striding off. Firebrands of agony shot through Axy's spine as he raised his head to look at his friend. Two pools of midnight stared back, and stared back until Axy reached out and released Edgar's soul by closing his eyes for the last time.

Axy's cup of bitterness was full, and now there was only one person to share it with. He held his head back, and when he screamed her name, his raging pain and anger tore at the heart of the world...

Naiba's own sightless eyes closed. Unaware that she was weeping – unaware of anything at all – she rose from her chair and fell onto the bed.

Gigi bobbed in the doorway of Dominica's study.
'Please, miss. Bursar said she'll be along in ten minutes.'
Dominica raised an eyebrow.
'Oh, did she, now? Thanks, Gigi. Tea, please.'
As Gigi left the Head of Faculties came in.
'Can I help, Dominica?'
'You can indeed, Marianna. Could you go and get Helena for me? She doesn't seem to understand urgency.'
'Then it'll be my pleasure to explain it to her,' Marianna replied and set off down the corridor.
Dominica was pacing in front of the fireplace when the Head of Personnel walked in, flicking through the diary part of her mighty black leather tome.
'Dominica, can't we reschedule this? I'm—'
'Sorry, Stephanie – not this one. Please. Sit down.'
Stephanie slapped shut her lifeline and sat down as Dominica continued her pacing. The Head Girl appeared in the doorway and was about to speak when Stephanie motioned to her to sit down and say nothing. This mime was repeated when Matron and JW came in together.

Marianna returned with a scarlet-faced Bursar, who came into the room as if she were trying to convince everyone that she and Marianna were complete strangers. Marianna closed the door, then Dominica closed the window and faced the bemused Senior Council.

'Now, what we're about to discuss is not for general consumption, so please don't say *anything* to *anybody* until we've got this sorted out. All right?'

The Senior Council nodded in baffled agreement.

'Good. I've had a letter from Eleanor's office. It says she left there in good time to get here for Imelda's funeral.'

'So where is she?' asked Matron.

'Well, she's not there, and she's not here, so I can only assume she's lost en route.'

'Lost?' said the Bursar. 'How can she be lost for over a week? Surely she can ask directions.'

'Not lost as in "can't find your way" – Mother Nature knows, it's a straight road from there to here – I mean lost as in "gone missing" lost.'

'Gone missing? Where?' said the Bursar.

'If I knew that, she wouldn't be missing, would she?'

'Perhaps she's taken a few days off.'

'Helena, she was coming to take up the most important post in her life, not going for a jaunt to the bloody seaside!'

The arrival of the tea prevented any serious name-calling or bloodshed. The sight of Gigi and – according to the name badge – Effie bringing in the tea trays distracted all except Marianna, who knelt down and rolled back the rug.

'Let's examine this logically,' she said, taking a chalk-end from her pocket. She looked up at Dominica. 'May I?'

'Be my guest.'

On the bare floorboards Marianna rapidly chalked a long squiggly line; not what she had intended, but the best she could do given that Gigi had tripped over her and landed rather heavily, part-way across Marianna and the rest of the way along the floor. Face down.

'Lucky you'd put the tray down, Gigi,' said Effie.

'Haaaaaa-aaaaa-aaaa,' said Gigi, as she and Marianna were helped up.

'Any damage, anybody?' asked Matron.

'No, I'm fine,' said Marianna, dusting herself off, not very successfully.

'I thik I roke e ose, iss,' attempted Gigi.

Effie brushed her sister down. 'Oh, don't fuss. You'll be all reight. Get off home and our Mam'll sort it out.'

Blood started to drip from the end of Gigi's nose.

'Nonsense,' declared Matron. 'She needs specialist help. I'll look at it.'

'Beggin' your pardon Matron, but our Mam saw to it last time and I'm sure she wouldn't want you to be put to any trouble.'

'No trouble. No trouble at all. Help me get her to sick bay. Dominica? Do you mind?'

'No… no… carry on, Matron. We do seem to be keeping you busy lately.'

'All good practice,' said Matron, although the word 'practice' didn't generate overwhelming feelings of reassurance for anybody. 'Now come along with me, and we'll soon have you as good as new.'

Matron and Effie helped Gigi out of the room, leaving behind the thought that for Gigi, 'good as new' was a prospect which could have been improved upon.

Marianna knelt down again. This time, on the bare floorboards she chalked:

W

W

W

H

W

W

Against the first W she wrote *Eleanor's Journey.*

'Was she definitely coming to the funeral?'

Dominica picked up a letter from the mantelpiece.

'It says – where is it? – "I shall be at The Union for the funeral". See for yourself.' She passed the page to Marianna. 'And she told her office she was coming up for the funeral. So I think we can safely say' – she looked pointedly at the Bursar – 'she wasn't going on holiday.'

Marianna wrote *To get to funeral* against the second W.

'Do we know exactly when she set off?'

Dominica knelt beside her.

'Eleven days ago, according to her office.'

'Which way she was coming?' said Marianna, chalking *11 days ago* alongside the third W.

'Presumably along the Great North Road,' said Stephanie, kneeling down and unfolding a small map from the back of her tome.

'It is the most direct route,' said the Head Girl, joining them on the floor and tracing the line on the map with her finger. *GNR* was chalked alongside the fifth W.

'And how would she be travelling?' asked Marianna.

'Broomstick, I suppose,' said Dominica.

JW shook her head and sat on the floor. 'Not if she'd got any luggage she wouldn't. It's a nightmare trying to pack trunks on a broomstick.'

'Horse and cart?' suggested the Bursar.

'What's she going to do with a horse and cart once she got here? She wouldn't need it – she'd have the Matriarchal coach to get about in.'

'Sell it,' said the Bursar.

'Horses and carts are ten a penny round here. It'd be a waste of good money.'

Despite the potential seriousness of the situation, Marianna was beginning to enjoy herself. This detective lark was just like mathematics – testing every theory, inspecting every element.

'All right, JW,' she said, 'how do you think Eleanor would be travelling?'

'My money says the mailcoach. It's easiest and quickest if you've got luggage. Just pay, get on, get off again at the other end. There's no worry about resting horses or paying out for fresh 'uns like you'd need to if you were horse-and-carting it, and if you want an overnight stop they do it all for you. And a businesswoman like Eleanor, she can use the time to catch up on paperwork, specially if she's got one of them new laptop writing desks.'

'Perhaps the mailcoach depot's our first port of call, then – ask a few questions,' said Marianna, chalking *Mailcoach?* by the H, and *Mailcoach Company?* by the final W.

The Head Girl checked her watch. 'The offices will be closed by now.'

'Tomorrow?'

'Graduation,' Dominica pointed out.

'You need to involve the proper authorities,' the Bursar piped up. 'Missing persons are their responsibility.'

'She's our Matriarch, Bursar,' said Stephanie, swivelling round to look up at the Bursar.

'Not until she's inaugurated,' snapped the Bursar.

'Hold on,' said JW. 'We could report her missing to the rozzers, and they could send somebody to the mailcoach depot tomorrow, while we're all busy with Graduation.'

'Do you think they would?' said Dominica.

Marianna grinned at JW. 'Fancy a walk?'

A **HEAVILY BANDAGED AXY** lay in his basket by the stove. His eyes were closed and his breathing was steady, but the impending evil still cut through his sedation.

'Mistress,' he said in a small, far-away voice, 'he is returning.'

Auregia gently stroked his head.

'I know, Axy. But you're safe. I'm not leaving you again.' She moved his basket inside one of the kitchen cupboards.

'Now sleep,' she said quietly. 'All will be well.' She closed the cupboard doors on him. Out of sight, out of Grandel's mind.

Grandel sauntered across the clearing admiring his handiwork, and entered what was left of Doughnut Cottage through the only exterior door remaining. In the kitchen, the kettle was boiling, but the witch was nowhere to be seen. Grandel heard a noise from behind a curtain, and pulled it back to reveal Auregia, tidying her pantry.

He stared, his mouth falling open. Crispbread shelves topped with royal icing supported phials, boxes, jars, canisters, bags and cones of every conceivable ingredient for baking. Grandel's imagination was not over-expansive – his limited list of 'conceivable' ingredients encompassed anything provided by the butcher, dairyman or the miller, and the things which fell out of the back of hens – therefore he'd never dreamt so many things could be used for food.

And everything was so clean. No sticky fingermarks, no vinegar rings, no floury deposits, no obnoxious brown knobbles grown by sauce bottles the world over. Everything was spotless – and labelled, not scrawled on quickly as a precaution against a bad memory, but labelled with love in an artistic hand. The writer of these labels was a culinary champion who respected food, was fascinated by its components and their interrelationships, knew its limitations and relied on its stability, marvelled at its versatility and expanded its capabilities. She just loved food.

Grandel noticed one jar in particular; it contained a powder which shimmered gold, bronze, brass and copper against a background of faded beige. Its neat label bore the inscription *Corpus Zingiber* and the jar gave off a warm glow, reminiscent of hot honey, cider and cinnamon, but it wasn't the glow attracting his attention.

It was the distant voice in the back of his head. Echoes of summer days, when his wife had been alive and the children had been innocent; before fate had thrust abject poverty upon him and quenched his spirit; before iron determination to wreak revenge upon that fate had invaded his heart and driven out softness; before bruising brutality and violence had hardened his soul; before the children had become fully paid-up members of the Young Thugs. Had there been a time before? He shook his head and sighed. No. Or if there had been, it was so long ago it was someone else's time.

He sensed unease in the jar, and was strangely drawn to it. At the back of his throat he could feel the dust of icing sugar: sweet, cloying, choking. In the pit of his stomach, he heard children's laughter, which faded as Auregia's monosyllable sliced through the air between him and the jar, deep into his reverie.

'Well?'

Grandel closed his mouth abruptly, like a goldfish which has suddenly developed a retentive memory and doesn't want to look stupid swimming round with its mouth open. He looked away from the pantry, and as he caught a glimpse of the wrecked gym through the kitchen door, he remembered why he was there.

'I can recommend a good builder, if you need one,' he smirked, in a way which normally made people feel they wanted to punch his pudgy smug face so hard he'd be able to talk out of the back of his head.

The only indication of any such emotion in Auregia was a

slight frosting of the floorboards where she stood.

'Thank you, no. Tea?'

'I just came for the children.'

'All in good time. First, we have a few things to discuss.'

'Oh, the fly wishes to discuss things with the spider?'

'If the spider wishes to flourish further, the fly has a proposition.'

Good woman. Come to her senses at last. 'Proposition?'

'Have you thought any more about the orphanage?'

'I've told you. I can't afford it.'

'What if you could afford it?'

'Even if I could, why would I? What's in it for me?'

Auregia smiled at him.

'You said yourself – and have amply demonstrated – that you are indeed a rich and powerful man. But wouldn't it say so much more about you if you were so rich you were able to give money away?'

'That *is* rich.'

'And you could be.'

'How?'

'You know the price people will pay for my baking. How they queue outside your shop for every new confection. Well, so far, they've been paying for ordinary cakes. You could make them pay more for even better confections.'

'Better?'

Auregia looked into his eyes and saw greed starting to sparkle…

~•~

NOTES ON

Rozzers

The Roster Of Persons Available To Deal With Incidents Injurious Or Potentially Injurious To Persons Or Property – otherwise known as the rozzers – were set up by a Maund Town Council committee and usually have very little to do, as there are only two classes of felonious offence to deal with: damage and theft. This simplifies the rule book immensely, particularly as there are only two items to which damage and theft apply: property and life.

Damage to property is rare; most of the possessions held by people have been passed down from generation to generation, being shortened, lengthened, widened, narrowed, fitted with doors, repainted, stencilled, distressed, cheered up and generally rebuilt many times along the way. So, on most things it is nigh on impossible to actually inflict any damage.

Theft of property crimes are few and far between: overcrowding is such that houses are rarely unoccupied and very few people own anything worth stealing anyway.

Damage to life and *theft of life* are generally considered too important to be left to the rozzers. Once again, overcrowding plays an important part in this: everybody knows everybody else's business, and therefore who's done what to whom and why. Retribution is swift and of equal measure, and if the culprits have fled town, there's always the family to get back at. Consequently, most people are decent law-abiding citizens, and those who aren't can usually be identified by their missing limbs, disfigured faces, surprised expressions or strange walks.

Theoretically, the rozzers are also supposed to be the people to call if there's an accident or medical emergency. However, there are so many druggists, pharmacists, faith healers, crystal healers, psychic surgeons, wise women and – of course – witches around Maund that if a rozzer is the first person you see peering down at you after an accident, you might as well give up because the rest of the town has succumbed to the plague anyway.

Finally, the rozzers are supposed to be sent for if fire breaks out anywhere, although there are so many people crammed into Maund that fires are usually quenched before they get out of control; if by some mischance a fire should take a good hold, there are always enough people to either form a human chain down to the river, or to extinguish the blaze by standing round together and widdling on it.

~✦~

'Good evening, sisters,' said the duty rozzer, trying to look like he knew this off by heart and it wasn't written on a card under the desk. 'Constable Jellicoe at your service. How may I be of assistance?'

'Evening, Erasmus,' said JW. 'We'd like to report a potential missing person.'

'You need Crime Prevention – down there, second left.'

'Why?' asked Marianna.

'Because that's where it is.'

'Why do we need Crime Prevention?'

'You said, and I quote, "We'd like to report a potential missing person" didn't you?'

'Yes…' said JW, in the tone of voice which students knew as a precursor to furniture flying across the room.

'Well, that's potential crime; we only deal in actual crime. Yer potential crime, being – by its very nature – potential, is crime which possibly can be prevented, having not actually happened yet. Unlike yer actual crime, which has already happened and therefore cannot be prevented and also, therefore, cannot be classed as potential.'

JW leaned across the counter, grabbed the constable's lapels and spoke into his startled face.

'Erasmus, how long have you been duty rozzer?'

He beamed. 'Seventeen years, man and boy.'

'Then you know sod all about potential.'

Marianna freed Constable Jellicoe from JW's grip. 'Let's divide this into smaller units, constable. Missing persons?'

Constable Jellicoe smoothed down his uniform.

'Down this corridor, second left, fourth right and through both sets of double doors. At the end, turn left, left again, then right, and out the door at the end. Go down the ginnel between the two buildings, left at the end, first left up Dragonslayer Gate until you come to Norman's Castle. Keep the church on your right-hand side, go through the graveyard past the Free Library and Paint Academy, left again, second right and it's the fourth blue door. You can't miss it.'

'Or go through that door behind you,' said Marianna.

'Swipe me. Yes, you could. How did you know that?'

Marianna looked at the door. The notice stuck on it said

Missing Persons Office. 'Oh, something just told me.'

'Ah. In the force, we call that intuition.'

'In The Union,' said JW, 'we call it literacy.'

'The Missing Persons Office hasn't been open very long, has it?' said Marianna, observing that the notice had been hastily scribbled and slapped on the door at a jaunty angle.

'Cor! You're good. Constable Sennet only arrived this morning. He should've been here last week, but he got lost.'

I COULD BAKE FOR YOU SUCH SWEET DELIGHTS that people would pay twice – three times as much as they do now. Much better. More expensive.' Auregia leant close to Grandel, and pouted her next words slowly and seductively. 'Much... more... mouth... watering.'

His gaze moved from her lips to her eyes.

She leant even closer. 'How does that sound?'

Grandel swallowed hard. He was all man, and felt he'd been on his own for far too long. His palms were damp.

'Sounds good to me.' And though he may have been all man, most of it was businessman. 'What's in it for you?'

She stood back. 'I want that orphanage.'

Part of the businessman was wallet.

'Will there be enough money?'

'Plenty of money. Money enough and to spare. You will get your share, and all I ask in return is the orphanage and its upkeep, plus a little help with the ingredients.'

'How can you be sure there'll be enough?'

'Easy,' Auregia said. 'You move up-market. Make your customers pay for luxury.'

'Luxury?'

'Luxury.'

He watched her tongue and lips form the word, and he gulped. She moved towards him. When she spoke, softly and lazily, he could hear the rustle of satin sheets, smell the perfume of pleasure, taste the salty heat of summer nights.

'Warm brioches and croissants, sumptuous gâteaux and caramelised fruits. There'll be chocolate éclairs and fruit tarts, maids of honour, devils' food cake and angels' whispers. You shall have crème brulée, mousses and soufflés, savarins and sachertortes and…' she leant closer, 'I'll give you maidens' kisses and cream horns.'

Grandel whimpered sweatily. His temperature was rising, and it wasn't alone.

'And as a sample,' she whispered, 'try one of these. They're a new recipe.' She passed him a dazzling white plate on which there were the most inviting biscuits he'd ever set avaricious eyes on. They couldn't have been more blatantly seductive if they'd had 'Take me, I'm yours' written across them in fondant icing. If a rozzer had been passing the door, he would have run them in for soliciting. They were like slices of a sunset.

Grandel's fingers intruded through the golden aura of the biscuits and took one. He turned it over and over, the rough surface intoxicating his fingertips. He held it flat in his hand and ran his thumb across it, listening to the rasp of demerara sugar. He could smell creamy butter from grass-fed cows and syrup which laughed as it poured and folded in on itself. Putting it to his lips, he felt the sting of spices, and it broke with such a satisfying crack when he bit into it. His teeth ground the biscuit into thousands of tiny crumbs, suffusing him with warmth and desire, and he would have signed any amount of blank cheques to prolong the feeling. He would have married this biscuit.

'Tasty, aren't they?' she breathed. 'There's as many of these as you want.'

Tasty? Understatement. As many as he wanted. What else was there to want?

'Wouldn't you pay extra to put your lips round these?'

The jagged crumbs massaged his tongue. 'Mmmmm.' His eyes closed as groans of pleasure echoed through his body. He never knew a biscuit could do so much for a man.

'So, if *you* would, others would. Just think how much you could sell these for.'

The businessman in him suddenly awoke and started whispering: all those bachelors and widowers – they'll buy a box of these week after week... better still: the old boys in the gentlemen's clubs – they'll lap these up... regular big orders, whopping premium, you'll be laughing... the witch knows that – that's why she's done all the talking so far... she's getting the better of you... don't let her have it all her own way... come on, make some demands of her...

Grandel opened his eyes and forced his face into a frown.

'They look so plain compared to the other things you make. Decoration attracts the eye of the customers; they wouldn't look twice at these.'

She smiled. 'I've thought of that. Take a look at these.'

She put a tray in front of him. Grandel's face forgot it was supposed to be frowning and broke into a huge grin as he beheld decorated gingerbread in the shape of stars, crescents, snowflakes, birds, butterflies, bees, fish, flowers, trees, four-legged animals and two-legged people.

'You can have any shape you want, and any decoration. And of course there's the seasonal presentations.'

She pointed to four decorated gingerbread pine trees tied together with a ribbon bow. 'Perfect for those family gatherings in midwinter. Wouldn't they look pretty in your own house?' She pulled the ribbon slowly and the bow came apart. 'Who wouldn't want to untie that silken ribbon?'

Something in the way she asked the last question made the back of his knees sweat.

Auregia still had more to offer. 'And as for the gingerbread children – the kiddies will love these. Think of the repeat business. Get them hooked at an early age and they're yours for the rest of their lives, aren't they?'

Curse her, she was right. He was hooked already. The businessman slapped him round the face. He coughed.

'So the deal is: I get the rights to sell these, these—'

'It's gingerbread,' she supplied.

'—this gingerbread… sole rights, mind you – and I can charge what I like?'

'Whatever money you can make.'

'And all you want is a few ingredients and the orphanage setting up?'

'Setting up and maintaining.'

He sucked air in through gritted teeth. 'I'm not sure…'

'Another?' Auregia asked, proffering the tray.

He took a gingerbread mouse. As his fingers closed upon the sweetmeat of pure pleasure, it occurred to him that if he didn't agree to the orphanage, he might never get another confection like this. He put it in his pocket; he would retrieve it later on in the quiet of his bedroom.

'Very well. These should make enough profit to cover the orphanage.'

'Good. And, of course, you get the children back.'

'And I get the children back.' He smiled broadly. 'Somehow, I just knew we'd be able to do business today.'

He rubbed his hands together, reached out, took a gingerbread girl from the tray and bit her head off. As he chewed, the spices spread inside his mouth and sent happy signals to all his favourite places.

She held out her hand. 'So it's a deal then?'

He put his hand in hers.

'A deal. It's funny,' he said, taking another bite, 'it's not like bread at all. Why did you call it gingerbread?'

She gripped his fleshy hand and chipolata fingers so tightly he could feel the bones grating and breaking.

'Because that's what they are. Ginger bred.'

'Father!' screamed Hansi from the cell.

Greta's voice was nowhere to be heard.

As pain spread from Grandel's broken bones to his brain, it delivered the realisation that everything had fallen horribly, grotesquely into place. Auregia had kept part of the deal already. He and his fate had been bargained and sealed with a curse. She released her grip. He fled outside, and was violently sick…

~•~
NOTES ON
Constable Sennet

There were many reasons why men joined the rozzers; almost as many reasons as there were rozzers. Some joined because they had delusions of herodom; others because they enjoyed the paperwork. A lot joined for the uniform, either because it was the only good suit they ever owned or it saved them having to decide what to wear every morning. Sennet had joined because he'd heard they needed men who could search for clues.

Sennet had spent all his life searching: socks, underwear, door keys, the right woman; but whatever he'd searched for, always at the back of his mind had lurked the Quest For The Answer, like some ancient rent man in a shabby olive-grey overcoat, demanding payment in full.

It was all the fault of his uncle. When he was a child he seemed to have hundreds of uncles, none of whom was around for more than a couple of months before dying in mysterious circumstances.

There was Uncle Joblat the Wanderer, who – according to Sennet's dear, white-haired old mother – had suffocated aboard a quinquereme when his ship had been hit by the tail of a giant mermaid. The ship went down, piercing a hole in the seabed, draining the sea and taking the mermaid with it. Sennet knew this to be true, for he'd looked up the grid references his mother gave him in his Boy's Book of What

The Rest of The World Looks Like, and found they converged on a point which appeared to be four hundred miles from the nearest tap, let alone anywhere near enough water to float a quinquereme.

There was Uncle Hubert the Malcontent, who – according to Sennet's recollection of his dear, white-haired, bandy-legged old mother – 'fell hapless victim to that old poisoned umbrella trick' so beloved of foreign spies. What she actually said was 'poison and umbrella trick', for Hubert's impromptu date with Death supposedly took place when he was demonstrating his fencing skills with an umbrella. Unfortunately, Hubert was in the druggist's at the time and knocked a bottle of curare off a shelf. More unfortunately, his footbladder skills were not on a par with his fencing ones and as he tried to head the bottle out of the way, it cracked itself and his head wide open.

That was according to Sennet's dear, white-haired, bandy-legged old mother whose favourite colour for lampshades was a comforting red, and who, whenever Sennet mentioned his uncles, smiled a secret smile.

There was Uncle Rennie the Fizzle Offer. That was him! He was the one who'd started him on the Quest For The Answer. If only the young Sennet had been able to say 'philosopher', he might have come to his senses much earlier and saved himself a great deal of heart-searching, not to mention money and a goodly portion of his life.

The brightest brains for centuries had been taxed by the philosopher's knot and the philosopher's stone, and Sennet was taxed by the philosopher's say-something-to-keep-the-kid-busy. Rennie had said to him one feast-day morning: 'When you really know what you're looking for, then you'll have the answer. That, my boy, is known as The Puzzle of the Laws of Zantak. See if you can work it out.'

Good old Uncle Rennie the Fizzle Offer. If only the young Sennet had known anything about the human mind, he might have realised not only is there no puzzle, but there's no Zantak Laws either.

So, whilst his mother and Uncle Rennie played horses, Sennet searched for what he was looking for to see if he knew what it was, and it did keep him busy. For years.

Eventually he joined the rozzers, where his natural abilities soon marked him out as someone who was continually posted to station after station.

~•~

'How can I help you, sisters?' said Sennet.

'We'd like to report a missing person,' said Marianna.

Sennet rifled through the desk drawers until he found the correct form. He put the form on the table and patted his pockets in search of a pen but they were empty, so he started to search the drawers again. JW lifted up the form, picked up the pen underneath and held it out to him.

'Oh. Right. Name?' he said.

'Marianna Land.'

He wrote the name carefully on the form.

'And when did you last see this Marianna Land?'

'See what?'

'Marianna Land.'

'Yes?'

JW slapped a hand down on the form.

'Before this turns into one of them plays where people rush in and out through doors and drop their trousers a lot,' she said, 'my friend here is Marianna Land, I am JW Arcrite and the missing person is Eleanor Lynin.'

Sennet tutted, screwed up the form, threw it away, searched the drawers again, pulled out another form and wrote *Eleanor Lynin* on it.

'Can you give me a description of her?'

Marianna looked at JW, then back at Sennet.

'Taller than JW but shorter than me, well built, stands very straight, fair complexion, sandy hair, hazel eyes, pink lips, all that sort of stuff.'

'Nose?'

'Yes, got a nose.'

'Is there anything special about her nose? Does it bend to one side? Is it long? Short? Fat? Thin? Bulbous? Retroussé? Aquiline? Is it a pug or a proboscis?'

If Sennet had had plants on his desk, they would have withered under JW's stare.

'Look, Mac, all we want you to do is go to the mailcoach offices tomorrow and ask if they've had anybody go missing from one of their trips up the Great North Road.'

Sennet looked as imperious as he could, bearing in mind these women knew he got excited about the shapes of people's noses.

'With all due respect, madam, I think I ought to be the judge of what needs to be done. I just need you to answer my questions, thank you.'

JW folded her arms. 'Suit yourself. If you want to waste time…'

Sennet stuck his chin out. 'And when did you last see this Eleanor Lynin?'

'Oh, about fifteen years ago,' said JW, watching Sennet's eyes widen.

'Fifteen years?' He screwed the form up. 'Madam, I hardly think we'll be able to trace somebody who's been missing for fifteen years.'

'Oh, she hasn't been missing for fifteen years, constable,' said Marianna. 'Only about eleven days.'

'But—' said Sennet.

'Just answering the question, Mac,' said JW with exactly the right amount of malice.

Sennet scowled at her and straightened the form out again. He cleared his throat and spoke to Marianna.

'About eleven days, you said. Don't you know precisely how long she's been missing?'

'We don't truly know if she *is* missing yet,' said Marianna brightly.

Sennet leaned on the desk and rubbed his hand over his face and ended up holding his nose, which was aquiline. He looked at the two women. Both were smiling broadly; one, he suspected, out of enjoyment and the other out of innocence. He let go of his nose and breathed down it. 'Just tell me what you know.'

By the time they had finished telling him and had left his office, Sennet had decided two things: one, he would make some preliminary enquiries at the mailcoach depot, and two, he didn't like JW very much.

'That bloke needs to get out more,' JW said to Marianna as they walked away from the rozzer shop. 'He spends too much time playing with the make-a-face books when things are slack.'

Naiba awoke feeling as if an ironmongers' co-operative had been squatting in her head and using her skull as an anvil. Normally she only felt so bad after copious amounts of Nouveau Château Brun, but an absence of bottles and a presence of manuscript said not this time.

She rubbed her eyes, yawned, stretched and waggled her fingers. The discomfort in her arm was such that writer's cramp would have been a pleasurable interesting diversion for her. She accepted the pain in her arm as a consequence of the writing; the pain in her heart came from the story. She knew there was only one way to get through this, and that was to get on and get through it. When the writing gets tough, the tough get writing; she went over to the desk and picked up the ginger root.

Twenty minutes later she had neither moved nor been moved. She saw nothing except her own room, her own desk, her own life all around her. She sniffed the ginger root. The warm, prickly smell invaded her senses then faded away to nothing. She tried to slice the ginger, but it was too hard and her arm too frail for a prolonged attack. She licked one of the fibrous ends of the root. She could again smell the warm, prickly smell, but taste nothing. All it did was suck most of the moisture out of her tongue.

The manuscript page in front of her remained blank. She reread the last few pages she had written, to see if she could pick up from where she had left off; she couldn't. The Muse had left her again, but this time without saying goodbye.

When the writing gets this tough, the tough make tea.

In the kitchens, lost in thought as disappointment, curiosity, relief and anger jostled for position in her soul, Naiba gazed at an oven door as she waited for the kettle to boil. Plates of biscuits sat on the worktop, and she absent-mindedly reached out for the comfort food whilst mulling over what to do next. As her teeth snapped a gingerbread man's leg, she became oblivious to the gleaming steel, well-scrubbed pine and whitewashed walls of the kitchen around her; her brain brought her visions of a wrecked cottage, a large black stove and a candywood chest, and hearts hardened by abuse, fractured in rage and broken in sorrow.

NOTES ON
Graduation

Passing through an educational establishment is rather like going in a washing tub. You get churned round in the system, absorb whatever's thrown at you and you can't leave until you've spouted it all back out again. For some people, once through the works is enough, especially if it's been a boil wash. For others, life's rich tapestry is all the better for having regular doses of softener; these are the ones for whom learning is not a preparation for life, but the main event itself.

If you study at The University of Nature you are expected to graduate at least once, and so sacred are the secrets of Mother Nature you're not allowed to leave until you do so.

Having graduated, you can assume your place in the world – ministering to others, raising a family and usually being so feared and respected by the community that you never actually buy anything because it's given to you immediately if you show the slightest bit of interest in it.

However, you're not forced to leave when you've graduated, and some witches can't be persuaded outside by a team of wild horses assisted by a tug-of-war champion.

If you wish to remain within the confines of The Union, the options are simple: continue learning, or help others to learn. The latter is a catch-all category covering not only teachers and teaching assistants, but researchers, exam-setters, translators, administrators, and everyone else whose nerves don't stretch to facing a bunch of first-formers.

Continuing to learn is simplicity itself, provided you graduate in each subject you study. However, the only way to graduate is to pass practical and theoretical examinations not only in the subject just studied but in all previous subjects as well. The reward for this is to go up a level in witchcraft each time, up to the maximum seventh level.

The first time you graduate you are presented with a Badge of the Black Cauldron, the Insignia and the Conical Chapeau of Systerhood, and a gift to symbolise your chosen degree. As the degrees – like the students – are many and varied, so are the gifts, which explains why, on the day before Graduation, the storerooms off the Globe Hall look like a maze of jumble sales.

Each of the seven Graduations brings a different colour cauldron badge, ranging from black to gold, and the choice of whether to stay or leave. However, it's generally agreed that once you've reached the gold standard you know so much you're too dangerous to be let out by yourself.

The ceremony itself starts after the Lunch of the Novices, stretches through the afternoon and evening – punctuated by a few tea breaks – and is rounded off by the Supper of the Initiated shortly before midnight.

On Graduation Day the Globe Hall is thronged with proud mums, aunties, grannies, sisters and nieces all in their best bib and tucker, all smiling, chatting and comparing outfits; the occasional nervous male relative present will look straight ahead, try not to catch anybody's eye and sweat a lot.

The graduating students sit in a circle surrounding the

time-blackened oak central dais and are dressed entirely in black, in stark contrast to the multi-coloured clothing of the relations who sit behind them in ever-wider concentric circles. Viewed from the galleried landings inside the Main Tower, the Globe Hall looks like one of the Town Council's flower beds with the middle burnt out, as they often are.

~•~

Naiba hated Graduation days. As an Assistant Graduation Administrator, she was not allowed to sit down from the start of the ceremony to the first tea break, which usually meant a good couple of hours on her feet. This was so she could rush to the aid of any relative who was overcome by nervousness at being inside The Union – an event which, though thankfully rare, still had to be anticipated. It was generally reckoned that after the first tea break everybody would be much more relaxed and so all members of staff could take a seat and enjoy the day.

As if the prospect of standing for two hours wasn't bad enough, Mother Nature had turned her benevolent weather face towards The Union and it was a scorcher of a day. Naiba's ceremonial garb weighed a ton and in the blistering heat she felt as if she were carrying a rucksack full of rubble through the desert. Once the Great Doors closed and the relatives were seated, all movement of air seemed to cease along with the chatter as the ceremony began.

'Sisters and friends.'

The voice of Rectrix Adamantha Sloop had such an edge it could have sliced bacon in the local butchers' shops; it was the kind of tinny, high-register vocal uttering which always sounded as if it should have been announcing the arrivals and departures at the mailcoach station. Only three words into her speech, the entire population of the Globe Hall stiffened. Crack military troops did not exhibit such precision as this hitherto pleasantly untidy party of polychromatic cotton. It was a transformation akin to knicker elastic suddenly being starched. As one, each amiable niece, plump mum, cuddly aunty, stooping granny and nervous male sat bolt upright and so far back in their chairs it seemed they were all trying to reverse out of the Globe Hall without actually being seen to do so. The graduating witches looked like a set of dominoes in a bucket of toy bricks. It was only a sense of occasion and a healthy respect for the purveyors of magic which kept everybody in their seats.

'Welcome to this most prestigious occasion in The Union calendar. Today we celebrate the culmination of another…'

The voice drilled through Naiba's ears and played ping-pong in her skull. Already tense, she involuntarily flattened her ears against her head and shuddered. Thank Mother Nature the Rectrix only pitched up on special occasions; as it was, the druggists had long sold out of earplugs and the young men of Maund had been standing on street corners covertly dealing cotton wool.

'…pleasure to be able once more to say a few words…'

And painful for us to listen to them, thought Naiba.

'…first asked to be Rectrix of this college…'

All eyes but four swivelled towards the Vice-Matriarch, whose own windows on the soul widened as she glared at the back of Adamantha's head with the same motionless expression that in the past had made stone lions get up and walk out declaring, 'OK, you win, I give up.'

Adamantha stopped talking and started sniffing.

'I say, can anybody smell smo—'

A line of fire was steadily travelling up the papers in her hand; with a scratchy scream she dropped them on the floor and stamped on them. Suddenly, she spun round to face Dominica. Only Adamantha heard the words, but everybody else in the Globe Hall could read them quite clearly in the Vice-Matriarch's face.

'This is not a college. It is The University of Nature, known fondly as The Union. If this were a *College* of Nature it would be known fondly as a section of the intestine. That is not so. Do you understand?'

Adamantha's head bobbed about like a daffodil in a hurricane.

'You do not need the remains of your speech, because you will now make way for the Roll Call, which I firmly believe will be a relief to all those present. Kindly introduce the Deaconess, then sit down and keep your strangulated vowels quiet.'

Adamantha spun back to face the assembled throng who immediately examined their fingernails, the hems of their garments and the finer points of the Globe Hall architecture. There were sporadic outbursts of throat-clearing, attempts at whistling tuneless songs, and much searching for non-existent items at the bottom of handbags. Eyes were looking anywhere but at the puce and slightly sooty Rectrix.

'And now Deaconess Glibly with the Roll Call,' she said,

so quickly the audience didn't have time to wince, but the sigh of relief they uttered was so strong it ruffled the feathers on both the Rectrix's hat and her personality. She flounced to her seat and folded her arms.

Deaconess Glibly walked slowly towards the ashes of Adamantha's speech. She was tall and stocky, and as befits a Music Mistress, she was always in great demand for recitals and concerts; no-one knew whether this popularity was because she was a witch, could produce the most mellifluous operatic cadences or was basso profundo.

She untied the scroll she was carrying. The roll whizzed past her hemline, boots, and the edge of the dais. The small conical gold weights hanging from the bottom edge chinked together comfortingly.

'Roll Call of the First Year of the McGinty-Lynin Interregnum, Vice-Matriarch Dominica Tort presiding.' The plush smoothness of her voice soothed everybody's nerves. The springiness returned to the knicker elastic and the whole building seemed to settle. 'Firstly, we welcome these novices into Full Systerhood of the Black Cauldron.'

As Naiba's ears regained their normal degree of protrusion she felt the tension drain from her body, being replaced by a hot flush which started at the very top of her head and oozed its way down to her fingers and toes. Its progress was as slow and steady as if someone had poured a vat of warm treacle over her. She wavered slightly.

Deaconess Glibly's voice flowed over the hall, as comforting and soothing as waves on the shore.

'We remind them of their duties under the Charter of

Enchantments. We present them with the Badge of the Black Cauldron which symbolises the attainment of First-Level Gramarye. We present them with the symbols of their chosen degree...'

As Naiba's eyelids began to droop her mind wandered back to her own first graduation where, as a graduate in First-Level Gramarye with Mechanical Engineering, she had been given her Badge of the Black Cauldron and a canteen of spanners. She imagined herself walking across the dais, getting too close to the edge...

When her head dipped forward she jerked back upright and put her hands out to stop herself overbalancing. She stumbled slightly, but luckily any resultant noise was drowned out by the applause for the first graduate. Naiba stretched the muscles in her face as discreetly as she could, and opened her eyes wide in time to see Geraldine Morpeth stepping off the dais, clutching a Badge, a degree in First-Level Gramarye with Licensed Victualling and a large brass bell. Geraldine came from a long line of brewers on one side and a long line of herbalists on the other, and the end-of-term parties were going to be all the duller for her departure.

Deaconess Glibly consulted her scroll. 'Catherine Shackle, First-Level Gramarye with Needlework.'

Catherine stepped onto the dais. She shook hands with Dominica and received her degree and a pair of golden scissors. As she walked across the dais to return to her seat, the black cotton housecoat she wore disintegrated, revealing a stunning creation of black silk, taffeta and chiffon, its off-the-shoulder neckline a broad band of black sequins and polished jet. This transformation drew gasps of admiration from the crowd, looks of resignation from fellow graduates and a raised eyebrow from Matron. It also assured her future in the fashion world as the Rectrix made a mental note to talk to Catherine after the ceremony.

Naiba put her hands behind her back and leant on the wall. Despite the accumulation of centuries of absorbed memories and excess magic, the stone was cool and provided a welcome relief from the heat generated by the number of bodies in the hall. Until she touched the stone, she hadn't realised quite how much her own temperature had risen. The rucksack full of rubble had become a backpack full of boulders, the band of her hat was trying to slice the top of her head off and she felt trapped inside a personal portable sauna. She stretched her neck and raised her shoulders, trying to subtly widen the neckline of her ceremonial outfit to release some of the heat trapped under it. The movement of the fans in the hands of the guests was hypnotising, and the glorious colours of their outfits swam before her eyes like the view through a kaleidoscope.

She looked through the network of glass panels which formed the domed ceiling of the Globe Hall, drawing comfort from the symmetry of the landings. This was the world she had inhabited for many years: solid, reliable, secure and far removed from the uncertain fantasy universe her brain insisted on visiting with increasing regularity.

The air seemed to be taking on the consistency of velvet, and starting to smell as if it had been shoved at the back of the wardrobe for a couple of centuries. The conical shape of the Main Tower seemed to concentrate the assault on Naiba's senses; the comforting symmetry gave way to oppressive uniformity, the security to claustrophobia. It was as though someone had built a prison inside a giant upturned ice cream cornet. She shook her head to try to clear the feeling, like an exam student with a headful of random facts trying to shake them into the right places so they made sense. She decided to marshal her powers of concentration.

There are certain places in the Globe Hall where, if you hold your head at the correct angle and close one eye, you can make your brain believe that the galleried landings are, in fact, just one huge spiral staircase. This requires intense concentration – not to mention architectural jiggery-pokery and the courage to run the risk of possibly disconnecting vital synapses in the process – and so although Assistant Graduation Administrators were supposed to be still, silent, alert and attentive during the ceremony Naiba very gradually tilted her head and closed one eye so slowly that tortoises contemplated buying running shoes.

Instead of the spiral staircase she had seen thousands of times before, her brain seemed to be fighting to get out of a giant ruff. The landings became circles which became tubes attached to circles which became tubes attached to…

She quickly closed her other eye and brought her head back to the vertical. She took a breath and the wind which scoured her nasal passages seemed to come straight from the frozen wastes. Its purity seared her lungs and its temperature made her eyes water. Her eyelids flipped open like spring-loaded shutters and for a second she fought a valiant battle with Mother Nature over the best course of action. Mother Nature won; Naiba coughed violently and turned to face the wall until she regained her composure.

Staring at the wall, trying to regulate her breathing, she pondered the carpeting she'd get from the Vice-Matriarch for breaking one of the cardinal rules of the position of Assistant Graduation Administrator – calm and serenity at all times. Having a coughing fit during Roll Call would not endear her to anybody. She knew what she must do. She must look the Vice-Matriarch straight in the eye and wait for the signal which meant 'Be in my office at eight o'clock sharp tomorrow morning'. With a sinking feeling and a pounding head, and whilst trying to make as little movement as possible, she turned back and looked at the Vice-Matriarch.

Naiba blinked several times then looked again. The Vice-Matriarch wasn't there – or if she was, she'd had the world's fastest head transplant. Naiba's eyes darted wildly around the dais. There was somebody reading the Roll Call, but it wasn't Deaconess Glibly. There was someone wearing the gown of the Rectrix, but it wasn't Adamantha Sloop.

Reason knocked on the door of her brain and said, 'Excuse me – there's something not quite right here.'

Panic elbowed Reason out of the way shouting, 'Let me in! Let me in!'

Fear Of A Carpeting wagged a finger and advised, 'I wouldn't do that if I were you,' but Naiba did it anyway.

She shut her eyes, slapped herself hard and opened her eyes again.

How empty the Globe Hall was, and how much cooler. A

minute ago this hall had been a seething mass of humanity and now it was barely a third full. It had been as colourful as an explosion in a paint shop, but now it was as sombre and muted as a gathering of monastic orders. The novices were still in black, but there were only about a tenth as many as there had been, and Naiba didn't recognise any of them.

Panic had laid out Fear Of A Carpeting with a left hook whilst Reason was still trying to pick the lock on the front door.

Naiba gingerly sat down on one of the empty chairs. This action, which would normally induce apoplexy in The Union staff, went completely unnoticed by everyone. The Deaconess, whoever she was, continued with the Roll Call.

'Auregia Skinton, First-Level Gramarye with Architecture and Confectionery.'

Naiba's bewilderment increased as the novice went up onto the dais to collect her degree, a full-size black cauldron, a pair of compasses and a fluted flan tin. As Auregia stepped off the dais, head high with pride, her gaze met that of Naiba, who screamed. It was the first time she'd seen somebody else's body wearing her own face.

She ran forward, putting her hands out to grab Auregia's shoulders, but momentum simply carried her straight through the recently graduated witch who, completely oblivious of anything untoward, made her way back to her seat. Naiba fell against the dais and scrambled onto it, snatching at the Roll Call, but again she could find no substance to gain a hold on. She waved her hand before the face of the Deaconess, who blinked not an eyelid but once again intoned, 'Auregia

Skinton, First-Level Gramarye with Architecture and Confectionery.'

'What?' exclaimed Naiba, whirling round to see Auregia ascending the dais, empty-handed, ready to once again receive the cauldron, the compasses and the flan tin. 'Stop! You've just done that! What's going on? Stop this!'

Reason was now unconscious on the front lawn next to Fear Of A Carpeting, and Panic had kicked down the door to her brain and was running through all the rooms, opening the cupboards and emptying the drawers onto the floor.

'Stop this, one of you, can't you?!' Naiba flailed her arms at the dignitaries. 'Who are you? Where are you? Stop it!'

Frustration fed ever-wilder arm movements, and as her hand swept straight through the head of the person wearing the clothes of the Rectrix, her reality grippers sprang apart and she passed out.

As she took forever to tumble to the floor, Naiba glimpsed Auregia rising from her seat again.

The morning after Graduation, a certain study was full. Apart from herself and Naiba, Dominica was also hostess to the Rectrix, Deaconess Glibly, the Head of Personnel plus assistant, and Mrs Ockstart, a lady whose daughter had been graduating, and whose normally cheerful personality had been temporarily replaced by a worried nervousness.

'First things first,' said Dominica. 'Thank you all for coming so promptly. Especially you, Mrs Ockstart, for coming back despite your unfortunate experience yesterday.'

Mrs Ockstart, who was sitting down and trying to be as

small as possible, clasped the top of her handbag tightly, smiled her bravest smile and said quietly, 'My pleasure.' When the witches send a coach to your house and tell you the Vice-Matriarch would like to see you, it's churlish – and stupid – to refuse.

Dominica smiled. 'And I believe Naiba has something to say to you.'

Naiba put her hand on the nervous woman's arm.

'Mrs Ockstart, I can't tell you how sorry I am that I sat on you yesterday.'

Mrs Ockstart patted Naiba's hand. 'It's all right, dear. Expect it were my fault. Expect I were in the wrong seat or summat.'

'You're very kind, but it wasn't your fault. You weren't in the wrong seat. I shouldn't have sat down at all, and especially not on you. But I've not been myself lately and…'

Naiba needed an explanation which – like a dieter's dream dinner – was both fully satisfying and completely devoid of content.

'…and I think Matron's pills were stronger than I was expecting,' she concluded.

Too strong to actually take, she didn't add.

Once she found out it wasn't her fault, Mrs Ockstart got off her tenterhooks and smiled at Naiba.

'Well, dear, if you was taking Matron's pills I'm surprised I only got sat on. I'm surprised I didn't get a black eye or something!' She laughed, but it quickly faded as she realised nobody else did. Not out loud, anyway. Especially not the Rectrix, who seemed to be sporting a new blue, purple and yellow eye shadow, but only on one eye. Mrs Ockstart coughed. 'Well, there you are, dear,' she said quietly, clasping the top of her handbag again. 'No harm done.'

Naiba smiled sadly. 'I am sorry.'

Dominica broke in. 'Thank you for being so understanding, Mrs Ockstart. I think we need detain you no further. Stephanie?'

The Head of Personnel helped Mrs Ockstart to her feet and said, 'We've got a little something for you as recompense for your inconvenience. If you'd like to go with my assistant, she'll sort it out for you and make sure you are taken home. Thank you again for coming.' She ushered Mrs Ockstart and the assistant out and closed the door behind them. 'One down, two to go,' she muttered.

'Right,' said Dominica. 'Who's next? Ah, yes. The Rectrix.' She looked up at Naiba. 'Away you go.'

The Rectrix burst forth.

'Well, I've never been so insulted in my—'

'Not you, Adamantha,' said Dominica, loudly enough to drown out the Rectrix's whine.

Naiba swallowed hard. 'Rectrix, please accept my humblest apologies. I'm truly sorry for what happened, but please believe me, it was done out of delirium, not personal animosity. As an apology, I've brought some soothing balms for you which will ease the discomfort and tone down the colour of your injury.'

'That won't be necessary.'

'But please, I'm so sorry—'

The Rectrix shrieked like a badly maintained lathe.

'I don't want your potions! I don't want anything more to do with you! Or your college! I resign! So there! Stick that in your cauldron and stir it!'

She stormed out, slamming the door. The remaining participants swapping wordless but meaningful glances.

The first person to break the silence was Deaconess Glibly, who said cheerfully, 'Well, there's a silver lining if ever I saw one.'

The second person was Naiba, who slumped to the floor unconscious.

As the coach drew up in Anniversary Street the place appeared to be deserted, but Mrs Ockstart knew the neighbours were watching from every available concealed vantage-point. She stepped from the coach and looked up and down the street; it was as empty as the windswept terraces at the local footbladder ground. She leaned back inside the coach and tugged at a leather strap. As soon as the first creak of wicker food hamper was heard, the street was heaving with people all shouting variations on 'What time's the party start, Mrs O?'

Mrs Ockstart smiled but said nothing as she carried the small picnic hamper into her house and the coach drove off. Nobody saw it trundle round the back of the house and unload three more hampers which, when emptied, Mrs Ockstart would be able to rent out as spare bedrooms.

The blackboard running along one wall of Marianna's study was covered in ticks, crosses, lines, arrowheads, half-sentences and question marks; pinned alongside it was a large map, with a long red line tracing the route of the Great North Road. Marianna and JW sat in large leather chairs, facing the blackboard with their backs to the desk. They were studying the evidence, analysing, rationalising and surmising when there was a knock on the door and a familiar figure entered, carrying a large tea tray.

'Please, mums, there's a rozzer wants to talk to you. Shall I show him in?'

JW swung her chair round. 'Yes, please. Thank you, er…' she squinted at the name badge, '…Deedee.'

Deedee put down the tray.

'Please, Mistress Arcrite, our Mam says to say thank you very much for our name badges. She says it's the first time in years she's been able to get somebody's name right in under two minutes, mum.'

'Tell her she's welcome.'

'And she's thinking of having some made for our twelve brothers. I'll show the rozzer in, mum.'

She bobbed and left.

Marianna swivelled her chair round and when Constable Sennet entered the room carrying his helmet under his arm, he felt as if he was about to be interviewed for promotion.

'What's this?' he asked, indicating the blackboard.

'Our Board of Enquiry,' beamed Marianna. 'Just waiting for a few constants to replace some of these variables.'

'Sorry?' said Sennet.

'My colleague means we're waiting for a few hard facts to back up our theories. Sit down, Mac,' said JW. He did so, and put his helmet under the chair. 'So what have you found out?'

It would have been nice to have had some tea first, but he supposed the sooner he told them what he knew, the sooner he could carry on his own investigations. He sighed and patted his pockets.

'Mistress Lynin did indeed travel by mailcoach on the days in question.'

Marianna bounded out of her chair with a 'Yes!' and started to tick things on the blackboard.

Sennet found his notebook in the top pocket of his uniform. 'There was an overnight stop at Stoneton. She reboarded the coach after the stop and the driver only noticed something wasn't right when the mailcoach arrived in Maund.'

'Did he report her missing?' asked JW.

'No.'

'Whyever not?' said Marianna.

'I asked him that very question. He replied – and I quote…' Sennet searched through his notebook to find the relevant pages, '…"She'd paid her fare. Where she gets off is her business".'

'You mean he thought she'd got off the coach at her destination? He didn't realise her destination was Maund?'

'Not until he had to unload her luggage.'

'The mailcoach company's got her luggage? Why didn't *they* report her missing then?'

'He said, "people are always leaving things on the coach".'

JW snorted. 'Full sets of luggage? Come off it. The odd trombone, maybe…'

'Well, her cases do have brass bands round them,' smiled Sennet. Blank looks greeted his attempt at levity, and his smile faded faster than a promise to keep in touch.

'Sorry?' said Marianna.

'I'm only reporting what the man said, sister. And if the luggage isn't claimed within three months the mailcoach company's legally entitled to dispose of it.'

'The thieving articles!' said JW. 'I'll go down there and claim it.'

'They won't let you if you don't have the proper papers.'

'I'll have the proper papers, don't you fret yourself. I'll have all the papers they'll need.'

Marianna scanned the blackboard. 'Exactly where did she leave the coach, constable?'

'Exactly somewhere between Stoneton and the depot. There's a few stops on the way, so she could've got off at any one of them.'

Marianna wiped clean an area of the blackboard, and wrote *Depot* at the top and *Stoneton* at the bottom.

'Well, JW, we can start at either end.'

JW tapped on the blackboard. 'Depot, I reckon. Ask a few more questions, get the luggage, go through it, see what's what and that.'

'We'll need Dominica's permission to search Eleanor's things.'

'In that case, you go see Dom and I'll get the luggage.'

Sennet coughed.

'Thanks, Mac,' said JW. 'That'll be all.'

'All, sister?'

'Yes, all. We don't need you any more.'

A smug expression settled on Sennet's face. 'I'm sorry, sister, but you don't have the necessary authority to dismiss me. Mistress Land is on record as having reported a missing person which makes it an official case and I'm the official whose case it is.'

'What?' said JW.

Sennet looked around for his helmet. 'I must continue to investigate this case until Mistress Land tells me otherwise.'

JW sighed. 'Marianna, tell him otherwise.'

'Oh, I think the constable may still be helpful to us, JW,' said Marianna conspiratorially. Sennet beamed, despite being anxious to find his helmet and even more anxious to get away to find anybody else who was on the mailcoach that day to see what they knew.

'Fine,' said JW. 'Then mebbe he can find somebody else on the mailcoach that day and see what they know.'

Sennet decided he *really* didn't like JW very much. 'I shall continue my investigations and report back when the case is solved.'

JW pointed underneath Sennet's chair. 'Oh, I think you'll report back before then.'

Sennet bent to retrieve his helmet. 'Why?'

'Because if we don't hear from you by the end of tomorrow,' Marianna smiled, 'I'll come down to the rozzer shop and close the case.'

Sennet twitched and made for the door. When he opened it, Deedee was on the other side with her hand poised ready to knock.

"Scuse me, mums, Vice-Matriarch says can you both go to her study for an emergency Senior Council meeting, please?'

After the emergency meeting, a certain section of the Senior Council thought that having Dominica Tort in charge, albeit temporarily, of The University of Nature was, at the least, a complete disaster: not only had the Matriarch Designate gone missing, *and* they'd had the first-ever Graduation ceremony presided over by a Vice-Matriarch, *and* there'd been a punch-up part-way through it, but now she'd manage to lose The Union a Rectrix as well.

However, the Bursar was in a minority and the rest of the Senior Council thought Dominica was the unluckiest Vice-Matriarch in the history of The Union, and wasn't she coping well, and sooner her than me, and getting rid of the Rectrix was a master-stroke and wasn't it time Matron's pills were checked out by an independent body if that's what they did to dependent bodies?

Back in her own room, the Bursar couldn't suppress a smile. Minnie's splendid display of incompetence was enormously pleasing. Whoever came after her would probably go down in history as the saviour of The Union simply by getting things back to normal. The Bursar knew it was only a matter of time, and she wanted to be ready.

From the box in her wardrobe she took the old envelope which had been opened so many times the flap had long since fallen off; the two pieces of paper inside the envelope were equally old and as the Bursar took one out and unfolded it she could see through a small hole in its centre where the well-used creases met.

Although she knew the written words off by heart, they shone with a new sense of urgency:

> *This curse hide one a grand will fall*
> *Four under pennant damage done*
> *The children shall the greedy pay*
> *Until the house and mine be one*
> *Until a single child they bear*
> *Until a child with gin jar new*
> *Be born unto a destiny*
> *His sack of pennants shall be two*
> *One time in every hundred year*
> *One of the children disappear*
> *And not a living soul to tell*
> *Cursed family shall prosper well*
> *But stop this magic by desire*
> *And fortune crumbles in the fire*
> *Until that single child be born*
> *And cross the path for you to meet*
> *The child releases then the bond*
> *His awful spell can be complete*

Time would tell; it usually does. It was only a matter of time. If not this time, next time.

Coming round, the first thing Naiba saw was Dominica sitting beside the bed holding a sheaf of manuscript papers.

She covered her face with her hands.

'Oh, Vice-Matriarch, I am just so sorry about everything. Everything, everything.'

'You'll only make yourself worse by worrying about it,' Dominica said. 'Come on out. Don't worry, I won't bite.'

Naiba took her hands from her face. 'Thank you.'

'Look, there's very little harm done. The only person you've really upset is the Rectrix, and to be honest, you've only done what quite a few people have wanted to do since she became Rectrix. It causes a few problems, but on the whole it's worth it and you're a bit of a heroine for that. Mrs Ockstart's quite happy – she's got an apology and a goodie bag – and Deaconess Glibly understands you were under some sort of hallucination at the time and so doesn't take it personally. I can forgive you the twitching, coughing, screaming and fainting, because the Tutor of Creative Chronicling tells me that you've been under some considerable stress recently on account of this manuscript. But why don't you tell me all about it in your own words?'

Naiba wept with relief. She told Dominica everything – about the ginger root and how she'd been possessed by it, the familiar unfamiliar voice that spoke from time to time, the writing that started and stopped and started and stopped, the vision in the kitchens and the hallucination which had caused the mayhem at Graduation.

'And do you truly believe it was Auregia's Graduation you were seeing?' asked Dominica.

Naiba nodded. 'I do. I heard them call her full name – and her degree. Mother Nature, if I could only remember her name! But I can't – I think the shock of seeing my own face made me forget everything else. Why would— why would she have my face?'

'Oh, any number of reasons. You're right in the middle of everything, so to speak: you're the one writing the story, you're the one being possessed, you're the one having the visions – it's only natural your face should figure quite prominently. It could be your mind's way of playing a practical joke on you – after all, you might've made all this up – or it could be an indication you're the one who's got to sort it out if it's true.'

'*Of course it's true*,' said a familiar unfamiliar voice. '*It's how I came to be.*'

'Didn't you get the luggage?' asked Marianna when JW walked in, carrying nothing but a rolled-up newspaper.

JW shut the door. 'It's coming in a couple of hours. The mailcoach company are just waiting for a dray to come back and then they'll send it round with a couple of blokes.'

'Ooh, nice. I love a free gift.'

JW chuckled. 'Have you seen the blokes on the mailcoach drays? I wouldn't have any of them as a free gift. Did you talk to Dom about the luggage?'

'I did. She says to put it in Imelda's old room – as long as we put a lock enchantment on it.'

JW sat down opposite her. 'Really? Is she worried somebody might tamper with Eleanor's stuff?'

Marianna screwed her face up. 'Well… she didn't say so in so many words, but…'

'The Bursar?'

'Given how erratic Helena's been lately, I don't think Dominica's taking any chances.'

'Don't blame her.' JW threw the folded newsprint onto the desk. 'I picked up a paper while I were out. Seems it's the season for vanishing acts. There's a kiddie gone missing from Spanniel Park.'

'Oh, no.'

'Aye. Pray Mother Nature they find her. That sort of thing makes my blood boil.'

'Mm.'

For a few moments they were silent. Marianna picked up the paper. 'Constable Sennet'll have two cases to deal with then. Won't be able to help us as much as he'd hoped.'

'Good,' said JW.

Marianna hit her playfully with the paper and laughed.

'Get on with you.'

'Well, that was interesting,' said Dominica. 'I think we can assume it's true, then.'

'Yes,' said Naiba sadly.

'But is it true as in a past event or true as in it's a presentiment for the future which could come true?'

'It feels like something that's already happened. And didn't the voice say, "how I came to be", not "how I'm going to be"?'

'Mm. In that case, let's assume for the moment it's a spell which needs signing off. All we have to do is find it.'

'Won't it be in the Dictionary?'

Dominica laughed. 'Oh, it'll be in there somewhere but so are millions of others. And we don't know how old it is. Was it cast last month? Last year? Twenty years ago? It could be any age. I'm afraid we need a bit more information before we go to the Dictionary.'

'Where do we start then, Vice-Matriarch?'

'Good question. We could trawl the archives for all the witches named Auregia who've been through these doors, but unfortunately there's no alphabetical record of who cast which spell.' She sighed heavily and flicked through the manuscript as she pondered. Eventually she said, 'I don't know of any cake shops called *Grandel's*, do you?'

Naiba shook her head. 'I don't know of any orphanages in Maund either. The nearest one's in Bayoake. Do you think that might be it?'

'No reason why it shouldn't be,' said Dominica. 'Mind you, there's no reason why it should.'

~•~
NOTES ON
Spells

The four phases of a spell are creation, activity, completion and sign-off. The great majority of spells sign off automatically, because most of them are of short duration (such as spells of disguise) or they're of a domestic nature (such as emergency house-cleaning when unexpected visitors are striding up the garden path) or they're training spells. It's nobody's pinnacle of achievement to be sitting all day manually signing off training spells; if you're of a mind to do that, it's not the kind of mind The Union wants or needs.

However, spells which are set to run for a year or more must be signed off manually – or as the romantic novelists would say, 'broken' – which hinges on two things: Spellcaster's Conditions, and the availability of someone high enough up the food chain to do the signing off.

Spellcaster's Conditions are the requirements which must be met before a spell is eligible for sign-off. They are usually of a random nature, very specific in detail and often quite bizarre, which is hardly surprising when you consider the state of mind of someone who's content to leave magic running for over a year. Spellcaster's Conditions have been known to encompass many things, such as an act of charity, a true declaration of love, tears of forgiveness dropping onto the hand of an enemy, a kiss from a prince or princess, the multi-coloured flowering of an erstwhile dead tree, a clock striking thirteen, and the rarely equalled 'when a virgin wipes a single drop of dragon's blood from the shield of a mighty iron-clad centaur warrior as the first eleven men return the trophy to its rightful home'. Rumour has it that a centaur with a dustbin lid, a dragon with a pin and a virgin with a dishcloth have been sharing a house for a fortnight once every four years, just in case.

Once the Spellcaster's Conditions are met the spell is considered to be 'completed' and ready for sign-off by whoever is allowed to. Depending on the duration of the spell, there's a sliding scale of authorised signatories. *O'Bridge's Table Book* – the small booklet of useful information given to every first-former – details it thus:

The Timetable of Existences

NB: Spellcaster's Conditions must be fulfilled before Sign-off unless the Spellcaster herself lifts the Spell.

Spell Duration (Years)	Persons permitted to Sign off the Spell
1 - 99	Spellcaster or Any graduate of The University
100 - 200	Any graduate of The University
200 - 300	Any Senior Council Member
300 - 400	Vice-Matriarch or Matriarch
400+	Matriarch

Any delay between completion and sign-off causes sorcerial uncertainty, which means one of three things: firstly, the spell just carries on working out of habit; secondly, the spell goes into a state of inactivity until the correct signatory can be found (this is known as 'sleeping'); thirdly, and most dangerously, the spell starts to decay, in which case anything might occur.

Which just goes to show what happens when magic goes past its spell-by date.

~•~

Dominica was poring over Naiba's manuscript, making notes, when Dennis leapt up and walked across her desk and tilted his head to look at her writing.

'That's a long apology for the Rectrix, isn't it?'

'She'll get no apology from me. I'd rather rip my own leg off and beat myself over the head with the soggy end.'

'What is it then?'

'A puzzle.'

'Why are you writing a puzzle?'

'I'm not. Somebody else has.'

Dennis clearly had nothing else to occupy his time.

'What sort of puzzle?'

Dominica put her pen down.

'Look at me. I've got a Matriarch Morte who can't start her Returning Journey, a missing Matriarch Designate, a vacancy for Rectrix, a Bursar who's— well, the Bursar, a junior administrator who's sporadically possessed by the spirit of a spell and I have to go through life with the Question Cat. I ask you – is that a fair load for one person?'

'What are you asking me for?' said Dennis smugly.

She laughed. 'Oh, very clever. Now listen. If I tell you about it will you shut up and go away?'

'Might do.'

'I'll take that as a yes. Right – pin back your lugholes. This puzzle might be a spell whose time has come. I just need to work out who cast it, when and where, and who has to sign it off, and all I've got to go on is this story.'

'What's the story about?'

'If you must know, it's about a sister called Auregia, a cat called Axy, two children and—'

'Axy?' said Dennis, pawing through the manuscript excitedly to find the name.

'Yes, Axy.'

'Not Axy the Tamer! Is the story about Axy the Tamer?'

Dominica looked at him. 'You know a cat called Axy?'

'Of course I don't! I wish! He's the stuff of legends is Axy the Tamer.'

'What sort of legends?'

'The sort that say he was so brave he could even tame dogs and he had all the dogs in the country working for him, but their masters didn't like that so one day they came round and tore his house down and he fought back and he gave the ringleader a punch in the face but they beat him up really bad and killed his best friend. Anyway, when he got better, Axy killed one of the ringleader's henchmen and *made the ringleader eat him*, and after that the masters were so scared they never bothered him again and he went back to taming the wild animals who lived in the woods. It's real *Cats' Own* stuff, is Axy the Tamer.'

Dominica took a long shot.

'I don't suppose you know his spirit name, by any chance?' she said nonchalantly.

Dennis assumed a stance suggesting he held a sword in one paw and a shield in the other. He put on his best warrior voice. 'Axy the Tamer – The Spirit of Friendship!'

Before she went through the gates, Naiba stood for a while looking through the railings. The orphanage was majestic: five storeys high, solid, proud, and built to impress. In the centre of a town it would have been a ducal residence or a government building and, as such, ignored on a daily basis; here, in its own parkland, those who passed by could not help but marvel at its classical proportions.

In front of the building was a large playground, affording plenty of space to the various activities of the orphanage's residents. The children were of all ages and sizes, and their boisterous games accompanied by whoops of laughter were testament to their welfare. They looked cleaner, better fed and downright happier than a lot of the children she'd seen in Maund; children who had a full complement of parents but whose cup of love and affection had a distinct ullage.

'Can I 'elp you, miss?' said a rough voice beside her, heavy on nasal congestion but light on refinement.

'Oh!' said Naiba, clutching at her chest. 'You startled me!'

She turned and saw an old man whose bald head was covered by a grease-blackened flat cap. His ancient face heavily lined with pain and loss, and only lightly etched with happiness. Its tanned, leathery skin told of a life spent outdoors, and the lightness and suppleness of its owner's actions suggested he was agile, had not rested for longer than he had to and was always ready to spring into action.

'Sorry, miss, din't mean to. We don't like folks starin' at the childer, is all.'

'Oh, I am sorry. It was thoughtless of me.'

'Not unless you knew what we know, miss. No offence meant, but the childer are safe 'ere, and we like 'em to stay that way. Can I ask your business, miss?'

Naiba felt that this man had a strength that far belied his years and he was quite prepared to strike down anyone who even looked likely to threaten the orphans.

'Would it be possible to speak with whoever runs this place?' she said, adding hurriedly, 'Please?'

'Do you 'ave a claim on one of the childer, miss?'

Naiba saw him tense up, and his tone of voice suggested that anyone having a claim on a child would be thoroughly investigated and possibly worked over to prove their intent before they were allowed to go anywhere near the child.

'A claim? No, no. I – er – I just want to find out about the – about the history of the orphanage, that's all.'

The old man relaxed a little.

'Oh. I'll see if the Head can see you. This way.'

He took her along a path skirting the playground at all times making sure he was between her and the children. The path led up to a wide stone staircase which narrowed as they approached the huge door at the top.

Once inside, their footsteps echoed as they crossed the

cavernous entrance hall. Naiba gazed around as she walked; the high vaulted ceiling glowed with rich frescoes of the four seasons; the upper walls were embossed with giant bas-relief friezes of different trades; the marble mosaics of the lower walls were mostly hidden by rectangles of paper, each bearing a child's name and a joyously painted artwork.

The old man stopped outside a door. The nameplate read *Head Mistress*, a sliding panel underneath it contained the name *Miss McOrly* and a smaller sliding panel below that said *IN*. The old man knocked on the door, waited for Miss McOrly to call 'Enter!' and then removed his flat cap and showed Naiba in.

'Sorry to disturb you, Head,' he said, 'but this young lady wants a word with you about the 'istory of our 'ome, if possible.'

Miss McOrly continued writing as she spoke.

'I dare say you'd be able to tell her more than I could, Meniel. You've been here longer than I have.'

She looked up, but Meniel had gone.

As she opened her door to set off for the Library, Dominica was met by the procession of Marianna, JW and four serving-girls bearing two brass-banded wooden trunks.

'We're just going to start looking through Eleanor's luggage,' said Marianna. 'Do you want to join us?'

Dominica shook her head. 'I think I can trust the pair of you, and I've just got some urgent business of my own to attend to.'

She walked off, then returned to Marianna and handed

her the manuscript. 'When you get time, read this. We'll talk later.'

Miss McOrly's accent marked her out as being from a place so far north that it was in another country. However, it was a country whose inhabitants were much respected as doctors, lawyers, engineers, educators and disciplinarians, and Miss McOrly was not one to let her country down.

'Why would you be interested in our history?' she asked.

'We've been investigating some old records at The Union,' said Naiba, as close to the truth as she was prepared to go at this stage, 'and an orphanage was mentioned. We realised we didn't know very much about it, and I volunteered to find out.'

Miss McOrly seemed as cagey as Naiba when it came to giving out information.

'Why would this orphanage be mentioned in The Union records?'

'To be honest, Miss McOrly,' said Naiba quietly, looking as baffled as she could, 'we're not even sure that this is the one mentioned.'

'Oh?'

'It's just… it's the nearest, and we had to start somewhere. If we can find out where the orphanage is, it'll add to our knowledge of the area and its history.'

'Surely the Union witches are interested in more than local history, are they not?' said Miss McOrly, hinting that there was something she was not being told.

Naiba whispered conspiratorially.

'We're trying to find out whether one of our number was a major benefactress of this place in years gone by. If this is the place, of course.'

Miss McOrly smiled. 'That would be very interesting.'

'Yes... so... can you tell me anything?'

'I can tell you all I know, which isn't very much, I'm afraid. This home has been here for well over four hundred years. There is a story that this was the family home of a merchant who underwent a... a religious conversion, would you believe, after which he bought a small house somewhere else in Bayoake and gave this house to be the orphanage. However, there's no hard and fast evidence to suggest any truth in such a story. My personal opinion is that it was built, for the good of the town, at the behest of a number of tradesmen. Did you see the frieze in the entrance hall on your way in?'

'Not very clearly – I just glanced at it.'

'It shows farmers, wheelwrights, millers, weavers, bakers and shopkeepers, whom I believe were the men who founded this orphanage, immortalised in the frieze as a measure of thanks for their generosity. To me, that is evidence, and it's preferable to believe in solid evidence rather than rumours and unsubstantiated stories, is it not?'

If Miss McOrly was expecting a challenge to her theory, she wasn't going to get it.

'Oh, definitely,' said Naiba. 'Are there any records to confirm it?'

Miss McOrly looked disappointed. 'Alas, no. All the early records were lost in a fire about four hundred years ago, which is why I can't be more precise about the age of the place. We do have records since then, of course; mainly about the children who have passed through our portals.'

'Could the name of our sister be in your financial records?'

Miss McOrly's eyes narrowed.

'How much is she supposed to have contributed?'

'I don't know exactly.' Naiba bit her lip whilst she tried to work it out, and failed. 'Enough to run the place for a year, or two, or ten or…'

Miss McOrly's interest levels rose considerably. She walked to one of her bookcases and took out a slim ledger which she leafed through. 'Is this some sort of bequest you're talking about?'

'Not exactly. Sort of, but – we're not sure.'

'Oh.'

'That's what we're trying to find out. With your help.'

'Of course.'

Miss McOrly put the open ledger on the desk and invited Naiba to look through it.

'There are rumours – again, rumours – that the orphanage is funded from the alleged house-owner's will, but again there's no evidence. I believe it is more likely our income derives from a trust fund set up by the tradesmen who had the house built.'

Naiba peered into the ledger. Although it represented four hundred years' worth of financial history there were very few entries, and no names which seemed familiar.

'The entry is the basically the same for every year,' said

Miss McOrly, 'although the amounts differ. As you can see, we receive a large – and I do mean large – donation twice per fiscal year. That is augmented by the proceeds from our summer fair – shown here, for example – and various small sundry donations throughout the year.'

'Where does this large donation come from?'

'I wish I could tell you.'

'Please, Miss McOrly. It's very important.'

'I appreciate that, and I wish I could tell you, because then I could thank the donor. But I cannot possibly tell you, because I do not know.'

One of the perks of being the Head of ADAM was ownership of a set of keys which would open virtually any lock in The Union, and a set of tools which would open the rest. Alchemists stood more chance of success than the nerds spending all their lives in a shed at the end of the garden trying to devise the physical fastening device that could defeat JW. As far as she was concerned, the term 'locksmith' meant 'someone who makes wrought iron wigs'.

'I don't think we're going to find much in here,' she said, peering at the luggage.

'How do you work that out?' Marianna asked, examining the conical hatbox, which yielded nothing more than a conical hat and an Insignia of Systerhood.

'They're only mortal locks. Specialist mortal locks, mind you, but mortal all the same. No enchantments, spells, invisible bindings; nothing, in fact, that can't be undone without a little thought and…' – JW held up a piece of thin bent wire headed by a tiny carved skull – '…a skeleton key.'

Seconds later she lifted the lid, which swung open as silently as a shadow, revealing neatly folded clothes. The lid of the second trunk opened just as silently, but this time revealed rows of cardboard filing boxes containing personal mementoes, work in progress and a lifetime's paperwork worth saving.

'Your call,' said JW. 'Clothing or correspondence?'

'She doesn't know?' said Dominica loudly, and several people looked up disapprovingly, sending irritated points of light tutting into the air. 'She doesn't know?' she whispered.

'It seems not,' said Naiba.

'But how can she—'

Someone coughed pointedly in their direction. It wouldn't be long before someone pointed out that this was a Library, after all. Dominica marked her place in the volume she was studying and motioned to Naiba. They went outside.

'How can she be sure they'll get the money?' asked Dominica.

'She says they've been receiving a large donation twice a year for over four hundred years, so she can't see any reason why they shouldn't carry on getting it. In fact, she's expecting the next one tomorrow.'

In the evening, Dominica stuck her head round the door of Marianna's study and noticed the blackboard.

'Very impressive,' she said.

Marianna swung round. 'Welcome to the Incident Room.'

Dominica smiled and went in. 'I think a missing Matriarch is more than an incident, don't you?'

'It doesn't sound right if I say "Welcome to the Major Catastrophe Room" does it?'

'Ah, never thought of that. Where's JW?'

'Taken a box of the correspondence up to her room, if that's all right.'

'Yes, fine, fine.'

Dominica closed the door behind her and leant against it.

'What's on your mind, Dominica?' said Marianna.

'Oh, is it so obvious?'

'Only to an old friend.'

Dominica walked over to the desk, sat opposite Marianna, and leant forward. 'Did you read that manuscript?'

Marianna passed it across the desk. 'I did.'

'Did you know Axy is the stuff of legends, apparently?'

Marianna's eyebrows shot up in much the same way Dominica's had when she'd checked the Registers in the Library. 'No!'

'Yes! Dennis told me.'

'Dennis knows him?'

'Only by repute. But he also told me Axy's familiar name is Spirit of Friendship.'

'So?'

'So I thought he might have been re-issued since the time of this story and he might be about somewhere and I could ask him... details.'

'Oh, good idea.'

Dominica's face took on that wide-eyed, wide-mouthed

rictus grin of someone who knows they've got some hot news, but doesn't know whether it's good or bad.

'So I trawled through the Register of Familiars with Systers for the last forty years to see if I could find him.'

'And?' said Marianna, eyebrows now somewhere down the back of her head.

'He was re-issued about twenty-five years ago.'

There was a short silence.

'To?' said Marianna.

Toffee-Nosed Claude couldn't remember when he'd last had so many thoughts. In this incarnation his life had been – on the whole – steady, if not as prestigious as some previous lives. Being the familiar of a Senior Council member was certainly a cut above the rest and not to be sniffed at, but in days gone by… ah, well.

That's the trouble with days. They go by. And in the days gone by since the Matriarch's death, life's placid lake had been whipped up by some very strong winds. At this moment, all was peaceful; the Bursar hadn't lost her temper with anybody for days. Volatility had once again been replaced by calm, but everybody knows what calm comes before. There was only one thing for it.

'Cookie – another beetroot, if you please.'

It's the early bird that catches the worm, but that's because the bird knows what the worm looks like. Naiba had no idea what her worm would look like as she sat in a tree opposite the orphanage soon after sunrise. Once she'd taken the saddlebag off her broomstick, only a trained horticulturist would have noticed that this otherwise healthy tree sported a new dead branch in its midst. Not knowing how long she'd have to wait, she'd packed a stakeout kit in the saddlebag: sandwiches, fruit, bottles of water, pencils and a notebook.

Apart from a tendency to numbness in the rear end from sitting on a branch, the day had been quite easy so far, as her notebook confirmed:

07:03 Pattantoni's Dairy: churns, yoghurts, cheeses
07:17 Royle's Fruit and Veg: potatoes and asstd. veg
07:22 Fishwick's Confectioners: breads and cakes
07:49 Courier took letters from red box on wall
Courier <u>did not deliver</u>

She had just written *11:00 All quiet* when the clattering of hooves rounding the corner proved her wrong. A coach which apparently had no driver stopped directly outside the orphanage's main gate. Its four black horses trotted up and down on the spot, the reins from their harnesses feeding through a small slit in the front of the coach.

The black coach had no windows and only one door, which was at the back and fastened by a large padlock and chain. On the roof of the coach sat four burly dwarves, one in each corner so between them they could see in every direction. The dwarves held large clubs, and carried throwing axes and knives on their leather belts. The sunlight bounced off their steel helmets and skittered down their chain-mail tabards. The lower halves of their leather trousers were protected by steel shinpads, and Naiba was willing to bet that their leather boots concealed steel toe-caps.

The dwarves leapt down from the roof and stood with their backs to the coach watching all the time for the least movement from anywhere. Slowly, one inched his way along the coach and hammered with the back of his studded gauntlet on a steel panel in the door of the coach.

Bang! Bang! Bang! Bang!

A small reply came from inside the coach. Tap, tap, tap.

Bang! Bang, bang bang bang!

Tap.

Bang! Bang bang, bang bang, bang bang!

Tap tap tap tap tap.

'Cover me!' shouted the knocking dwarf, and the other three started to pace slowly round the coach, always with their backs towards it.

A small panel slid open in the back of the coach and a key was passed out. The dwarf unlocked the padlock, removed the chain, and then passed the key back inside.

Tap tap.

The dwarf opened the back door with his right hand whilst guarding it with the club in his left. A cloaked figure descended from the coach and was immediately surrounded by the dwarves, who jogged alongside as the figure approached the door of the orphanage.

Naiba strapped her saddlebag onto her broom, unhooked the broom from the tree, jumped down, walked over to the coach and stepped inside.

The interior of the coach was dimly lit by small candles which could be easily extinguished to plunge the coach into darkness in case of trouble. She looked around for the horses' reins, but they were nowhere to be seen. She felt along the front wall of the coach, finding that it vibrated much more readily than the other walls; obviously there not for substance but for show – or hide. A false wall to hide the driver. Along it ran a bench seat, and at the end of that was a large grey safe, the door of which was covered in high-security deadlocks, bolts, dials and levers. And wide open.

She heard the hurried crunching of five sets of footsteps, so she flattened herself against the coach wall by the open back door.

The coach swayed as the cloaked figure was almost thrown inside and the door slammed behind it, blowing out the candles. Naiba could hear the padlock and chain being slung across the door. The coach rocked violently to the tune of four thuds as the dwarves took up their lookout posts on the roof. Two heavy slams from a studded gauntlet indicated to the driver that he could pull away, which he did with a 'Yee-hah!', a loud crack of the whip and as much thrust as he could muster.

As the coach lurched away, the thick door of the safe slammed shut with a deafening clang and a rattle of levers. Over the pounding hooves Naiba heard the cloaked figure slide across the floor and hit the back wall of the coach.

'Dammit! There's me elbow again,' it said.

A chocking noise was followed by a sliding noise, then that light tinkle which only occurs when a box of matches empties onto a hard surface.

'Oh, hell!'

'Here, let me help,' said Naiba.

'Aaaagh!' yelled the voice.

Naiba clicked her fingers and all the candles lit.

'Oh, mind me eyes!' cried the cloaked figure, putting its arm over its face.

Naiba crouched down and helped it as upright as possible. As they both swayed with the movement of the coach, she found she was holding the arm of a bulging-eyed hunchback who was clutching his chest with his free hand and gasping for breath.

'Hello,' said Naiba brightly. 'You must be Igor.'

'Men...' Igor heaved, 'all around... I just need to... call.'

'They won't hear you through all this reinforcement.'

'Driver's only... through that wall.'

'He won't hear you for the clattering of hooves.'

'I can knock on the wall.'

'They'll just think it's the coach rocking.'

Igor was regaining his composure.

'You're wasting your time. Nothing of value in here.'

'It all depends on what you call value.'

'Just done a delivery, not a pick-up. Nothing left.'

'Knowledge is a treasure which accompanies its owner everywhere,' said Naiba, and waited until this sank in.

'I'm not telling you anything!' said Igor, in the true spirit of his profession.

'All I want is information. That won't hurt you, will it?'

He bristled and jutted out his chin. 'Client security and confidentiality are paramount in this business.'

'I should think so. What you tell me will be in the strictest confidence.'

'I'm not saying another thing. My reputation is built on reliability and the highest regard for security of goods and information.'

Naiba pointed. 'You see that broomstick? It doesn't mean I'm one of the cleaners.'

Igor laughed bitterly. 'I'm already hump-backed and goggle-eyed. If you turned me into a frog it'd only be a change of colour.'

'Fair enough. But if you don't tell me what I want to know, I'll tell everybody what I already do know.'

'Which is?'

'How easy it is to get past your security.'

'What?'

'Once they find out I just strolled in here when the door was open, your precious reputation will be shot.'

Igor gulped.

'And,' said Naiba, 'nobody will ever use Secure-Igor again.'

As Dominica and Marianna walked towards JW's room, Marianna said quietly, 'Eleanor's not the only one who's vanished. A little girl's gone missing as well.'

'Do you think there's a connection?'

'Not sure. Seems an unlikely coincidence, but coincidence, by its very nature, is unlikely. The fact that it happens on a regular basis is neither here nor there.'

'It wouldn't be coincidence if the same person had kidnapped them,' Dominica pointed out.

'But we don't know that they have been kidnapped yet.'

'You mean they could both have met with an unfortunate accident in the same place?'

'If it's a particularly dangerous place,' said Marianna. 'For example, what if there's a hidden pit somewhere they've both fallen into?'

'Why would there be a hidden pit unless someone had dug it and then hidden it? Someone like a kidnapper?'

'But we haven't had a ransom note, have we? And would someone who kidnaps women also kidnap children?'

'So there could be two kidnappers at work?'

'Could be two, could be none. Who knows? It's all just theory at the moment.'

They knocked on JW's door and went in.

'Hello, supersleuth,' said Dominica. 'Found anything yet?'

JW looked up from the midst of Eleanor's papers.

'Not much. Though I didn't know she were an orphan.'

'An orphan?' said Dominica.

'All right, not strictly an orphan, but as good as.'

From the smallest of the boxes which had been inside the trunk, JW lifted a baby's shawl, intricately crocheted. Pinned to the top was a yellowing note.

> *Forgive me, but the mother of this child has died, and I, her father, am so far gone in grief I can no longer give her the care she must have. Please take her under your protection, for she will be safe with you. Soon I shall be out of her life and it is better she not know me at all.*
>
> *When the time comes she must leave your care, please give her this letter. At that time also shall another letter be*

delivered to her which will explain more. Can you please let her know her mother and I loved her very much, and we gave her the name Eleanor Lynin. I and generations to come are forever in your debt.

'Oh, that's so sad,' said Marianna, 'but he gave her the best start in life he could. Did you find the other letter?'

'Not yet... not that I'm aware of anyway, but then again, would I recognise it? Would it be that obvious?'

'Talking of obvious,' said Marianna, 'Dominica's pointed out something we've missed, JW.'

'Oh aye?'

'Where's Eleanor's familiar?'

'I don't know who the client is,' Igor said, as he and Naiba clung grimly to the bench seat during the buffeting ride back to his office. 'I just get an envelope twice a year, delivered to the office, and in it there's the goods, all the instructions and the fee.'

'Who delivers it?'

'No idea. It's just there waiting for me one morning.'

'Aren't you even curious about it?'

His look suggested that curiosity had killed not only the cat but the dog, the budgie and the hamster as well and had done it right there in Igor's office as a warning to him.

'In this business it pays not to ask too many questions.'

This was not a policy Naiba subscribed to. 'Have you still got the envelope and the instructions?'

He pointed. 'They're in the safe.'

Naiba looked at him unblinkingly for a few moments, then a few more, and then a few more.

Igor sighed. After a moment's consideration he decided that as she was between him and the safe, it was probably for the best if he didn't climb over her, so he dropped onto the floor and crawled across to the safe, bouncing and jerking with each lurch of the coach. Every so often he would land on one of the dropped matches, which was not only painful on the knees but brought with it the constant danger of self-immolation. By the time he reached the safe, he was thinking of giving up Secure-Igor and opening a flower shop.

He wrenched open the door of the safe. It swung violently and he had to let go of it before its weight broke his arm against the false wall. He fell off the bench with a dull thud, and sucked in air through his teeth.

'The next coach I get is having padded walls,' he muttered as he clambered onto the bench. 'I was six foot ten and straight as a die before I started this job, you know.'

He reached into the safe, retrieving an envelope just before the safe door clanged shut. He twirled some of the dials with a flourish to lock the safe, and handed Naiba the envelope. 'There you are. Now please, no more questions.'

The coach halted as Naiba put the envelope in her saddlebag and took out her notebook and pencil.

'Thank you,' she said. 'You've been most helpful.'

She picked up her broomstick and stood by the door. Igor stood up then dropped back down onto the bench clutching at his throat.

'What's the matter?' asked Naiba.

A hoarse whisper emerged from Igor's face, which was red from choking and embarrassment.

'I've trapped me cloak in the safe.'

The back door of the coach opened; Naiba stepped out into the middle of four very surprised dwarves and flashed her notebook.

'Independent Quality Assurance Auditor,' she said. 'Igor asked me to do a QA check on his operation, and it's not a pretty story. Call yourselves security guards? You're lucky to be in employment at all. Not only was I able to gain access to the most secure area without any form of check whatsoever, but I was also able to incapacitate the Head of Operations.'

The dwarves hung their heads.

Naiba called to Igor.

'My report will be on your desk first thing, sir.'

She strolled off. The shamed dwarves watched her go.

'She's right! It's just not good enough!' yelled Igor.

As one, the dwarves rushed into the coach, sustaining various cuts and bruises as they got jammed in the doorway.

'Solved the case yet, Mac?' said JW by way of greeting as Constable Sennet entered the Incident Room.

Sennet glared at her, cleared his throat and sniffed.

'According to one of the other passengers, Mistress Lynin did not reboard the coach after its wee stop at a roadside inn outside Deartreen Wood.'

'Do you hail from the very far north, constable?' asked Marianna.

Sennet looked puzzled. 'No, sister, why? Because Mistress

Arcrite calls me Mac?'

'No, it was just you said "after its wee stop" and I thought you must be—'

'It's not wee as in little, Marianna,' JW broke in. 'He means they stopped for a—'

'Comfort break,' supplied Sennet.

Marianna blushed. 'Got you. Ah. Yes.'

'Carry on, Mac,' grinned JW.

'Mistress Lynin did not reboard the coach, and was last seen heading off into Deartreen Wood after her dog.'

'Her dog?' said Marianna.

'Her dog,' he repeated, then saw that neither witch appeared to understand what he was saying. '*A* dog,' he tried.

Still no sign of comprehension.

'*There was a dog involved,*' he said in desperation.

'Fancy that,' said JW.

Inside, Sennet jumped for joy. He'd told that woman something she didn't already know.

'What could there possibly be in Deartreen Wood that would make Eleanor go in there?' said Marianna.

'Her dog,' said Sennet smugly.

'I think we ought to go find out,' said JW. 'Meet us back here in an hour, Mac.'

'Sorry, sister, I'm working my other case this afternoon.'

'The little girl?' said Marianna. Sennet nodded.

'Well, then,' said JW. 'Spanniel Park's on the way to Deartreen Wood, so we might as well pool our resources. We'll help you at the park for a bit before we go on to the wood, so bring a rozzer coach.'

'A rozzer coach?' said Sennet.

'If we're going up and down the Great North Road, we don't want anybody getting in the way, do we?'

'I'll see if I can find one,' said Sennet, leaving the room.

'I'm not having him on the back of my broomstick,' said JW when he'd closed the door. 'Besides,' she giggled, 'I want to know how they make that woo-woo noise.'

As Naiba entered the study Dominica rubbed her hands together in expectation.

'So tell me, tell me, did you find anything out?'

Naiba frowned as she walked towards Dominica. 'Not much. Secure-Igor delivers the package, but he doesn't know on whose behalf. He gets the money and the instructions along with his fee in a sealed packet and he just follows the instructions.' She gave Dominica the envelope.

'Don't tell me,' said Dominica, opening it, 'he never sees who delivers it to him.'

'It just appears in his office overnight.'

Dominica flattened the letter of instruction on her desk.

Please deliver this parcel to the head of the orphanage on the day you receive it. Confidentiality and secrecy are paramount. Fee enclosed.

Dominica's brow furrowed as she studied the letter.

'You know, I've got a feeling…'

'I know what you mean,' said Naiba. 'I got that as well when I read it. There's something… familiar, almost…'

'Yes... but you can't quite put your finger on it.'

'No.'

There was a knock on the door which opened to admit JW and Marianna.

'Oh, sorry,' said JW. 'Didn't realise you were with— aren't you the girl from Graduation?'

'The one who wrote that story?' said Marianna.

Naiba's face fell.

'Neither of which were her fault,' said Dominica, 'being possessed at the time, and now we're trying to work out why. Naiba, go and get some lunch and have a bit of a rest, then meet me back here in an hour.'

'Yes, Vice-Matriarch.'

After she'd gone, Dominica said, 'So what can you two tell me?'

'The sum total of our knowledge has increased,' said Marianna. 'Eleanor was last seen getting off the coach and going into Deartreen Wood.'

Dominica was as surprised as JW and Marianna had been.

'Deartreen Wood? What's in Deartreen Wood apart from trees and legends?'

JW grinned. 'We're off there this afternoon with our pet rozzer to see if we can find out.'

'And we're going to look round Spanniel Park to see if we can help him with the missing girl,' added Marianna.

'Spanniel Park?' said Dominica. 'Spanniel Park right on the edge of Deartreen Wood, Spanniel Park?'

Marianna nodded. 'Probably too much of a coincidence.'

Toffee-Nosed Claude looked up from his post-lunch relaxation as the door of the Bursar's study opened.

'Good day, dear lady,' he said.

'Good day, Spirit,' said Dominica. 'Would you happen to know where your mistress is?'

Toffee-Nosed Claude's answer was given with a large dollop of I'm-only-telling-you-what-she-told-me.

'As far as I know, my mistress is in the Natural Beauty Department for a hair treatment. However, as my mistress's information has proved to be unreliable in the past, I cannot be certain.'

'How has her information been unreliable?'

Toffee-Nosed Claude was about to launch into his favourite topic when he remembered who he was talking to, and how much closer to the position of Matriarch Dominica was when compared to the Bursar.

'Oh,' he said, laughing lightly, 'it was merely a difference in… expectations. My mistress and I do not necessarily work at the same… pace. Please, think nothing of it, dear lady. I am sure you will find my mistress in Natural Beauty.'

'Thank you, Spirit.'

Toffee-Nosed Claude inclined his head a little.

As she made her way back to her own study, she met Naiba on her way to the same place.

'Come on,' said Dominica. 'Let's go for a walk.'

As they went down the stairs Naiba said, 'Vice-Matriarch, I think I know what it is about that letter.'

'Yes,' said Dominica. 'I do as well. You first.'

'It's the handwriting. Or bits of it anyway. It's the capital letters. They remind me of the letters Fishwick Confectioners use on their bags and on the side of their delivery carts. I wouldn't have thought about it but one of their carts delivered bread and cakes to the orphanage this morning.'

'Oh, really?'

'Mm. You don't think Fishwick's could be dropping the money off and this Secure-Igor thing is just a blind, do you?'

'I suppose it's possible, but the orphanage would know if there was a cache of money hidden in with the loaves, wouldn't they? Unless Miss McOrly's lying to you, but why should she?'

'But what's so secret Secure-Igor needs to be involved?'

When they reached the doors into the Globe Hall, Dominica rested her hand on the door-handle.

'I think Secure-Igor delivered the money, and Fishwick's were just dropping off the daily bread order.'

'So it's just coincidence then?' said Naiba.

'There's a lot of it about,' said Dominica, opening the door. Like her own feeling that elements of the handwriting resembled that of the Bursar and the Bursar being in charge of The Union's funds.

Dominica had gone five steps into the Globe Hall before she realised Naiba was not at her side but standing in the doorway, holding the door. 'Naiba? What's the matter?'

Naiba blew out her cheeks.

'I'll be all right in a minute. It's just... I haven't been in here since... since the hallucination.'

'Are you frightened it'll happen again?'

'Not frightened, exactly, but... but I want to be prepared

for it if it does.' She walked slowly towards Dominica. 'It seems difficult to believe it now, but it was all so – so real then,' she said. 'I felt so – oh, I don't know – disorientated. It was like being a stranger in your own home.'

Her eyes started to fill with tears.

Dominica put her arm around Naiba's shoulders.

'All right,' she said softly.

'I looked at you, and it wasn't you, I looked at Deaconess Glibly and it wasn't her, I looked at the Rectrix and it wasn't her – you were all different people! And none of you – them – could see me!'

'Come on, come on, it'll be all right,' said Dominica, desperately trying to think of something to focus Naiba's energies on. 'Tell me what I – she – whoever you saw looked like. Could you draw a—'

Dominica gripped Naiba's shoulders.

'You didn't recognise anybody?'

Naiba shook her head. 'No.'

'Not even from these portraits?'

Naiba walked round the Globe Hall, scrutinising the paintings of previous Matriarchs. 'No, she's not here.'

'Come on, then – we'll go to the Art House.'

'The Art House?'

'The Art House. Let's take a look at the Old Mistresses.'

As they left the Main Tower, a rotund figure with a large white towel round her head was walking towards it. From a distance the Bursar looked like a pear which had been dipped in chocolate and topped off with a squirt of whipped cream.

'You go on without me,' Dominica said to Naiba. 'You

know what you're looking for, don't you?'

'I do.' Naiba went off to the Art House alone.

'Ah, Helena – the very person,' said Dominica.

'Can't stop, Minnie,' said the Bursar, pointing to the towel. 'Just going to fetch my final rinse conditioner then I'm off back to Natural Beauty.'

'How long will you be?'

'Why, are you waiting to get your hair done?'

'No, I'd like a word with you, if possible.'

'With Mother Nature, all things are possible, Minnie.'

Dominica wanted to say, 'Like you being Matriarch one day, I suppose?' but she settled for, 'In that case, will you come and see me when you're ready?'

In the Art House, room after room of portraits looked down on Naiba. The further back along The Union's history chain she looked, the more eloquently the portraits illustrated that being a guardian of all Mother Nature's secrets was not a job for the faint-hearted or those without a good moisturiser. One or two pictures were candidates for hanging over the mantelpiece to keep the children away from the fire, and if these were merely the portraits, what had the women looked like in real life? If a picture paints a thousand words, some of these could have written novels that would make you scared to go out in the daytime, let alone at night.

Dominica was at her desk when the newly coiffed Bursar strolled in.

'You wanted to see me, Minnie?'

Suddenly, Dominica's patience shattered and hurtled off in all directions, mostly towards her hands where it had its work cut out trying to stop them going round the Bursar's neck. She shivered.

'Helena. Please sit down.'

The Bursar fitted herself into the most comfortable chair.

Dominica studied her, trying to decide whether there was any credence in the theory that you could tell if people had criminal tendencies just by looking at them. She came down on the side of no, it's a load of hogwash.

The Bursar soon got fed up of waiting to find out why she'd been summoned. 'Are you all right, Minnie?'

Dominica was startled. 'Mm?'

'You were staring at me.'

'Was I? Oh, sorry, didn't mean to.' There was a short pause, then Dominica steepled her fingers and said, 'What do you know about the orphanage in Bayoake?'

'Bayoake? Nothing, I don't think. Why?'

'You don't know *anything* about the orphanage?'

'I know there is one, but nothing more than that.'

'So, you wouldn't know anything about…' – Dominica spread her hands in a manner which suggested she was oh, I don't know, just picking this out of the air at random, you understand – '…the way it's funded, for instance?'

The Bursar looked puzzled. 'How should I know how it's funded? I've always assumed it was donations from the local community that kept it going.'

'Has The Union ever made any donations to it?'

'What?'

'It's a straightforward question. Has The Union ever made any donations to the Bayoake orphanage?'

'Why should we?'

'That's what I'm trying to find out.'

'What's all this about?'

Dominica's spirits sank. Ask somebody a simple question and what do you get? This could go on for the rest of the day. Only one way to know for sure.

'Forget it. I'll get the books out myself and look.'

The Bursar almost stopped breathing. The accounts were her domain, her empire, and in common with all other emperors and empresses, she was paranoid about defending it. After all, it only needs some fool to leave the empire's back door open for five minutes while they take something out of the oven and before you know where you are, you're overrun with infidels, the whole thing's crumbling around your ears and you're on trial for being a despot, when you were only taking care of things for everybody. The Bursar wasn't having any of that, thank you very much.

'You'll do no such thing!' she said, putting her foot down with a firm hand but forgetting to check what sort of ground she was on.

Dominica's eyebrows leapt. 'Won't I?'

'Accounts are a specialised area,' said the Bursar, smiling sweetly but insincerely.

Dominica matched the Bursar's sweetness with innocence.

'It must be reasonably easy to check.'

'It can't be done by just any old f—, by, by just anyone!'

'I know a woman who can do it.'

'You don't trust me, do you, Minnie? You've never trusted me! You've never even liked me! That's why you stopped me becoming Matriarch, isn't it? Isn't it?'

Dominica hated getting into a spat with the Bursar; she always felt the situation rapidly dropped to playground level. Unfortunately the Bursar was the red rag to her bull.

'There's nothing in the rules that says I have to like you, Helena, just like there's nothing in the rules that says I can stop you if you are nominated. And as you've brought it up, just why are you so keen on becoming Matriarch?'

'I'd give you the sack for a start,' snapped the Bursar.

'You wouldn't need to. Come on, let's hear it. Why do you think you should be Matriarch? No – I'll rephrase that. Why are you convinced you *will* be Matriarch?'

The Bursar was silent.

'What are you hiding?'

The Bursar reddened, her mouth twitching. 'Hiding?'

'Yes, hiding. There's something you're keeping to yourself, Helena, and I want to know what it is.'

'Well, there's nothing in the rules that says I have to tell you, so there.' The Bursar stuck her tongue out.

Dominica closed her eyes for a second then looked at the Bursar again.

'You've no conception of how your behaviour looks to other people, have you?' she said slowly.

'If this is another one of your decorum lectures—'

'Look at it from my point of view. You were *convinced* you'd be nominated Matriarch. Everybody knows that. Imelda dies, and you start going about like a frog that's just found out there's a ban on dissection. When Eleanor's nominated, you throw one of your princess paddies and stomp out. Then Eleanor fails to turn up, and suddenly everything's right with your world again. You're back in with a chance, because if Eleanor fails to turn up entirely, we have to hold an election, and if you win, you'll be the Matriarch, just like you told everybody you would be.'

'So?' said the Bursar petulantly.

'What better reason is there for ensuring Eleanor never turns up?'

The reddening became purple as the Bursar shot to her feet, her eyes like organ stops above a snarling keyboard.

'I don't believe this! You're accusing me of – of – of – doing away with Eleanor? Dominica Tort, how can you say such a thing?'

Dominica was so surprised at hearing her full name she was almost thrown off-balance. Almost, but not quite.

'I'm not accusing you of anything. You are convinced you will be Matriarch; the only way you will get there is by Eleanor's disappearance or death, and you are known to have a violent side to your nature.'

The Bursar strode towards Dominica's desk.

'Me? Violent?'

'You threatened to strike me down quite recently.'

'But I didn't – I – I wouldn't,' the Bursar blustered.

'Maybe not in the everyday course of life—'

'Not in any course of life!'

'But the very idea of not being Matriarch of The Union sparks very strong emotions in you.'

The Bursar leant on her knuckles on the desk.

'And you think that allows you to accuse me of murdering Eleanor?'

'I'm not accusing you of any such thing. I'm just telling you what it looks like from where I'm sitting.'

'Well, thank Mother Nature that's only your opinion,' said the Bursar as she swept towards the door.

'At the moment.'

The Bursar wheeled round.

'You've really got it in for me, haven't you?'

Dominica curled her fingers like claws and bared her teeth. 'Aaagh!'

She stretched back in time to her teaching days. Illustrate by example.

'No, I haven't got it in for you. But from *your* point of view, *that's what it looks like.*'

Unfortunately, this hint sailed straight over the Bursar's head and hit the door, slid down it and crumpled up on the floor, unheeded.

'Because that's how it is, Minnie.'

Dominica slumped onto her desk. 'For the love of—'

'You can't stop me becoming Matriarch. You said so yourself.'

'Will you ever frigging listen? I said I couldn't stop you if you were nominated.' Dominica hauled herself upright. 'But if Eleanor fails to turn up and we hold an election—'

'Yes?'

'—then unless you give me a good reason to change my opinion, I will apply to have you de-registered—'

'What?'

'—and thrown out of The Union.'

The Bursar's sound mechanism went way up into the short pipes.

'Struck off?! You'd have me struck off for an opinion?'

'If I have to.'

'You wouldn't. You wouldn't risk the scandal.'

'*You* can't *afford* to.'

'Oh, can't I?' said the Bursar in a last act of defiance.

Dominica slammed both hands on the desk.

'Helena, how on Mother Nature's good earth did you ever get to be Bursar? You can't even put two and two together! You can't afford it because *if you're struck off*, you will never, *ever*, be Matriarch!'

The silence could have been sliced up and served with lumpy custard.

The Bursar tightened her lips into a momentary snarl, closed her eyes, and then suddenly sagged as if someone had cut her strings.

'All right. Come to my study in about ten minutes. I'll tell you what I can.' She left the room and closed the door.

It was only when Dominica listened to herself sigh with relief she realised she was shaking.

'Can I come out now?' said a voice emerging from under the bed.

Dominica almost broke The Union's High Jump From A Sitting Start record. 'Hell's bells! How long have you been there?'

'Long enough,' said Dennis, like a bloodthirsty schoolboy

with a great tale to tell. 'You don't really think she's killed the Matriarch, do you?'

Dominica sucked her teeth. 'My heart says no, but my eyes and ears are keeping an open mind.'

Dennis walked towards the window. 'Wow!'

'Before you go,' said Dominica, 'you are not to breathe a word of this to anybody, and I mean anybody.'

His evening's entertainment evaporated. 'Aww?'

'If you do, I'll be pussona con grata round here.'

'What's that mean?'

'The woman with the grated cat.'

Dennis stuck his tongue out at her and sloped off in search of clean slates to draw new mischief on.

Naiba burst through the study door. 'I've found her!'

'Auregia?'

'The Matriarch!'

'What?'

'Auregia's Matriarch!' She checked a piece of paper in her hand. 'Constanza Prevarios.'

'Constanza Prevarios? That's a fair way back, isn't it?'

'About five hundred years.'

Dominica winced. Five hundred years; right up there with the fairy at the top of the sign-off tree. A spell needing a live Matriarch to sign it off, and Dominica only had a dead one in stock at the moment.

'On the bright side, Vice-Matriarch,' Naiba beamed, 'at least now we know it's not a presentiment for the future.'

'True, true.'

'So what do we do now?'

'Now we go to— no, now I go see the Bursar, and you go look in the Dictionary.'

'I've never spoken to anybody about this,' said the Bursar quietly. Ever. But you've forced me into it, Minnie. I don't know if I'll ever forgive you.'

'I understand.'

'I hope so.' The Bursar held her head high and closed her eyes. 'I must be Matriarch because it is my destiny.'

Dominica remained silent, waiting for the rest of the story to come tumbling out, but it didn't. 'I'm sorry?' she said.

'It is my destiny to be Matriarch,' said the Bursar, as if this would make any muddy waters crystal clear.

'Could you explain a little further?'

The Bursar looked irritated. 'Explain why it's my destiny?'

'If you could, please.'

The Bursar sighed tetchily. 'Very well, as you insist. There is a spell – a curse – on my family, and I am the only one who can sign it off.'

Oh, great. Just what the world needs: another bloody spell causing havoc in The Union.

'You don't need to be Matriarch to sign off a spell,' said Dominica.

'It's old enough to need Matriarchal sign-off.'

Wonderful.

'How do you know it's got to be you?'

From an old envelope missing a flap the Bursar took one of two pieces of folded, well-thumbed paper. 'This letter.'

My darling daughter,

Full is my heart to write this, but the time has come for you to know the task fate has laid upon you.

Many generations ago, an ancestor of your mother's laid a curse upon an ancestor of mine, for what reason now I know not. All I do know is the curse hangs over our family to this day, and can only be lifted when a child of the curser loves a child of the cursed, and produces a child of that love.

Sweet angel, you are that child and that is why you learnt the arts of your ancestor. You must solve this riddle, for you are the child who alone can lift this curse from our lives and the lives of those to come.

I have written it as I know it, as it has been handed down to me through the generations. We will never speak more of this, for indeed I have told all I know, and at such time as you hold this in your hands, I will be beyond reach.

Constantly I pray you keep well and remember you are and ever have been and ever will be in my heart.

'I take it you got this from your father,' said Dominica.

'During the summer recess when I was about thirteen, I was working in Father's shop and somebody came in and wanted something I couldn't deal with. So, I went into Father's study to fetch him, and he was writing a letter. He went to deal with the customer, and…'

'Curiosity getting the better of all young people?'

The Bursar nodded. 'That night I crept back down to his study and copied it out so I could study it further. And before you ask, I was their only child.'

Dominica pointed to the other piece of paper.

'Is that the spell?'

'It is,' said the Bursar, handing it to her.

Dominica read it. 'Not exactly clear, is it? What does it mean?'

'That's just it – I don't know. I only know I'm the child mentioned and it's up to me to lift the spell.'

'How can you lift a spell if you don't know what it is?'

The Bursar winced. 'I was, well, sort of hoping that it – that I – that once I became Matriarch it would just sort of – present itself.'

Dominica frowned at her. 'There's always hope, I suppose. But perhaps we ought to lend hope a bit of assistance.'

~•~
NOTES ON
The Dictionary

As spells go through their various stages, they write themselves up in ledgers kept in a department housed at the very bottom of the basement of the Library. This department is called the Dictionary and is made up of two parts, the Stable Block and the Unstable Block. The Stable Block holds shelf after shelf of ledgers containing spells which have run their course and are successfully completed and signed-off, and can therefore be said to be 'stable'. The Stable Block is so pitch black and silent that sometimes it's difficult to believe it's there at all.

However, the Unstable Block of the Dictionary is – to put it mildly – a potentially catastrophic place. The ledgers in there are full of spells being created, alongside active spells fizzing away until their time is up plus a proportion of stable spells. Spell ledgers cannot be transferred from the Unstable Block to the Stable Block until all the spells in a ledger are stable. This serves two purposes: firstly, it saves wear and tear on the carpet carrying individual spells across the corridor; secondly, the element of stability within each ledger helps to stop the active spells sending the whole of the Library up in brightly coloured smoke.

Spells being created write themselves on a blank ledger page with an iridescent blue edge; on the back of the page the spell writes up notes on who cast the spell and where it was cast. Once the spell is active, the edge of the page changes to green; as it completes, the green changes to a vivid red, and as they are signed off the border self-ignites and burns like a fuse, giving off a pure white light, leaving behind a black-bordered page containing a stable spell. This enables you to see at a glance the state of any particular ledger, providing your eyes are up to it.

O'Bridge's Table Book gives another useful guide:

The Colour Status Table

Edge Colour	*Spell Status*
Blue	In creation
Green	Active
Red	Completed
Black	Signed off

The sheer number of spells extant in the universe means that at any one time there's an awful lot of unstable magic about, which brings with it the possibility – however remote – of disaster. Long-term spells tend to release small magical resonances into the air which hang smokily in waves and drifts until they can gather enough energy to make a prank; the changing of edge colours gives constant illumination; the fizzling and burbling of active spells provides unending background noise. Combine that with the power of active magic and the odd spell stuck in limbo between completion and sign-off, and you can't blame people for feeling that being in the Unstable Block is like being the match-seller at an arsonists' convention in a dynamite factory.

Absolute authority in the Dictionary comes in the shape of the Spellchecker, although what shape the Spellchecker is can't always be guaranteed. Close proximity to unstable magic has led to an ability to temporarily shapeshift. More often than not she does retain control over her shape, but sometimes she is overridden by the magical resonances forming a practical joke. However, she has warned the resonances with the utmost vehemence that she will personally destabilise the entire Dictionary should things get too out of hand. Or paw. Or claw.

~✦~

At the Dictionary, the reception desk was deserted.

'Good day, Spellchecker,' Naiba called tentatively.

'Good day to you. How may I help you?' said a voice, the location of whose body was not exactly apparent.

The hairs rose on the back of Naiba's neck, then settled again once she realised that this disembodied voice was not the familiar unfamiliar one. She looked around for a vague hint of where the voice might come from but found none, so she carried on with her half of the conversation.

'The Vice-Matriarch sent me to investigate a spell.'

'Oh, yes. You're the girl from Graduation, aren't you?'

Naiba drooped. 'Is that how I'll be remembered?'

'Cheer up. By the time you're eighty you'll have a cult following among the younger students as the only witch ever to punch a Rectrix. In public, at least. Now, this spell. How far back are we talking about?'

Naiba was still wondering what it would be like to be eighty, let alone a cult figure.

'Sorry? Oh, er…' – she looked at the paper in her hand to make sure she got it right; after all, she didn't want to spend too long in the company of excess magic and a voice that came out of thin air – '…Matriarch Constanza Prevarios.'

'Ooh! You don't do things by halves, do you? Stable or unstable?'

'Unstable.'

'Sleeping or non-sleeping?'

'Possibly active, hopefully sleeping,' said Naiba, adding in her own mind, probably decaying.

'Fingers crossed, then. Open the door behind you and we'll get going.'

Naiba looked behind and saw a door she hadn't even noticed previously. She realised it gave an excellent vantage-point for keeping an eye on the reception desk without seeming to be there. Instantly relieved, she opened the door.

'Thank you, Spellchecker,' she said, smiling warmly into an empty cupboard. She blushed.

'Don't worry,' said the voice. 'Everybody makes that mistake. Just put it on.'

The cupboard may have been empty, but the back of the door held an expanse of material which Naiba fought her way into. It had a hole for the head, two sleeves and an absence of any other fastenings.

'What is it?' she asked as her head emerged through the knitted welt which formed the collar and hugged her neck.

'It's a stopcoat.'

Naiba's hands popped through the knitted cuffs like opening flowers. 'A stopcoat?'

'Oh, yes. Mischievous magic in the Unstable Block loves an idle body, you know.'

Naiba felt slighted. 'But I won't be idle.'

'Your head and hands will be busy looking for a particular spell, but the rest of your body will be hanging about with nothing to do, and therefore technically idle and at risk.'

Naiba wondered whether there wasn't some way she could convince the Vice-Matriarch to do this bit. 'At risk?'

'At risk of over-exposure to excess magic, and at risk of magic attaching itself and hitching a lift out of the Dictionary. The stopcoat stops all that.'

The coat draped steadily from the neck to the floor, where the excess material gathered in folds around Naiba's feet, making her look as if she'd been piped out like the soft ice cream sold from carts during the summer. Somewhere in the midst of the surplus surplice piled on the floor was the hem, which was lined with lead shot to keep it on the floor.

'There's a pair of cotton gloves in one of the pockets,' continued the Spellchecker, 'but they're to protect the ledgers as much as to protect you.'

The inside of the huge poncho was covered with enough hidden pockets to remedy the dove-storage problems of the most ambitious conjuror. Naiba pulled her hands back inside and found the gloves.

'Skin secretions play havoc with old manuscripts,' said the Spellchecker. 'It may be just a thumbprint to you, but it could be the kiss of death to a page three hundred years from now.'

Naiba had never thought of herself as dangerous.

'Doesn't the magic protect the pages?'

'It's usually too busy working or mucking about. How do you think I got to be in this state?'

'I'm not quite sure what state you're in, Spellchecker.'

'Put it this way: have you got a notebook and pencil?'

'Yes.'

'Well, if your pencil breaks, use another from the extra supply in one of the stopcoat pockets. Don't even think about sharpening it.'

'The trouble with these,' said the Tutor of Creative Chronicling, re-folding the well-thumbed pages, 'is there's no telling what state they've been mangled into.'

The Bursar was horrified. 'Mangled?!'

'Oh, yes. Half the time they're not worth the paper they're written on.'

The Bursar's face indicated either a torrent of tears or an apoplectic fit.

Dominica acted quickly. 'How do we know which half this falls into?'

'You don't. That's the excitement of it, you see.'

'Excitement?'

'Hey,' said the Tutor, 'in this job you've got to get your kicks where you find them. Each new document is a mystery to be unravelled – a different detective story every time.'

A mixture of disbelief and dread prompted the Bursar to speak. 'How do they get... mangled?'

'Well, just imagine what sort of state you'd be in if you'd been passed down for hundreds of years.'

The Bursar screwed up her face in bewilderment. 'What? What are you talking about, Chronicles?'

The Tutor seized the opportunity to prove there was more to her craft than a stack of postcards, infinite patience and an ability to find something positive in the most appalling text.

'Words are like food,' she said. 'Best preserved when fresh. Unfortunately, because in those days hardly anybody could read and write, things like this curse were originally handed down orally. By the time they *were* written down – usually a good couple of hundred years after the event – they've gone from original source to family legend, often changing location, action and personnel along the way, because of people's bad memories and mondegreens.'

She took the Bursar's open-mouthed blank look as a cue to continue.

'You know when someone finally gives you the words to a song and you find out that what you've been singing for years as *over the fence and into the yard* is in fact *honour, defence and enter the guard?*'

'Oh,' said the Bursar. 'I've always sung *on the defence, an end to regard.*'

'There you go – that's a mondegreen. You see my point? Generations of people could've mondegreened this. Then throw in the fact it might have been passed through someone with a hearing or speech impediment – or both – and you could find yourself up an end that's deader than a cremated cardboard coffin.'

'Indeed,' said Dominica.

The Tutor hadn't finished yet. 'And then there's age. If the story has to be passed to someone very young, the likelihood is they'll get some of the words wrong because they don't know what they're saying, and as they learn new words they'll modify what they thought they heard anyway.'

The Bursar looked for hope. 'But once it's written down, it's all right, isn't it?'

The Tutor shook her head, letting the Bursar know she could look for hope until the cows came home, slept it off and went out again the next night.

'Not necessarily. There's often transcription errors.'

'Transcription errors,' repeated the Bursar, leaving hope to find its own way home.

'With an important family document, whoever's given it to look after usually transcribes it – makes a copy for safekeeping. However, unless they're absolutely scrupulous about it, things can get accidentally changed from one version to the next – that's a transcription error. If that changed version gets passed to the next generation, the error gets passed on. Then the next person takes a copy, could make a mistake, and so on. Plus, spelling hasn't always been standardised so you can get several different versions of the s-a-m-e word within the s-a-y-m text, and even within – or inwith – the s-a-i-m sentence, which leads me on very nicely to comprehension.'

The Bursar was slowly sinking. 'Comprehension.'

'People might not understand what they've been told?' said Dominica.

'Or what they've read,' said the Tutor. 'Both children and adults might modify what they've heard or what they've read so it makes sense to them. Do you want me to explain the theory of clear communication to you?'

Dominica smiled. 'Another time, perhaps.'

The Tutor took the hint.

'Nice,' she smiled. 'I can see you don't need it. Anyway, if a transcription error has occurred and whoever reads it next can't make sense of what's there, they'll put their own value judgements on what they think must have been meant. For example, I once spent ages trying to decipher a story about someone polishing the sunshine. Turns out it was originally *polishing the son's shoon*, shoon being the old plural of shoe. A transcription error meant *shoon* became *shon*, but the next person didn't understand it and so changed it to what he thought it meant.'

'I see,' said Dominica.

'And documents do suffer at the hands of those phoneticists who think it doesn't matter how words are spelt as long as they—' she broke off and scribbled on a sheet of paper which she then held up.

'S-o-w-n-d write?' read the Bursar.

'Exactly. Plus there are intellectual deficients who think punctuation doesn't matter and usually stand at the top of Weetly Hill to throw full stops into a document which means their prose drones on and on and on and by the time you get to the end of their first sentence the subject and object are miles apart in separate counties and the verb is stuck in the middle of no-man's-land while you're well on your way to

Chapter Two without having had the chance to draw a mental breath.'

'Ah,' said Dominica, mainly to prove she was still paying attention.

'But then,' growled the red-faced Tutor, 'they'll get right up close and put apostrophes in like spots on a leopard whose mum's got the measles and in their book that'll end up as spot-apostrophe-s on a leopard who-apostrophe-s mum-no-apostrophe-s got the measle-apostrophe-s.'

'Which means?' asked the Bursar.

'Which means,' came the unenthusiastic reply, 'that all in all, it's a miracle old documents make any sense at all, and frequently many of them don't without an enormous amount of spadework. So you need to ask yourself if this piece of paper's worth even going to the shed for a spade.'

'Please can you tell me which way to go, Spellchecker?' asked Naiba, hoping to find what she was looking for and be out again in the shortest possible time.

'You don't think I'd let you go in there by yourself, do you?' answered the Spellchecker. 'You'd better put me in one of your pockets.'

Naiba put her hand out towards the reception desk, then withdrew it and looked distinctly worried.

'What's the problem?' asked the Spellchecker.

'Erm – I'm not quite sure how to pick you up.'

'I'm a small metal pencil sharpener,' came the reply in a tone which suggested the Spellchecker was rolling eyes that she didn't presently have. 'There's only so many ways you *can* pick me up. And just to make it easier I've even got indentations on the side. Put your finger in one of them, your thumb in the other and grip. You won't hurt me – just don't cover up the hole otherwise I might not be able to breathe. Mind you, I'm only surmising. I'm not sure what I'm breathing through at the moment.'

Naiba gently picked up the pencil sharpener and pulled it through the knitted cuff and along the sleeve of the stopcoat until she was able to place it in one of the pockets. She pushed her arm back down the sleeve again and brushed down the front of the stopcoat to straighten it.

'Ow!' said a voice from inside the stopcoat as Naiba inadvertently brushed too hard and caught the pencil sharpener a glancing blow.

'Sorry,' she winced.

'Let's go,' said the Spellchecker wearily, 'before one of us gets hurt. Go through the door marked *Staff Only.*'

Naiba expected the weight and volume of the stopcoat to restrict her movements. Unfortunately she hadn't passed her expectations onto the stopcoat, which had been designed not only for total body protection, but to anticipate the wearer's movements. So when she set off with more enthusiasm than normal in order to drag the stopcoat along, the stopcoat did the same. She crashed through the door and had hurtled halfway down a dark corridor before surprise tripped her up and she went sprawling and sliding along the polished floor, only coming to rest when she hit a length of carpet which lay across the corridor between two sets of double doors.

'My, my, we are impatient,' said a muffled voice.

'I'm sorry, I'm sorry,' quavered Naiba. 'Are you hurt?'

'No, though I may never sharpen properly again. Where are we?'

Naiba looked up. To her left, the double doors were marked *Unstable Block*. 'I think we're here.'

'Good. We'd better go in then.'

Slowly Naiba got to her feet and pushed open the doors. Once they closed behind her it was as though someone had turned off the world and left her to find the switch, and as her senses became accustomed to the all-consuming blackness, she heard a faint hiss not too far away.

'Just step forward two paces,' said a voice from somewhere round by her knees. 'There's another set of doors just in front of you.'

She put her hands out in front and took two steps, but still jumped when she touched the doors.

'Go on,' said the Spellchecker. 'Push them open.'

Naiba did as she was bidden, and was assailed by so much light and sound she thought she'd stepped out of a black velvet sack into an electrical storm in the middle of a rainbow. She stared for a few seconds at the aurora thaumatalis, and then fell over as she became incredibly heavy on one side.

Any passing observer might have worried that Naiba was about to break the world's fastest birth record, for suddenly there was a large extra lump under the voluminous cloth of the stopcoat and a very surprised look on Naiba's face. However, a cheery call of 'Sorry – only me. Forgot to tell you that bit' reassured her and when she stood up again, she found she was minus a pencil sharpener but plus a full-size Spellchecker, who crawled from under the stopcoat, muttering and waving away curious resonances.

'Ah!' shouted the Spellchecker, dusting herself down. 'Welcome to the Unstable Block of The Union Dictionary.'

Naiba took a good look around because she couldn't help it; the intensity of light and sound simply demanded her attention. She'd heard tales of what it was like in the Unstable Block, of course – every witch trained in The Union was told of its existence and purpose – but no amount of dry educational fact or late-night exaggerated tale-telling could prepare you for the actuality of it all. It was the difference between being told about ice cream and being thrown head-first into a vat of it.

All around, spells were fizzing into life and just as quickly fizzling out again. The newest ledgers would sparkle and glow, changing from blue to green to red to white to black with a brilliance which would have caught your attention even in a fairground. The spells that had moved into black, black stability provided a perfect backcloth for this living kaleidoscope, and just as the sable midnight of the stable spells seemed to heighten the brilliance of the active spells, so the flashes of colour seemed to intensify the inky blackness, as if they knew their fate. For the most part a spell's life was short, powerful and intense and therefore necessarily dramatic.

Sparks flew in every direction from the ledgers, tracing large arcs and swallow-dives in the air as they had their brief moment of glory in a perpetual fireworks display. Channels set into the floor caught the sparks and carried them away to drain into the Magic Pool, jostling and skittering, chafing and chattering like schoolgirls on a day out. It resembled the foundry where the ends of the rainbow were welded together before they fell into the crock of gold.

Occasionally there would be a loud whoosh and a thump as a completely stable ledger would fly from its life-shelf and land on the departure shelves by the double doors, waiting to be transferred into the Stable Block.

'Is it always like this?' shouted Naiba.

'Come on!' shouted the Spellchecker. 'This way!'

They moved through the colourful cacophony.

'Is it always like this?' repeated Naiba.

The Spellchecker nodded as the noise receded a little.

'As it was in the beginning, is now and ever shall be. Mind you,' she added, 'they're only the spells cast by graduates. You should see the vault where the training ledgers are. Even I won't go in there without earplugs and dark glasses. And then only if absolutely necessary.'

She led Naiba away from the riotous party of the recent spell ledgers, passing through the large public bar of the slightly more mature enchantments and into the residents' lounge of the older spells. Here things were much more sedate; there were a couple of large, heavily padded armchairs, a desk and chair, and the lighting was for the most part a gentle, relaxing green with just the occasional red accent light here and there like single poppies in a field. Smoky resonances drifted in the air, some amalgamating and gathering strength as they worked their way back towards the party to get some action, and others languidly posing in the peace and quiet. As Naiba moved, weak wisps of colour coruscated around the stopcoat, trying to find a way in. She lifted her arms as slight wraiths of magical resonances wreathed and chased around her.

'Just brush them off,' said the Spellchecker.

Naiba smoothed down the front of the stopcoat and chuckled as the vapours mingled and shimmered across her hands prior to being cast into the air where they writhed for a few seconds before separating and hanging like smoke rings waiting for a breeze.

The Spellchecker tapped her fingers on the shelves as she walked along.

'Prevarios... Prevarios... ah! Here we are,' she said, reaching up to a ledger.

'Oh, I think this piece of paper's definitely worth it,' said Dominica, much to the Bursar's surprise.

'Great,' said the Tutor, cheering up. 'Then let's see if we can find some word that teems with hidden meaning.' She unfolded the paper again. 'Well, the first line seems plain enough – a cloaking spell – *this curse hide one*. If we put a full stop in there, then *A grand will fall* – a grand what?'

'A grand person, like a duke or a king?' said Dominica.

'A grand is an old accounting term for a thousand,' said the Bursar. 'Could it be a thousand men will fall?'

'Could be. *Four under pennant damage done* – four under a flag?'

'Soldiers?' said Dominica.

'Under the flag of the duke?' suggested the Bursar, sensing aristocratic blood coursing through her veins.

'Possibly. *Damage done* – sabotage? A special mission to the enemy camp? Hmm.' The Tutor chewed her bottom lip in concentration. 'I think the next five lines are all one sentence. Look: if we put commas in and a full stop at the end, we get *The children shall the greedy pay until the house and mine be one* – the owner of a big house gaining control of a mine? – *until a single child they bear, until a child with gin jar new* – could be a reference to brewing, or even glass-making, producing a better gin bottle – *be born unto a destiny.*'

'So that means,' said Dominica, 'the children shall pay something to someone until a certain child is born?'

'Looks like it.'

'*Until the house and mine be one,*' repeated the Bursar. 'Mines are usually underground, and houses above, so... until the house is flattened and the mine filled in?'

'It's possible,' said the Tutor, 'but *house* can also be used to mean a family, as in *the house of Jacket* or *the house of Tort*, and as it goes on to talk of a child, that's probably the more likely explanation. A *mine* was often used as a symbol for trade or industry, and we've got military references in at the start, so it could be that this child will be born when the military family – presumably quite high-ranking, as in the duke or king – marries into a family in trade.'

The Bursar was almost beside herself, which wouldn't have left much room round the desk. She'd made Dominica promise that the origin of the document remained secret, so she couldn't very well give the game away by shouting, 'My father was in trade! My father was in trade!'

'*His sack of pennants shall be two*,' the Tutor went on. 'A *sack* was often used to denote an amount or quantity, and there's an echo of the *pennant* from the first few lines. You've got to remember that people in trade were classed as being of a lower social order than all but the very lowest military ranks, so such a marriage would be considered to involve a drop in status for the military family.'

The Bursar looked indignant, but only Dominica noticed.

'However,' continued the Tutor, 'the birth of this child appears to restore and indeed augment that status – going from one pennant to two. Maybe this child was born to be more prosperous than its antecedents.' The Bursar now fizzing like a glass of fresh lemonade didn't distract the Tutor as she concentrated on the written words. 'Oh, now that's interesting,' she said. 'That's very interesting indeed.'

'What? What?!' shouted the Bursar. The Tutor and Dominica both looked at her. She giggled and put her hand over her mouth until she was sure she wasn't smiling any more, then took her hand away. 'Sorry,' she said diffidently. 'I had no idea old documents could be so... interesting.'

'Quite,' said Dominica. 'So what is *interesting* about it?'

The Tutor pointed at the paper. 'See here – the rhyme scheme's changed.'

'Rhyme scheme?'

'The first half rhymes every second line, then you get a block of six rhyming couplets, then it's back to rhyming every second line. That's very interesting.'

'But does it matter?' asked Dominica.

'On the whole, I'd say yes, it does. As I said, these things were handed down orally to start with, and one way of prompting people to remember is by using a regular rhythm and rhyme scheme. Like *Maisie had a little sheep.*'

'What?' said the Bursar.

The Tutor's eyebrows lifted. 'You know:
*Maisie had a little sheep,
Its fleece was just like wire,
It played around with matches and
It set itself on fire.*'

'What the hell has Maisie got to do with anything?'

'Maisie? Nothing. The rhythm? Everything. Having heard the word *wire* and knowing the rhythm of the thing, you'd never say *It went up like a rocket* as the last line, would you? Get it?'

'But what does it *mean*, Chronicles?' exclaimed the Bursar. 'What does it *mean*?!'

'Well, some people think Maisie is a metaphor—'

The Bursar stabbed at the paper with her forefinger. 'This one! This one!'

'Oh, I see. Well, the first part and the third part seem to be dealing with the birth of this child who will restore the family fortunes and lift the spell. The middle bit seems to be from something completely different.'

Naiba's heart beat faster as the Spellchecker gripped the ledger. Fact said it was possible that the spell she was looking for was green – still active and therefore still under control –

but intuition said it was probably red: completed, and therefore a law unto itself. And whilst fact, possibility, intuition and probability were usually at the same party, it was rare they stood in the kitchen talking to each other. Naiba shut her eyes.

The Spellchecker pulled the ledger down.

'Looks like the only book left for Prevarios... yes, that's it.' As she placed it on the desk, she noticed Naiba's eyes were closed. 'Take your time,' she said gently. 'I'll just be over here if you need me.' She settled into an armchair and knotted resonances together to make a cat's cradle.

On the premise 'never put off till tomorrow what you can do today, because if you do it today and it's awful, at least it hasn't buggered up tomorrow', Naiba opened her eyes.

Most of the page edges were black – black enough to let you know they had been black for a very long time – except for a single, very obvious red one. Naiba's heart sank. Intuition and probability were dancing a drunken jig with their fists in the air, whooping up another victory whilst fact and possibility got their hats and coats and went home with the monk on. There was only one thing to do. She opened the ledger. Before her, a thin trail of red resonance steaming from the edge of its page, lay a completed spell which could be sleeping, decaying or working on out of habit, but wasn't about to let on which. She groaned and scanned the notes on the back of the spell.

'Found it?' asked the Spellchecker.

'*Oh yes, I'm here,*' said a familiar unfamiliar voice.

'Sorry?'

'Nothing,' said Naiba gloomily. 'May I copy this out?'

The Tutor peered over the top of her spectacles. 'Are you sure it's all one thing?'

'As sure as we can be,' said Dominica.

'Then I'd say there's definitely something missing. You don't mess up your rhythm and rhyme scheme for no good reason, not if you want something to be preserved. However, it might have been bolerised.'

'Bolerised?'

'Mm. A couple of hundred years ago some chap called Boler decided that a lot of the entertainments of the time were too bloodthirsty, or showed people in the wrong light, that sort of thing, and so he sanitised them to make them more' – she bent and flexed the first two fingers on each hand – '"acceptable".'

'You think he might have sanitised this?' asked the Bursar.

The Tutor laughed. 'No, no, not personally. But if this had to be handed down to a child, somebody might have taken out the gorier bits as long as they preserved as much of the original meaning as they could. So, *One time in every hundred year* – that's self-explanatory – *One of the children disappear* – could be kidnap, or murder—'

'Murder?' choked the Bursar. 'W— why mur— why— why couldn't it be… invisibility?'

'Emigration?' suggested Dominica.

'Bingo!' said the Tutor, clicking her fingers. 'Precisely my point. Somebody's taken out the detail, yet kept, presumably, the overall sense of the thing. It says *Cursed family shall prosper well* from the child's disappearance, but doesn't explain how.'

'One less mouth to feed?' hoped the Bursar.

'Could be anything from adoption to zoological interference. But I'd say it was something unpleasant, else why bother taking the detail out?'

Dominica sighed. 'So, what is seems to be is: as long as the family gives up one of their children—'

'Ah,' said the Tutor. 'It's not necessarily *their* child – it might be that as long as *a* child disappears once every hundred years, the family fortune is secure, but if something happens to prevent a child disappearing, the fortune will be lost. Probably in a fire,' she added helpfully. 'Then, when a certain child is born – the child whose coming has been foretold – the spell is lifted.'

'Leaving the family fortune intact?' enquired the Bursar.

'Who knows? It might mean the prosperity of the family no longer depends upon the disappearance of a child. Why do you ask?'

'Oh, just curious.'

'What about the end?' asked Dominica. 'It says *His awful spell can be complete*. Why *His*?'

The Tutor tapped her fingers on her chin. 'Yes, interesting that. It might mean it's not one of our spells.'

'What?' exclaimed the Bursar. 'Not one of— why wouldn't it be one of ours?'

'Well, *His* would seem to indicate the spell has been cast by a man. And we haven't had any men graduate from The Union, have we?'

Dominica could almost hear the Bursar's heart plummet to the floorboards. 'Remember, Helena – nothing is certain.'

But the Bursar wasn't listening. The Bursar couldn't hear anything except her own voice repeating 'a wizard's spell… a wizard's spell…' as she stood up straight, and withdrew so far into herself it looked as if it would be a day's journey to get her back again. She walked trance-like out of the room.

'Don't worry – I'll go after her in a minute,' said Dominica. 'Could it really be a wizard's spell?'

'Could be. Or *His* could be a transcription error.'

'How? It's only three letters long!'

'Ah, but centuries ago, one of the ways of writing the sound *th* was to use a special letter of the alphabet. Trouble is, that special letter looked a bit like a y, so words that looked like *yat* and *yis* were actually *that* and *this.* Are you with me?'

Dominica concentrated. 'With you so far.'

'Good. When spelling was standardised, somebody decided the y-looking thing was too confusing and it was dropped from the alphabet.'

'Which is why we spell words like *this* with a th?'

'Correct,' said the Tutor. 'But there's still all these old manuscripts knocking about with the y-looking thing in. Years later somebody comes along who doesn't know about the y-looking thing and they transcribe what they think the words are, based on what the words look like. Get me?'

'Get you.'

'So *yat* becomes *yet* – or *gate* or *get* or *got* because sometimes they thought it was a g. And by the same token, *yis* becomes *yes* or *his*.'

'Why *his*?'

'Context. In this case, it wouldn't make any sense to say *Yes awful spell shall be complete*. But *yis* sounds a bit like *his* and that makes a lot more sense. So you've gone from *Yis awful spell* to *His awful spell*.'

'I see.'

'It's either that or they've just missed the T off the beginning of the line.'

'Oh.'

'I told you, these things are notoriously unreliable. We've got a story out of this that could be a complete load of rubbish.'

In his basket, Dennis was just on the twitching-point of sleep, where half his brain was convinced he was awake and the other half was convinced he was just about to fall off the pavement. The latter half won and a spasm shot down his leg. He moaned, and as he stretched, his waking half was alert enough not only to see the study door open and two figures enter but also to reclaim all the cells lost to the dreaming half of his brain.

'Dom?' said a voice.

Dennis spoke through a yawn. 'She's not here, JW.'

'Ah. Know where she is, flower?'

'Bursar.'

'Cheers. Night, Dennis.'

'Night, JW.'

'Night, little kitty,' said Marianna, behind JW.

'Grr.'

As they walked towards the Bursar's study, Marianna said, 'He calls you JW?'

'Course he does. What's he call you?'

'Cheat, mostly.'

'What are you doing, Helena?' asked Dominica, although it was obvious from the half-filled suitcase and open drawers.

'Packing,' said the Bursar flatly, scooping up clothes from a drawer and dropping them into the case. 'Claude, have you got your things together yet?'

'But why are you packing?'

The Bursar continued to throw clothes into the case.

'Because I'm leaving. Leaving this place, this life, this – this identity. Get a move on, Claude!'

Toffee-Nosed Claude looked as though someone had taken his brain out and replaced it with a slack rubber band, rendering him incapable of thinking and moving at the same time, so he was concentrating on thinking about what she'd said. Leaving The Union? Going out – out there? After all she'd promised him? Oh, my dear, it was too much to bear.

'But why?' Dominica persevered.

The Bursar moved to the bookcase and selected three volumes. Her voice was calm and steady.

'Because I don't want to be here any more. I don't want to be me any more. There is no me. It's all been a lie. A huge, vast joke at my expense. Well, the joke's over.' She threw the volumes into the case. 'Claude, if you don't make a move I'll take you as you stand.'

Toffee-Nosed Claude could only stare at her as she strode across the room to open her wardrobe.

Dominica was genuinely shocked. She'd never heard the Bursar give her a straight answer without some form of jibe attached, even if it was only 'Minnie'. This was something different. All the points-scoring one-upmanship had vanished. It was as though the real Helena Jacket had stepped out from under the personality of the Bursar and the weight of generations of family expectation.

'You don't know—' Dominica started.

'You were right. I'm not going to be Matriarch.' The Bursar threw the broom part of her broomstick in the case, then folded the stick and threw that in as well. 'I'm not going to sign off this spell.' She put on her cloak and hat, and jammed the collapsed hatbox on top of the broom and stick and clicked the case shut. 'I'm not going to achieve my destiny, because I don't have one.'

She picked up the case and hooked her arm under the still-static Toffee-Nosed Claude, who promptly fainted with shock. She straightened up and walked towards the door.

'You heard her,' she said. 'It's not one of our spells.'

Dominica grabbed the Bursar's shoulders and looked straight in her eyes. 'I heard her. You didn't. She said it may not be one of ours, but it may well just be a transcription error. You can't leave until we've found out for definite.'

There was a knock on the door.

'In a minute!' shouted Dominica.

'I don't want to know any more. Please let me go.'

Dominica saw a woman let down not only by many

generations of revered ancestors but by her adored father, and that was a generation too many. For perhaps the only time in her life, Dominica felt sorry for the Bursar. She let go of her.

'As you wish.'

The Bursar was silent. Dominica opened the door, and the Bursar walked out of her study and down the corridor with suitcase, cat and dignity intact. Dominica stared after her and whispered to herself. Down in the Dictionary, an iridescent blue edge flashed emerald green.

'Ooh, trouble at t'mill, Mistress Tort?' said a voice from the shadows.

'Aye. Trouble at t'mill, Mistress Arcrite.'

The sleek, dark-eyed cat winked seductively at Dennis and inclined her head in a 'follow me' gesture. He padded after her, the curve and swish of her tail sending new life through him. She led him into a softly lit room and across to a huge cat-basket sumptuously padded with red leather cushions. She stopped, lowered her head and looked up at him from under half-closed lids. He gently rubbed his head against hers, the meshing of their fur massaging his skin.

The door to the study burst open courtesy of Naiba, who had declaimed the words, 'Vice-Matriarch, I've got the spell!' before realising the room was empty. Well, almost.

Dennis's lady-love faded.

'Not here!' he snapped. 'With the Bursar.'

The rude awakening had set his fur on end, and he rippled as it calmed. He closed his eyes and tried to reconjure a sleek lady cat with dark eyes, but she had gone to enrich the dreams of others. Lucky buggers.

'Thanks, Spirit,' said Naiba.

'Oh, don't mention it,' he muttered bad-temperedly, but she had gone also.

The Bursar put the case on the floor behind the main front door. Toffee-Nosed Claude had come round but, as he was in the biggest sulk of his life, he still hung limply over her arm. She turned the large iron ring which lifted the latch, and gently pulled. The door did not move. She pulled harder. All the door did was rattle. She looked up at the top bolt.

'Fool,' she muttered, drew back the top and bottom bolts and turned the ring again. The bolts shot home. The Bursar snorted. She draped Toffee-Nosed Claude across the case, drew back the top bolt and held it in place with her right hand, drew back the bottom bolt and held it in place with her right foot, and tried the latch ring again. No use. The door would not open. She let go, stood back and said, 'Door?'

The bolts shot home again.

'Can't do it,' said the iron ring, bending and flexing to form the words like a disembodied mouth.

'Can't do what?'

'Can't let you out.'

The Bursar stared hard at the iron ring.

'I command you to let me out.'

'Nothing I'd like better, believe me. My raisin detra, you might say, but unfortunately—'

The Bursar raised her hand, a spell forming in her mind.

'Won't work,' said the ring. 'I'm under orders.'

The Bursar's hand dropped. 'Whose orders?'

'Vice-Matriarch's orders, so, sorry, no can do— oof!'

The bolts drew back, the latch lifted and the door swung inwards. The Tutor of Creative Chronicling walked in, and out of politeness held the door open until the Bursar had hold of it.

'Hello again, Bursar,' she said.

'Evening, Chronicles.'

There were many questions the Tutor wanted to ask the Bursar about the spell, but she saw the suitcase and decided to walk away. The Bursar propped open the door with her foot, tucked Toffee-Nosed Claude under her arm, picked up her case and looked out at the clear, uninterrupted, obstacle-free view. She glanced at the iron ring.

'So, can't let me out, eh?' she said, striding past the wide open door.

'Afraid not,' said the ring, as the Bursar's case bounced off an invisible wall and dropped out of her jarred hand. 'Only letting in, not out.'

The Bursar knocked on the view. It rang like glass.

'Very well,' she said, 'I'll go out of the back door.'

'You can try,' said the iron ring.

The study door opened slightly.

'She's with the bloody Bursar!' yelled Dennis.

The door shut quickly. In the corridor, raised eyebrows indicated that it was the first time this particular form of naming had been used. To her face, anyway. By a cat.

Dennis snorted, left his basket and stomped towards Dominica's desk.

'Anyway,' said Dominica as she, Marianna and JW entered the Incident Room, 'now you're up to speed on Helena, tell me how you two got on today. Find anything?'

'Oh, yes,' said Marianna. 'We found that Deartreen Wood consists of hundreds of trees and dozens of paths, all of which were thoroughly searched with a net result of one.'

Dominica sat by the desk. 'One what?'

'One deaf old bloke,' said JW.

'And again I say: one what?'

'All we saw,' said Marianna, 'was one deaf old man walking through the woods. We did send Constable Sennet to ask him a few questions but he lost him.'

'Typical rozzer,' commented JW.

There was silence for a few moments then Dominica said, 'Can I ask a question?'

'Ask away, old thing,' said Marianna.

'How do you know he was deaf?'

JW chuckled. 'Put it this way: I'd back that rozzer against anybody in next year's Town Crier contest.'

'But the old man didn't hear him,' said Marianna.

Dominica drummed her fingers on the desk. 'And you're sure you checked the whole wood?'

'Every last inch.'

'Show her your plan, Chalky,' said JW.

Dominica laughed. 'Chalky?'

Marianna pulled a face and took a playful swipe at JW,

then laid a large-scale map of Deartreen Wood on the desk. Dominica was not surprised to see a grid plan marked on the map; in each of the boxes of the grid was a large cross.

'Every time we started or ended a path, we marked the nearest tree on that path, so we wouldn't check the same one over and over,' Marianna explained. 'And every time we completed a square, we crossed it off.'

'Very systematic is our Chalky,' grinned Dominica.

'If systematic doesn't work, we may have to resort to systermagic,' said JW.

Marianna gave her a withering look. 'I can see the fresh air hasn't done *you* any good.'

JW yawned and stretched. 'It's worn me out. Next time, I'm having the chalk and you' – she prodded Marianna – 'can get yourself up the trees. Honest, Dom, I've climbed more bloody trees than ivy. So if you don't mind, I'll get some shut-eye.'

'I think we all need to,' said Dominica, getting to her feet. 'Fancy a nightcap? Chalky? Ivy?'

JW's comment was forestalled by a knock on the door. She opened it. 'Whatever you're selling we don't want any.'

It was Naiba. 'I'm not selling anything, Mistress Arcrite. I'm looking for the Vice-Matriarch.'

'In you come; there she is.'

Naiba went in. 'I've found her, Vice-Matriarch.'

'Found her?' chorused Dominica, Marianna and JW.

Naiba looked startled. 'You did send me to find her.'

JW shut the door.

'Where is she?' said Marianna.

Dominica managed to leap from one train of thought to another with only a slight stagger. 'Hang on, Marianna – it's not what you think. Naiba's been trying to find the witch in that story. So who is she?'

'Her name was Auregia Skinton,' said Naiba, 'and she lived in Deartreen Wood.'

'Deartreen Wood?' the other three said in unison.

Naiba looked apologetic. 'Look, no offence, but I wish you wouldn't do that. It's really spooky.'

'Sorry,' they said, one after the other.

Naiba gave the copied spell to Dominica. 'And it's red. Completed and awaiting sign-off.'

'Whereabouts in Deartreen Wood?' asked Marianna.

'Sorry, it doesn't say. Just – in the wood.'

'Well she's not there now,' said JW, just before the door opened and knocked her sideways.

The Bursar walked in, carrying cat and case. 'Please let me out of the building.'

Behind her the door swung shut again, revealing JW with bared teeth and raised fist about to gladly punch the Bursar off the premises. She was only prevented from doing so by Marianna, who struggled to restrain her and said, 'I'm sure it was an accident, JW.'

The Bursar looked round at them.

'Sorry, I didn't know you were there,' she said and looked back at Dominica.

Marianna and JW stopped struggling and stared first at each other, then at the Bursar. Sorry? The Bursar said sorry?

'I must be tired,' said JW. 'I'm hallucinating.'

'No,' said Marianna, 'I heard it as well.'

Dominica, staring at the spell, was oblivious to all this until the Bursar said, 'Vice-Matriarch?'

'Mm? What? Oh, Helena. You're here.'

'*Please* let me out of the building.'

'No.'

Toffee-Nosed Claude sprang into life, jumped from the Bursar's arm and ran to Dominica. She looked down at him, then at the Bursar, who seemed on the verge of tears, then back at the spell.

'Nobody's going anywhere,' she said, 'except to bed to get a good night's sleep. Go on – all of you. And if you can't sleep, take something. I want you all fresh, awake, alert and in my study first thing in the morning.'

Toffee-Nosed Claude hugged Dominica's leg, his face a mixture of relief and total adoration.

The next time Dominica looked up from the spell, she was surprised to see someone standing watching her.

'Marianna? Why haven't you gone to bed?'

Marianna shrugged. 'It didn't seem polite to get undressed while you were still in my room.'

As she approached her own study, Dominica was intrigued to see a note stuck on the door. Drawing nearer, she smiled as she read the message which had been written by a paw dipped in ink: *She is with the Bursar. Go away.*

Naiba thought she'd be reluctant to close her eyes, scared of what dreams the night may bring, but her body knew what it lacked and soon she was in peaceful oblivion, much like JW and Marianna who, in their respective studies, both felt they'd done a good day's work and deserved a good night's rest. Dominica knew she needed sleep to be ready for the following day and so, quite sensibly, refused to have any truck with staying awake worrying. The Bursar didn't even bother getting undressed but passed the night in her cloak and boots on top of the bedclothes, exhausted from the day's disappointments.

It was that same hour of the morning when bone-tired night-shift workers all over Maund were climbing into beds still warm from their previous occupants. Marianna, JW, Naiba and the Bursar were gathered in Dominica's study, along with enough tea to keep even JW happy. Various papers were laid out on the desk.

'Now bear with me on this,' said Dominica. 'I think I know where all this is leading physically, but thaumaturgically is another matter. First of all, I need complete co-operation *without question* from each and every one of you. Clear?'

Four people nodded but only three people knew she wasn't talking to them.

'Good. So let's start with Naiba. She's managed to get to the root of the unfortunate incidents at Graduation.'

Dominica picked up two pieces of paper, handed one to Naiba and walked round the room. 'It's a spell needing sign-off. We're going to read it to you, and I want you to pay very close attention.'

She stopped behind the Bursar's chair and signalled to

Naiba. 'Ready? Very well. Slowly, please.'

The atmosphere thickened as the sound of Naiba's voice all but overrode Dominica's whisper.

> '*Thys curse I do on Grandel call*
> *For unrepentant damage done:*
> *Thy childer shal thy greed repay*
> *Until thy house and mine be one*
> *Until a single child they bear*
> *Until a child of gynger hue*
> *Be born unto our dynastys*
> *Thys acte of penance shal ye do:*
> *One time in every hundred year*
> *One of thy childer shal ye tak*
> *And grynd them, skyn and bone and all*
> *The corpus zingiber to mak*
> *To use to bak the swete deleights*
> *To sell to mak the shyning geld*
> *To kepe the orphan home alyve*
> *And not a lyving soule be teld*
> *Cursed family shal prosper well*
> *And have the geld ye did desyre*
> *But try to stoppe thys magyck and*
> *Theyrn fortune crumbles in the fyre*
> *But when a single child of ourn*
> *Shal cross thy path and ye shal mete*
> *That child releases then thy bond*
> *Thys aweful spell shal be complete.*'

The Bursar looked up at Dominica. 'You weren't saying what she was saying, were you?'

'Not exactly, no.'

The Bursar whimpered and gripped the arms of the chair so tightly her knuckles whitened.

'Are you all right, Helena?' asked Marianna as the colour drained from the Bursar's face.

'Put your head between your knees,' said JW, and to her surprise, the Bursar obeyed, letting out a long moan as she did so.

'Will you tell them, Helena?' said Dominica.

The Bursar's thick chestnut tresses shimmered as she shook her head.

'Then I shall.'

The Bursar did not protest.

'What I was reading,' said Dominica, 'has come down through the Bursar's family for generations. You probably gathered it's a curse spell which needs to be signed off by a certain child born into the family. The Bursar believes she is that child who has to sign off the spell.'

'When you say "for generations",' said Marianna, 'exactly how many generations?'

'Over five hundred years' worth.'

'So to sign off the spell, she'd need to be— ah…'

Around the room there was much dropping of pennies and wise nodding of heads.

'So that's why me and Marianna are here,' said JW. 'I did wonder.'

'Correct. And now everybody's in the picture, let's recap. As you've heard, it's not pleasant, although *that is not the fault of anyone here*,' said Dominica. 'It seems every hundred years one of the family's children is… er, um, let's say… turned into this thing called corpus zingiber.'

The horrified Bursar sat bolt upright. 'WHAT?!'

'Now before you go off the deep end…'

'Deep end? Deep end?!' she shrieked. 'Do you know what you've just said?'

'Calm down, Helena,' said Dominica quietly.

The Bursar leapt from the chair.

'Calm down?! After what you've just said? I'm not stopping here to—'

'Oh yes you are.'

'Not this time. I've had it up to here with you. You must really hate me. You stop me becoming Matriarch, accuse me not only of stealing from The Union's funds but of murdering Eleanor, and you blackmail me into co-operating with you just so you can accuse my family of murdering children!'

'BURSAR! SIT DOWN!'

The temperature dropped by several degrees, the pictures straightened themselves on the wall and even the curtains stood to attention. Three people were holding their breath, watching the other two who were breathing hard enough for all of them. The Bursar sat, silently fuming.

If words had weight, she was in for a burying.

'We all,' said Dominica, '– including you – heard the spell. We all – including you – know what it said. So we all – including you – know what we're dealing with. And if you accuse me one more time of stopping you becoming Matriarch, then as Mother Nature is my witness, *I will have you thrown out of The Union*. Now sit there, and don't say another bloody word until you're asked. Understood?'

The Bursar said nothing, but the veins in her temples throbbed and everyone heard her teeth grinding.

'Shall I put a personal restraining order on you?'

The Bursar shook her head by a fraction of a degree.

'Good,' said Dominica, turning away from the Bursar. 'Now, where was I?'

The three others breathed again.

'Zingiber?' Marianna prompted.

'Oh yes, zingiber.' Dominica paused. 'Perhaps it's better if I tell you a story. Once upon a time…'

By the time Dominica had finished telling a cut-down version of the story, Marianna had drawn flow diagrams, JW's tea was cold and the Bursar was breathing normally.

'Just tell me one thing,' said JW.

'What?' said Dominica.

'Just tell me all our cakes and biscuits are home-made.'

'Of course.'

'And the spell is red, isn't it?' asked Marianna.

'It is.'

'Red?' said the Bursar. 'But that means it's completed.'

'I know,' said Dominica levelly. 'It means Spellcaster's Conditions have been fulfilled, so you must have met Grandel already.'

The Bursar's eyes widened and her mouth opened.

'Is there something you're not telling us, Bursar?' asked JW, and Dominica's heart sank.

'JW…' she reproved.

'Now look,' said the Bursar. 'I know no more about this than you do. I've met hundreds – thousands – of people in my life. How do I know whether I've met him or not?'

'I'd've thought you'd remember if you'd met somebody that were five hundred year old,' said JW.

'Ah, but he might not look that old,' said Marianna. 'Long-term spells don't work like that, do they?'

'What?' said the Bursar.

'Mother Almighty,' said JW. 'Did you graduate at all?'

'What? What are you talking about?'

JW sighed and shook her head. 'It's first-level stuff! If you want a prince to wake up the princess in a hundred years' time, you don't want him waking up someone who looks like his great-granny. And if you curse somebody to do something for a thousand years, you don't want him dropping dead after the first ninety – it'd be a waste of time and magic. In long-term spells, time slows down, or even stops. The Law of Preserved Time, remember?'

'Yes! Yes, of course!' cried the Bursar.

'Which means,' said Naiba, 'he might look just the same as he did the day he was cursed, or any age after that.'

'Which means I could have met him at any point during my lifetime! When I was a baby, even! How am I expected to remember that?'

This morsel of food for thought lodged in the back teeth of four brains, where it was subconsciously chewed over.

'So what's the next step?' asked Marianna.

'Well,' said Dominica, 'I want you and JW to go back to Deartreen Wood and give it another thorough going over.

There must be something there we're not seeing. Helena, you go with them. Another pair of eyes won't hurt. Naiba and I will go to Fishwick's Confectioners and see what we can find out about where they get their ingredients from.'

'Fishwick's?' said JW.

'They're not the only bakers around, I know. But they are based in Bayoake, where the orphanage is, and they do deliver bread and cakes to the orphanage, and Naiba thought the writing on the letter to Secure-Igor looked like the writing on Fishwick's food bags and delivery carts. Why?'

'It's Ashton Fishwick's bairn that's gone missing.'

'I'm not seeing anyone,' came a voice from the office.

'It's the Vice-Matriarch of The University of Nature,' said the secretary.

'Show her in.'

The secretary stepped aside as Dominica and Naiba entered Ashton Fishwick's office. Ashton leapt up from behind his desk and greeted them.

'Good day, Mistress Tort, Mistress...?'

'Hudwicz,' supplied Naiba.

'Please, sit down. Why— what can I— do you— do you bring help to find my daughter? Do you bring news?'

Dominica hoped fervently that no news would be good news.

'No, unfortunately we have no news, I'm afraid, Mr Fishwick. But we are here to help, and in order to do so, we just need a bit of... um... information from you.'

'Information? What information? I'll tell you anything.

What can I tell *you* that I haven't told *anybody* who'll help me find my daughter?'

Dominica swallowed hard. 'Now, I know this is going to sound a little odd, but... the information we need is... where you get your ingredients from.'

Ashton couldn't have looked more bewildered if he'd just found out he was his own grandfather.

'Sorry? Mistr— Mistress Tort, my daughter is missing and you – you want to know—'

'Mr Fishwick. Believe me, I only ask because it may be the key to your daughter's disappearance. One of your suppliers may be involved.'

'A supplier? Who? Which supplier? Why—'

'It *may* be a supplier, Mr Fishwick. Which is why we need to know—'

'But why a supplier? We pay a fair rate for everything, we support the local economy, we keep people in jobs—'

'So everything is produced locally?'

'Absolutely. And if one of the farmers has got a grudge against me—'

'Including the corpus zingiber?' Dominica threw in, not quite knowing what reaction she would get.

First of all, Ashton looked as though someone had told him his backside was on fire, then he shot a glance over to a painting hanging on the wall and his face assumed a look of innocence as convincing as a green beard. 'I'm sorry? Corpus...?'

'*Corpus zingiber*,' said a familiar unfamiliar voice.

'Uh?' said Ashton, looking at Naiba.

'For every item to be produced: one grain of corpus zingiber to be added to the mixture of flour, butter, sugar, ginger, treacle, cinnamomum, saleratus... Do you wish me to give you the exact amounts of the other ingredients?'

Ashton went more the colour of meringue than gingerbread. He walked over to the painting and pulled it aside. The safe behind it didn't look like it had been tampered with. 'Er – no, no... no need.'

'*Good,*' said the voice, '*because I'm not sure I could remember them. It has been five hundred years, you know.*'

'What do you mean "rum goings-on"?' asked the Bursar.

'When we were here yesterday we marked all the trees at the start and end of the paths,' explained Marianna.

'And now they're all as clean as a whistle,' said JW.

The significance of this did not come within orbit of the Bursar, let alone striking distance. 'So?'

'So somebody has rubbed the marks off.'

'Why?'

'It's obviously "Keep Deartreen Tidy" week, why do you think?' snapped JW.

'Somebody is trying to put us off the scent,' said Marianna, cutting off the bickering. 'And that means the scent leads somewhere. Let's start again.'

Ashton turned the dials on the safe, but kept missing the correct numbers because his hands were shaking. When he spoke, his voice had obviously caught what his hand had.

'C-corpus zingiber is our t-trade secret, Mistress Tort. I

could be doing irreparable harm to the business just by… just by talking about it.' He managed to open the safe and took out an ancient piece of paper which he looked at then locked away again. He faced Dominica and mopped his brow with a handkerchief. 'I… I shouldn't even be acknowledging its existence.'

'But we already know it exists,' she said. 'And – Mother Nature help us – we even know roughly how to make it.'

Ashton's eyelids opened so wide Naiba thought his eyeballs were going to fall out.

'Do you?' he squeaked. 'Then you already know more than I do.'

'I'm glad to hear it,' said Dominica.

He opened a large window and sat down unsteadily on the sill, loosened his collar and fanned himself.

'But how— how do you know about this? And w-what do you want from me?'

'All we need to know,' said Naiba, 'is where you get it.'

Ashton looked down through the open window at his bakery workers and sighed as if it were his last breath.

'I can't tell you.'

'You must and you will, Mr Fishwick,' said Dominica. 'Because whoever supplies the corpus zingiber may be responsible for the disappearance of your daughter.'

Considering he'd never been on the back of a broomstick before, Ashton Fishwick was doing a remarkable job of hanging on to Dominica, his sanity and the contents of both ends of his digestive tract.

'Whereabouts exactly?' called Dominica.

Ashton dared not open his eyes, and was surprised he was able to open his mouth.

'I can't tell you from up here,' he shouted back. 'Only ever done it on foot.'

They hovered low on the edge of Deartreen Wood.

'You can let go now,' said Dominica.

'I don't think I can,' he said. 'My fingers are locked.'

Cold water and willpower, she thought, prising his fingers open. She heard the start of the long, heartfelt scream of someone falling from the sky; a scream that never had time to get into full swing before it was cut off by a thud as Ashton met the ground much sooner than expected.

'It's a lot easier if you just put your feet down,' she said.

'I'm not sure I'm cut out for flying,' said Ashton.

'Of course you're not. If you'd been cut out for flying, you'd have been cut out in the shape of a bird.'

They walked through the wood with Ashton leading the way.

'Shouldn't we wait for Mistress Hudwicz?' he asked.

'She'll be here later. She's going back to The Union first to pick something up for me.' Dominica paused. 'Why didn't you want to tell me where you get the corpus zingiber?'

'As I said, it appears to be the secret of our success as a business.'

'Appears to be?'

'The gingerbread's our most popular line – it brings in the most money – and although the zingiber is hideously expensive, we can't make our gingerbread without it.'

'Can't?'

'I've tried. I couldn't exactly see what it did for the biscuits. I examined it and tested it, and couldn't find out what it was, so I thought we'd leave it out. For a month we experimented with no end of different recipes but the damned stuff wouldn't bake.'

'Did you vary the cooking time?' said Dominica, immediately regretting it as she realised she was getting the eggs out to show Granny a new trick.

'Do you know what gingerbread should look like after a fortnight in the oven?'

'Tiny lumps of charcoal?'

'Exactly. Not this. Oh, no. As fresh, soft, pliable and unbaked as the day it went in. Well, obviously we couldn't sell it. We lost a good portion of our income, we had to lay people off, and the whole business looked like it was going to suffer. Once I put the corpus zingiber back – fine. In the end I just had to accept that we have a unique product, and therefore a trade secret which needs to be protected.'

'At least you didn't say it's an old family secret handed down for generations and you're bound by the family code of honour not to reveal it.'

At these words, Ashton stopped walking and could almost hear Dominica's heart sinking as she said, 'Oh great. It is, isn't it?'

He nodded sadly. 'But how did you know?'

'Let's just say there's a lot of it about, although why people can't just stick to handing down furniture and clothes is beyond me. You'd better give me the full story.'

They carried on walking.

'All I know,' said Ashton, 'is that it's been a condition of the Fishwick wills for generations that whoever inherits the business becomes guardian of the secret and must never reveal it or else dire consequences will follow.'

'What sort of dire consequences?'

'The exact words are "*else stops the business there with he who tells this for whatever sake, and from this sweet he shall have no prosperity nor money make*". So, I think I've probably just condemned my family to a life of poverty and put all my workers out on the streets.'

'Not to mention the effect on the orphanage.'

'The orphanage? What's that got to do with it?'

'If you can't afford to keep supporting the orphanage, it'll have to close and all the children will be homeless.'

'I'm flattered you think me so public-spirited, Mistress Tort,' he said, 'but I don't support the orphanage. My concern is for my own children, not other people's.'

Marianna consulted her map, marked off another completed square and pointed along a well-worn path.

'This way now, straight down here. JW, if you carry the map I'll mark these trees as we go.'

JW took the map. 'Which way do we go at the junction?'

'Right,' said the Bursar, red in the face from having to trot occasionally to keep up with Marianna's stride.

'Left,' said JW.

'No difference,' said Marianna. 'It brings us out at the same place whichever way we go – don't you remember?'

'Oh, aye.' JW smiled. 'All right then, we'll treat it as a carousel and go left.'

The Bursar narrowed her eyes at JW. 'You said that just because I want to go right.'

'As if,' teased JW.

'We can't all go right, anyway, Bursar,' said Marianna.

'And why not?'

'Because that would be going widdershins.'

'Aye, and you know what happens when you go round something thrice widdershins,' added JW.

'But we wouldn't be going thrice – only once.'

'Ah, but there's three of us,' said Marianna. 'It adds up to the same.'

'We wouldn't be going all the way round, anyway, so it doesn't count.'

'Look,' said Marianna firmly. 'You go right, we'll go left and we'll meet up round the other side. Happy?'

The Bursar grimaced. 'All right. But don't go hiding and pretending you're lost and leave me all alone here.'

'As if,' teased Marianna.

'I wouldn't put it past you.'

'Here! Take the bloody map!' snapped JW, stuffing the folded paper into the Bursar's hands. 'Just get on with it!'

Ashton stopped.

'What's wrong?' asked Dominica.

'Nothing,' he replied. 'We're here.'

Dominica looked around, and even though she used to study botany – albeit quite a few years ago now – the trees all looked exactly the same. There were no distinguishing marks, not even knobbly bits of bark which in the right light might have vaguely resembled somebody famous.

'How can you tell? There's nothing here!'

'Believe me, when you've been here as often as I have, you can tell.'

Dominica looked more closely at the trees. Maybe there were slight variations in them. 'So what happens next?'

'I wait, the old man turns up, he gives me the corpus zingiber, I pay him, we go our separate ways. Are you sure this is going to help me find my daughter?'

'As sure as I can be. Tell me about the old man.'

Ashton pulled a face which suggested he didn't quite know how to expand on 'old' or 'man'.

'I don't know where he lives or what his name is. He seemed to be an old man when I started coming here with my father. Still, everybody looks old when you're young, don't they? He comes from that way,' – Ashton pointed straight ahead – 'and goes back the same way.'

'Have you ever followed him?'

'Once, but – would you believe it – he was too quick for me. He turned right at the end, I got there – and I was only just behind him – I turned right and he'd gone. Just vanished into the wood.'

'Show me,' said Dominica.

They walked to the T-junction end of the path.

'He went off down there,' said Ashton, but Dominica was not listening. She was staring at the trees which formed the thicket on the far side of the other path, and something in her bones was telling her that her botany was not as rusty as she might have thought. She looked back along the path to where she'd thought the trees looked alike, then again at the thicket straight ahead. Compared with the trees in front of her, those behind her could have taken first prize in a chalk and cheese competition.

Tilting her head from side to side and raising a finger in front of her, she counted branches. The word 'identical' was insufficient to describe the similarity of the trees ahead of her. It was as if someone had planted the same tree over and over and over again, throwing in a degree of rotation to give the illusion of difference. She crossed the path and leant her head against one of the trees. It certainly felt like a tree, no doubt about that. But there was something missing.

'What's the matter?' said Ashton.

'Shh! Can you hear something?'

Ashton strained to listen, desperately clutching at any audible straw which might lead him to his daughter.

'No,' he said dejectedly.

'Listen!'

He sighed and listened again. 'Birds singing... leaves rustling... branches creaking... nothing else.'

'Exactly,' said Dominica. 'I'm not getting any of that.' She concentrated on the tree. 'I can't hear any sap rising, any insects burrowing, any bark cracking. Nothing. Which way did you say he went?'

'That way.'

The path he indicated curved gently to the left before disappearing from view. She turned a half-circle and looked along the path to where it swung to the right and was swallowed up by the rest of the wood.

'Stay there.' She plunged into the thicket, took five paces, faced him and waved her arms. 'Can you see me?'

Ashton waved back. 'Of course I can see you.'

'What am I doing?'

'It looks like you're doing charades and it's a play.'

She took another five paces further in. 'Now what?'

'A song. Mistress Tort—'

'Just tell me.' Another five paces, another wave. 'Now?'

'I don't know,' he said irritably. 'A menu?'

She dropped her arms and walked out of the thicket.

'I don't understand,' he said. 'Why are you—'

'Quick, hide! Somebody's coming!'

Dominica pushed Ashton into the thicket and they each hid behind a tree.

Just as Marianna had predicted, she and JW and the Bursar met up round the other side.

'Which way do you want to go now, Bursar?' asked JW, staring along the only path available, which stretched out in front of them.

'Don't move,' said a voice behind them.

'Waaggh!' yelled the Bursar, to the accompaniment of a jettisoned map fluttering in the breeze.

'I know that voice,' said Marianna, and the three of them turned to see Dominica emerging from behind a tree.

'Dom?' said JW. 'I thought you went to see Fishwick.'

'And so I did, and after what he told me, we came here.

It's all right, Mr Fishwick,' she called. 'You can come out now.'

Ashton Fishwick did not respond.

The old man stared at Ashton. 'You? Here? Now?'

'A very interesting experience, miss,' said Sennet as he and Naiba disembarked at the edge of the wood. 'If the forces of crime detection were airborne, we would solve many more crimes with much greater efficiency.'

Naiba laughed, which shocked Sennet.

'What are you laughing at, miss? Do you not consider crime detection to be a serious business?'

'Oh, of course. But I can just imagine what JW would say. "Flying rozzers? Flying pigs are as likely!"'

'Mistress Arcrite has a wicked tongue.'

'I think everyone does, constable. It's just JW chooses not to hide hers behind a thin veneer of social grace as often as the rest of us. She's a sweetheart, really. When you get to know her.'

'That's a big price to pay.'

Naiba took her saddlebag from the broomstick and was about to sling it over her shoulder when Sennet said, 'Let me carry the bag, miss. It looks rather heavy.'

'Oh, er, yes, thank you.' She passed him the bag with one hand. The weight of it pulled him violently to one side.

'It's even heavier than it looks, isn't it?' he said, straining to lift it an inch and wondering how on earth the stitching was holding out.

'It's not so bad once you get used to it,' said Naiba, staring at the bag.

'*The longer you carry, the lighter it seems,*
Until all its weight is as light as your dreams.'

Down in the Dictionary, a blue edge flashed green as a spell burst into life. She looked back at Sennet and smiled.

'Isn't that what people say?'

'I don't know, miss. I've never heard it before. You're right, though. It feels lighter already.'

'Are you sure you brought him with you, Minnie?'

The Bursar's question brought Dominica up short. *If she calls me Minnie one— Minnie!* Dominica smiled to herself, then faced the Bursar with a look of exasperation.

'Oh, Helena – back to normal I see.'

'What do you mean back to normal? Have I ever been abnormal?'

'Mph phlmph!' muffled JW, as Marianna's hand covered her mouth.

'Ashton Fishwick was in here,' said Dominica slowly. 'Behind one of these trees. I pushed him in here myself!'

'Then we need a systematic search of this area,' said Marianna. 'Easy enough with four of us.'

'Three,' said Dominica. 'Helena, don't come anywhere near this thicket until I say so.'

'Oh, now what? Not allowed to play with the big girls any more, eh?' sneered the Bursar. Marianna and JW winced as they felt Dominica's inner spring wind up a few notches. When it was overwound, the person holding the key had better be prepared to have a few lumps taken out of their hands from the recoil.

'Helena, if I have to, I will kick your spiteful backside all the way back to The Union to keep you out of here right now. I'm trying to save your life, you moron!'

'Oh, yes, trees are really dangerous, aren't they?'

Click, click, snap, twang.

'Come here!' blazed Dominica. The Bursar did not move. Dominica strode over, clamped her hand round the Bursar's wrist and dragged her to the edge of the thicket – no mean feat as the Bursar was usually considered to be a standard immovable object.

'Hold your hands out!' She lifted the Bursar's arm. The Bursar limply lifted the other arm. 'Straight out!' Steel rods apparently shot from the Bursar's shoulders down to her fingertips. 'Walk forward slowly, and watch your hands.'

The Bursar closed her eyes.

'BURSAR!'

The Bursar's eyes jerked open. She didn't know whether she was more scared of Dominica or of what might happen. She soon found out.

Still gripping the Bursar's wrist, Dominica pulled her forwards. The tips of the Bursar's fingers began to fade.

'Uuuuuurrrrggghhhh...' moaned the Bursar.

Dominica felt her stiffen and dragged her onwards.

'Come on. You wanted to do this.'

The outline and substance of the Bursar's fingertips became finer and finer until they disappeared completely, her fingers following suit. Like some creeping deadly colourwash, transparency crawled across her hands.

'Let me go! Let me go!' she yelled, and shook and tried to pull away from Dominica, but her terror was no match for a Vice-Matriarch's anger. The Bursar slapped her free arm down by her side as Dominica twisted her wrist and thrust her arm into the air. The Bursar watched wild-eyed as the colour drained from her arm until it seemed Dominica was white-knuckling a fistful of fresh air.

Suddenly, Dominica let go of the Bursar who sprawled on the floor and scrabbled away backwards, rubbing her fat pink arms to make sure they were back. Red weals started to form round one of her wrists.

Dominica strode after her. 'Now stay on the path!'

'But – but – how did you know what would happen?' choked the Bursar.

Dominica towered over her. 'I didn't. But I know who you are.'

The old man was as surprised as Ashton to see two fat pink hands appear out of nowhere, shake in the air, and then disappear one after the other.

Marianna paced the circumference of the thicket, divided it by three and chalked three starting points on the ground. She, JW and Dominica each took up their positions equidistant from one another. 'Go!'

Dominica hoped, without much conviction, that as the three of them walked through the trees, they'd find Ashton Fishwick hiding behind one.

When they met up in the centre of the thicket, there were still only three of them. Marianna marked the place where each of them stood, and drew a triangle joining the three points. Inside the triangle stood a well, a perfect round well, complete with a wooden roller to haul up whatever hung deep inside. JW cranked the handle of the roller and reeled in a tattered and fraying rope until it hauled up a slimy, dribbling, rust-banded bucket.

'I don't like the looks of them weeds,' she said. 'They look like noodles.'

Dominica had a look. 'So they do. What colour would you say the water is?'

'Black— no, no, dark green. Nearly black.'

'Ready for round two?' said Marianna, marking out points half-way along each side of the arrival triangle.

Dominica's optimism was not at its highest. 'I don't think it'll do any good.'

'Best to be sure, though,' said JW.

'Right girls, places please!' said Marianna. They each stood on one of the half-way points, backs to the well. 'Go!'

The second search proved as fruitless as the first.

'Don't you think,' said Naiba to Sennet as they walked further into the wood, 'it'd be better to prevent crime rather than detect it? Prevention's better than any cure.'

At this Sennet laughed, which shocked Naiba.

'What are you laughing at, constable? Don't you consider crime prevention to be a serious business?'

'That way lies anarchy, miss.'

'Anarchy?'

'Anarchy. The easiest way to prevent crime is to not have crime in the first place.'

Naiba chased this around in her head but couldn't find an end to grasp. 'But... how can you prevent what you don't have?'

'Why would you want to, miss?'

'I think I'm missing something here.'

With his free hand, he started patting his pockets for his notebook. 'When did you notice it was gone?'

'What?'

'The thing you're missing. Has it been lost or stolen?'

'Unravelled, I think.'

'Miss?'

'I meant I was missing the point of your argument. Before I lose my sanity as well, tell me how crime prevention leads to anarchy. In simple steps, please.'

Sennet stopped patting. 'Simple steps are all that's needed, miss. A crime happens when someone breaks the law. The easiest way to stop that happening – to *prevent* crime – is to get rid of all the laws.'

'But if you don't have laws...'

'...you have anarchy. And that's why crime prevention is a non-starter in my book.'

Naiba thought someone ought to take Sennet's book back to the library and get him one with a few more pages in it.

They turned a corner.

'Do you know where we're going, miss?'

'No,' said Naiba.

'*Yes,*' said a familiar unfamiliar voice.

'Pardon?' said Sennet.

'Sort of,' said Naiba. 'Oh, look – isn't that the Bursar?'

Drastic times, drastic measures.

'Helena, I want you to climb up this tree and take a look,' said Dominica.

'You said you didn't want me anywhere near it!' the Bursar protested, quite correctly.

'You'll be all right on the edge. It didn't take effect until you were past the first row of trees. Stick to the outside and you'll be fine.'

'What if it drags me in?'

'It won't. Just don't lean too far forward, will you?'

'I'm no good at climbing trees!'

'We'll help,' said Marianna.

JW put her face close to the Bursar's. 'Come on, Bursar. I'll go up with you and make sure you don't get' – JW widened her eyes – 'sucked in.'

'Good idea,' said Dominica. 'If JW holds on to you, you won't fall in.'

'I don't trust her,' said the Bursar.

'You don't trust anybugger,' called JW, halfway up the tree already.

'I only want you to take a look and tell me what you see,' said Dominica as she and Marianna frogmarched the Bursar to the tree.

'Can't Faculties, do it?' jabbered the Bursar. 'She's taller than the rest of us and she can see further and—'

'And,' said Marianna, 'I couldn't see it when I was in the middle of it. Up you go.'

JW reached down from a branch. 'Come on – it's easier than it looks.'

The Bursar chewed her lip and reached towards the tree.

'Good day, sisters,' said a voice some way behind her. 'Can I help?'

The Bursar saw a rozzer and her chance. She ran to him.

'Officer, these people are trying to make me climb a tree!'

'Are they really?' he said, walking over to the tree and looking up. JW sat on a bough, swinging her legs and smirking. He smiled and looked back at the Bursar.

'Tree-climbing's not actually a crime, madam.'

'But you don't understand! They're trying to force me—'

'*Quiet!*' roared a familiar unfamiliar voice.

A silence fell, swift as a blink and deep as a snowdrift.

'*All right,*' said the familiar unfamiliar voice softly. '*You can come out now.*'

People's reactions differ when their world is transformed, literally, within the length of a full stop.

The first thing Sennet noticed was that a good number of trees had vanished. The second thing was that suddenly he'd dropped the saddlebag and was holding something quite different: JW. This might have been a romantic moment, but the fact she'd arrived in his arms from a vertical trajectory and not a horizontal one rather took the shine off it. He coughed and reddened.

JW laughed and winked at him before turning round and

saying 'Bloody hell' in a voice which went up and down through several octaves.

Marianna said, 'Ten out of ten, Dominica.'

The Bursar's mouth and eyes opened so wide she looked as if her face was constructed entirely from ping-pong balls, and it was only when Marianna slapped her on the back she remembered to breathe.

Dominica said simply, 'Mother Nature.'

'It's here,' whispered Naiba. 'This is it. It's here.'

And it was. The smashed rock rollers and torn liquorice strip. The ripped punchbag. The piles of broken shortbread bricks, grissini roof trusses and crispbread slates which had once been the parlour, the dining-room, the bedroom and the wash-house. The kitchen and the utility room were the only two rooms left in what had been Doughnut Cottage. Despite the sunshine which now flooded the clearing, over the whole place there hung an air of infinite sadness, regret and weariness, given solid form by a small grave to one side of the debris of the gym. It bore a posy of fresh flowers.

So many emotions swept over Naiba she began to sway. Sennet and JW moved to her side in case she collapsed.

The kitchen door opened; the old man walked out slowly.

'The deaf old man,' whispered Marianna.

'He's not deaf,' said Dominica. 'He was ignoring you. He wanted you to go away.'

'Meniel!' said Naiba. 'Meniel from the orphanage!'

'Is it over?' he asked, his voice an orchestra of hope, fear and disbelief, led by a longing, longing for release.

'Almost,' said Dominica. 'So it was you – the money Mr

Fishwick gave you went straight to the orphanage.'

'That was the whole point, wasn't it? She wanted the orphanage.'

'You bought the children?!' cried Naiba.

'In a way,' said Dominica, never taking her eyes off the old man. 'He bought their lives. He kept them fed and clothed… and safe. But it came at a cost.' She hesitated for a moment. 'We will not leave a child in harm's way.'

Her words cut him as badly as any knife, and the pain showed in his face and his voice.

'I never hurt any of the childer at the home. Not one of them. Never. I never harmed a child. Never. Not in all my long, long life. The childer have always been safe. When will it be over?'

'What about *once in every hundred year*?' spat Naiba.

'No!'

'You killed children!'

She rushed forward. Dominica grabbed her arm.

'NO!' he screamed, and started to shake. His eyes brimmed over with tears that would follow numberless others which had streamed down well-worn courses. '*She* took *my* baby! *She* did! *She* took my girl! *I* couldn't! Not ever! I had to beg and beg and beg of her!'

Naiba wasn't finished. 'What about *One of the children shall you take—*'

'A boy be a grandfather but he's still someone's boy! Someone's child. A grown child, but…' His voice trailed off. 'Old ones,' he said quietly. 'I took the old ones. *My* childer,' he whispered. 'Always *my* childer.'

'Your children are long dead!'

'Their line goes on! My line goes on! My blood in their veins, however little.' His words were drenched in bitterness and regret. 'Childer of my line – for generations! She gave me the power to see who is mine and who is not. Clear as day, I see… through to the bad blood, she called it. No mistakes, she said. My family to suffer, she said. My family misdeeds, my family to pay. We have paid. I have paid. When will it be over?'

'What about Mr Fishwick's little girl?' asked Dominica.

He wiped his eyes with the back of his hand. 'I didn't take her. As I still live and breathe, I didn't take her. She'd been in the park. She was wandering, lost. She followed me. I didn't know she was his – but I knew she was mine. Just as *she* is.'

He pointed at the Bursar.

'What?' shrieked the Bursar.

The old man looked back at Naiba. 'And you are.'

Naiba was horrified. 'Me?'

'You.'

She started to back away from him. 'No… no…'

'The blood is thinner in you, but it is there. I see it.'

Naiba walked to the edge of the clearing, pushing away those who tried to comfort her. She sat down, hugged her knees close to her, and rocked gently to and fro as her heart broke for reasons she did not fully understand.

He sobbed. 'When will it be over? When?'

'Will somebody tell me what's going on?' said the Bursar.

'You don't know this man?' said Dominica, suddenly bewildered by the Bursar's ignorance.

'Never seen him before in my life!'

'Helena…'

'Truly, I haven't!'

'Do you swear on your father's letters you've never seen this man before?'

'I swear! I swear!'

'Oh, Helena. I am so sorry.' There was far too much sadness in Dominica's voice for it to have been absorbed solely from her surroundings. 'This… is… your many-greats grandfather.'

'What? What are you talking about? This isn't my grandfather!'

Any softening towards the Bursar which Dominica might have felt evaporated in an instant and she rounded on the Bursar.

'Death's head on a shitty stick, Helena! For the love of everything in Mother Nature, will you just, for once in your sodding irritating life – I'm begging you – will you *just frigging listen*!'

Everybody listened. Nobody dared blink.

Dominica licked her lips. When she spoke, she spoke very, very deliberately.

'I'll say it again. This is your many-greats grandfather. He is living under a curse, and wants to be released from it.'

The Bursar took a breath, but Dominica pointed sternly at her which stopped her saying anything.

'His name is Grandel. The curse he is living under – and wants to be released from – is your family curse. Yes, that one. That curse you've been carrying round with you. That curse which can only be signed off by a Matriarch.'

'But I can't do it! I'm not Matriarch! You won't let me be Matriarch!'

'Helena…' growled Dominica through gritted teeth and clenched fists.

'Then which amongst you is Matriarch?' asked Grandel.

'None of us yet,' replied the Bursar.

'Then it is not over.' He walked back towards the cottage.

'Wait!' shouted Dominica.

Grandel stopped.

'Did we miss anything?' said a voice at ground level.

Dominica closed one eye and raised the other eyebrow in the manner of a saint who's been given a lemon to suck. She searched for the source of the voice, as did everyone else.

From under one end of the flap on Naiba's saddlebag stuck the head of a black cat with a white eye-patch; from under the other end stuck the head of a marmalade cat of the three-fruit variety. The whole thing looked as if it were the product of an illicit liaison between a small pushme-pullyou and a canvas rucksack.

Dominica glared. 'What… Mother Al-sodding-mighty give me strength. What the… what are *you* doing here?'

'Stowaways?' Dennis offered, hoping his soft answer would turn away her wrath.

That's the thing about hope. It's chance, not certainty; a chance which even the most ardent anti-gambling righteous fanatic will readily cling to when it appears. And, like so many of us, Dennis found out that hope doesn't give a damn about us and should be treated with the same healthy scepticism as a vote of confidence.

Dominica's words fell with such force that gardeners could have planted rockery alpines in between them.

'*Do not get into any trouble. Understand?*'

He and Bertie nodded meekly. Marianna winked at them and tilted her head; they squeezed out of the saddlebag and padded over to her. Grandel looked at them, the scars on his cheek twitching as he thought of another cat, another time.

'Let them go, Grandel,' said Dominica. There was silence. 'Please.'

'No.'

'The girl and her father can't help you.'

'No.'

'We will take their places until it's over.'

'You said it can't be over without a Matriarch.'

He turned to leave.

Dominica took her courage in both hands and twisted the strands together for strength. 'There is one here who will be Matriarch. One who has been called to sign off this curse.'

Grandel turned back and stared at her, as did everyone else. 'Forgive me if I cannot believe you.'

'Give me the others and I will give you a Matriarch.'

'No! I will not be the fool of a witch's trickery again.'

She held out a well-folded sheet of paper. 'Then read this.'

'My letter!' said the Bursar.

Grandel took the letter and read it.

'Written by a man to his daughter,' said Dominica. 'Written to the child who will release you.'

'She is here?'

'I'm here! I'm here!' yelled the Bursar.

Dominica ignored her, and concentrated on Grandel.

'You told us you have always seen who is yours and who is not. Now I tell you: there is one here who is of both your line and Auregia's.'

'Then let her release me and let it be over!'

'She cannot release you until I say so.'

'Why you?'

'Because at this moment I am the highest authority in The University of Nature. Without me, she cannot become Matriarch, and without her being Matriarch, you cannot be released.'

'Why should I trust you?'

'I will not lie to you, nor will I hide the truth. She is the last of her line, the last one who can help you. But she is powerless until I give her power. Release those you hold, and you shall be released.'

'No. Once bitten, however long ago, twice shy.'

Dominica groaned. 'Why condemn yourself to an eternity of…' – she gestured round the clearing – '…this? Unless, perhaps, we came too late.'

'What?'

'Perhaps you cannot release them because they are already dead.' She started to walk away.

'No! Wait! They still live.'

'Then let them go.'

'Will you release me?'

'Let them go and you shall have your Matriarch.'

'Do you swear?'

'I swear.'

Grandel looked into her eyes, and saw his only hope for release. He went into the kitchen; when he re-emerged, much to everyone's relief, he brought out Ashton. On a normal day Ashton's unruly mop of black hair only accentuated the pallor of his thin face; now, he seemed one step away from the coffin lid. Red blotches around his eyes were a testament to his tears; tears for the daughter sleeping in his arms.

'Mistress Tort!' he cried. 'She is safe! She is safe.'

'Mr Fishwick,' said Dominica, 'please go and stand by the constable.'

Grandel looked affectionately at the child in Ashton's arms and stroked her dark, glossy hair. 'Goodbye, little lamb,' he said tenderly. 'Be good for your father.'

Ashton walked over to Sennet. Naiba scrambled to her feet and ran over to join them. 'Mr Fishwick, is she truly safe? Is she unhurt?'

'Unhurt and it seems... well cared-for.'

Grandel walked over to face the Bursar. 'Release me.'

Terror and helplessness vied for supremacy on the Bursar's face.

'She cannot,' said Dominica flatly.

'You swore she would release me!'

'I said you would have your Matriarch.'

Grandel's sigh held all the bitterness of a monk who has been forced to break a thirty-year meditative silence just to give somebody directions.

'Word play!' he spat. 'I should have known better.'

'Yes, you should,' snarled Dominica

'What?!'

She strode over to him, grabbed his leather jerkin and violently pulled him towards her. 'Five hundred years ago you took Auregia for a fool and you have lived with the consequences ever since. And I am the first person – the *only* person – in five hundred years to offer you salvation, and yet you take me for a fool as well. So yes, you should have known better.' She pushed him away.

'You swore I would be released!'

'I said release those you hold and you shall be released!' she shouted.

Grandel threw his arms out. 'Have I not done so?'

Dominica clenched her fists, put them up to her face, bent double and let out a deep-throated growl of anger which lasted for a long, long time. The world held its breath.

When she straightened up, she cleared her throat before speaking.

'Very well. As you still insist on treating me like a simpleton, I will speak very simply. No, you have not released those you hold. You have released *half* of those you hold.'

'The time is close,' Grandel said dismissively. 'I need raw material.'

'Raw material that can only come from very specific people, which is why you let Mr Fishwick and his beautiful dark-haired daughter go so easily.'

Grandel shrugged. 'What of it?'

'I will tell you what of it. The one that you propose to use for raw material is the future Matriarch.'

'She's the one?' he gawped.

The world let go of its breath.

'Eleanor?' said Marianna and JW.

'Ohhhh,' said the Bursar.

'No! No! You lie!' Grandel shrieked.

'Why should I?' said Dominica.

He rushed towards her. 'To save her! You just want to protect your own kind, to carry on your trickery and condemn me for ever! I should kill you where you stand!'

'Then do so.'

'What?'

'Take my life in exchange for hers.'

'No!' gasped Marianna. 'Not you, Dominica. The Union needs you. Now more than ever. Let me go instead.'

'No,' said Sennet. 'I must go. I am trained for this sort of thing,' he bluffed, stepping into a situation the instructors at rozzer college had not even dreamt about.

'How noble,' the old man laughed bitterly. 'So eager to be martyrs. I would take you all, but this is a family affair.'

Naiba pushed past Sennet. 'You said I am of your family. Take me.'

'It cannot be you,' said Dominica.

'But—'

'Trust me. It cannot be you.'

'Then it must be me,' said the Bursar calmly. 'Me. My letter. My family. Your family.'

Several jaws dropped as she walked towards him.

'You? You said you were the Matriarch,' he scathed, turning to walk away.

'I believed I was.'

She spoke with such heaviness of heart that Grandel stopped and studied her for a while.

'No,' he said at length, 'I will not take you.'

'I am family.'

'But I will not take you. The one I already have must die. The one I already have is what I need – ginger. Ginger skin and bone. This…' – he put his hand out and lifted the Bursar's hair which glowed and glinted in the sunlight – '…this is ginger bottle.'

A wave of surprise in the clearing underlined the moment when Dominica's profound concentration once more snapped like an over-bent ruler. The Bursar looked as if she wished the ground would open up and swallow her, and if the subterranean rumblings of Dominica's anger were anything to go by, it might just do that.

Dominica stared at the Bursar.

'You dye your hair?' she said, in a manner normally reserved for such utterances as 'You eat razor blades for a living?' and 'They've been elected again?'

'You dye your hair?' she repeated. 'You mean to tell me that all this – that five hundred years of magic – that the future of The Union – depends on a sodding hair-do?'

The Bursar was visibly withering.

'I have one who is ginger skin and bone,' said Grandel. 'It is all I need.'

He walked back inside the kitchen.

'You can always count on the Bursar in a crisis,' muttered Marianna.

'Aye, to be right in the middle of it looking overly innocent,' said JW.

Dominica interlocked her fingers and put her hands on top of her head.

'She dyes her hair, Naiba,' she said, walking round the clearing. 'She dyes her hair, JW. She dyes her hair, Marianna.'

Something in Marianna's face made Dominica stop. She stood with her hands on her head watching Marianna's eyes dart back and forth between the Bursar and a point down by her side. Little lights of recognition went on all over Dominica's brain. She bobbed down by Marianna's side and said nonchalantly, 'She dyes her hair, Dennis.' She reached out and stroked him, and he went into her open arms, glad to be back in the good books again. She stood up and cuddled this soft, floppy bundle of devotion.

'But you don't, do you, Dennis?'

'No mis— now hang on a minute!' Dennis went from being a warm and cuddly cushion to something made entirely out of fur-covered pokers. 'You're not giving me to him!' he screamed, pushing against her.

It took nearly all Dominica's strength to restrain him.

'Not you, just your body.'

'I'm not finished with it yet!'

'You owe me one, Dennis. Remember?'

He stopped struggling but did not relax. 'Oh, I know, but... there are limits!'

'Then push them back a bit, boy.'

'You said I hadn't got to get into any trouble,' he tried.

'I didn't say I couldn't get you into it.'

'It's no good. He's not family,' said the Bursar.

'He will be,' said Dominica.

'What?!' shrieked Dennis.

'You're going in the Bursar's body, and the Bursar's going in your body.'

This time it was the Bursar's turn to shriek. 'What?!'

'You heard.'

'Are you out of your mind?'

'Very probably. But at this stage of the game I don't really care.'

'Well, I do,' said the Bursar, striding off across the clearing. Dominica watched with a certain amount of satisfaction as JW and Marianna cut off the Bursar's exit, took hold of an arm each and brought her back, heels kicking on the ground.

'You're as mad as she is!' she shouted. 'You don't think she knows what she's doing, do you?'

'Oh, I think she does,' said Marianna.

'You would.'

They set the Bursar back on her feet, but did not let go of her arms.

'Ah, now, fair's fair, Marianna,' said JW. 'I think the Bursar's raised a very good point there.'

The Bursar's self-preservation overcame her surprise at finding an ally in JW.

'See? See? Even she agrees with me!'

'Dom?' said JW.

'Mm?'

'Tell me you know what you're doing.'

'I know what I'm doing, JW.'

'There you are, Bursar – she knows what she's doing.'

JW smiled sideways at the glaring Bursar. Marianna chuckled.

The Bursar broke free.

'I'm going to walk out of here,' she snarled, 'and none of you is going to stop me, because if you try to, I'll—'

'You'll what?' said Dominica. 'Use magic?'

'Yes, if necessary.'

'No you won't, because I will stop you. And I know what you're thinking now: "Could I take her down? Is she a level six witch, or only a five?" Well, in all honesty, it doesn't matter, because I'm the Vice-Matriarch – the most powerful witch in The Union at the moment – so you've got to ask yourself one question: "Do I feel lucky?" Well, do you, Bursar?'

The Bursar took a breath.

'Go ahead,' said Dominica. 'Make my frigging day.'

The Bursar thought for a moment then waggled an arm in the direction of Naiba. 'Why not use her? He said the blood runs through her!'

'Not as thickly as through you.'

'I'll bet it's as thick as bloody ice cream in the Bursar,' JW whispered to Marianna.

'But it's still—'

'HELENA!' Dominica exploded. 'Enough! This is *your* family curse. The one that *you* have carried about for years. The one that *you* have been desperate to lift. *You will play your part.* Do I make myself clear?'

The Bursar looked at her feet. 'You do.'

'Good. And you will also play your part, Dennis.'

He sagged. He had been trying to take advantage of the distraction to stage a small but significant getaway, but Dominica's grip was tight.

She looked into his eyes. 'I'm going to give you to this nice rozzer to hold, and if you struggle, kick, bite, scratch or generally try to get away, I will send you into the Bursar's body before it's empty and the two of you will live together for the rest of your lives. Is that understood, little kitty?'

'There's no need to add insult to injury,' he bristled. She handed him over, and he knew better than to put up a fight.

'Right,' she said, rubbing her hands together, 'all we need now is something empty to put the Bursar in.' She looked around the clearing. 'Hmm. Can't use anything living, because that'll have a spirit of its own and therefore be full…'

Dennis's ears pricked up. 'But you just said—'

'Shut it, Dennis.'

'Will this do?' said Naiba, picking up one of the many royal-icing gargoyles which lay scattered in the rubble of Doughnut Cottage.

'Excellent!' said Dominica.

'You can't put me in a downspout!' cried the Bursar.

'Bursar, I'm in charge. I can put you where the hell I like. Now if you don't want to spend the rest of your life throwing up rainwater, I suggest keep your mouth shut while you can.'

'Well, I've never been so—' chomped the Bursar.

'No, you never have,' said JW.

Dominica held the gargoyle in her right hand and put her left hand on the Bursar's head.

'I call a spirit transfer spell:
From full to empty make the leap
And 'til a transfer next be made,
Then empty vessel, spirit keep.'

A small, bad-tempered purple cloud shot from the Bursar to the gargoyle. Irritable spirits always move faster than happy ones, usually because they can't wait to get where they're going and complain about the new accommodation.

'Ohhhh... ohhhh... ohhhhh,' wailed the gargoyle. 'Ohhh... 'ish ish aw-hul! Get 'e ou' o' here!'

Dominica handed the gargoyle to JW, who put her hand over the spout to keep the noise down. The wailing escalated to a high-pitched whine. 'I ca' hreeed! I ca' hreeed!'

'I think she's saying she can't breathe, JW,' said Marianna.

JW looked at the gargoyle which was slowly turning blue.

'Oh, sorry, Bursar,' she smirked, and took her hand off the spout.

The gargoyle wheezed for a few seconds then said, 'Herry hunny!'

Dominica put her right hand on the now-empty Bursar's head and her left hand on Dennis's head, and repeated the spell. This time, a small orange cloud rushed half-way to the Bursar's body then stopped and swirled around.

'Wow!' it said. 'Wheee!'

'Get a move on, Dennis,' said Dominica.

'Cor! This is brilliant!'

'Dennis!'

'Oh, soz.'

The cloud gathered itself together and rushed into the Bursar's body, which promptly fell over.

'Ow!' said Dennis.

'Are you all right?' asked Dominica.

'I'm not used to this two-legged business,' he said. 'I suppose I'll get the hang of it.' The Bursar's body writhed on the ground. 'Hey, isn't there a lot of room in here?'

'Heeky hugger,' said the gargoyle.

Naiba tapped Marianna's arm and began a whispered conversation as Dominica took the gargoyle from JW.

'Now for stage three,' said Dominica. Stage three saw a small, bad-tempered purple cloud flash from the gargoyle to Dennis's body, and the first thing the Cat-Bursar did was to open her mouth as wide as she could and stick her tongue out.

'Oh, Mother Nature, what do you give this cat to eat? Yeeuuurrgh!'

She wiped her tongue on her hand to get rid of the taste before realising her hands were paws, recently used for walking about on.

'Blech! Blech! Blech! I hate you! I hate you!'

She struggled so much Sennet dropped her and she ran towards Dominica.

'Don't even think about it,' said Dominica, as the claws came out.

It was then the Cat-Bursar became aware of a new and unnerving sensation.

'And I'm a boy!' she screamed. 'Ohhhh…'

The significance of this was not lost on Dennis, who started to pat his nether regions. 'Where's my— what have you done with my—?'

He started to pull his skirts up, but Dominica's foot on the hems stopped him revealing too much.

'And if you want them back,' she said, 'you'd better do as you're told.'

'You're in charge,' he said.

'Good boy.'

'Just tell the Bursar I don't want to see any stretch marks in that fur when I get it back.'

The Cat-Bursar lashed out at him with one of his own claws. He tried to roll out of the way, but he'd forgotten about the extra bulk which came with the Bursar's body. The claws scraped across his leg, drawing blood.

'Ow!' he yelled.

'Serves you right,' crowed the Cat-Bursar.

'Maybe so,' he replied, 'but it isn't half going to hurt you when you get back in here.'

'Children, children,' said Dominica, putting down the gargoyle and picking up the Cat-Bursar.

Marianna coughed. 'Dominica? A quiet word, please?'

'What, now?'

'It could be important.'

Dominica handed the Cat-Bursar to Sennet again, and joined the small huddle of Marianna, JW and Naiba.

'The thing is,' said Marianna quietly, 'do you think he literally meant blood when he spoke about "bad blood"?'

Dominica seemed surprised. 'I don— no, no... he said

Auregia called it "bad blood", didn't he? I'm sure he just meant it's got to be someone of his family line, that's all.'

'It's just... well... we don't want to be disqualified on a technicality.'

'Technicality?'

'Dennis the cat doesn't have that blood, does he?' said Naiba. 'I mean, the Bursar now has Dennis's blood, which isn't "bad", is it?'

'Fair point, Dom,' said JW.

Dominica saw three worried faces. 'Oh, I'm sure he just needs somebody of his family who's ginger skin and bone, and now she's in Dennis's body the Bursar fits the bill. The "bad blood" thing's just a... just a...'

She waved her hands as if trying to physically pull words out of the air.

'...technicality?' said Marianna.

'Figure of speech,' said Dominica.

'Best be on the safe side,' said JW. Naiba nodded.

Dominica sighed and thought for a moment. 'Very well. You three hold the Bursar's body down.'

Marianna, JW and Naiba moved off towards Dennis, who was too busy trying to stand up to notice he was being approached.

'Blood,' Dominica muttered as they walked away. 'Now they want blood.' She took the Cat-Bursar from Sennet. 'Constable, come with me, please.'

Before Dennis knew it, he was flat on his back with witches immobilising three of his limbs.

'Ow! What the— put me down! I mean let me up! Will

you gnph smph fnlfn!'

'Nothing personal, just aural,' said Marianna, whose hand was a gag so effective it left Dennis only one channel of expression – his free leg, whose violent swinging was born of rage and perpetuated by Dennis's lack of control over a human body.

'Constable, grab hold of that foot, will you?' said Dominica matter-of-factly.

'Certainly, ma'am.' After a couple of wild and inelegant lunges, Sennet managed to capture the foot and braced it against his body, which shook sporadically with the effort.

'Oh, do calm down, Dennis!' snapped Dominica. 'You've been in worse scraps than this in Concentric Yard!' Her tone of voice surprised him, and she took his momentary calm as a chance to push back his skirts and rub the Cat-Bursar's fur across the bloody scratches on his leg.

'Errgh! Oh, yeeuck! Oh, yow! Ohhhh!' strained the Cat-Bursar. 'I cannot believe you did that! *I cannot believe you did that!*"

'You'd better believe it, honey.'

Dominica carried the disgusted Cat-Bursar over to the kitchen and knocked on the door. Grandel opened it. Dominica held the Cat-Bursar up.

'I bring you one who is of your family, and who is ginger skin and bone. Take her in exchange for Eleanor, and you shall have your release.'

'Her?' said Grandel, staring at a certain area of fur.

The Cat-Bursar crossed all her legs and blushed. 'Didn't anybody ever tell you it's rude to stare?'

'This is another one of your tricks,' he said.

'Oh, no, believe me, this is real enough,' said the Cat-Bursar. 'I only wish it wasn't.'

'Are you ginger skin and bone?'

'Apparently so and I hate every last little furball of it with every fibre of my ginger skin and bone being. Now can we get on please? I have vengeance of my own to wreak.'

'You're my family, right enough,' said Grandel.

'Then take her,' said Dominica. 'She will be your raw material, so you will lose nothing. Give me Eleanor in return and I will pass to *her* the mantle of power. She will be the Matriarch and she will release you.'

'No more word play? I will have my release?'

'You will have your release. It will be over. You will have rest.'

'I am so very tired,' he said heartbrokenly, his words heavy with the weight of every one of his hundreds of years.

'And so am I. Then take her, and give me Eleanor.'

He looked at Dominica, and could see no deception, no trickery, no-lose situation. For the first time in five hundred years he truly trusted someone, but not without a fallback. He took the Cat-Bursar.

'Very well,' he said. 'Let it be over.'

He retreated into the house.

Dominica called to the others.

'You can let him go now.'

As one, Dennis's captors released him.

'You wait till I get my own body back!' he screamed, all limbs flailing like an extremely large new-born babe. 'I'm gonna come and visit each and every one of you late at night and—'

'Oh, belt up!' commanded Dominica, and much to everyone's surprise, Dennis did so. She walked over to him and put her face very close to his. 'Do you want us to go back and tell everybody what a big cissy you are? Whingeing and whining because he got a wittuw scwatch on his wittuw weg?' There was silence. 'Well, do you?'

More silence piled up. Everybody started to look embarrassed – everybody except the two protagonists who scowled at each other in the ever-thickening soundlessness. Eventually Dennis stuck out his bottom lip.

'Not *my* leg, is it?' he said with a hint of a smile.

He was saved from further injury by the creaking of the kitchen door as into the clearing stepped a woman for whom the term 'statuesque' might have been coined, for not only was Eleanor of imposing proportions, but she showed as much awareness of her surroundings as a carved marble icon. She held a lead, at the other end of which a large dog snarled at Grandel.

'What's wrong with her?' asked Naiba.

'She's suspended,' said Grandel. 'That's how I... Auregia taught me... she said it'd be easier that way. I just wish it worked on animals. He's not very friendly.'

'Strange,' said Dominica, 'considering he is Spirit of Friendship.'

The dog stopped snarling and looked at Dominica.

'Spirit of Friendship?' squeaked Dennis. 'Bertie! Bertie! Come and see this! Axy the Tamer's a dog!'

'Axy?' said Naiba.

'A dog?' said Bertie.

The dog's head swivelled round as he looked at each one in turn.

'Good day, Spirit,' said Dominica.

'Good day, mistress.'

'You know him?' said Grandel.

'Not exactly,' said Dominica, 'but you do.'

'Me?'

'You broke his legs once, I believe.'

'So don't stand too close,' growled Axy.

'Oh, boy,' Dennis beamed. 'A living legend!'

Bertie gaped. 'Wow!'

'Right,' said Dominica. 'If you'll just unsuspend Eleanor, we'll get started.'

'Ah,' said Grandel.

'What do you mean, "Ah"?'

'I can't do it.'

'Can't or won't?'

'Can't.'

Dominica put her hands on her hips. '*What?*'

Grandel looked sheepish. 'Auregia taught me how to… but she never taught me…'

'Wonderful.'

'I've never had to let anybody go before.'

'Don't you understand? In order for the Matriarch to release you, she's got be functioning!'

'You never said that!'

'I didn't know you had her suspended, did I?! How did

you put her under?'

'All I did was say *"Be dreams, go sense, see darkness from hence"* and that was it.'

And that was it.

There was silence. Nobody moved. At all. Grandel looked around and groaned. The clearing had become the world's most bizarre stonemason's yard, full of living, breathing, suspended statuary.

'Oh, no,' he whimpered and flapped his hands. 'Not now! Not now!'

'Oh, excellent,' said Axy witheringly. 'Now we're stuck in here forever.'

'What?' exclaimed Bertie.

'This useless, worthless waste of space and time has only gone and put the fluence on everybody, hasn't he?'

Grandel waved his hands in front of Dominica's face.

'I didn't mean to!'

'But you did, didn't you?'

Bertie ran over to Axy. 'What can we do?'

'I don't know. You any good at this kind of magic?'

Bertie shook his head.

'Well, then,' said Axy, 'the waste of space'll have to go get someone who is.'

'What?' said Grandel.

'You'll have to go to The Union and fetch somebody.'

'I'm not going anywhere near that place. I've had enough dealings with witches to last me a lifetime. Several lifetimes, in fact.'

'Then my friend here will have to go, won't you…?'

'Bertie,' said Bertie.

'Won't you, Bertie?'

'Why don't you go?' said Grandel. 'You've got longer legs than he has – you'll get there quicker.'

'Oh, no. I'm not leaving my mistress. And if you let me off this leash the first thing I'll do is rip the flesh from your bones.'

'That's no good – I wouldn't die.'

'Good enough for me – I wouldn't stop.'

'I'll go,' said Bertie.

'Go where?' said a marmalade cat of the three-fruit variety strolling towards them. Dennis's body was ginger skin and bone, and it had curiosity right through to its corpuscles.

'Dennis!' said Bertie.

'Try again,' said the Cat-Bursar.

'Bursar!'

'How did you get out?' snapped Grandel.

'Through bars on the cell window. I never realised cats were so flexible. I couldn't have got through as me.'

'Well, now you're out,' said Axy, 'maybe you can rescue the situation.'

'What's the matter?'

'Let's just say that in a quite unparalleled display of foot-shooting, the Magnificent Mayhem here opened his mouth and uttered the words which suspended everybody who could possibly help him. Hence all this lot standing about like tailors' dummies.'

Grandel was determined to defend himself.

'Look, all I said was—'

'Shut up!' shouted two cats and a dog.

'Write it down!' said the Cat-Bursar. 'Then we'll have a look at it.'

Whilst Grandel was in the kitchen writing down the words which had caused so much trouble, the Cat-Bursar strolled around the clearing.

'So they're just stuck there?' she asked, looking up at Ashton Fishwick.

'They are,' replied Axy.

She pawed at Marianna's shoe. 'Can they feel anything?'

'I don't think so.'

She stood on her back legs and pushed at Dominica's knees. 'Will they remember anything?'

'Probably.'

She walked over to JW and looked up at her. 'But there's nothing they can do when they're like this?'

'Not a thing.'

She stood by JW's ankles, tilted her head and opened her mouth wide.

'Bursar!' reproved Bertie.

'What?'

'That's cannibalism!'

She shut her mouth abruptly. 'Hmm. I suppose you're right.' She walked round and round JW's feet until she had another idea. 'But territory marking isn't, is it?'

'Aw, Bursar, no!'

She stood on her back legs again and rested her front paws on JW's calf.

'And with this thing I can point it wherever I like!' She

wiggled her hips to prove it. 'Right into her boots!'

'No, Bursar!' shouted Bertie. 'No. Not nice. Not the done thing. Not... elegant.' He'd spent many years moving in Senior Council circles and was well aware that inside the small, round, shirty Bursar they all knew and loved – well, they all knew, anyway – there was a tall, thin, poised, refined, graceful society hostess just waiting to get out, put on a fringed frock and be languid over cocktails.

'No... not elegant,' agreed the Cat-Bursar, suddenly realising exactly what she'd been about to do. 'Being in this fur must have got the better of me. Strange how potent a cheap skin is.'

'Here,' said Grandel, shambling across to the Cat-Bursar as fast as he could. He laid a piece of paper on the ground, and the Cat-Bursar walked across it, moving her head from side to side as she read the words.

'Easy,' she said. 'You just take the first word off, stick it at the end, read the whole thing again and shout "Gone!".'

'Are you sure?' said Grandel.

The Cat-Bursar glowered. 'Am I sure? Am I sure? Do you think I want to be stuck in this bloody fur coat for the rest of my life? No thank you, mate.'

She sighed irritatedly. 'If you move the first word to the end and shout "Gone!" it'll reverse the polarity of the whole thing, and that'd better be a good enough explanation for you 'cos you ain't getting another.' She sat on her haunches and folded her forelegs across her chest. 'Read it. It'll work. You see if it doesn't.'

So he read it, and waited to see if it didn't, and it did.

'Am I sure?' she muttered. 'I ask you. Am I sure?'

There was a communal sigh of relief accompanied by much shaking and stretching of limbs and fingers.

'Thank you, Helena,' said Dominica, silently hoping that now the Bursar knew what it was like dealing with herself.

'Thank you,' said Grandel, for the first time in a very, very long time.

'Yes, thank you,' said a new voice in the clearing.

Axy leapt up at Eleanor and she fussed over him.

'Eleanor,' said Dominica. 'Welcome back.'

'Glad to be back, Dominica. Everything all right? You're looking a bit fraught.'

'Let's just say we've been through a trying time.'

'Mostly trying to find you,' JW chipped in.

'JW! Got your flask on you? Pity. I could murder a cuppa. Being suspended's all very well but it gives me a raging thirst. Marianna! How are you?'

'Absolutely average, thanks, Eleanor.'

'Release me,' called Grandel. Axy snarled.

'Just wait your turn, there's a good chap,' said Eleanor.

'I've been waiting for over five hundred years.'

'Then a few more minutes won't make a vast amount of difference, will it?' She turned her attention to Naiba, and smiled. 'And this is?'

'Assistant Graduation Administrator Naiba Hudwicz, Matri— Mistress Lynin,' said Naiba holding out her water bottle. 'I'm afraid it's only water, but you're welcome to it.'

'Excellent! Thank you.' Eleanor glugged the water. 'Ah! Mother Nature's own wine. Can't beat it.' She poured some in her hand and Axy lapped it.

'Naiba has been what you might call instrumental in helping us to find you,' added Dominica.

'Well, bless you for that, dear. And who's that cluttering up the floor over there?'

'Pardon me if I don't get up,' said Dennis.

'It's a long story,' said Dominica, 'but it's actually my familiar, Spirit of the Wind.'

'Really? Looks just like a junior accountant we used to have. What was her name, now? Bucket? Crockett?'

'Jacket,' supplied the Cat-Bursar, wearily.

Eleanor clicked her fingers. 'Jacket! That's it!'

'Will you release me?' pleaded Grandel.

'Yes – as soon as the Inauguration's finished.'

Grandel's face started to crumple. 'Inauguration?'

'I must inaugurate Eleanor as Matriarch before she can release you,' explained Dominica.

'There's always something else to be done! When will it be over?'

'It would've been over a lot sooner if you'd just let Eleanor go in the first place,' Dominica reproached him. 'And then I wouldn't have had a cat for a Bursar and a familiar who can't stand up!'

'Oh, I don't know,' said JW. 'I've seen Dennis staggering out of Cookie's.'

'I gave the woman back. You promised it would be over! Please, please, just do it!' begged Grandel.

'Oh, stop whingeing – we're just about to start,' said Eleanor, clearly displaying the talents for which Imelda had chosen her to be Matriarch. 'You wait here, but everybody else outside. Come on, clear the area!'

'Outside?' said Grandel.

'Yes, outside. You don't think I'm going to be inaugurated in the middle of a spell, do you? No, no, no. Far too dangerous – way too much nested magic – and besides, something about this place gives me the willies.'

'Me too,' said the Cat-Bursar, lifting a paw to walk off.

Dominica blocked her exit. 'And where are you going, Helena? Don't forget, you've got to stay as well.'

The Cat-Bursar stopped. 'Me? Stay? Why?'

Dominica stiffened. '*Why*? Did you just ask *why* you had to stay?'

'Yes. Eleanor's here now and she'll release him, so—'

Further words were cut off by Dominica clamping the Cat-Bursar's mouth shut. The only sound in the clearing was that of nobody else moving a muscle to help the Cat-Bursar.

'I have never,' Dominica growled, 'do you hear me, *never* met anybody whose doors of perception were so firmly welded shut as yours are. I will tell you, as simply as I can, why you must stay. You must stay because you are of that man's family and you are ginger skin and bone. You must stay because I traded you for this lady here. You must stay because we gave that man there our word and we don't break our word. You must stay because should this lady here – for some reason – not release that man there, he will take you and he will grind you skin and bone into tiny little pieces and then sell those pieces to this man over here and he will make ginger biscuits out of you and I will be the first in the queue to buy the buggers!'

She pushed the Cat-Bursar's head aside. 'Now get off over there!'

The Cat-Bursar staggered away, panting for breath.

'Jolly good,' said Eleanor. 'Now if we can have everybody where they should be, we can get on with it. Old father, are you prepared for release?'

Tears wet his face again. 'I have been prepared for five hundred years.'

'Very well.'

The clearing emptied, Dennis's progress slowed somewhat by the Bursar's voluminous skirts.

Just as JW was about to step on to the path, she turned.

'Oh, Bursar?'

'What?'

'Remember when the rest of us were suspended?'

'Yes…'

'So do I, and I shan't forget, either.'

The Cat-Bursar slumped. JW left the clearing, and its only remaining occupants were a resentful cat and a forlorn old man.

'Mistress Lynin?' said Sennet.

'Yes, officer, what is it?'

'I can understand you not wanting to see the man again, but is it possible you could come down to the rozzer shop and give evidence?'

'Evidence?'

'Against Grandel.'

Eleanor laughed. 'Oh, that won't be necessary. I shan't be

pressing charges, officer, and neither will Mr Fishwick, will you, Mr Fishwick?'

Ashton gave a wide-eyed, rapid shake of the head indicating that anything Eleanor wanted was fine by him, thank you very much for asking.

'See?' said Eleanor. 'And before you go getting all public-spirited yourself, officer, you should know that Grandel won't be here to prosecute, so just write "lost two, found two, case closed" across all your notes, there's a good chap.'

She called to the others.

'Attention please! Civilians, stand over there if you would, and sisters over here. Officer, will you hold Axy, please?'

Sennet, having just had his purpose for being there taken away, resignedly took Axy's lead as the group divided into its constituent parts, the animals going off with the civilians.

'So what's your part in all this, Bertie?' asked Axy.

'I was the old Matriarch's familiar. I've been helping them to find your mistress, but... well, I suppose I'm out of a job now. I'll probably end up back in the office waiting for a new mistress.'

'You don't sound too keen.'

'I'm not, really. I hate all that hanging about, and you know what it's like: by the time you do get re-issued you find a lot of your mates have been re-issued as well and they're all in different bodies and you've got to re-learn who they all are, and oh, it's just a nightmare.'

Axy could see the weight of despondency bowing Bertie's head.

'Well,' said Axy, 'I've been many things in my times, but

I've never been a Matriarch's familiar before, so... I'm going to need a bit of help with... protocol and... stuff. So don't throw yourself back into the pool just yet.'

Bertie's head shot up. 'You mean it? Really?'

Axy looked stern. 'Let me tell you I don't say anything I don't mean!'

'Wow, thanks! That's brilliant!'

A rotund figure slumped down next to them. Bertie pawed at it.

'Dennis! Dennis! Axy says I can stay! Isn't that brilliant! He says I can stay and help him! We can both help him, can't we?'

Dennis closed his eyes. 'I think I'm the one who's going to need help.'

'Dennis!' called Dominica. 'Over here! We need a full complement of sisters to witness the Inauguration.'

'But I'm not— oh, I am, aren't I?'

He started to crawl back across the path. 'Oh, this is hopeless. How do you manage with these things on? Wait a minute.' He sat on his haunches and slowly stood up, putting his arms out to the side to balance. He wavered for a few seconds then tottered at an angle across the path before collapsing on the ground at Dominica's feet.

'Bravo!' said Dominica.

'Splendid,' said Eleanor. 'Now, do you think you could stand up again? I know it's not easy but I do think it would be better if you were upright during the Inauguration.'

'But I'm not really the Bursar, though, am I? How can I witness something as her when I'm not really her?'

'Helena can see us from where she is,' said Dominica, 'but we need her body here. Then, should anybody ask, she can truthfully say that her own eyes witnessed what happened. Now will you stand up?'

Marianna and JW moved to stand on each side of him.

'Come on, little— come on, Bursar,' said Marianna.

'Up you get, Dennis,' said JW.

They helped him to stand and supported him as he gently swayed like a teetotaller after half a pint of shandy.

From Naiba's saddlebag Dominica took *The Book of Procedures Volume VIII: The Procedure of Inauguration* and *The Book of Ceremonies Volume XII: The Ceremony of Transference.*

And so began the first, heavily edited Inauguration of Eleanor Lynin as Matriarch of The University of Nature.

NOTES ON
Inauguration

'1. As a Mark of Respect for the Matriarch Morte, there should be a general Fast from Midnight to Midday on the Day of Inauguration.

2. At Noon, the Fast should be broken by a symbolic Meal, with the Matriarch Designate serving Bread and Water to the youngest Novice.

3. The Matriarch Designate should be presented with her Entrandements of Office, namely:

- The Box of Earth -
symbolic of Mother Nature's Bounty.

- The Ring of Water -
symbolic of the Fluidity of Time
and the cyclical Basis of Mother Nature's Works.

- The Vial of Air -
symbolic of the Fact that Mother Nature's Resources
are to be shared, and her Methods are not always visible.

- The Ball of Fire -
symbolic of Mother Nature's all-consuming Power.

- The Sachet of Seeds -
symbolic of the Work of The University of Nature
as an educational Establishment.

- The Pot of Red Nose Paint -
symbolic of the Fact that Mother Nature
provides Life to be enjoyed, not just worked at.

4. The Matriarch Designate should be presented with the Two Triangles of Tecton, the six Points being symbolic Reminders of the six Entranclements of Office.

5. The Matriarch Designate should don the Mantle of Power.

6. The Vice-Matriarch shall execute the Transfer of Power as laid down in The Book of Ceremonies Volume XII: The Ceremony of Transference.

7. The Matriarch should be presented with a Key, symbolic of the Safety of The University of Nature, which is now in her hands.

8. The Matriarch should be presented with a Magnifying Glass, symbolic of the Eye she must keep on The University of Nature.

9. Those Members of The University of Nature who are present at the Inauguration shall renew their Vows of Allegiance,

after which Toasts and Speeches may be made, subject to a strict five-minute Limit on Duration per speech so that there may be no unnecessary Delay to the Dancing.'

> *The Book of Procedures Volume VIII:*
> *The Procedure of Inauguration*

Inauguration is usually a very grand affair, bringing with it – as do many of the ceremonies of The Union – a day of feasting, fun and firewater.

Being served bread and water by the incoming Matriarch is enough to put the fear of Mother Nature into any novice, particularly after a twelve-hour fast, but to eat bread and water without coughing or spluttering when hundreds of people are watching you takes nerves of steel.

When the symbolic meal has been eaten, then everybody else gets to exercise their teeth as the Inauguration Banquet is served, the first course consisting of a bread roll and a glass of water for everyone. A different course of the banquet is consumed each time an Entranclement of Office is presented, a pragmatic system which has three benefits: it saves everybody having to sit through the whole ceremony on an empty stomach and therefore stops people fainting from hunger, it gives everybody something to watch and talk about whilst the dishes are being cleared away, and it gives the kitchen staff time to get everybody served.

The drawback is that by the time it gets to the renewing of the Vows of Allegiance, the empty wine bottles are piling up like legends round an archaeological dig, the noise level has risen considerably and there's a very real danger of an unsavoury song breaking out to the accompaniment of bodies sliding under the table. It's a situation only saved by the fact that a witch knows her Vows of Allegiance so well she could say them even if she were comatose, which some of them are at this stage.

The Vows of Allegiance they swear are to The Union, not to any particular Matriarch. Long and sometimes bizarre experience has taught that whilst individual Matriarchs may sometimes be notoriously unstable, it is highly unlikely that the whole of The Union will go off its collective trolley and hurtle headlong into megalomania. So, put your loyalty where it's least likely to be tested.

To inaugurate Eleanor, Dominica used a greatly slimmed-down version of the Procedure of Inauguration – in fact, just points 6 and 9. As she realised, they are the crux of the whole ceremony, and the rest is just a load of symbolics.

~•~

~•~

The Ceremony of Transference

'The Ceremony of Transference shall be witnessed by no less than three Members of the Senior Council.

1. The Vice-Matriarch shall clasp the Right Hand of the Matriarch Designate and say: "Into thy Hand I pass the Responsibility for The University of Nature. Be not afeared." The Matriarch Designate shall reply: "I am not afeared."

2. The Vice-Matriarch shall clasp the Left Hand of the Matriarch Designate and say: "Into thy Hand I pass the Power of The University of Nature. Be not abusive." The Matriarch Designate shall reply: "I shall be not abusive."

3. The Vice-Matriarch shall clasp both the Hands of the Matriarch Designate and say: "You have undertaken to be neither afeared nor abusive." The Matriarch Designate shall reply: "I have."

4. The Vice-Matriarch shall clasp both the Hands of the Matriarch Designate and say: "Then welcome, Matriarch, but forget not that we shall be watching."'

The Book of Ceremonies Volume XII:
The Ceremony of Transference

~•~

After the Inauguration JW, Marianna and Naiba applauded; even Dennis managed to figure out how to clap before the congratulations died down. Ashton Fishwick and Constable Sennet smiled at each other in slight embarrassment, primarily because they genuinely had no idea of the significance of what had just happened.

'Right. Stand clear, everybody,' said the Matriarch, now with full authority. She and Dominica discussed the next stage of the proceedings whilst JW, Marianna and Naiba herded the others behind the first row of trees in the non-magical wood opposite the clearing. The Bursar's body dropped to its haunches and lay down in the undergrowth.

'I'm starting with backache,' Dennis groaned. 'How do you lot stay upright for so long? You must be in agony.'

JW sat beside him and gently rubbed his back. 'There, there, old love. It'll soon be over.'

Marianna took a crumpled paper bag from her pocket and bent down beside him.

'Here, suck one of these,' she said, holding out the bag.

Dennis may have been in a different body, but he had his own suspicion. 'What are they?'

'Painkillers. They'll make you feel much better.'

'They're not Matron's, are they?'

'No, no, I made them myself.'

'What flavour are they?'

'Placebo.'

'What's that?'

'Any flavour you want.'

He stuck his hand into the bag and rootled round.

'I can't get one,' he whined.

'Bend your fingers and thumb,' said JW. Dennis clasped his hand quickly, causing Marianna to stagger and four placebos to leap out of the bag and roll away. 'Slowly,' JW demonstrated. 'Just use the tips of your fingers.'

He opened his hand then closed his fingers slowly, and when he withdrew his hand he was holding a small, smooth ball of orange painkiller. 'Hey, these thumb things are brilliant, aren't they?'

'Marvellous,' said Marianna. 'Now suck the placebo and you'll feel much better, little… Bursar.'

'Hmm.' Dennis frowned at her, not altogether trusting her, but he put the placebo in his mouth and found that for once she was not cheating him. His backache miraculously disappeared as he tasted fresh wild salmon, chilled lapping cream and clear spring water. Ooh, he thought, what this needs is… and there it was, suffusing his taste and smell buds. 'Mmm… mmm! This is wonderful! I'll take a bagful of these if you're selling 'em.'

Marianna laughed and stood up again.

Dennis opened and closed his hands.

'Don't fingers bend well?' he said, testing his grip up and down his arms. 'Not very sharp, mind. No good in a fight.'

The sound of Eleanor clapping attracted everybody's attention.

'Silence, please, ladies and gents,' she called. 'We are about to begin. Vice-Matriarch? The spell, please.'

From Naiba's saddlebag Dominica took a scroll of paper and handed it to Eleanor who unrolled it, read it, rolled it up again and turned to face the others.

'Stand well back and hang on to your hats – this could be a bumpy ride.' She spoke to Grandel. 'Goodbye, old father, and go to your rest. We shall not meet again.'

'Thank you,' he whispered through his tears.

She held both arms above her head. With the spell in her right hand, she clamped her left hand over a finely engraved silver bangle on her right wrist.

'By Matriarch command now willed:
Enchantment from this man be gone.
Conditions for thy end fulfilled,
Then, spell now cease: thy time be done.'

She ripped the spell in half.

It's not often the opportunity arises to witness five hundred years of forest activity taking place in five minutes, so everybody except the still-sleeping child paid close attention.

The sun continued to blaze over the rest of Deartreen Wood, but over the clearing the sky flashed hyperactively, day following night, week after month after year as half a millennium of weather rushed through its party pieces. Dark flecks of thunder-cloud whipped across the roiling sky. Millisecond-long black flashes were the shadows of migrating flocks flying overhead. Wisps of torrential downpours evaporated, leaving behind brief colour bursts which were but the echoes of long-dead rainbows.

The earth boiled and sprayed as the birth of plants tore at its skin. Gouges opened up as seeds became saplings became great verdant warriors, hurling rocks and the remains of

Doughnut Cottage to one side as they vied for space, air, light and water. The losers tentatively held out ailing limbs before crumbling away as the victors soared skywards, stretching their branches in a lush canopy whilst their surface roots were giant worms, writhing and gnarling across the ground. Whole bushes appeared as a single bloom, and a blazing paintbox of colours flashed on and off as shrubs flowered and fell with each year. A burst of flame told of small forest fires. Tumbling storms of gold and orange showed the passing of the autumns, and tempests of white marked the winters. A grey-brown haze hung around the forest floor, the blurred images of animals which passed through, nested, reared their young and returned to the earth.

The accelerated growths of massive trees, the accumulated beating of millions of wings and every zephyr from gentle summer breeze to raging hurricane sent huge clouds of dusty, soily air billowing from the clearing, curling and looping across the woodland paths. Heady summer perfumes lived side-by-side with leaf mould and the damp soil smell of heavy rain, punctuated by throat-catching smoke.

Concentrated centuries of noise were released in a column of sound, a great barrage of birth, life, exuberance and death. Birdsong, wing flap, animal howl, insect tick and bee buzz were the choir against the orchestra of earth rumble, rock fracture, stem crunch, twig snap, bark split and leaf rustle. Cracks of thunder, crunches of snow and slaps of rain applauded the performance.

Just as the audience were becoming attuned to the roaring

rush of speeding centuries, suddenly the opera was over and the orchestra had downed instruments.

In the Unstable Block of the Dictionary a brilliant red border burned purest white, fading to impenetrable black.

Dominica felt a palpable absence of noise, as if she'd been standing under a waterfall when someone had turned the tap off. The silence wrapped her in a thick towel, dried her hair and said, 'Now listen.'

She listened, and heard only the normal sounds of the forest. The gentle susurration of the leaf canopy, the twit-twit-twit of birds, the occasional snap of a twig or shush of a lizard shimmying through the undergrowth. Life lived at its everyday speed.

She smiled. 'Congratulations, Eleanor.'

'Hell of a show, don't you think?' Eleanor beamed.

Dominica nodded. 'Hell of a show.'

They walked towards the others, who spontaneously applauded. Eleanor took a theatrical bow and Axy ran to her. She bent and held his face in her hands.

'It's over now, Axy. It's over. He's gone.'

Tears streamed down his face. 'Thank you, mistress. Thank you.'

She fussed over him and he licked her face.

Dominica walked over towards the others.

'Very impressive,' said JW.

'It's a good start, isn't it?' said Marianna.

Dominica smiled at them and looked down at Dennis.

'When was the last time you said thank you to me?'

'Thank you? You want me to thank you, when you do

things like put me in this tub of—'

Dominica's laugh cut off the rest of his rant. She spoke to Naiba, and then they both walked over to Ashton Fishwick.

'Mr Fishwick,' Dominica began.

'Please, call me Ashton.'

'All right, Ashton. As you probably guessed, you won't be seeing the old man any more.'

'I can't say I'm sorry.'

'However, I must admit I have no idea what effect this will have on your business.'

'I have my daughter back, which was all that mattered to me. As long as nobody else has to die, I don't care if it bankrupts me.'

'Well, we need to make sure it won't, because not only do you have your workforce to look after, you now have an orphanage to support. If you'd like to, of course.'

'Gladly.'

'Thank you for being so understanding.'

'What is there to understand? Our children are our future selves. I have my daughter; she has her parent. Other children and other parents are not so lucky. If any need help, we must give it. We must.'

'We must,' Dominica smiled. 'So, to continue your business you'll need some new recipes. And that's why Naiba here will be working with you over the next few weeks to sort things out. She's our new... how shall we say... Community Liaison Officer.'

'Sort of a Neighbourhood Witch,' said Sennet, only to find himself the object of many withering stares.

'So now, Ashton,' said Dominica, 'I think you need to take your daughter home. I'm sure you're both very tired.'

His eyes filled up again. 'Thank you, Mistress Tort. I can't thank you enough.'

'You are more than welcome. She is safe, that's all that matters. Constable, could I ask you to accompany Mr Fishwick and his daughter back to their home? We don't want anything else happening to them.'

Sennet slyly looked across to JW. 'Well, if there's nothing else I can do here…'

Only those paying close attention saw JW's head give a sharp, very small tilt.

'…then I'll be off,' he said. 'Reports to write, that sort of thing. Mr Fishwick, do you know how to get out of here? I think I'd probably lose my way.'

'Follow me,' said Ashton and, carrying his daughter, he led Sennet away, leaving the rest of the group to gather themselves and their belongings.

'I think that about wraps it up, ladies, don't you?' said Eleanor, rubbing her hands together. 'Time to get home for a quick snifter and a long chat, I think.'

The others could find no argument against such a plan, and soon a band of six witches, one dog and a black cat with a white eye-patch were walking away from a very undistinguished part of the forest.

'Stop!' commanded a voice behind them.

They all stopped.

'Oh-oh,' said Dennis.

'I could have sworn it had worked,' said Eleanor.

'Me too,' said Dominica.

'Get me down! Get me down now!' yelled the voice.

'The Bursar?' said Naiba.

Perched precariously in the lower branches of the tallest tree in what had been the clearing was a marmalade cat of the three-fruit variety.

'Helena?' said Dominica, as JW rolled her eyes and tutted. Marianna began estimating the height of the branch.

'What on earth are you doing up there?' asked Eleanor.

'I was just sitting there when this thing shot straight up my— I was just sitting there and now I'm sitting here. Get me down!'

'Jump!' shouted Dennis.

'Dennis!' reproved Dominica.

'If she jumps, she'll bend and flex and land on her feet – no harm done. I've fallen out of beds that were higher than she is. Jump!'

'Are you mad?' shouted the Cat-Bursar.

'You'll be all right! You'll land on your feet! Jump!'

The Cat-Bursar temporarily forgot what and where she was. She sat up and put her hands on her hips. 'If you think I'm waaaaggghh!'

There were two schools of thought about what happened next. The first said putting her hands on her hips meant letting go of the branch therefore precipitating her fall. The second said it was a good job she had her hands free or else she wouldn't have had anything to grab hold of the branch with when her bottom fell off it. Either way, she was suspended by her front paws and getting heavier every time she breathed. 'Help!'

When the Cat-Bursar slipped, the Bursar's body sprang into life with a swifter turn of speed than anybody would have put money on. Dennis sprinted back along the path and collapsed at the bottom of the tree in time to break the fall of his own body before it slammed into the ground and wasted another of his lives. He didn't understand why his body hadn't flexed as it usually did; perhaps it was something to do with the fact it had its paws over its eyes and was busy screaming like a banshee.

'It's all right. You can open your eyes now,' shouted Dennis, holding his body at arms' length to reduce the volume. The Cat-Bursar stopped howling and opened her eyes in relief, but fainted clean away when she saw herself holding her.

'Is everything all right?' called Dominica.

'Yes,' he shouted. 'I— she— we fainted, that's all.'

He struggled upright, and tottering out of what had been the clearing he haltingly carried his own apparently boneless body to Dominica, laid it at her feet and collapsed.

'Swap us back, Mistress, please,' he begged. 'Please swap us back. I promise I'll say thank you.'

'So will I,' said the Cat-Bursar.

The rescuers and the rescued sat in what was now Eleanor's study with Axy lying stretched out on the hearth-rug.

'But why me?' asked Naiba. 'Why should the spell choose me to write its story?'

'Well, you are family, dear, however distant,' said Eleanor.

'But that's my point. Why me, and why not the Bursar?'

'There doesn't have to be a reason,' said Dominica. 'These things happen. And you were studying Creative Chronicling, after all, and what better person to tell a story than someone who *wants* to tell a story?'

She broke off and looked towards the dressing table where Dennis and Bertie were apparently doing feline yoga in front of the mirror. Dennis reached up as far as he could and tugged at the fur on his legs. Bertie stood behind him like a hairdresser and pulled Dennis's facial skin tight.

'Dennis, what *is* the matter with you?'

He winked at her. 'It's my fur. It doesn't fit properly any more. She's stretched it!'

JW splurted tea halfway across the study.

'You cheeky bugger!' railed the Bursar, as Dennis and Bertie collapsed with laughter. 'After what you've done to my body? My knees are shot, I've got chronic backache and grit stuck in the palms of my hands and all thanks to you scrabbling about on all fours! Not to mention all the other bloody bumps, bruises and scratches!'

'You did the scratches yourself!'

'Children, children,' said Dominica. 'If you want to fight, go out into Concentric Yard and do it. Although you'll have to wait until we've drawn up some rules about fair fighting.'

'Yeah, I don't want to win too easily,' said Dennis.

'*Whatever happened,*' said Eleanor, brooking no further argument, 'happened in a good cause and I'm sure that in a couple of days you'll both be back to normal. And while I thank you all most heartily for my rescue, I feel a special mention is due to the Bursar and Dennis for service above and beyond the call of duty.'

'Hear, hear!' said the others, applauding.

'Especially the Bursar, for helping to save the life of a rival, I understand.'

The Bursar laughed hollowly. 'A rival, Matriarch? Surely not. I think you're mistaken with that one. I don't know what you're talking about.'

'But I was under the impression you thought you would be Matriarch.'

The Bursar glared at Dominica. 'You just couldn't keep it to yourself, could you? You just had to tell her. You just had to, didn't you?'

'No,' said Marianna, 'I told her.'

'You? Why?'

JW couldn't resist. 'So if she wakes up one morning stabbed in the back she'll know who's done it.'

'What?!'

'Bursar,' said Marianna calmly, 'I told her because I thought she should know.'

'Without wishing to rub it in,' said Eleanor, 'I am the Matriarch. I ought to know these things.'

'And she would've found out anyway, so it's best if it comes from one of the Senior Council.'

The Bursar groaned. After all she'd been through, people still insisted on kicking her in the teeth. 'Well, you know now. Though I can't see what difference it makes.'

'It could make a *big* difference,' said Eleanor gravely.

'Why? How?'

'I'm not sure there's any precedent for having two members of the Senior Council from the same family.'

'Especially when they are half-sisters,' said Dominica.

'What? What do you mean? Why does everybody know something I don't?' flapped the Bursar.

'Because if it doesn't involve money, you can't work it out,' said JW.

'Because you never pay any attention!' said Dominica. 'It's very simple. Eleanor is your half-sister.'

'She can't be! I was their only child! I told you that!'

Dominica lifted her arms, palms upward, in a gesture of helplessness. 'What did I just say about paying attention? I give up. I bloody give up.'

'You were *their* only child,' said Eleanor, 'but not *his*. My father was your father. My mother died when I was a baby and Father couldn't look after me, so he gave me up as an orphan. Years passed, he met your mother, and…'

'But my letter!'

'My letter,' said Eleanor gently.

The Bursar went white. 'You're the child in the letter?'

Eleanor nodded. 'I am. To complete the spell, there had to be a child descended from both Grandel and Auregia. My father – our father – was descended from Grandel, and my mother was descended from Auregia, but yours was not.'

'Is this true?' said the Bursar. 'Really really one hundred percent gold-plated no questions asked true?'

'I have the original letter, if you want to see it.'

The Bursar's mouth dropped open and she held her breath; the movement of her eyes was the only sign of life in her at all. The others waited and watched as she replayed events and sorted out facts in her mind.

'Helena?' said Marianna. 'Are you there?'

The Bursar went off like a firework. 'Do you know how long I've had to live up to the prospect of signing off that spell? How long I've carried it around with me? The hours I've spent trying to decipher it? The struggle to keep it a secret? The things I've had to give up just to concentrate on a family responsibility that wasn't even mine? The work I've had to do to get anywhere near a chance at being Matriarch? The toadying and fawning and not putting a foot wrong?'

JW's mouth opened, but the Bursar was in full flow.

'Well, not any more, mate. Not me. It's your pigeon now. You won the big prize, but you can kiss goodbye to your life. Somebody just handed me my life on a plate and I'm going to make the most of it. And first, I'm going down to the Brew Shed to get absolutely slammed!'

She wrenched open the door and disappeared in the direction of a new life.

'I like a good, positive attitude,' said Eleanor.

'I think we all might venture down to the Brew Shed tonight,' suggested Dominica, 'to celebrate your safe arrival, and Naiba's promotion to... what did I call it?'

'Community Liaison Officer,' supplied Naiba, smiling.

'Fine idea,' Eleanor chortled. 'Let off a bit of steam, eh?'

'Great!' said Axy. 'I haven't had a beer for ages.'

From the doorway came the tin-reinforced chink of china on a tray.

'More tea, mums?' said a familiar face.

'Excellent!' said Eleanor.

'Truda!' cried Dominica. 'You're back! How's the foot?'

'Right as rain, thank you, ma'am. And me new uniform fits a treat.'

'Oh, yes. I must have a word with... maybe later.'

'How's your sister?' asked Marianna. 'The one who... the one with the er...'

She waved a hand in the general area of her nose.

'Not too bad in herself, ma'am, although she's worried about Cedric.'

'Cedric?'

'The courier,' supplied Dominica.

'Yes, ma'am. He's said he hopes the accident ain't going to spoil her looks, ma'am.'

Truda put the tray on a table in the middle of the floor. Gleaming china surrounded a plate of biscuits, in the centre of which were two gingerbread men.

'Oh, goody,' said Eleanor, reaching down to the biscuits. 'My favourites. Don't you just love custard creams?'

Thanks

The biggest thanks go to my husband Martin for his love, support and not so gentle hints that I should 'get on with it'.

Thanks also to...
...the very talented Lisa-Marie Damant for her marvellous illustrations, her ideas and her friendliness...

...Terry Pratchett, whose book *Mort* opened my eyes to a world of possibilities...

...Hilary Johnson and her SF/Fantasy reader at *The Hilary Johnson Authors' Advisory Service* for much-needed and invaluable advice...

...and to you, for picking up this book to have a look at.

About the author

Carol Carman is a former shop assistant, computer programmer, systems analyst, fog-knitter, treacle-weaver and BBC journalist and radio presenter.

She edits and illustrates the *Grunty Fen* series of books by Christopher South (dennisofgruntyfen.co.uk), she writes fiction and poetry for the website *The Reaper* (thereaper.rip) and just for her own amusement she leads a double life as the poet and sporadic blogger Fifi Fanshawe (fififanshawe.co.uk).

She is currently working on a second novel, and possibly even a third. She's not sure where she finds the time, to be honest, but she does enjoy it.

If you'd like to know anything else, please email:

info@mccawmedia.co.uk